REVELATION HOOFBEATS

When the Riders of Apocalypse Come Forth

RON J. BIGALKE, JR.

General Editor

Dedicated in memory of brother Dave Breese who passed away shortly after completing his chapter for this volume. His God-given eloquence in communicating the prophetic Scriptures motivated many to study diligently in order to rightly divide the Word of God. His earnest devotion for his Lord was evident in his evangelistic and discipleship ministries, and his passion for holy living in light of the soon return of Jesus Christ. He truly demonstrated that the study of Bible prophecy not only affects our doctrine, but also our manner of living.

Read pgs. 20 & 21
24

CONTENTS

ACKNOWLEDGEMENTS

Revelation Hoofbeats is a labor of love. It did require intensive work, but my spirit was always joyful as I strove to uphold absolute integrity and care with regard to the handling of the Word of God. A project of this nature would not have been possible without the blessing of God and the support and assistance of many friends.

First and foremost my deepest gratitude is to my *Lord and Savior Jesus Christ* for His testimony is "the spirit of prophecy" (Rev. 19:10). I give glory and honor to Jesus Christ for His grace and mercy in providing His children a preview of things to come. He has a wonderful future in the making for those who love Him and are the called according to His purpose.

Second, I am deeply indebted to *Terry James*, my consulting editor and dear Christian brother, without whom I would not have attempted this project. His many valuable recommendations, enthusiasm, willing support, patience, and professionalism were necessary for the publication of this book. God has blessed my ministry with his friendship. May the Lord continue to bless you, your work for Him and reward you according to His good pleasure.

My greatest appreciation for the ministries of *Dr. John Walvoord* and *Dr. David Breese*, who went home to be with the Lord the past year. Both have greatly influenced my thinking and touched my life deeply through their faithful service to the Lord. What a joyful day it will be when the roll is called in heaven and all the saved will come together.

Of course, I am thankful for the love and patience of my mother, *Arlene*, and sister, *Mary*. They do deserve a special word of thanks for putting up with my busy schedule and preoccupation with the work at hand. Thank you for your endless support of all the ministries that God calls me to.

Many thanks to my dear friends *Josh and Julie Hofstede*, who are as close as family, for their faithful prayers and financial support. I am not capable of expressing the depth of my love and gratitude for your friendship. Also an earnest thank you to all who supported Eternal Ministries through gifts and prayers so that I could concentrate on the task at hand.

Thanks especially to my darling wife, *Kristin*, who took the time to format and read the entire manuscript providing many helpful suggestions and criticisms. Words cannot express my greatest love for all you mean to me. God is gracious to bless my life with such a wonderful wife and friend with whom I can "run the race" together. Soli Deo Gloria!

Introduction

HOOFBEATS OF THE APOCALYPSE

RON J. BIGALKE, JR.

The hoofbeats of the four horsemen of Revelation 6 are impending each day the cry is made "There must be peace in the Middle East." Although Bible prophecy is not being fulfilled today, there are "signs of the times" that are drawing the world closer to the period called the Tribulation, or Daniel's Seventieth Week. The start of the Tribulation will begin with the Antichrist confirming a peace treaty with the nation of Israel. Today, the world is ripe for such a time. Truly, Jerusalem is "a cup of trembling unto all the people round about" (Zech. 12:2). The world is crying out for the rider on the white horse, the Antichrist (Rev. 6:2). The terrorist attacks taking place in Israel, and now America, are unexplainable apart from the fact that this is a spiritual war stemming back all the way to the Genesis record. In such tumultuous times, it is critical to understand where the future is headed according to God's prophetic Word.

THE COMMUNICATION OF PROPHECY

Using media and fiction. The first section in this book recognizes the fact that communication is absolutely essential to resolving questions about Bible prophecy. This includes the increasingly popular medium of using fiction to present Bible prophecy. It is appropriate to use fiction and media as an evangelistic tool since there is great benefit in taking teaching out of the Bible and making a fictional presentation about it. The perennial best sellers *Pilgrims Progress* and *Ben-Hur* are two examples.

The use of fiction and media is a wonderful vehicle to spread the biblical teaching of the pre-tribulation rapture. This method is quite familiar since the Bible itself is filled with parables (events that are not historical but teach a certain point). The best manner in which one is able to produce a fictional portrayal of prophetic events is, of course, based on the literal interpretation of Scripture. A faithful presentation of Bible prophecy is important because one's understanding of the future will determine how one will live in the present and plan for the future. The most important factor to consider is not so much the fictional story line; rather, it is to pursue the non-fictional truth about future events in the Bible.

Proclaiming and teaching prophecy. The God-given ability to accurately proclaim the prophetic Word is equally important. All too often Bible classes and study groups have turned into Christian sensitivity sessions where people discuss themselves rather than converse about the inerrant Word of God, yet we read in 2 Timothy 3:16, *all of Scripture is given by inspiration of God.* Prophecy is part of the canon of Scripture. Therefore, it is *profitable for teaching, for reproof, for correction, for training in righteousness; that the man of God may be adequate, equipped for every good work* (2 Tim. 3:16, 17). Prophecy is not the only content of Scripture, but it should be approached using personal involvement and interaction with a view to producing a changed life for the eternal glory of God.

The proclaiming of Bible prophecy is essential to the spiritual growth of believers because it is an integral part of the whole counsel of God's Word. We need to be challenged to live our lives in light of Christ's soon return. Communicators of Bible prophecy must stay true to the prophetic text (this includes parents, Sunday school teachers, pastors, etc.), avoiding a quest for experiences to the exclusion of understanding regarding the intent of Bible prophecy passages. Furthermore, there is the need to remain relevant to the people as they minister regarding the daily issues of life and godliness.

Consistent interpretation. Unfortunately, in an effort to draw attention to the prophetic Word, some have not been careful in their interpretation of Scripture using "newspaper exegesis" which forces current events to fit the Bible rather than drawing out of Scripture the truth of future events. The method of interpretation that one uses is crucial to understanding the whole counsel of God's Word. A consistent literal interpretation must be applied from Genesis to Revelation.

Defining dispensationalism. In treating the subject of consistent interpretation, it will be important to define the word, "dispensationalism," which may not be familiar to most readers. The word "dispensation" is simply a compound of two Greek words, *oikos* ("house") and *nomos* ("law"). The central idea of dispensationalism is "house law" or (as one scholar indicates) "managing or administering the affairs of a household."[1] The Greek word for dispensation is *oikonomia* and is found in passages such as Luke 16:2-4; 1 Corinthians 9:17; Ephesians 1:10; 3:2, 9; Colossians 1:25; and 1 Timothy 1:4. Literally, the word means "house dispensing" or "house managing." The word is used to describe the manner in which God manages His house. Dispensationalism is that biblical system of theology which views the Word of God as unfolding distinguishable economies in the outworking of the divine purposes for the nation of Israel in a distinct and separate manner from His purpose for the church.

Essentials of dispensationalism. Since there may be many misunderstandings of dispensationalism, Charles Ryrie (editor of the *Ryrie Study Bible*) reviews the basics (*sine qua non*) of dispensationalism: (1) Dispensationalism keeps Israel and the Church distinct. This is the most basic tenet of dispensationalism. (2) The distinction between Israel and the church is the natural result of a system of hermeneutics that is usually called literal (plain) interpretation.

Dispensationalism interprets words in the normal or plain meaning; it does not spiritualize or allegorize the text. The strength of dispensationalism is its consistently literal, or plain, interpretation of the Scripture. (3) The underlying purpose of God in the world is the glory of God. Salvation is a component of the glory of God but it is not an end in itself.[2]

Without equivocation, the major area of difference in prophetic interpretation relates to the lack of a distinction between the nation of Israel and the church. This confusion is most apparent in the false teaching that the church has replaced Israel in the present age. Dispensationalists believe that God promised eternally to establish the New Covenant with the literal nation of Israel (Jer. 31:31). Particularly in relation to salvation, the New Covenant amplifies the blessing aspect of the Abrahamic Covenant, the greatest of redemptive covenants. All of God's blessings, for both Jew and Gentile, spring forth from the Abrahamic Covenant (Gen. 12:1-3, 7; 13:14-17; 15:1-21; 17:1-21; 22:15-18). This covenant is not an elaboration of the Mosaic Covenant; it ultimately replaced the Law (Jer. 31:31, 32; Rom. 6:14, 15). The key aspect of this covenant is the blessing of salvation that will include the national regeneration of Israel (Jer. 31:34; Ezek. 36:29; Rom. 6:22; 11:25-27). The national salvation of Israel will extend to every individual Jewish person. This salvation will be true in succeeding generations from the time that the initial regeneration of Israel begins. The covenants with Israel are not negated because of her disobedience. It is because the covenants are dependent upon God for fulfillment, that their literal fulfillment can be expected.

The relationship of the church to the New Covenant has caused some confusion because the prophet Jeremiah specifies that the covenant is with Israel, not with the church. Nevertheless, there are numerous passages that connect the New Covenant with the church (Mt. 26:28; Mk. 14:24; Lk. 22:14-20; 1 Cor. 11:25; 2 Cor. 3:6; Heb. 7:22; 8:6-13; 9:15; 10:16, 29; 12:24; 13:20). Scripture is clear on the following: Israel, not the church, will fulfill the New Covenant. However, the church does partake of the spiritual blessings of the Abrahamic and New Covenants (Rom. 15:27).

Some have tried to teach that there are two New Covenants: one made with Israel and one made with the church. That particular view is quite difficult to defend from the Scriptures. Others have tried to teach that there is only one covenant, but that there are two aspects of the covenant. The solution to the problem is found in Ephesians 2:11-16 and 3:5, 6. The two Ephesians passages teach that God made 4 unconditional covenants with Israel. It is through these 4 covenants that all of God's spiritual blessings will be mediated.

The Mosaic Covenant was the "middle wall of partition" between Jew and Gentile. The Law prohibited the Gentiles from experiencing the blessing of the 4 unconditional covenants. In order for a Gentile to experience the blessings of the 4 unconditional covenants, he had to completely submit himself to the Mosaic Law. Since this was not possible because of the weakness of human flesh, the Gentiles were "aliens from the commonwealth of Israel." When Jesus Christ died, this "middle wall of partition" was broken down. Christ ratified the New Covenant. The church celebrates the New Covenant and the ratifying of it through the death of Christ (1 Cor. 11:23-26).

Although the church is partaking of the spiritual blessings of the covenant (Eph. 1:3), it is the nation of Israel who will receive the material and national promises. This relationship of the church to the New Covenant is explained in Galatians 3:13, 14. Through Christ, the church partakes of the New Covenant between God and Israel (Rom. 11:28, 29; 11:17).

All of the biblical covenants contain two types of promises: physical and spiritual. The physical promises are, and will continue to be, fulfilled by and limited to Israel. Nevertheless, some of the spiritual blessings of the covenants will extend to the Gentiles. Since the death of Christ is the basis of salvation for all people, for all time, the church has become a partaker of the Jewish spiritual blessings. The church is not a taker-over of the Jewish covenants. Only Israel will fulfill the New Covenant as promised in the Old Testament. The New Covenant was given to Israel and will be fulfilled by Israel. The church participates in the promises but she will in no way fulfill the covenants given to Israel. One's ability to understand the Bible, particularly relating to God's general dealings with humanity, depends on how well one understands the biblical covenants.

In approaching this subject, it is important to emphasize, as the late Dr. Walvoord stated succinctly: "The real issue is whether the Bible is inerrant, whether it is verbally inspired, and whether it should be interpreted literally. The concept of literal interpretation is the real issue in the interpretation of prophecy today." Consistent, literal interpretation is the *sine qua non* of any theological system since it allows no fuller or extended meaning beyond the original intent of Scripture.[3]

Importance of prophecy. Though there are Christians who seek to undermine this field of theology, the study of eschatology is important because it encompasses the totality of Scripture. For instance, 6,641 of the Old Testaments' 23,210 verses are prophetic (amounting to 28.6%) and 1,711 of the New Testaments' 7,914 verses are prophetic (amounting to 21.6%). Therefore, 8,352 of the entire Old and New Testaments' 31,124 verses are prophetic (amounting to 26.8% of the entire Bible)!

Furthermore, prophecy is important to study for at least 6 reasons. First, Bible prophecy demonstrates the veracity of God's Word (Isa. 40-49; 2 Pet. 3:13). There are over 300 prophecies that speak of Christ's first coming and about 1/2 of the New Testament is prophetic. Second, Bible prophecy demonstrates the sovereignty of God in real history. God has stated history before it commences. Third, Bible prophecy demonstrates the believer's responsibility in the current age. One's view of the future will determine how one lives in the present. Fourth, an understanding of Bible prophecy should be an impetus for evangelism. Christ will judge the world of sin and unrighteousness thus the gospel message needs to be proclaimed loudly and clearly. Fifth, Bible prophecy should be an impetus for godly living. One does not want to be caught in shame when Christ returns for His church. Sixth, Bible prophecy gives comfort in the midst of sorrow and facilitates perseverance with a hope of the future.

The issues in Bible prophecy are important because they deal with the whole counsel of God's Word and the eschatological hope of the Christian. The study of Bible prophecy also follows biblical admonitions (cf. Mt. 16:1-3; 24:3). Hebrews 11:13-16 (cf. Lk. 21:34, 36) refers to those who lived in light of God's future promises. Second Peter 3:11-14 emphasizes the urgency of being ready when Christ returns. First Thessalonians 5:1-11 contrasts the "you" (those who are able to understand the times in which they live) and the "they" (those who are unaware of God's prophetic decrees).

Bible prophecy is important because Jesus commended the study of prophecy. The world today desires to make sense of the events currently transpiring. Matthew 24-25 answers the question concerning the sign of His coming and the end of the world. The Jewish understanding of the end of the age and Messiah's subsequent coming are intricately related. The reference to the "coming" in verse 3 (also vv. 27, 37, 39) means the kingdom of God will be established by Messiah as a literal, earthly reign. It is when Christ establishes His kingdom on earth that the unconditional promises made to Israel in the Abrahamic covenant will be fulfilled. Prior to that time, Jerusalem will be *a cup of trembling unto all the people round about* (Zech. 12:2). The present turmoil in the world today is leading toward the fulfillment of Bible prophecy.

Spiritual wisdom. The children of Issachar stood out among the tribes of Israel because they *had understanding of the times, to know what Israel ought to do* (1 Chron. 12:32). In contrast, the Pharisees and Sadducees were rebuked by the Lord for not having understanding of the times. *He answered and said unto them, When it is evening, ye say, It will be fair weather: for the sky is red. And in the morning, It will be foul weather today: for the sky is red and lowering. O ye hypocrites, ye can discern the face of the sky; but can ye not discern the signs of the times?* (Mt. 16:2, 3). God expects His people to understand the times in which they live in order to respond in a manner that is consistent with His revealed will.

The book of Revelation recognizes this necessity to understand the times with phrases such as "here is wisdom" and "the mind which has wisdom" (see also Dan. 12:10). It appears that the "wisdom" is a component of the spiritual insight to understand the events taking place during the Tribulation (Rev. 13:18; 17:9). The "wisdom" is the God-given ability to understand the nature of the revelation. Christians have the mind of the Spirit so that they are not irresponsible spiritually (see 1 Jn. 2:20, 27).

Although the Antichrist will attempt to prove himself as God, he will fail to deceive the elect of God (Mt. 24:24). On the other hand, the world will fall under his deception (despite all of its wisdom and culture) and will worship the Antichrist as God. It is not by wisdom alone that man knows God; rather, man must obey the revelation of God. Despite the horrors of the Tribulation, believers will look to the Word of God understanding that He is still in control as in indicated in His revelation. The phrase, "the mind which has wisdom," indicates the complexity of the revelation that God provides to the reader of the sacred text (cf. Dan. 12:4). True spiritual wisdom will be necessary to understand the events of the Apocalypse. It is during the Tribulation that those who have not been martyred for the cause of Christ will be given eschatological insight to discern the times they are facing.

THE NATIONS IN PROPHECY

God's Judgment upon Individuals. The nature of the Tribulation will center on Israel. Jeremiah 30:7 refers to the Tribulation period as a time of "Jacob's trouble." During this period, God will prepare Israel for restoration and conversion (Deut. 4:29, 30; Jer. 30:3-11; Zech. 12:10). God will also judge an unbelieving world during this time for its sins against God (Isa. 13:9; 24:19, 20; Rev. 4-19). All nations and communities will be affected by this judgment. However, for those who turn to belief in the Messiah, there will be salvation. This time of wrath will also lead to worldwide evangelization and mass conversions (Mt. 24:14; Rev. 7:1-17). Luke 21:24 calls this period the "times of the Gentiles" as a reference to Gentile domination of Jerusalem. At the end of this time period, God will judge the Gentiles for their wickedness and anti-Semitism. The Old Testament prophets understood that, prior to the coming of Messiah in power and glory to rule upon the earth, He would first execute judgment upon the nations and then establish His kingdom in fulfillment of the covenants given to Israel as a nation.[4]

Matthew 25:31-46 and Joel 3:1-3 prophesy of the judgment of the Gentiles. While some believe that the judgment will occur in the valley of Jehoshaphat (based on the passage in Joel), it is possible that this place of judgment will be a future site yet unknown to man since the earth will experience great catastrophic changes during the Tribulation.

The judgment of Matthew 25:31-46 also concerns the Gentiles individually. At this judgment, some will inherit the kingdom while others will be eternally condemned. The basis of the judgment is whether or not Gentiles extended help to the godly remnant of Israel (*one of these brothers of Mine, even the least of them*) because, to extend such help, will be a true evidence of saving grace (cf. Jas. 2:14-26). This judgment will coincide with the final restoration of the nation of Israel (Joel 3:1-3).

Unfortunately, these verses have often been called "the judgment of nations" since they have been misinterpreted to mean that there will be "sheep" or "goat" nations. Matthew 25:31-46 reveals that this is not a judgment of national entities since even the most wicked nation will have some believers. Furthermore, justice would not be served if believers were rejected simply because they lived in a nation that is rejected by God. According to Zechariah 14, *all* nations will come against Israel so it is impossible that there will be any "sheep" nations. Therefore, it must be concluded that this will be a judgment of individuals, not of nations.

Although there will be a brief "taking away" of the unrighteous at the return of Christ (Mt. 24:37-42), it will not be *in toto* since the passage does not specify that all unbelievers will be taken at that time. Some unbelievers ("goats") will live after Christ's Second Coming. It is during the 75-day interval that Christ will judge the sheep and goats. Based on decisions made on earth, some will enter into the millennial kingdom and others will be cast away into eternal punishment. The sheep represent the Tribulation saints, whereas the goats represent the unbelievers. The sheep Gentiles were the ones ready, watching, and laboring in light of the Lord's return to earth. This judgment is distinct from the Great White Throne judgment of Revelation 20:13-15, since, at that judgment, only the wicked will appear before the Judge.

America and Islam. According to *World*, the September 11 terrorist attacks may prove to be a major catalyst toward one-world

19

religion. The irony is that while Americans and Christians (in particular) "are targets of Islamic jihad, all of a sudden Muslims are getting so much good press."[5] The new enemy is not Islam but intolerance. The attack is turning toward those who believe that their faith is the sole means of salvation. This charge applies to the Taliban, but it can also be brought against evangelical Christians.

In a *New York Times* editorial, Thomas L. Friedman writes, "World War II and the cold war were fought to defeat secular totalitarianism—Nazism and Communism—and World War III is a battle against religious totalitarianism." The alternative to religious totalitarianism "is an ideology of pluralism."[6] Religious pluralism is not new to Christianity since it is ultimately rooted in the fall of mankind. Historically speaking, it has become more dominant in the 20th century than in times past. Actually, the whole of the American saga is the story of expanding pluralism and the toleration that follows it. In an interview with Thomas Friedman, Rabbi Hartman said, "America is the Mecca of that ideology, and that is why bin Laden hates and that is why America had to be destroyed."[7]

According to Friedman, World War III will be a battle among those who will not "know that God speaks Arabic on Fridays, Hebrew on Saturdays and Latin on Sundays, and that he welcomes different human beings approaching him through their own history, out of their own language and cultural heritage.... [Various faiths must] reinterpret their traditions to embrace modernity and pluralism, and to create space for secularism and alternative faiths."[8] Christianity cannot reinterpret inspired biblical doctrines to fit the culture. Furthermore, in a pluralistic society, faith in Jesus is no longer the sole way of salvation. From the pluralistic viewpoint, Jews, Muslims, and others are just as likely to enter heaven. Jesus is said to have led people to the heart of God in the same manner as a slice of pie touches its center. In other words, there is a lot of God beyond the slice. In biblical times this view also dominated the culture. The pagans worshipped gods and goddesses, Christ confronted numerous religious sects, Greek philosophy and mystery religions were prevalent, and the Romanist religion mixed politics and religion by glorifying the Caesars.

At least in a democratic society, emphasis is placed on persuasion as opposed to coercion. One cannot coerce an individual to believe what he wants; yet, an individual may be persuaded. The European state churches, for example, are much like a business monopoly that is coercive. In America, separation of church and state fashions a religious equivalent to a free market economy, which is an important distinction between coercion and persuasion. In other words, it is the persuasion of the biblical apologetic that will be effective and is deeply needed today to combat the pluralistic society.

The call for a one-world religion today, based on the premise that all are one, is indeed becoming louder.[9] Such beliefs are clear nonsense. For instance, the world religions cannot all disagree with each other and yet claim they all lead in the same destination. Gene Edward Veith summarizes this thought in his article for *World*:

> The only way to bring them [world religions] under one umbrella is to deny their distinctive teachings and to construct a totally new religion. To not allow different beliefs, to deny the validity of any kind of distinctiveness, and to insist that everyone conform to one overarching ideology—that is totalitarianism. If the culture is indeed drifting toward a new syncretic religion... Christians will find themselves demonized as "intolerant," perhaps our culture's worst form of abuse.[10]

Babylon and Jerusalem. "It was the best of times, it was the worst of times, it was the age of wisdom, it was the age of foolishness, it was the epoch of belief, it was the epoch of incredulity, it was the season of Light, it was the season of Darkness," writes Charles Dickens in his classic *A Tale of Two Cities*. The Bible presents another tale of two cities from Genesis to Revelation identified as Jerusalem and Babylon. Jerusalem is the city of God and Babylon is the city of Satan. Both stand at odds to one another.

The Bible depicts Babylon as the beginning and continual nurturing of the kingdom of man (Gen. 11:1-9). The Satanic reign of Antichrist incorporates all economical, political, religious, and social aspects that are identified with Babylon. Daniel describes Babylon as the beginning of the Gentile kingdoms that will dominate earth's history during the "times of the Gentiles" (Dan. 2, 7; Jer. 30:7; Lk. 21:24). This period will not end until Christ returns to the earth in judgment. Babylon will be revived in the end times to play a significant role in the Tribulation (Rev. 14:8; 16:19; 17-18).

Revelation 17-18 depicts Babylon as the fountainhead of all godless economy, government, and religion. Nearly all ungodliness during the Tribulation period is connected to Babylon. The apostle John writes speaks of "Mystery, Babylon the Great, the Mother of Harlots and Abominations of the Earth" (Rev. 17:5). Babylon, or Antichrist's harlot, is the "mother" of all false religion in the end times from Genesis 11 to Revelation 17. All the religions of the world, including an apostate Christianity, will unite with ecclesiastical Babylon during the Tribulation period (Rev. 17). Nevertheless, God, at the end of the Tribulation, will pass judgment upon these false religions.

Democracy in world government. A major element of Bible prophecy is the belief that there will be a revived form of the four Gentile world powers described in Daniel 2 and 7. It is clear from Daniel 2:36-39 that the first kingdom identified is Babylon. The Medo-Persian Empire will overtake the Babylonian Empire (2:39a) and the Grecian Empire will overtake the second empire (2:39b). The fourth empire that breaks apart the three previous empires is the Roman Empire (2:40-43). The dream of Daniel clearly reveals the succession of Gentile world powers. There is an obvious succession of these powers that exert dominance over the nation of Israel. In the analysis of the democracy in world government remember that there are four empires which dominate not only the nation of Israel, but also the entire Earth. The destruction of these Gentile world powers will only take place when Christ returns and establishes His everlasting kingdom (2:44-45).

Whereas Daniel 2 records the Gentile powers as man sees them, Daniel 7 records them as God sees them – as beasts. Daniel 7:4 describes the first beast, Babylon, like a lion with eagle's wings. Daniel 7:5 describes the second beast, Medo-Persia, like a bear raised on one side. This is a fitting description since the Medes and

Persians produced one empire, but the Persians were the stronger of the two. Daniel 7:6 describes the third beast, Greece, like a leopard with four wings and four heads. The accuracy of this description is fitting to the swift conquests of Alexander the Great. After his death, the Greek Empire was divided into four parts. Daniel 7:7 describes the fourth beast, *dreadful and terrible, and strong exceedingly*. The fourth, and final, beast, with ten horns, personifies Rome as the last Empire. The ten toes in Daniel 2:42 and ten horns in Daniel 7:23, 24 correspond to the fourth beast. It is because Rome is the last empire depicted that it is often taught that a revived form of that empire will be the last earthly kingdom before Messiah returns and establishes His kingdom (Rev. 16:13-16; 19:17; 20:6).

Revelation 13 and 17 also testify that there will be a ten-nation confederacy that is revived in the Tribulation. The ten-nation confederacy is to represent the ten kings that will rule with the Antichrist (Dan. 7:19, 20, 24; Rev. 13:1; 17:12). These toes mingle together into iron and clay forming what many Bible scholars believe to be an accurate picture of the unstable, democratic governments that exist today. Nevertheless, the Antichrist will seize world domination through this confederacy. Dr. Walvoord indicates the importance of understanding this revived Roman Empire according to Bible prophecy. The reunification today of Europe is a clear indicator that God is setting the stage for prophetic events that He inspired the biblical writers to record thousands of years before the actual fulfillment. Walvoord writes,

> The prediction that there will be a ten-kingdom stage of the revival of the Roman Empire is one of the most important descriptive prophecies of the end time. This prophecy anticipates that there will be ten countries originally related to the Roman Empire that will constitute the Roman Empire in its revived form.... Since the names of the countries are not given and there are many more than ten countries in the ancient Roman Empire, it leaves some flexibility in the fulfillment. The prediction, however, requires a political union and then a dictator over the ten countries.[11]

THE MOVEMENT OF PROPHECY

Coming world religion. The last 3 1/2 years of the Tribulation period will be a time of intense persecution for the nation of Israel. It is at the midpoint of the Tribulation period that the Antichrist will break his covenant with Israel (Dan. 9:27; Mt. 24:15). The resultant outcomes will be both political and religious. For instance, the Antichrist will stop the Jewish sacrifices in the rebuilt temple (Dan. 9:27). At this point, the period of time called the "Great Tribulation" will begin (Mt. 24:15, 16, 21).

Daniel 12:11 adds the following: *from the time that the daily sacrifice shall be taken away, and the abomination that maketh desolate set up, there shall be a thousand two hundred and ninety days.* In others words, from the time of the Abomination of Desolation until the beginning of the millennial reign of Christ will be 1,290 days. The extra 30 days after the time of Christ's Second Coming is necessary for the judgment of the sheep and goats to determine who will enter the millennial kingdom and who will be cast away into eternal punishment (cf. Mt. 25). Therefore, the Antichrist will stop both the worship of God and the Jewish sacrificial system in order to declare that he is the one to be worshipped (2 Thess. 2:4).

Religion of the last days. The Bible indicates that the Antichrist (or Beast) will expand his rule from a revived Roman Empire to the entire world during the last half of the Tribulation period (Rev. 13:12-17). Revelation 17-18 indicate that the Antichrist's one-world government will focus upon economic, political, and religious concerns. The world today believes that the only hope for mankind will be a one-world economy, government, and religion. This idea would certainly make sense in an unstable world. However, such attempts are a rejection of God's authority and the attempt of mankind to build heaven on earth.

The move toward a global religion is stronger than ever today. For instance, the New Age movement has infiltrated every area of Western thought including the business world, healthcare, education, and even the church at times. Organizational religious unity and theological heresy are rampant in the current day. Clearly, the stage is set for the rise of the Antichrist from a revived Roman Empire.

The Satanic trinity. The Satanic trinity will be a counterfeit of the true and living God. Satan (representing God the Father), Antichrist (representing God the Son), and the False Prophet (representing God the Holy Spirit) will comprise this false trinity. The Antichrist and the False Prophet will collaborate to develop a one-world government and religion. The False Prophet (or "another beast") will be the spokesperson for the Antichrist (Rev. 16:13; 19:20; 20:10). It is written of the False Prophet: *he deceived them that had received the mark of the beast, and them that worshipped his image* (Rev. 19:20). He deceives the world through "signs and wonders" to worship the first beast, Antichrist.

It is near the end of the Tribulation that the Antichrist grows weary of the counterfeit religion and makes *her desolate, and naked, and shall eat her flesh, and burn her with fire* (Rev. 17:16). The destiny of both the Antichrist and the False Prophet is to be thrown into the lake of fire at the return of Jesus Christ (Rev. 19:20).

Great discernment must be exercised today in light of these future prophecies. Furthermore, any so-called "Christian" movement that is working toward a kingdom on earth should be viewed as working toward the kingdom of Antichrist. The responsibility of each and every Christian is to share the Gospel with the lost and to be ever watchful for the glorious hope of Christ's return.

Kingdom of Antichrist. The Antichrist is known as the "beast" (Rev. 13:1), "the man of lawlessness" (2 Thess. 2:3), "the son of perdition" (2 Thess. 2:3), "Wicked" (2 Thess. 2:8), "the abomination" (Mt. 24:15), the "little horn" (Dan. 7:8), "a king of fierce countenance" (Dan. 8:23), "the prince that shall come" (Dan. 9:26), "a vile person" (Dan. 11:21), the strong-willed king (Dan. 11:36), and the worthless shepherd (Zech. 11:16, 17). The Antichrist not only stands against the true Messiah, but also, in the most diabolical manner, he comes in the place of Christ. The Antichrist will be the one who is able to make the peace process in the Middle East succeed. He will bring about a false peace that will end in sudden destruction (1 Thess. 5:3).

The man of lawlessness (2 Thess. 2:3), or the "wicked," is depraved in his nature and deeds. He is certain to break any and all laws that God has commanded. Specifically, his rebellion is against

God and His law. The Antichrist will actually exalt himself as God and set up an image of himself to be worshiped (Dan. 11:36; 2 Thess. 2:3; Rev. 13:8). The New Age movement will find great joy in this world leader, as he will likely encourage the lie that man can become a "little god." Through "lying signs and wonders" he deceives a wicked and unrepentant world (2 Thess. 2:9-10).

Stories given from the King. Matthew 12:31-37 addresses the national rejection of the Messiah by Israel. The basis for His rejection was their accusation that Jesus was demon possessed. To refuse the testimony concerning Christ could not be forgiven in the Jewish age, in this or any other age to follow. Nevertheless, the scribes and Pharisees approach Jesus, perhaps trying to rescind their accusation demanding that He give them a sign (12:38). The national rejection of Jesus' Messiahship resulted in no more signs given to the Jews. The policy concerning signs changes from the nation of Israel to the apostles; only one sign will be given to the Jews, "the sign of the prophet Jonas" (12:39).

Committing the unpardonable sin by the generation of Jesus' day resulted in the official postponement of the kingdom. The unpardonable sin was a national sin not an individual sin. The nation of Israel fell under physical judgment, resulting in the destruction of the Temple in 70 AD by Titus and his armies. The unpardonable sin was unique to the generation of Jesus' First Coming. Committing the unpardonable sin will result in changes to Jesus' ministry.

Previously, when Jesus performed a miracle, faith was not required. Now, He only performs a miracle if the individual demonstrates faith in Him. When Jesus healed someone previously, He would tell him to spread the news; now, He will instruct him not to speak of the miracle. Proclamation of the message of the kingdom is now silenced. His teaching method, as well, will no longer be readily discernable; rather, He will speak in parables that only His disciples will understand. Using parables provides an outstanding method of memorable teaching while simultaneously hiding the message from the unsaved. The parable is also an excellent vehicle to communicate spiritual truth.

In Matthew 13, Jesus now presents the mysteries of the kingdom. He specifically outlines the course of this age between the two mountain peaks of His First and Second Coming. The mystery kingdom will be composed of both believers and unbelievers, in all parts of the world and in societies that profess devotion to Christ. The mystery kingdom is limited to this earth and lasts from the national rejection of Jesus until the Jews accept Him as Messiah (Mt. 12; 23:39).[12]

Christ's purpose for speaking in parables is to hide the truth; no more light will be given to Israel. *It is given unto* [His disciples] *to know the mysteries of the kingdom, but to* [Israel] *it is not given* (13:11). Another purpose of the parables is to fulfill prophecy (13:35; Ps. 78:2). Matthew 13 describes various points concerning the outworking of the mystery kingdom. The mystery kingdom is "Christendom," which is distinguished from either Christianity or biblical faith. Christendom includes the cults, such as Catholicism, Jehovah's Witnesses, and Mormonism.

The outline of the parables allows us to observe their relationship to one another. For instance, the parables of the mustard seed and leaven are the results of the sower. The mystery kingdom will be characterized by the sowing of the gospel seed throughout this age. However, the true sowing will be imitated by a false countersowing. Two results of this false countersowing will include: 1) the mystery kingdom will assume huge outer proportions, and 2) it will be marked by an inward corruption of doctrine. The results from the true sowing will be: (1) God will gain a believing remnant from Israel, and (2) He will gain believers from among the Gentiles. This age will end with the judgment of Gentiles, bringing the righteous into the Messianic Kingdom, while excluding the unrighteous. Finally, the mystery kingdom will have similarities, and dissimilarities with other facets of God's kingdom program (e.g. eternal, spiritual, theocratic, and messianic kingdoms).

Setting the Stage for Prophetic Sequence. Understanding the sequence of end-time events draws the conclusion that the stage is being set for prophetic fulfillment. It is consistent to believe in future prophetic fulfillment and to believe that God is presently setting key players and allowing key to occur on the world's scene that will be center stage after the Rapture of the church when God resumes His eternal purpose with the nation of Israel. Current world events are setting the stage for the fulfillment of end-time events even though these future events will not be fulfilled during the church age. John Walvoord wrote:

> In the present world scene there are many indications pointing to the conclusion that the end of the age may soon be upon us. These prophecies relating to Israel's coming day of suffering and ultimate restoration may be destined for fulfillment in the present generation. Never before in the history of the world has there been a confluence of major evidences of preparation for the end.
>
> The fact that in our day there is again movement and development in relation to this ancient nation [Israel] is a sign that the stage is being set for the final world drama. Certainly as Israel's promises are being fulfilled in our eyes other aspects of prophecy such as the resurrection of the dead in Christ and the translation of living saints become a real and an imminent possibility. The hope of Israel is also the hope of the church. With John the Apostle all faithful students of the prophetic Word can say: "Amen: come, Lord Jesus."[13]

Though many signs are given for Christ's Second Coming there are none given for the Rapture. There is nothing that must precede the Rapture, and yet nothing that precludes prophesied events from transpiring before the Rapture of the church—it is an imminent event. It is consistent with a futuristic perspective to believe the Rapture is imminent and to also believe that we are living in the last generation of the church age.

Controversy over Prophetic Fulfillment. For many Arabs, the return of the persecuted Jewish people to the Promised Land is abhorrent. Some even believe that Jerusalem and the Temple Mount are Arab property. The events of 11 September concern the religious faith of some in Islam. The recent terrorist attacks relate to God's promises with Israel. God is dealing with Israel as a nation. Nevertheless, there is great controversy over the role of Israel's present state. Some Bible scholars believe the existence of the nation is mere coincidence while others believe Israel's existence harmonizes with God's eternal purpose. There are 2 primary systems of theology that have developed over the past 3 to 4 centuries which address the issues. Those systems, respectively, are dispensationalism and covenant theology.[14] Both systems affect one's perception of Scripture and one's philosophy of God's dealings with humankind throughout history.

The common presupposition for all varieties of covenant theology is an overriding unity for the 66 books that comprise the Holy Scriptures. Rather than having wisdom to discern the real difference among things which resemble one another, the covenantist is driven to find an "integrating principle" (key) that produces theological uniformity with the hope of discovering what the Bible is really all about. Their "key" is the erroneous concept that every relationship between God and man must take the form of a covenant or legal agreement. Their apocryphal Covenant of Works and Covenant of Grace subsequently arise from this notion.

Not all covenant theologians agree when, in history, the Covenant of Grace began. Louis Berkhof believes that it was not formally established until Abraham's time. "Further the Covenant of Grace is predicated on several things of the people who are in it. It requires faithful, devoted love, agreement to be God's people, saving faith in Christ, continual trust in Christ forever, and a life of obedience and consecration to God."[15] In fairness, the covenant theology viewpoint is not all wrong and possesses some excellent features. It emphasizes the grace of God and Christ's redemptive work on the cross resulting in salvation to those who believe. It also centralizes Jesus Christ as the focus of both the Old and New Covenant. It truly attempts to be faithful to the Scriptures while exposing the biblical philosophy of history.

However, this writer has several concerns regarding the covenant theology position. For instance, the ultimate goal of covenant theology in history is too limited. Covenant theology views God's ultimate goal as the redemption of the elect. It is true that God has different roles for different nations in His overall plan, but Israel has a different program than that of the Gentiles. He also has a unique plan for Satan, the non-elect, and nature. Covenant theology denies the existence of distinctive gospels in the Bible. The language of Jeremiah 31:31-34 indicates that the Mosaic and New Covenant are not essentially the same. In Jeremiah 31:32, God declares that the New Covenant is not like the Mosaic Covenant.

DISPENSATIONALISM AND COVENANT THEOLOGY UNMASKED

The Relationship between Law and Grace. What is the relationship of the Old Covenant to the New Covenant today? This is a question that both dispensationalists and covenant theologians seek to answer. The New Testament explicitly states that some of the Mosaic Laws are no longer applicable to Christians, such as dietary restrictions and the stipulations regarding "clean" and "unclean" animals. However, the Ten Commandments appear to be applicable in some sense to the church today since they are part of New Testament morality. The Ten Commandments are not defined as a legal system whereby man can find salvation, but simply as a guide and standard. The only commandment not mentioned in the New Testament pertains to the Sabbath. It is possible that God has allowed freedom of choice on this issue since the church may set aside any day of the week for rest. As the church developed, the first day of the week was traditionally set aside as the day of rest in remembrance of Jesus' day of resurrection.

Classic dispensationalism would argue that the Mosaic Law has been completely abolished as a whole and as a system, although certain elements of the Mosaic Law may be "reincorporated" into the moral standard of the church. This would appear to be the only consistent manner in which to state equivocally that the Law has indeed "ended." McClain writes the following:

> The law had only the "shadow of good things to come," but "not the very image" of those things (Heb. 10:1). Let us recognize the value of the shadow, but let us beware even of seeming to put one iota of the shadow in the place of the substance.[16]

Covenant theology would argue that the ceremonial and civil elements of the Law have been abolished, but the moral element still remains intact. From this perspective, the ceremonial element was temporary since it prefigured the sacrifice and priesthood of Christ. The civil element was applicable to God's people under a theocracy, and since that theocracy no longer exists, neither does the civil element.

Theonomy, which is covenant theology (especially pertaining to replacement theology of Israel with the church), argues that the entire Mosaic Law is in effect because Jesus taught that not one part of the Law would pass away (Mt. 5:18). Therefore, the church should urge society to follow the Mosaic Law in order to bring in the conditions of the millennium. Theonomists would argue that the "law of God" is the will of God today.

The differences in these various perspectives have to do with the issue of continuity and discontinuity. Is there more discontinuity or continuity between the Old Covenant and the New Covenant? There are differences, of course, but the question requiring an answer is whether those differences are relatively minor or major in terms of significance. Theonomy and covenant theology witness more continuity between the 2 covenants. Classic dispensationalism argues for more discontinuity. Progressive dispensationalism, an aberrant form of classic dispensationalism that changes rather than develops the classic view, looks for indicators in the New Testament that parts of the Mosaic Law have been laid aside for the Christian and that the remaining parts can be applied in the sense of deriving eternal principles.

In the progress of dispensations there is gradual unfolding of God's truth, which is called progressive revelation. As God reveals His purposes to man, he is able to learn more concerning God's expectations. Since the transition between dispensations brings radical changes, especially in changing from the Old Covenant to the New Covenant, there is evident discontinuity.

Furthermore, classic dispensationalism understands the Law as the rule of life for the nation of Israel. It is a code of behavior specifically bespoken to a theocratic, earthly nation. The church has laws, yet the presence of the Holy Spirit enables the believer to obey those laws. Covenant theology, on the other hand, states that the Law can be applied today in the same manner under the Old Covenant. Therefore, the nation of Israel is not all that distinct from the church today.

Israel and the Church. Truly, one of the greatest theological battlegrounds of orthodox Christianity throughout the centuries has been the nature and character of the church, in relation to its biblical predecessor, Israel. The covenant view is that the church replaces Israel, becoming "spiritual" or "new" Israel, a continuation of the concept of Israel in the Old Testament. The dispensational view is that Israel and the church are distinct. According to dispensationalism, the church is an entirely new entity that was born on the Day of Pentecost and will continue until she is taken to heaven at the Rapture (Eph. 1:9-11). None of the blessings or curses upon Israel refer directly to the church.[17]

Any view of eschatology that does not give full biblical import to the New Testament teaching that the church differs significantly from Israel is incorrect. The church is a mystery (Eph. 3:1-13) comprised of Jews and Gentiles who are now being united into one body through Christ (2:11-22). Interpretative views that confuse general terms like "elect" and "saints" (which apply to saints of all ages) with specific terms like "church" and those "in Christ" (which refer to believers in the church age only) are misinterpretations of Scripture.

Covenant theology emphasizes that Israel and the church are one entity. They insist that people throughout history are included in the church. However, Jesus Himself spoke of the church coming into existence as a future event (Mt. 16:18) and the Apostle Peter declared that the Day of Pentecost (Acts 2) was "the beginning" of the church (Acts 11:15).

Another error taught by covenant theology is that each of the biblical covenants is a continuation and newer phase of the Covenant of Grace. Grace has always been an element of God's dealing with humankind, but its administration has been handled differently under the Law versus the Church Age. The New Covenant arises from what was not previously there. The writer to the Hebrews states, *Jesus [is] the mediator of a new covenant* (Heb.

12:24). The New Covenant was a mystery not known in the Old Testament. The mediator, Christ, through the shedding of His blood, ratified this covenant in the Dispensation of Grace.

Another serious issue with covenant theology is the use of double hermeneutics it employs when interpreting Scripture. Instead of applying a single meaning to the text, covenant theologians employ a double meaning. In all fairness, the system mainly uses a system of literal interpretation. However, it does use a second method of interpretation when exegeting certain areas of Scripture (specifically prophecy). Covenant theology introduces an allegorical or spiritualization of the Scripture creating an unacceptable method to interpret the plain sense of God's Word. Covenant theology claims that previous prophecies are fulfilled literally (as history verifies), but future prophecies are often allegorized to prove the interpreter's point of view. This mixture of hermeneutical methods is unacceptable and ultimately leads to a distortion of the prophetic teachings in Scripture.

Historical Divisions. Most dispensationalists believe Scripture affirms 7 dispensations. However, all would agree that there at least three main historical divisions in God's dealing with man: Law, Grace, and Kingdom.[18] The Apostle Paul clearly distinguishes between the Dispensation of Law and the Dispensation of Grace in Colossians 1:25-27. Paul also alludes to the Dispensation of the Kingdom in Ephesians 1:10. By analyzing the Bible carefully, other dispensations seem to naturally surface in the historical narration. All the dispensations begin with a *responsibility* from God to man and end with the *moral failure* of man followed by the *judgment* of God.

- Dispensation of Innocence (Gen. 1:28-3:6)
    Responsibility: "do not eat the fruit"
    Failure: "ate the fruit"
    Judgment: "curse and death"

- Dispensation of Conscience (Gen. 3:7-8:14)
    Responsibility: "do good; offer sacrifices"
    Failure: "great wickedness"
    Judgment: "world-wide flood"

- Dispensation of Human Government (Gen. 8:15-11:32)
    Responsibility: "scatter and multiply"
    Failure: "did not scatter and multiply"
    Judgment: "dispersion; confusion of tongues"

- Dispensation of Promise, or Patriarchal Rule (Gen. 12:1-Ex. 18:27)
    Responsibility: "dwell in Canaan"
    Failure: "dwelt in Egypt"
    Judgment: "Egyptian captivity"

- Dispensation of Law (Ex. 19:1-Mt. 27:51)
    Responsibility: "obey the Law"
    Failure: "broke the Law"
    Judgment: "world-wide dispersion"

- Dispensation of Grace (Acts 2:1-1 Thess. 4:18)
    Responsibility: "trust Christ by faith"
    Failure: "reject Christ; apostasy"
    Judgment: "Bema"

- The Seven-Year Tribulation (after the Rapture and ends in Rev. 19:11)
    Transitional period

- Dispensation of Kingdom
    [*Fulfillment of the Biblical Covenants: Abrahamic Covenant (Gen. 12:1 and on), Land Covenant (Deut. 30 and on), Davidic Covenant (2 Sam. 7 and on), and New Covenant (Jer. 31 and on)*]
    Responsibility: "obey and worship God"
    Failure: "final rebellion"
    Judgment: "eternal hell"

- Eternity
    New heaven and new earth

Although Dispensationalism was not systematized as a doctrine until the 1800s, there were men throughout the history of the church that held to a dispensational system of thought. Regarding the ante-Nicene (church) fathers, Justin Martyr (110-165), Irenaeus (ca. 120-202), Tertullian (ca. 150-225), Methodius (d. 311), and Victorinus of Petau (d. ca. 304), Crutchfield remarks:

> Regardless of the number of economies to which the Fathers held, the fact remains that they set forth what can only be considered a doctrine of ages and dispensations which foreshadows dispensationalism as it is held today. Their views were certainly less well defined and less sophisticated. But it is evident that the early Fathers viewed God's dealings with His people in dispensational terms.... In every major area of importance in the early church one finds rudimentary features of dispensationalism that bear a striking resemblance to their contemporary offspring.[19]

John Darby (1800-1882), a Church of England pastor, visited the United States on several occasions teaching many the dispensational viewpoint. Beyond the 7 dispensations, Darby's teachings had a definite program of eschatology delineated through five steps. First, Darby held to a two-stage coming of Christ, that is, the Rapture and *parousia* (coming). Second, he believed in 7 years of tribulation on earth for those who were not raptured. During that period, the last 3 1/2 years will be the time of the Antichrist and 144,000 Jews will trust Christ and become evangelists. Thirdly, Christ will return with the church, conclude the battle of Armageddon, and rule for 1,000 years. Fourthly, he believed in an unconditional covenant between God and Israel. According to Darby, God is working through Israel and the church. In the millennium, national Israel will be restored. Lastly, he taught that all Old Testament prophecy will be fulfilled literally.[20]

Ryrie demonstrated that prior to Darby, Pierre Poiret (1646-1719) expounded a rather complete system of theology that was both premillennial and dispensational. Jonathan Edwards

(1637-1716) published *A Compleat History or Survey of All the Dispensations* (1669), providing a dispensational scheme even though he spiritualized Christ's millennial reign. Isaac Watts (1674-1748) gave an extensive outline of dispensations in works. It is noteworthy that Scofield's dispensationalism is closer to the teaching of Watts than Darby.[21] The obvious conclusion is that men long before Darby taught dispensational concepts and that dispensationalism and eschatology are closely related. It was not systematized until recently because it was not a subject of great discussion until the present time since doctrine always arises out of a theological void.

 Some of the more popular advocates of dispensationalism have been C. H. MacKintosh, W. E. Blackstone, Donald Grey Barnhouse, James Brookes, H. A. Ironside, Warren Wiersbe, J. Dwight Pentecost, Charles Ryrie, John Walvoord, and A. C. Gaebelein. More recently in this century, Hal Lindsey espoused dispensational thinking in his best-selling book, *The Late Great Planet Earth* (1970). The books of Daniel and Revelation are key to the dispensational system. For instance, dispensationalists see the church mentioned in the beginning chapters of Revelation (chs. 1-3), but the remainder of Revelation (chs. 4-18) deals with the 7 years of Tribulation after the Rapture of the church. Revelation is primarily written for those who will be on earth during that time of Tribulation.

Grace in Dispensationalism. One accusation leveled at dispensationalists relates to the aspect of grace. Some contend that dispensationalists define the different economies of God in such a manner that grace has not been the overriding element in God's dealing with humankind. This is misstating the issue since all dispensationalists believe, as Scripture clearly teaches, that salvation has always been by grace through faith.

God's grace has always existed through faith. During each dispensation, God deals with His people in accordance to what He revealed to that generation. When Cain slew his brother Abel, God's grace was administered to Cain although he had taken the life of his brother. Instead of killing Cain, God sent him to wander the earth through the administration of grace. Grace is always by faith (Eph. 2:8). God's grace has always been in effect according to New Testament teaching.

> Whom God hath set forth to be a propitiation through faith in his blood, to declare his righteousness for the remission of sins that are past, through the forbearance of God (Rom. 3:25).

Paul affirms the necessity of Christ's sacrifice at Calvary to make the forgiveness of sin a reality for all who will believe. The writer to the Hebrews maintains the same view:

> And for this cause he is the mediator of the new testament, that by means of death, for the redemption of the transgressions that were under the first testament, they which are called might receive the promise of eternal inheritance (Heb. 9:15).

The first covenant required that a price be paid for all the sin committed under it for which Christ was the propitiation. He was therefore, as stated in Revelation 5, the Lamb that was slain from the creation of the world. It was since the foundation of the earth that God decreed a plan of grace that was a mystery until it was revealed to the Apostle Paul.[22] Even for those who have not heard the gospel, man is without excuse since he will be judged according to the evidence in the created universe.

> For the invisible things of him from the creation of the world are clearly seen, being understood by the things that are made, even his eternal power and Godhead; so that they are without excuse (Rom. 1:20).

Therefore, it can be witnessed that Christ is the Redeemer for both the Old and New Covenant. The Mosaic Law was given to establish moral absolutes and to convey the penalty for sin. The grace associated with the Law did not appear because of the reality of breaking it and its subsequent punishment (often death). Ephesians 2:15, 16 supports this. Even under the Law, grace was administered by the temporary covering of sin through animal sacrifice. However, the actual covering of grace did not occur

THE PENALTY OF DEATH

until Christ's death (Rom. 3:25). In Romans 7:4, Paul asserts that Christians have become dead to the law through Christ's physical death. The law came through Moses, but grace came through Jesus Christ.

Modern System of Theology. Another fallacy propagated in many theological circles today is that dispensationalism is a modern theology of the church. This tendency does not necessarily prove the reliability or falsity of a particular view, but it is germane to the discussion. Opponents of dispensationalism attempt to divert the issue by claiming that Scripture does not use the word "dispensation" in the same theological sense that is often taught. Ryrie states that 2 facts should reverberate in response to this charge. Foremost, on at least 2 occasions, Scripture does use the word in the same way as dispensationalists (Eph. 1:10; Eph. 3:2). In both of these verses the Greek word *oikonomia* is used, which is translated as administration (of a household or estate); or specifically as a (religious) "economy"—dispensation, or stewardship. Second, Ryrie contends, "it is perfectly valid to take a biblical word and use it in a theological sense as long as the theological use is not unbiblical."[23] He then clarifies this point stating that all conservatives use the word "atonement" in such a way. The word is never used in the New Testament, yet theologically it represents what is involved in the death of Christ on the cross.

As a developed theological system, dispensationalism did not appear until the 17th century when Pierre Poiret wrote about it in *The Divine Economy: or An Universal System of the Works and Purposes of God towards Men Demonstrated.* In these writings Poiret outlined 7 dispensations. A thorough systemization of dispensational theology took place later under John Nelson Darby. As a Church of England pastor, Darby became disenchanted with the state-church religion and began to write about the fact that the church had not taken the place of the Jews in Scripture. Throughout his extensive writings Darby developed a systematic view of Scripture during the next 30 years of his ministry. Acknowledged as the father of modern dispensationalism (that is, Darby developed the system the most systematically), he is remembered for calling the church to be prepared for the imminent return of Christ in the

Rapture. Darby stated in his works, "A dispensation is an economy, any order of things that God has arranged on earth. The primary characteristics of a dispensation include governmental administration, responsibility, and revelation to fulfill both. Secondary characteristics include testing, failure, and judgment. When a group fails the test to exercise their responsibility given to them by God, judgment falls and ends the dispensation."[24]

Other well-known modern day dispensationalists are Cyrus Ingerson Scofield (1843-1921), John Flipse Walvoord (1910-2002), and Charles Caldwell Ryrie (1925-). Scofield is widely known for his *Scofield Reference Bible* with extensive notes concerning dispensational premillennialism. Scofield popularized the dispensational system in his study Bible printed in 1909. He set forth 7 dispensations regarding God's dealing with human beings: (1) Innocence (Gen. 1:28), the period of time in the Garden of Eden; (2) Conscience (Gen. 3:23), the awakening of human conscience and the expulsion from the Garden; (3) Human Government (Gen. 8:20), the new covenant made with Noah, bringing about human government; (4) Promise (Gen. 12:1), the new covenant made with Abraham; (5) Law (Ex. 19:8), the period of acceptance of the Jewish law; (6) Grace (Jn. 1:17), beginning with the death and resurrection of Jesus; and (7) Kingdom (Eph. 1:10) constituting the final rule of Christ.

Does it Matter? Does it really matter whether one adopts a dispensational or covenant theology position? Both adhere to the shed blood of Christ as man's Redeemer from the penalty of sin. Yet, on the other hand, one's theological position impacts one's view of God's ultimate purpose for history and the unfolding of future events in Scripture. Doctrine determines attitudes and practice. Therefore, the system of doctrine to which a person is committed does make a difference. In light of this thought, it is crucial that every Christian diligently search the Scriptures to determine whether it is covenant theology or dispensational theology that accurately represents the biblical view.

Os Guinness is one critic of premillennial dispensationalism stating that it "has had unfortunate consequences on the Christian mind."[25] He accuses dispensationalism as being anti-intellectual "by its general indifference to serious engagement with culture" and associates it with a "careless crossover between the Bible and historical events of its day."[26] The problem with such a statement is that all conservative evangelicals, regardless of their theological viewpoint, reacted to the liberal social gospel of the 19th and early 20th century when all stepped away from "serious engagement with culture" because of the social gospel that was so prevalent at the time.

Ryrie emphasizes the importance of dispensationalism in history and in the present:

> If one does not interpret the Bible this way, will it mean that he cuts down some of its parts? Not at all. Actually, the Bible comes alive as never before. There is no need to dodge the plain meaning of a passage or to reinterpret or spiritualize it in order to resolve conflicts with other passages. God's commands and standards for me today become even more distinct, and His program with its unfolding splendor falls into a harmonious pattern. The history of dispensationalism is replete with men and women who love the Word of God and promote its study, and who have a burden for spreading the gospel to all the world.[27]

One last statement is a particularly relevant admonition from Ryrie:

> Dispensationalists are conservatives and affirm complete allegiance to the doctrines of verbal, plenary inspiration, the virgin birth and deity of Christ, the substitutionary atonement, eternal salvation by grace through faith, the importance of godly living and the ministry of the Holy Spirit, and hope for the future in the coming of Christ. Those who are divided from us in the matter of dispensationalism or premillennialism may remember the areas in which they are united with us....Some doctrines are more important than others,

so it particularly behooves us not to cut off our fellowship from those who share similar views about these
important doctrines.[28]

THE PRACTICAL VALUE OF BIBLE PROPHECY

Though terribly saddened and grieved by the heart-wrenching world
events of today, the understanding of the coming Tribulation has led
many Bible teachers to uphold the truth that the entire world is moving toward the prophetic events described in Scripture. Scripture
states that scoffers will come in the last days questioning the return
of the Lord (2 Pet. 3, 4). Today's current events have scoffers on the
run with no explanation of what is taking place in our world. When
terrible times come, people need more than ever to think of eternity,
and of what really matters in life. They need to have their eternal
salvation secure in the work of Christ on the cross. Pastors need to
explain what is behind current events. Christians need to be
reminded to use the New York terrorist attack as teaching points
about the dangerous and depraved world in which we live. Each
moment should be seized to proclaim to men and women the marvelous grace and the eternal life found only in Jesus Christ.

Bible prophecy is an impetus to believers to warn the lost. Since
these events have not yet occurred, it proves *that the longsuffering
of our Lord is salvation* (2 Pet. 3:15). Peter's words of exhortation
are both dramatic and sobering as he prioritizes the believer's
responsibilities to live a diligent life, in peace, spotless and blame-
less in Christ.

The future is certain for all those who are in the Lord Christ
Jesus. The duration of all the saints in eternal fellowship with the
God of peace, who has reconciled the elect unto Himself, will be
everlasting. Since God has given such a great hope for the church,
His people should take comfort that *God hath not appointed us to
wrath, but to obtain salvation by our Lord Jesus Christ* (2 Thess.
1:9; 2 Tit. 2:13). Christians are to warn those that do not have such
hope that the coming of God in judgment will be swift (2 Thess.

TRIB IS SATAN'S WRATH

41

2:1-3). Indeed, God is setting the stage in our day for the time known as the Tribulation when the riders of the Apocalypse come forth. Are you proclaiming the prophetic truth and do you understand the times in which we live?

The early church would greet each other (in the form of a petition) with the word "maranatha" (1 Cor. 16:22) meaning "our Lord come." It was spoken to indicate their eager expectation for the coming of the Lord Jesus to deliver the church from the coming Day of the Lord (1 Thess. 1:10). As Christians, we should live each day with an eternal perspective knowing that our future in Christ is certain. Maranatha!

THE COMMUNICATION OF PROPHECY

Chapter 1

PRESENTING BIBLE PROPHECY THROUGH FICTION

RUSSELL S. DOUGHTEN, JR.

A*nd with many such parables spake· he the word unto them, as they were able to hear...But without parables spake he not unto them* (Mk. 4:33, 34)

From time memorial, and throughout the history of man, the storyteller has been a focal point of all known cultures. In fact, much of the Bible is factual history presented in story form. Moses begins Genesis with a factual, historical story of creation. He then tells the stories of Adam and Eve in the Garden, Cain slaying Abel, Noah and the Flood, Abraham's willingness to sacrifice his son, the accounts of Joseph, Joshua and Caleb, and many more.

The Bible stories of historical fact are filled with colorful characters, stirring events, challenging themes and often a surprising plot twist—elements that grace all good storytelling, whether fact or fiction. The stories that Moses wrote are Scripture—the Word of God. They are true! We can rely on them for information and instruction. We can also apply the insights they bring to our lives, our families, our relationships, even to our business, knowing that we are on safe ground.

The writers of the New Testament are equally reliable. Matthew and Mark, for instance, both reveal the historical fact that to reach the "ears" of His audience, Jesus prefers a unique type of story-telling prophesied by Asaph in Psalm 78:35 and repeated in Matthew. *I will open my mouth in parables; I will utter things that have been kept secret since the foundation of the world* (Mt. 13:35). Jesus uses stories of non-historical events or persons to communicate true spiritual concepts to us. His purpose appears to be to implant each concept deeply into our spiritual awareness. Then, if we are yielded to His Spirit, or "have ears to hear", the hidden meaning blossoms within our minds and hearts. Both Gospel writers emphasize that Jesus uses only this method to communicate these most important spiritual concepts about Himself, the Father and the kingdom of heaven. They both report that...*without parables spake he not unto them* (Mt. 13:34b and Mk. 4:33a).

Since the parable is so important to Jesus and since He demonstrates its great effectiveness as a way to communicate spiritual truth, should not we who follow Him try to master the use of the parable? Should we not seek to use the parable to tell others about His great salvation and His imminent return? Especially in the realm of prophecy, which constitutes 28% of the Word of God and over which so many believers puzzle and unbelievers speculate, should not the parable be used to bring believers to a deeper spiritual understanding of God's eternal plan and to bring unbelievers to Christ? For me, I believe His answer to all of these questions is, "Yes!"

However, I also believe that God has some pre-conditions, cautions and limitations for those of us who would use the parable (stories of non-historical events and persons, in other words, fiction) to reveal scriptural and, particularly, prophetic truth. First, I believe that those of us telling parables about eternal life and prophetic events should understand from personal experience what it is to be "born again". From that perspective I offer my personal testimony.

BEGINNING

I was 24 years old when I reccived Christ on 14 June 1951. I had grown up in the church, learned many Bible stories, sang in two choirs, and was even baptized two times. I also had a degree in drama and was enrolled to study for a second degree in directing, producing and writing from the Yale Graduate School of Drama in September.

My wife and I were working that summer in her hometown of What Cheer, Iowa. A simple invitation to a Bible study from an interim pastor of a little church there led to a momentous change in my life. Through a few simple verses, I learned the profound truth that, like all of mankind, I was a sinner. I learned that my sin had separated me from God but that Jesus Christ, out of his great love for me, had died for me. I learned that he said *I am the way, the truth, and the life. No man comes to the Father except through Me* (Jn. 14:6). I learned that if I truly believed that He is the Son of God with the power to forgive my sin and asked for His forgiveness that He would forgive me, give me the gift of eternal life and make me a child of God.

Wow! How I wanted his forgiveness! How I prayed for the gift of eternal life! How wonderful if I could actually become a child of God! When I told the pastor what I was thinking and feeling about Jesus, he said, "You should be baptized right away." I agreed to the baptism but having already been baptized twice I secretly wondered "How many baptisms must one experience before it takes?"

Somehow it seemed very important to recognize the exact time when I would pass from being a lost sinner to becoming a newborn child of God. So I prayed that the Lord would help me know the precise moment during the baptismal ceremony when I was being saved. As I put on the baptismal robe, I silently asked "Lord, is it now?" No answer came. As I walked down the steps into the baptismal water, I asked" "Lord, is it now?" No answer. I recited a Bible verse to the onlookers ...*for it is by grace that you are saved, through faith...*(Eph. 2:8). "Lord, is it now?" Still no answer. The pastor took me by the shoulders, one hand on my head. He recited "In the name of the Father, and of the Son..." "Lord, is it now?"

Under the water I went (buried with Christ in baptism). "Lord, surely it must be now!" Still no answer! I came up out of the water, walked up the steps, and changed into dry clothes. No answer. By this time I was disappointed and greatly puzzled. "Why didn't the Lord answer my fervent prayer?"

For a few days I pondered the situation. I searched the Scriptures. I went back over the verses we had studied. *For all have sinned and fall short of the glory...*(Rom. 3:23). *For the wages of sin is death, but the gift of God is eternal life through Jesus...*(Rom. 6:23). *For God so loved...that He gave his only begotten Son, that whosoever believeth on Him shall not perish but have...*(Jn. 3:16). *As many as received Him, who believed on His name, He gave the right to be children of God* (Jn. 1:12).

And then the light dawned!

It had already happened! Right there in the pew, during the Bible study, as I *repented* and *confessed* that I was a sinner! As I believed that Jesus was the Son of God who could forgive sin! As I gave my heart to Him knowing that He was the "way" to the Father. At that moment! At the *moment of my faith!* Jesus saved me! *I was then and am now a child of God!* He had answered my prayer of faith by giving me eternal life and He had verified this by also answering my prayer to know the exact moment of my salvation. Hallelujah!

DISCOVERY

I did not fully realize it then but this knowledge was to be very important in framing my lifetime service to the Lord as a film evangelist. I have come to understand that it is important for the evangelist to know without question that...*faith cometh by hearing and hearing by the word of God* (Rom. 10:17). It is important for him to know that...*now is the accepted time; behold, now is the day of salvation* (2 Cor. 6:2). It is important to realize that once the Word of God, the "good news" about Jesus Christ – who He is and His power to forgive – reaches the heart of the non-believer then, at that moment, life-giving faith, in Jesus Christ instantly occurs. It can be in the middle of a conversation, while reading the Bible or a novel, during prayer, alone or with someone or in the middle of a crowd. It can even occur while viewing a prophetic motion picture that glorifies Jesus Christ!

Second, I believe the teller of prophetic parables should be "called". He should feel comfortable that he is being guided by the Lord in the telling of the parable for the Lord's purposes.

After my salvation experience I continued reading the Bible, searching for my life direction. I was greatly impressed by the realization that Jesus told so many parables. I thought, "What a wonderful means of communication! What a subtle, dramatic way for Him to connect His infinite, spiritual thoughts to the finite minds and hearts before Him." "Could it be," I mused, "that the Holy Spirit had guided me to study drama even before He graciously gave me the faith in Jesus that brought me salvation?"

I had been fascinated by the study of the book of Job, the earliest extant drama, and deeply moved by the great Greek tragedies and comedies, the highest religious expressions of pre-Christian culture, which are still impacting the world today. Gripped by His Spirit, the thought broke through, "Why shouldn't the truly great dramas of this age center on Jesus, the 'only wise God', the Giver of eternal life?" As I prayed, I realized, "He has been preparing me to tell parables for Him!"

Third, I believe that the effective teller of parables must believe that the Bible is true. Although the Yale Graduate School of Drama is a secular school, it was recognized at that time as the finest drama school in the country. I thought the Lord wanted me to receive a first-class education in acting, writing, directing, and production. So in September my wife Gertrude and I moved to New Haven, Connecticut.

I was determined to take every opportunity to apply Scripture and Christian principles to my drama studies. To do that, I knew that I needed a solid understanding of the Bible. So I also enrolled in a Yale Divinity School "Old Testament" course. The very first day in the class the Old Testament professor began by saying that the Bible "is not true." He said, "Although Mama believes that the Bible is true, Mama is not aware of the multiplicity of writers of Scripture who contradict each other and have their own agendas of truth."…"Whoa!"…My solar plexus kicked in. He went on to list a dozen or so of these writers, giving each one a letter identification. I felt like I had stumbled into a nest of vipers. Fortunately, the Lord moved me quickly out of the "higher criticism" and into a sound conservative Bible study.

As I continued in my drama studies, the Lord arranged for me to work on several dramatic presentations of spiritual significance. Among these was a play called *The First Born* about the Pharaoh's tragic loss of his first-born son after he defied the God of Moses. Also, I was cast as Paul in the play *Paul in Corinth*, was able to perform in *Phaedra*, a Racine adaptation of the Greek tragedy of Hypolytus and was able to direct the Irish tragedy, *Riders to the Sea* by John Millington Synge. I was also privileged to work with the play write and to be the first director of a play based on the book of Jeremiah called *I Believe in Rubble*. Following that was my master's thesis production, *Judas Iscariot*, another original script based on the twelve Apostles as they are depicted in the four Gospels.

Implausible as it seems, through my drama work at Yale, God had forced me into an in-depth study of the Pentateuch, the Prophets, the Gospels and Paul's letters. All this, plus a thorough study of the book of Hebrews at my church, led me to the conclusion, contrary to the Old Testament professor, that the Bible is, indeed, true and filled with truthful facts, characters, action, relationships, emotions, desires, history and prophecy. It appeared to me that the purpose of the Book is to reveal Jesus Christ as the Messiah, the only Son of God and His mission of creation, salvation and eternal rule.

One of the strongest proofs to me, of the accuracy of the Bible, is the 28 % that is prophecy, of which about half has already occurred exactly as predicted. Since prophetic statements are scattered throughout the Bible in nearly every book and since only God perfectly knows the future, that is proof that the writers were inspired by God. Moreover, it offers proof that the prophetic events that have not yet happened will occur in the future exactly as predicted. My conclusion was that faithful men guided by the Holy

Spirit wrote exactly what God wanted and the Bible is true! I can base my life on it! I can base my work of telling parables on it. And even though I may fail, if I put the Word in my work, it will not fail for God has promised, "My Word will not return void".

After graduating from Yale, the Lord led us to Good News Productions, a Christian film company in Chester Springs, Pennsylvania. As I began to master filmmaking, I continued to read the Bible eagerly, learning to trust it more and more. However, no matter how much I poured over it, I found much of prophecy confusing. Seeing my quandary, a friend at Good News, gave me a copy of the book *Dispensational Truth* by Clarence Larkin. As I read Larkin and considered the charts, I went to the Bible and re-read the prophecies of Daniel, Ezekiel, Revelation, Isaiah, Zechariah, Thessalonians, Peter, Matthew and the prophetic statements of Jesus in all the four gospels, searching for the truth about these prophecies. I wondered, "How can Larkin know this? How can he be so confident in the meanings and sequence of prophetic events? How can he know enough to make the charts and visualizations?"

The more I studied the more I became convinced that not only were the historical events and facts of the Bible true, but also, the prophecies about Jesus' first coming actually did happen as they were prophesied. That seemed to be strong evidence that the scriptural prophecies of the future would also occur according to God's sequence of events revealed therein. I was amazed to find that studying Biblical prophecy brought more certainty that the whole Bible was truly God's Word, that it is based on historical facts written by faithful men urged by the Holy Spirit in such a manner that all parts interrelated in ways that verified not only the parts but also the whole. I found that it seems to make the best sense when taken literally. Even the poetic and metaphorical languages seem to be used by God to illustrate and communicate specific Godly truths. It appeared to me that God "says what He means" and "means what He says" in His Word. I did not learn until several years later that the view of Scripture I had adopted is known among scholars as the "grammatical - historical" approach to interpreting them.

PROPHETIC FILMS

After beginning to open my understanding and passion for prophetic Scripture, the Lord allowed me to deviate in the area of making feature films that did not have explicit gospel content. Although these films enjoyed modest success from a worldly viewpoint, at the local premiere of one of these films, while everyone was celebrating, He quietly struck a blow to my heart when He asked in that wee small voice, "What have you told these people about My Son? Has He been lifted up in all this excitement and activity? Will this crowd of people leave this show knowing any more about Jesus than when they came?" I was deeply chastened. I resolved right there not to make another film that did not focus on honoring Jesus Christ.

Shortly after that incident the Lord brought Donald W. Thompson and me together and gave us the impetus to make a prophetic film that He would honor. That film was *A Thief in the Night*. It was about the Rapture of the church, a subject that we have since discovered interests almost everyone who hears about it. *A Thief in the Night* grew into a series of films that God uses even today to reach many lost souls for Christ. The first three, *A Thief in the Night*, *A Distant Thunder*, and *Image of the Beast* were a phenomenon. Shortly after the release of the fourth film in the series, *The Prodigal Planet,* our records showed that an estimated over 300,000,000 (more than most Hollywood blockbusters) persons had seen the series at film showings around the world. At that point we had reports estimating over 6,000,000 people had received Christ after viewing the films. Since then they continue to be popular and many more have viewed the films in additional languages through many showings on television, on videocassettes and now on newly released DVD with added material.

There are so many prophetic elements in the Scriptures that a single fictitious story, novel or film cannot possible include them all. Therefore, very cautious selection is necessary or even a series of stories might be desirable as has been demonstrated in our prophetic film series, *A Thief in the Night, A Distant Thunder, Image of the Beast, The Prodigal Planet*, with a fifth, sixth and seventh film projected to complete the story. Recently we have seen the extraordinary success of the *Left Behind* series of novels by Tim LaHaye and Jerry Jenkins. Nine volumes of stories about the same characters followed *Left Behind* with three more books projected in the series. There are reports of over 30,000,000 books sold to date. Several other apocalyptic films have been released by Cloud Ten including *Left Behind, the Movie* and *Tribulation Force*, as well as films by other producers like *The Omega Code* and *Megiddo*. These examples help us see that people gravitate in great numbers to prophetic fiction in the form of novels and motion pictures. Therefore, it is incumbent on those of us who are called to work in the media of novel and film to inquire of ourselves "what are the proper, the Godly guidelines for expressing the 'good news' and prophetic truth of Jesus Christ in these vehicles of prophetic fiction'?"

"Eye has not seen –"

Eye has not seen, nor ear heard, neither has it entered into the mind of man, the things that God has prepared for them that love him (1 Cor 2:9)

As a story teller, I cannot hope to express either the fullness of the exquisite joy and ecstasy that is experienced in heaven when one sinner is found by our Lord, forgiven, and brought into His family, nor the agonizing depths of the groaning and gnashing of teeth experienced by those who are thrown into "outer darkness" by their own folly of disbelief. The "Hollywood" approach might be to labor through a myriad of the most graphic technical effects in order to try to technically impose the experience upon the viewer. That will cost millions and cannot be accomplished because filmmakers are men and it "has not entered into the mind of man the blessings that God has prepared" – so it can only fall short. It is better for us, the storytellers, to suggest, reveal in part, direct and captivate the mind and heart of the viewer so that he, the viewer, will open his heart and mind to the Holy Spirit who will, through the Word, reveal the depths of love, vision and understanding to the fullest measure that the viewer can receive.

We, the story tellers, can and I believe, must, use the Word of God in the storytelling in order to direct the viewer to the truth, validity and application of the Word to their present condition and circumstances. Therefore, I as the storyteller must consciously work prayerfully, and openly with the Holy Spirit as all the elements are created which will lead the viewer to a fully receptive condition. I must be careful not to limit the work of the Spirit. In fact, I must faithfully try to remove those elements that "bedim and obstruct" and thus limit the full effectiveness of the communication that God's Word is making to the experience and growth of the viewer.

Moving unbelievers to belief, believers to serve

How does the story telling in a motion picture move the unbeliever to belief and the believer to serve and witness? As the story is revealed the viewers mind is engaged and his emotions stirred. As he identifies with the character and is drawn into the plot his spirit is opened. It is then that the Holy Spirit becomes involved with the viewer's spirit. It is then that the well-told parable can have its desired effect because *things of the spirit are spiritually discerned* (1 Cor. 2:14). The spirit of the lost person viewing will become increasingly aware of the majesty and sovereignty of God and will greatly desire to be in His presence. He will begin to see that in his present sinful state he is separated from God by sin and cannot, of himself, be cleansed enough to enter into God's presence. As he sees Jesus Christ being lifted up in the story and sees how others have been cleansed by Christ's blood, he finds himself repenting of his sins and turning to Jesus for forgiveness. As he sees the character in the story with whom he has identified, cleansed, freed from his sin and entering into a close relationship with Jesus, then he sees that he also can experience a close relationship with Jesus, that he also can truly repent of his sins, and ask Jesus for forgiveness and that Jesus will then freely forgive him and give him the gift of eternal life – an eternal total relationship with Jesus Christ. Hopefully, joyfully he finds that happening.

When the viewer who is already a believer and a born again child of God sees these same characters and events happening and when his mind and emotions are similarly engaged by the storyteller, he begins to see his role of serving his Savior in a deeper more meaningful way. As the Christian viewer begins to open his spirit to the Holy Spirit's voice, he starts to see how important it is for him to tell his family and friends who do not know the Lord how they too can be forgiven. He sees more clearly that the certain destiny of each person he knows will be either joy in heaven and eternal life with Jesus Christ or eternal separation from Christ in the eternal agony of the "outer darkness" reserved for those whom Jesus "never knew". He will leave the film inspired with the desire to be a "servant and a witness", to know the Bible and the prophecies more thoroughly, to be obedient to the Word and especially to tell others about the "Wonderful Counselor" who is his Savior.

THE "CRACK"—ENTERTAINMENT VS. REVEALING CHRIST IN THE STORYTELLING

Evangelism

I am impressed by the evangelist who said that, in leading someone to Christ, you must love him or her. You put your arms around them and "feel" for "the crack" that is the opening to the heart. When you find "the crack" you pour the gospel of Jesus Christ into it. The gospel then trickles through the crack until it touches their heart, at which time; the Holy Spirit creates their own individual faith in Jesus Christ as their Savior and Lord.

It does not grow into Christian morality or popular Christian family values, or 'doing good to the poor and indigent' or giving your life as a missionary to deepest Africa. These very desirable ends cannot properly develop before the regeneration that comes only with faith in Jesus Christ and receiving His forgiveness of sins and gift of eternal life. Only then can a new believer by studying and following the Word (the whole Word, including the 28% which is prophecy) and being obedient to it, develop and properly pursue these highly important Christian goals with certainty.

The young Christian who tells me he is "called" to make a film frequently dismays me. He does not want to call it a "Christian" film because that name has the bad reputation of being a poorly told tale with very little production excellence. "The Christian film," he says, "tends to be 'preachy' in presenting Scripture and salvation through Jesus Christ and has very little to offer in terms of entertainment." He wants to "fill the gap" between the "Christian" film and the "Hollywood" sleazy motion picture that has slick production values but upholds the degenerate behavior of infidelity, depraved morality and blasphemous dialogue. His film will show Christian morality and family values (without calling attention to them). His film will win wide acceptance among both believers and non-believers because of its excellent production techniques and storytelling. He will avoid insulting the audience by telling them that they are sinners who need forgiveness and saving faith in Jesus Christ. Little does he realize that "filling the gap" in that manner very likely will be falling into the abyss of actually deceiving his audience into thinking they can please God by ignoring His Son. He may even be teaching them to seek the gift of eternal life by "working their way to God", through imitating the "moral life", and "family values" depicted in his story.

What he must do is to use all his knowledge of excellent production techniques and storytelling to create a compelling work which reveals the source of "Christian" morality and true family values – that source is the redemptive power of Jesus Christ, the cleansing power of His blood, the inspiration of His Word, the guiding comforting power of the Holy Spirit and the blessed hope of Christ's imminent return. These elements should be so inextricably woven into the texture of the plot and characters that to remove them or to avoid them would destroy the effect and beauty of the story. These elements should be an inherent part of the "interest creating" or "entertainment" value of the story.

God's Special Provision
Since the invention of the printing press God has greatly used the printed word to spread the gospel. However, even today a large percentage of the people in the world cannot read. *The Holy Bible, Pilgrim's Progress, Left Behind,* and the works of Aristotle will not be read by hundreds of millions in every culture in this present generation

because they cannot read. If a story is being told or visually shown people who cannot read, they will cluster to a radio, watch television, view a videocassette or a motion picture. Even though they cannot read, they can receive the full gospel message. I believe that God has raised up these technical wonders in this special age before Jesus' Second Coming to make it possible for a witness of Jesus Christ to go out to every one of the 6.5 billion inhabitants of the earth.

CAUTIONS TO OBSERVE IN PRESENTING PROPHECY THROUGH FICTION

Over the years, as I have worked on several prophecy films, I have found it important to keep in mind the following list of things to avoid while trying to communicate the gospel message through prophetic films.

- Making the prophecy seem fictitious, allegorical or symbolic, that is, not literal in fulfillment. You do not want to mislead the audience to think things about prophecy that God does not intend, such as setting dates or suggesting the following:
- Mid-Tribulation or Post-Tribulation Rapture
- A Post-Millennial Return of Christ
- Millennialism, that is, no literal Millennium
- Preterism – the idea that the Rapture, Tribulation and the Second Coming occurred in 70 AD
- Suggesting that prophecy will only be partially fulfilled.
- Making up "biblical" events that are not revealed in Scripture.
- Adding "biblical" characters to the prophetic events.
- Omitting biblical characters that are predicted to participate in prophetic events.
- Changing the sequence of biblical prophetic events.
- Attributing to the church (believers) prophetic events that are predicted for Israel.

- Attributing to Israel prophetic events predicted for the church.

The reader or viewer of any fictional story about prophecy is cautioned to refer to his Bible often to verify that the prophetic story he is witnessing truly follows the prophetic events revealed in the Scripture.

THE CREATOR CAN AND CANNOT

The creator (writer/filmmaker) of popular fiction *cannot* assume that the reader or film audience:

- Knows anything about the content of Scripture.
- Knows anything about sin or repentance and the for-giving, caring power of Jesus Christ.
- Knows anything about prophecy prior to the birth of Jesus Christ or after His death and resurrection.
- Knows anything about the Rapture, the Tribulation, or the Second Coming.
- Knows anything about the church being made up of individuals saved (born again) by the grace of Jesus Christ and the power of the Holy Spirit.

The creator of popular fiction *can* assume that:

- God loves the reader (audience).
- The Holy Spirit is devoutly interested in creating faith in Jesus Christ in the heart of the reader (audience).
- The reader (audience) has witnessed God's creation around him and within himself and has observed that a great power (and not himself) has brought this universe into being and continues its existence (Rom 1:20).
- The reader (audience) has noticed his own imperfec-tion and that he has not gained total mastery of that problem.

- The Holy Spirit has been at work throughout the life of the reader (audience) to give testimony of Jesus Christ and is instantly ready and able to change the heart that has faith in Him, to convict that person of sin, to urge his repentance and to build redeeming faith in Jesus Christ.

CONCLUSION

In the end, the writer of prophetic fiction or the filmmaker of a prophetic film must ask himself:

- Have I represented Jesus Christ in a truthful manner?
- Have I lifted up my Creator/Savior in such a way that all the readers or viewers can be drawn to Him?
- Will those who are lost be able to recognize the One who died for their sins?
- Will this story help them to sense their need for a Savior?
- Do they now see Jesus as the answer to their heart's yearning?
- Will the believers who read this story or view this film be stirred in their hearts to love Jesus Christ more deeply?
- Will they be stimulated to serve Him daily? To share the good news of their salvation with their family and neighbors and fellow workers who also need their sins forgiven?
- Are they inspired to look forward daily to the imminent return of Jesus for His church? And live lives worthy of His coming?
- Have I been true to the prophetic utterances of the Holy Spirit as He spoke thorough Moses, through Daniel, thorough Isaiah, Ezekiel, Joel, Zechariah and the other prophets?
- Have I been guided by the prophecy revealed by Matthew, Mark, Luke and John, Peter and Paul?

- Have I been true to John's Revelation of Jesus Christ?
- Will my readers or viewers turn quickly to the Bible to verify the truths of Scripture that are revealed in my story? And will they find in personal study of the Scriptures that my fictional story has not led them astray, but rather led them to the heart of Jesus Christ our Lord?

If he finds it so, I have been a faithful servant. It is the measure of a steward to be found faithful.

Chapter 2

PROCLAIMING THE PROPHETIC WORD

REG DUNLAP

Today, most people believe the sermon to be the dominant feature of the worship service. It ranks higher than any other aspect of Christian worship. That being said, the tragedy in all of this is that often what comes across from the pulpit is not relevant and pertinent to life and its problems. This must change!

I believe that the best way to get people *into* God's Word and to *live by* God's Word is through the expository preaching of God's Word. Such preaching must include the total message that God has given the minister to proclaim. A message not only about a PERSON – the Lord Jesus Christ, but also a message of a PROSPECT – His personal coming in glory. A prophetic message which encompasses resurrection as well as redemption, judgment as well as mercy, the crown as well as the cross, and the eternal hope of Heaven as well as the everlasting horror of Hell.

All of these messages are an essential part of God's revelation given not only to those early disciples to preach, but also to every minister of the Gospel of Jesus Christ. Yet, such prophetic truth must be presented in a sane, sound and sensible way. It must follow the example of the Apostle Paul who declared to the Colossians: *...of which I became a minister according to the stewardship from God which was given to me for you, to fulfill the word of God...To them God willed to make known what are the riches of the glory of this mystery among the Gentiles: which is Christ in you, the hope of glory* (Col. 1:25, 27). Let us now consider together the nature of prophetic expository preaching.

THE DEPARTURE OF PROPHETIC EXPOSITORY PREACHING

In approaching our topic, "Proclaiming the Prophetic Word," I want us to realize that such preaching on the whole has largely vanished from the today's pulpits. I recognize there are exceptions to this observation, but in reality we have to admit that for one reason or another, the vast majority of preachers today very seldom, if ever, attempt to preach on Bible prophecy. Whatever the reasons, I am fully persuaded that we are in need of a revival of sane and sound prophetic preaching today. It is part of the minister's total package of proclaiming God's Word. Give ear to the words of the Apostle Paul who declared to the believers at Ephesus: *For I have not shunned to declare unto you all the counsel of God* (Acts 20:27). Bible prophecy to Paul was part of the total message God wanted His people to hear.

Now as to the reasons why Bible prophecy is not a popular subject among many of today's preachers, let me mention the following:

- *Feelings of Inadequacy*
  Some pastors do not feel adequate for what is required to proclaim the subject of prophecy. They feel uncomfortable in setting forth their own eschatological beliefs in sermon form, perhaps realizing they are not certain of their own views of Last Day events. So they hesitate, not feeling up to the task. This is particularly true of

pastors whose ministry has very little of the teaching element to it.

- *Fear of Difficulty*
  All preaching involves time and toil, but this is especially true of proclaiming the prophetic Word. It demands diligent study and pastoral sweat. **"Hard work"** are the two words that describe prophetic expository preaching. It demands careful preparation that some ministers are not willing to undertake through the searching and study of Scripture. Far too many preachers today are not prepared to pay the price of proclaiming the great prophetic truths of Holy Scripture.

- *Failure of Relevancy*
  Too often prophetic sermons fail to relate to life as it is being lived in the 21st century. It does not connect with today's problems. It is not pertinent to the difficulties at hand. This situation becomes a real problem to the preacher who does not bring last day events to bear upon present day experiences.

For these reasons, and others not mentioned, the prophetic voice emanating from the churches has become a rarity among us. That is not to say that prophetic preachers do not exist, but only to sadly confess that the vast majority of ministers very seldom touch the subject of Bible prophecy. The day must come when every evangelical preacher will make Bible prophecy a regular part of their preaching and teaching program. For who can forget the words of the Apostle John in writing the book of Revelation: *Blessed is he who reads and those who hear the words of this prophecy, and keep those things which are written in it; for the time is near* (Rev. 1:3). Let us now explore the next point in our study.

THE DESCRIPTION OF PROPHETIC EXPOSITORY PREACHING

A descriptive word now needs to be said regarding the meaning and nature of the prophetic expository sermon. First, we will define the distinctive character of expository preaching. An expositor of Scripture is a teacher who analyses and explains the Word of God by applying its truths to life. The explanation may be a passage of Scripture, a paragraph, or an entire chapter, as the expositor seeks to illuminate the meaning of a section of the Bible, and to make it applicable to life. Jesus was the greatest example of this kind of preacher. It says of Him: *He expounded all things to His disciples* (Mk. 4:34, KJV). Again we read of Him: *And beginning at Moses and all the prophets, He expounded unto them, in all the Scriptures, the things concerning Himself* (Lk. 24:27, KJV).

By a prophetic sermon that is expository in nature, I mean one that has both a text and a context by which theological truth and practical application are drawn from those verses. Prophetic expository preaching is expounding passages of the Bible which address Bible prophecy, and discovering the prophetic truth the author of those words was endeavoring to communicate to his readers. It is the unfolding of the prophetic text of Scripture by which the hearer may come to understand the meaning of the text and its application to life in today's world.

It is my conviction, based on the exposition of Scripture by both past and present great preachers, that there are many variations and shades of the prophetic expository method of preaching. Words from a single prophetic text may be expounded upon to bring forth eschatological truth, or the preacher may use a series of verses in a chapter or book of the Bible as prophetic truth is gleaned from the cluster of verses being preached upon. Prophetic expository preaching may be accomplished in various ways if the preacher is in fact exposing his listeners to what is revealed in the biblical text. From an explanation of the portion of Scripture being studied, the preacher endeavors to apply the theological truths to the lives of his listeners.

Permit me to illustrate the above concepts from two expository sermons preached recently at a prophetic Bible conference: The first sermon was entitled "Heaven - The Home of the Believer," based on the verses in John 14:1-6. The body of this message consisted of four main points as found in the Bible passages, plus other supporting paragraphs of Scripture to provide further development of my theme. The following were my four points:

1. The REALITY of Heaven – *I go to prepare a place for you...that where I am, there you may be also* (vv. 2, 3).

2. The REVELATION of Heaven – *In my Father's house are many mansions* (v. 2).

3. The RECOGNITION in Heaven – *I will come again, and receive you* (v. 3). (Jn. 20:16, 28).

4. The REQUIREMENT for going to Heaven – *believe also in me* (v. 1).

The second sermon was entitled: "Antichrist - The Devil's Dictator" taken from 2 Thessalonians 2:3-12 where we read these words in verse 8: *And then shall that wicked one be revealed, whom the Lord shall consume with the spirit of His mouth, and shall destroy with the brightness of His coming.* The main divisions and sub-divisions of this message are found in the text and context of the chapter. The points were:

1. The APPEARANCE of Antichrist – *And then shall that wicked one be revealed* (v. 8).
   • The Time of it – *And then shall* (v. 8).
   • The Titles given to him – *man of sin...son of perdition* (v. 3); *wicked one* (v. 8).
   • The Traits that characterize him – *with all power and signs and lying wonders* (v. 9).

2. The ACTIVITY of Antichrist – *Who opposes and exalts himself above all that is called God, or that is worshiped so that he as God, sitteth in the temple of God showing himself that he is God* (v. 4).

3. The ANNIHILATION of Antichrist – *Whom the Lord shall consume...and shall destroy* (v. 8).

These two samples leave a lot to be desired, but they illustrate, I hope, how the teacher can preach an expository message on some aspect of Bible prophecy from a group of prophetic Bible verses, and, instead of becoming just a peddler of interesting facts, he becomes a proclaimer of helpful, meaningful, and relevant truth in preparing the non-christian listener for the coming prophetic events, and preparing the believer to live life the way Christ desires in light of His sure return.

THE DRAWBACKS OF PROPHETIC EXPOSITORY PREACHING

We will now have a candid word concerning some of the hazards in the expository preaching of prophecy. There are dangers which must be avoided by preachers at all costs. Let me mention some of these perils that the expositors, and teachers (either in a home Bible study, Sunday School class, Bible college, etc.) of prophecy must evade.

There is the fear that the preacher will take too much prophetic liberty in dealing with certain segments of Scripture. The Bible expositor of prophecy must never go beyond what is contained in the Bible verses before him. This practice is being done by a large number of preachers, thus bringing disrepute and disfavor upon the field of prophetic preaching. Thus, the voice of the preacher becomes nothing more than an echo of sensationalism and an exploitation of Bible prophecy.

There is the peril that the expositor of prophecy does not relate the prophetic passages of the Bible to contemporary life here and now with its perplexing problems and mounting difficulties. Let us be certain, as ministers of Christ, that whenever we attempt to preach on Bible prophecy it will be relevant for living life today, it will have a bearing upon the problems at hand, and it will offer pertinent help for present trials. Prophetic preaching must meet the immediate cares of people's lives.

There is also the hazard that the preacher of prophecy will miss the literal meaning of many of the symbolical and figurative passages used by the prophetic writers of the Bible. The preacher must realize that, though parts of Bible prophecy may be symbolical in language, symbols do have a definite literal fulfillment. It is up to the dedicated student of Scripture to seek out the true meaning behind the prophetic words of the writer. A good rule of Bible interpretation for the expositor of prophecy is something that was passed on to me early in my ministry. It was this: *Take the Bible literally where it is possible. If symbolic, figurative, or typical language is used, then look for the literal truth it intends to convey!*

Although you may not be a Bible scholar or a student trained in Hebrew or Greek, you may still be a fruitful prophetic preacher of God's Word, for you have at your disposal the abundant works of the great scholars of Bible prophecy to assist you. Be a partaker of the indispensable works of these spiritual giants!

THE DEMAND FOR PROPHETIC EXPOSITORY PREACHING

In our discussion of preaching on prophecy, we must realize that, though there are drawbacks to it, there is an urgent demand for its necessity. At this point in time, it is imperative that we have a resurrection of sane and sound prophetic preaching. Those who use it for their own advantage and profit today use a large amount of Bible prophecy in an unethical manner. It is so easy for the self-imposed preacher to exploit this avenue for his own gain. But for all of its liabilities, preaching on Bible prophecy has its advantages. Here are a few:

- Prophetic expository preaching demands the minister immerse himself in the total Word of God. Not certain segments of it, but he must preach the "whole counsel of God" of which prophecy is a very important part. The biblically sensitive communicator of the Word of

God will realize that he is called to expound prophecy in all its scope and in all of its consequences.

- Prophetic expository preaching demands the preacher to do justice to the selected Bible verses as they endeavor to interpret correctly what the inspired writer had in mind when he penned those words. What was the purpose behind the inspired words of the writer? The expositor of prophecy will be a flaming herald of those doctrines dealing with death, resurrection, judgment, immortality, and many others as the preacher does precisely what the Apostle Paul encouraged Timothy to do: *Study to show thyself approved unto God, a workman that needs not be ashamed, rightly dividing the word of truth* (2 Tim. 2:15).

- Prophetic expository preaching, if soundly interpreted and correctly explained, presents the preacher with the greatest opportunity of sharing God's future plans with the laity. In a day when there is so much heretical teaching and misleading information regarding Last Day events, it gives the Bible expositor an effective way to uncover and disarm the false prophetic teachings of so many self-imposed last day prophets. If the pastor wants his people to know God's divine program for the future, the prophetic expository sermon is one of the best ways to accomplish it.

- Prophetic expository preaching, above all other kinds of preaching, touches all bases involved in man's future destiny. Preaching on Christ's return gives *hope* to the believer. Preaching on judgment gives *accountability* both to the sinner and saint. Preaching on Heaven gives *comfort* for those who know Christ while preaching on Hell gives *incentive* for the unbeliever to receive Christ. The prophetic sermon provides the best opportunity for preparing the listener to be ready to meet his or her

Maker. The unforgiven sinner will meet God the Father as Judge, while the forgiven sinner will meet God the Son as Savior and Lord.

THE DEVELOPMENT OF PROPHETIC EXPOSITORY PREACHING

Before we take leave of our topic, "Proclaiming the Prophetic Word," I would like to mention how a minister might go about developing a series of prophetic sermons.

One possibility is to take a theme such as "Great Events for the Future." The subdivisions in such a series could include messages on death, the state of the dead, the Second Coming of Christ, the resurrection, the judgment and rewards, the punishment of the wicked in Hell and the eternal blessings of the redeemed in Heaven. If one is a convinced premillennialist, such as I am, without being conceitedly dogmatic, it could include additional topics such as the Rapture, the Tribulation, Antichrist, Armageddon, Israel and the Millennium. Here again these sermons must not be preached only to impart eschatological truths, but also to stimulate the non-believer into the realization that Christ is indeed coming back again and encourage the believer to live a life of Christian holiness and become involved in Christian ministry.

Another possibility is to preach a series of messages on how to live one's life in light of the fact that Jesus is coming again. Here, the emphasis would not be on one of the major views of interpretation in the way Christ is coming, but on the responsibility of the believer to be ready for it. For as Jesus Himself declared: *Therefore be ye also ready; for in such an hour as ye think not the Son of man cometh* (Mt. 24:44). Or as the NKJV renders it: *Therefore you also be ready, for the Son of Man is coming at an hour you do not expect.* The prophetic preaching of the pastor would be to set forth the scriptural incentive for living a life of purity in anticipation of our Lord's coming.

Still another way of handling this subject of prophecy would be to deliver a series of messages aimed at reaching the lost. The special emphasis here would be strictly evangelistic in nature. For let us always remember that the major calling of every evangelical pastor is to confront men and women to turn from the power of Satan that enslaves them and turn unto the living God that emancipates them and establishes them in the Christian faith. Every prophetic sermon should aim at this fruitful result. There are without doubt many evangelistic opportunities when it comes to prophetic preaching.

For more solid Bible study on the actual events of Biblical prophecy, a pastor may well give himself to a thoroughly prepared series of sermons on his own denominational view of Last Day events. Congregations will be that much more the wiser on future events whose pastor has spent a number of Sundays analyzing, explaining and applying eschatological truth to his people. I have done this both on Sunday morning and Wednesday night and have found our attendance to triple because of the interest.

One more suggestion needs to follow under this heading. One may develop a chain of sermons in which the various signs leading up to Christ's return are discussed with respect to the part they play in relation to His coming. Would there not be great value in preparing a series of sermons based on the words of Jesus when He stated: *And when these things begin to come to pass, then look up, and lift up your heads; for your redemption draweth nigh* (Lk. 21:28). I am absolutely convinced that such a preaching program can be presented if the pastor at all cost will avoid the pitfall of sensationalism, date-fixing and reading his own self-imposed prophetic beliefs into a situation which does not warrant it. But remember: Behind all prophetic preaching must be the cross of Christ as it reveals not only man's ruin through sin, but God's remedy through His Son.

I dare not conclude this chapter of the book without encouraging and challenging the expositor of God's Word to include regularly in your preaching schedule the prophetic sermon. Expound, explain, and expose your people to the great prophetic events God has planned for the future. I beg of you who are communicators of the Word of God, with holy abandon, give of yourself to this kind of preaching. If you do, the rewards will be eternal.

Chapter 3

TEACHING THE PROPHETIC WORD

HAROLD L. WILLMINGTON

What we are going to do in this chapter is help you to understand "Fifty-Five Future Facts" concerning Bible prophecy. I will provide you with the chronological sequence of coming events, along with the appropriate Scripture verses. My goal is to help you not only understand the major prophetic events, but also help you use this information to teach the prophetic Word to others in your church, home, college, or anywhere else that you have the opportunity to proclaim the inerrant Word of God. I invite you to fly (so to speak) with me now as we scale the prophetic city. I want you to envision this flight as a survey of fifty-five buildings. We will look at each building basically, survey some of the main buildings, then perhaps land the plane and visit some of these buildings.

BUILDING ONE

The first of these great buildings is the fact of **The Rapture of the Church** (Jn. 14:1-3; 1 Cor. 1:7, 8; 4:5; 15:23, 51-53; 1 Thess. 1:10; 2:19; 3:13; 4:13-18, 5:23; Phil. 3:20, 21; Col. 3:4; 2 Tim. 4:8; Tit. 2:12, 13; Heb. 9:28; 10:25, 37; Jas. 5:8; 1 Pet. 5:2, 4; 1 Jn. 2:28; 3:2; Rev. 2:25; 3:10, 11; 4:1). Immediately, you need to look at Building 43, "The Second Coming of Christ," and distinguish the differences between the Rapture of the church and the Second Coming.

The Rapture of the church will occur when Christ comes for His people, which will introduce the Great Tribulation shortly thereafter, whereas seven years later Jesus will come with His people and that will conclude the Great Tribulation. It would be difficult to understand how Jesus will come *with* His people unless He had first come *for* His people.

Now, you should know that there are three views concerning the Rapture of the church and the timing of that blessed future event. First, there is the Pre-tribulation Rapture that Jesus will come before the Great Tribulation. Secondly, there is the Mid-tribulation Rapture that Jesus will come in the middle of the Great Tribulation. Third, there is the Post-tribulation Rapture that occurs at the end of the Great Tribulation. At this point, I would not like to give you an argument, but a non-Scriptural (yet hopefully not unbiblical) suggestion that might indicate a pretribulational and premillennial coming of Christ.

A certain event occurred 60 years ago on Sunday, 7 December 1941. I was 9 years old and I remember living in Mount Vernon, Illinois when we heard my dad say that the Japanese had bombed Pearl Harbor and this means war. Now, on 8 December we went back to school because it was too early for the Christmas vacation. At 12:55 pm, the principal of that little school herded all the students into the gymnasium and we stood at attention. We knew something big was about to happen. Our speculations became apparent when the workers and the janitors came pushing this gigantic radio (not the transistor kind), but one of those big radios with a vacuum tube, which was about the size of a refrigerator. The proper station was located and we stood to hear the President of the

United States, Franklin D. Roosevelt, make an 8-minute speech. I remember hearing it, as I have an excerpt of some of what he said.

Roosevelt said, "Yesterday, 7 December 1941, a day which will live in infamy the United States of America was suddenly and deliberately attacked by naval and air forces of the empire of Japan. Yesterday, the Japanese government also lashed an attack against Malaysia, Hong Kong, Guam, Philippine Islands, etc." He said, "As commander-in-chief of the army and navy, I have directed that all measures be taken for our defense." Roosevelt ended by saying, "Hostilities exist; there is no blinking of the fact that our people, our territory, and our interests are in great danger. With confidence in our armed forces, with the unbounded determination of our people, we will gain the inevitable triumph. So help us God." Roosevelt ended his speech. Well, that was Monday.

Do you know what the President of the United States did on Tuesday? He sent three telegrams to the three American ambassadors: one in Tokyo, Japan, one in Berlin, Germany, and one in Rome, Italy. They all said the same. In essence, here is what the telegrams said, "Pack your bags and come home as quickly as you can." Why? It is because the state of war now exists between your country and the country that you are in as a representative of America. What I am trying to say is that usually the last thing that a President or King will do before he declares war on another country is to call his ambassadors home. Someday God is going to declare an all out war on planet Earth; it is called the Great Tribulation. However, before He declares war on Earth, God is going to call His ambassadors home and that is the Rapture of the church. *ALTERNATE VIEWPOINT: THE TRIB IS SATAN'S WRATH A R. AT END OF T. REMOVES SAINTS BEFORE GOD'S WRATH IS POURED OUT. AFTER MARRIAGE SUPPER THEY COME BACK (IMMORTAL TO RULE W/ MESSIAH) DURING THE M.*

BUILDING TWO

The Judgment Seat of Christ is the next building (Rom. 14:10-12; 1 Cor. 3:11-15; 9:24; 2 Cor. 5:10; Gal. 6:7-9; Col. 3:24, 25; 2 Tim. 4:8; Heb. 10:30; 13:17; 1 Pet. 1:7; 4:17; 1 Jn. 4:17). It is important here to distinguish between the Judgment Seat of Christ and the Great White Throne Judgment. The Judgment Seat of Christ, or the

Bema, will take place in the heavenlies, perhaps shortly after the Rapture. Only believers will stand before that judgment. The issue there will be rewards as opposed to the events of the Great White Throne Judgment. It is not only after the Tribulation but also after the Millennium, that the apostle John writes, *I saw the dead, small and great, stand before God...and whosoever was not found written in the* [Lamb's] *book of life was cast into the lake of fire*. The Great White Throne Judgment will only involve the unsaved to stand before God. The criteria will not be whether those judged are saved or lost; rather, it will be the degrees of punishment they will receive in Hell.

When I was a boy, (I was saved when I was 16) and I did not know anything about the Bible, I had a wrong concept on future judgment. I thought that one day all humanity would stand in a single file line before God, and I thought that line must be probably a billion miles long. Afterward, one angel would come out carrying a set of books and another angel would come out carrying scales and balances. It would then follow that the angel with the books would open them and say, "John Jones, born Chicago, Illinois 1900, died New York City 1950. Step forward." With great fear and trepidation, brother Jones would step forward. What would then happen is that all the good things that brother Jones ever did, all the good words that he had ever said, all the good thoughts that he had ever thought would be placed on one side of the scales and all the bad on the other. My former thinking was that if the good outweighed the bad he would go into a door marked "Heaven" and if the bad outweighed the good he would go into a door marked "Hell." I must admit at that age, I was not sure what would happen if it matched. Now, I must say the following: you will find that description of final judgment in the Bible where it talks about Rudolph the Red-Nosed Reindeer (that is to say, it is not in the Bible).

Actually, there are a number of judgments and some have already come to pass. Second Corinthians 11 states that there is a judgment taking place right now. However, in the future judgments there will be two special ones. Every person here, and everybody you know, and everybody they know, will someday be arraigned before one of two judgment seats. The saved will appear before the

Judgment Seat of Christ and the unsaved will appear before the Great White Throne Judgment.

BUILDING THREE

The third building is **The Marriage Service of the Lamb** (2 Cor. 11:2; Eph. 5:25-32). It is important to distinguish between the Marriage Service and the Marriage Supper. The Marriage Service takes place in heaven (perhaps shortly after the Judgment Seat of Christ). God knows we will need something to cheer us up after that! The Marriage Supper will take place at the beginning of the Millennium.

I think it was Dr. Dwight J. Pentecost of Dallas Theological Seminary who suggested that the Marriage Service and the Marriage Supper between Christ and His church would possibly follow the Middle Eastern scenario. In other words, there will be three stages: the betrothal stage, the presentation stage, and the celebration stage. Pentecost points out that the betrothal stage would consist of two steps: the selection of the bride and the payment of the dowry. Maybe years later (because this could be done when the children were small), there was the presentation stage where the bride and groom would be officially married, followed by (and this marriage service would take place in the house of the groom's father) the great celebration.

If the above were the case, then the church is now in the betrothal stage, since the bride has been selected (chosen in Him before the foundation of the world) and the dowry has been paid. We have been redeemed, not with corruptible things, but as silver and gold. Therefore, the presentation stage will take place at the Rapture.

Where will this service take place? According to Jesus, *I will come again and in my Father's house are many dwelling places, if it were not so I would have told you. I go to prepare a place for you, and I will come again to receive you to Myself* (Jn. 14:2, 3a). Therefore, the presentation stage will take place in the home of the Father, that is to say Heaven. Afterward, the celebration stage that follows the presentation stage will be at the beginning of the

Millennium. I do not think it is any accident that the presentation stage is described in Revelation 19: *Let us be glad and rejoice, and give honor to him: for the marriage of the Lamb is come, and his wife hath made herself ready.* In contrast, the Millennium is described in Revelation 20, which indicates to me that the Father is ready to throw a party to celebrate the marriage between His Son and the church. He owns the cattle on a thousand hills so He will pull out all the stops and there will be a one thousand year celebration. I believe that is one of the reasons for the Millennium.

BUILDING FOUR

Building Four involves **The Singing of Two Special Songs** (Rev. 4:10, 11; 5:9, 10; 14:3; Ps. 96:1, 2; 98:1, 2; 100: 1, 2). I have read many books on Bible prophecy, and written a couple of books on Bible prophecy, but I do not remember reading too much about these all-important chapters of Revelation 4-5. Suppose you are taking a test, and suppose there is one question requiring you to put down everything that God has ever done on a sheet of paper and everything that God is doing right now, and everything that God will ever do.

You are probably thinking if that is the final test, we will be working right into the Millennium. Not really! If you know your Bible well enough, you could pass the test by writing your answer in about 30 seconds, or however long it would take you to write two words. The twofold answer would be creation and redemption. Revelation 4 gives the background of the singing of the first song praising God for His work in creation. Revelation 5 provides the background of the singing of the second song praising God for His work in redemption. We sing a little chorus from time to time in my church that summarizes both. We say, "my Father is omnipotent and that you cannot deny, a God of might and miracles written in the sky [that is, creation], it took a miracle to put the stars in space, it took a miracle to hang the world in place, but when He saved my soul [that is, redemption], cleansed and made me whole it took a miracle of love and grace." After the first four events, we leave the heavenlies, and the world will enter the Great Tribulation.

BUILDING FIVE

Building Five takes us from heaven to hell. This building contains **The Appearance of the Antichrist and His False Prophet** (Dan. 7:24, 25; 2 Thess. 2:2, 3; Rev, 6:2; 13:1, 8, 11, 12). Here there is a need to distinguish between the appearance of the Antichrist and the full manifestation of the Antichrist (see Building Twenty-Four). As I understand the Scripture, the Antichrist does not come upon the world scene announcing that he is Antichrist. He will come pretending to be the friend of Israel and the world, but it is not until the middle of the Tribulation that the Antichrist will drop all pretence and declare himself to be god of very gods (2 Thess. 2). The false prophet will be to the Antichrist what John the Baptist was to the true Christ.

At this point, I would like to draw attention to basic facts about the Antichrist. For instance, he will be an intellectual, oratorical, political, commercial, military, and religious genius. He will begin by controlling the Western power block. He will make a seven-year covenant with Israel but will break it after 3 1/2 years. He will attempt to destroy all of Israel. He will destroy the false religious systems so that he can rule unhindered. He will set himself up as god. He will do everything according to his own selfish will. He will not regard the god of his fathers; his god will be the god of power. He will be a master of deceit. He will profane the temple and will be energized by Satan himself. He will briefly rule over all nations. Yet despite all his best efforts, he will be utterly crushed by the Lord Jesus Christ at the battle of Armageddon.

BUILDING SIX

Following, the appearance of the Antichrist, there will be **The Organization of the Super Harlot Church** (Acts 20:29, 30; 1 Tim. 4:1; 2 Tim. 3:1-5; 4:1-4; 2 Pet. 2:1; 1 Jn, 2:18, 19; Jude 4; Rev. 17:1-6). I often say the following: we do not know the identity of the Antichrist, but if the coming of Christ is as close as many feel it to be then certainly there is the possibility (if not the probability) that the Antichrist is on earth right now. Furthermore, I do know this that the Hollywood people are grinding out horror films, apparently preparing their people for the coming of a world dictator. I think of the movie many years ago, *Omen I*, followed by *Omen II*.

In *Omen I*, little Damon is born and he is the Antichrist and he kills his mom and dad. When Hollywood writes the script the bad guys always win. There is a little funeral dirge in that movie and this is the gospel according to Hollywood. "When the Jews return to Zion, and a comet rips the sky, and the Holy Roman Empire rises, then you and I must die. From the eternal seas he comes creating armies on either shore, turning man against his brother till man exists no more."

BUILDING SEVEN

The next building is **The Revival of the Old Roman Empire** (Dan. 2:41; 7:23, 24; Rev. 12:3; 13:1; 17:12). Of all the prophetical teachings that I have come across, I have found that there is more confusion among the average church member concerning the revival of the old Roman Empire than any other subject.

Where in the Bible does it say that the old Roman Empire will be revived? I say we have to go back to a dream (really a nightmare) of a monarch named Nebuchadnezzar. The time is about 6 centuries before the birth of the Messiah in the city of Babylon. It frightened him so he called all of his Chaldeans, cabinet members, soothsayers, and magicians to inquire the interpretation of his dream. Whereas the prophets and soothsayers of Babylon were unable to give the interpretation of the dream, Daniel prayed to God and He revealed to His servant the interpretation.

Daniel told Nebuchadnezzar that he had a dream of a huge statue and that he noticed that the statue consisted of four parts. The head was gold, the next part was silver, the third was brass, and the fourth part was iron and clay. Daniel also revealed to him that he heard a terrible grinding noise and that some invisible hand was clawing out a huge rock from out of a cliff and this rock hovered over the statue. It was this rock that fell upon the statue and smashed it, which turned it into dust and powder, and the wind blew it away.

Daniel told the king that this dream was God's way of depicting Israel's future in addition to four world Gentile powers. Nebuchadnezzar was the head of gold until the Medo-Persians took over Babylon in 539 BC, followed by the Greeks who took over from the Medo-Persians, and then the Romans annexed the city of Jerusalem in 63 AD. The Romans were the last to take over so that during the Roman Empire, Jesus was born.

Here is a small problem. Jesus grew up during the Roman Empire, related His miracles, and told His parables, but He did not crush world Gentile powers. In fact, humanly speaking, He was put to death at the command of the centurion representative of the Roman government. Here is the problem: there is now one of two possibilities. Either Daniel was wrong or the empire is going to strike back. During the revived Roman Empire, the Savior will come and at the battle of Armageddon He will crush world Gentile power.

BUILDING EIGHT

The **Antichrist's 7-Year Peace Treaty with Israel** (Isa. 28:18; Dan. 9:27) is next. The Jewish people will think that they have entered into true peace, but halfway through the Tribulation the true nature of the Antichrist will be revealed. At that point, they will flee for their lives since the Antichrist will seek to kill all the Jews.

BUILDING NINE

Building Nine is **The Mass Return of the Jews to Israel** (Isa. 43:5, 6; Ezek. 37:1-12; 38:8). In the 1870s, Mark Twain visited the land of Palestine and said, "Someone has referred to the God of the Bible as a dirty bully, but He also has a weird sense of humor to call that cursed piece of real estate the land of milk and honey." In addition, he said, "These wind-sunken preachers and these jack-legged preachers that squeal, yell, spit, and slobber about the Jews going back in the last days, it will never happen." Well, it will happen, and it has happened (in part) in modern times.

BUILDING TEN

Building Ten is **The Ministry of the Two Witnesses** (Mal. 4:5, 6; Rev. 11:3-6). In connection with this future fact is the martyrdom of the two witnesses (see Building Twenty-One). I believe that these two witnesses will most likely be martyred during the middle of the Tribulation.

BUILDING ELEVEN

The next building is the **Ministry of the 144,000** (Mt. 24:14; Mk. 13:10; Rev. 7:1-8; 14:1-5). I think the 2 witnesses and 144,000 will begin their ministry shortly after the Rapture. The ministry of the two witnesses will end with their martyrdom in the city of Jerusalem. According to Revelation 7:1-8, the other witnesses will be 144,000 Jewish Billy Sundays, D.L. Moodys, or Apostle Pauls. These witnesses will be the witnesses spoken of by Jesus in Matthew 24 who preach to all the nations. We are never told to bring the entire world to Christ, but we are commanded to bring Christ to the world. These witnesses will accomplish that command.

BUILDING TWELVE

Following those buildings is the **Rebuilding of the Third Jewish Temple** (Dan. 9:27; 12:11; Mt. 24:15; 2 Thess. 2:4; Rev. 11:1, 2). The first, of course, was built by Solomon and later destroyed by Nebuchadnezzar. The Temple was then rebuilt and completed by Herod, only to be destroyed by the Romans. There will be a rebuilt third Jewish Temple since, according to the above passages, it would be impossible for the Antichrist to desecrate a Temple that does not exist. When John is told to measure the temple in Revelation 11:1, the year was about 95-100 AD, so the second Temple had already been destroyed. Therefore, he is talking about a future Temple.

BUILDING THIRTEEN

This involves the **Rebuilding of Babylon** (Jer. 51:7; Rev. 18:3, 5, 7, 24). When I first started writing these future facts, I had a question after this coming event. However, after reading Dr. Charles Dyer's book, *The Rise of Babylon* (Wheaton: Tyndale House Publishers, 1991), I think that I would put an exclamation mark after this event.[1]

I am convinced that Babylon will be rebuilt. For instance, in Isaiah 13:19, 20, God predicts the destruction of Babylon. Isaiah states that this destruction will be supernatural (God Himself will do it), it will be sudden (in an hour or a day), and it will be absolutely total (by fire). The problem with this prophecy is that it has never been fulfilled. The Babylon of Daniel and Nebuchadnezzar (like the old soldiers) rather faded away. Therefore, Babylon will be rebuilt as the headquarters of Antichrist on the banks of the Euphrates, where sin began in Genesis 11, and that is where it will end.

We are now introduced to seven seal judgments. The seventh seal will then introduce the seven trumpets.

BUILDING FOURTEEN

The **First Seal Judgment** is a symbolic picture of the Antichrist (Rev. 6:2; Mt. 24:5; Mk. 13:6; Lk. 21:8). At this point, he will take control of the revived Roman Empire.

BUILDING FIFTEEN

The **Second Seal Judgment** reveals the uneasy peace of the rider on the white horse (Rev. 6:3, 4; Mt. 24:6; Mk. 3:7; Lk. 21:9, 10). The peace of the Antichrist will be temporary and counterfeit.

BUILDING SIXTEEN

The **Third Seal Judgment** will bring famine upon the earth (Rev. 6:5, 6; Mt. 24:7; Mk. 13:8; Lk. 21:11).

BUILDING SEVENTEEN

The **Fourth Seal Judgment** will result in the death of one-fourth of all humanity (Rev. 6:7, 8; Mt. 24:7; Mk. 13:8; Lk. 21:11). The riders, "death" and "hell," will apparently bring physical and spiritual death upon numerous unbelievers.

BUILDING EIGHTEEN

The **Fifth Seal Judgment** reveals the martyred souls of the Tribulation (Rev. 6:9-11; Mt. 24:9; Mk. 13:12; Lk. 21:16).

BUILDING NINETEEN

The **Sixth Seal Judgment** is the most frightening of all the seals before the trumpet judgments come (Rev. 6:12-17; Mt. 24:9; Mk. 13:25; Lk. 21:25).

BUILDING TWENTY

Building Twenty is the **Gog and Magog Invasion into Israel** (Ezek. 38:1-6, 8-12; 39:1-12). I was taught in the 1950s when I attended Moody Bible Institute that Gog was probably the leader and Magog was the land of Russia. In other words, he is talking about the Russian invasion in the last days.

Something very interesting took place 26 December 1991. For the first time in recorded history, shrimp learned to whistle. I remember in the 1960s when Nikita Khrushchev came to the United

Nations and pounded on the podium saying, "You out there in the Western world and you waiting for Communism to collapse. We Russians have a proverb, 'you will have to wait till shrimp learn to whistle.'" Well on 26 December 1991, shrimp learned to whistle.

Some prophecy teachers suppose that we have to throw in the towel concerning the Russian nation, but I am not quite ready to give that thought up. Russia is still pictured as a bear. What is the most dangerous kind of a bear? A polar bear? A grizzly bear? A black bear? No, none of the above. The most dangerous kind of a bear is a starving, insecure, and freezing bear. What I am thinking is that if things keep getting worse and worse in Russia, and the economy is still declining, then the nation will become so desperate that rather than negate this invasion because of their weakness, their situation will actually necessitate it. Thus, I still think it is possible that Ezekiel 38-39 speaks of the Russian invasion and subsequent destruction upon the mountains of Israel.

BUILDING TWENTY-ONE

This building is the **Martyrdom of the Two Witnesses** that were mentioned in Building Ten (Rev. 11:7-13). About the time that we reach this point, I think that we are at the middle of the seven-year Tribulation. I believe that Revelation 11:7 is one of the most comforting verses in the entire Bible. For example, before you read about their death you read...*and when they shall have finished their testimony.* This tells us that the man (or woman) of God living in the center of the will of God is absolutely indestructible until he or she has finished their testimony. I hope that all of us will be able to say as Paul said *I have fought a good fight.... I have finished my course.... I have kept the faith.*

BUILDING TWENTY-TWO

The next building is the **Casting of Satan out of Heaven** (Rev. 12:7-12). This event should be distinguished with the casting of

Satan into the bottomless pit. Scripture would seem to teach that at the middle of the Tribulation, Satan will be cast out of the heavenlies and he will come down having great wrath because he knows that he has but a short time before his judgment.

One day, when the Devil did not have anything else to do but read *Playboy*, *Penthouse* and other sinful magazines, he read Daniel 9 in the Bible and figured out the time of his judgment. Therefore, Satan will be cast into the bottomless pit at the end of the Tribulation and the beginning of the Millennium. There is great rejoicing in heaven knowing that the accuser of the brethren has been kicked out of heaven.

BUILDING TWENTY-THREE

The next event to survey is the **Abomination of Desolation in the Temple** (Mt. 24:15-20; Mk. 13:14-18; 2 Thess. 2:3, 4; Rev. 13:11-15). Obviously, this passage is referring to a rebuilt Jewish Temple on the present day Temple Mount. Jesus warned about this event in Matthew 24. He said, in essence, "When you see this happen, then all hell itself is going to break loose." And about that time, the Antichrist will declare himself to be god.

At this time, the False Prophet will construct the statue that represents the Antichrist. Of course, the statue will be able to speak and, in essence, it may say the following: "For the last 3 1/2 years I have allowed people to look about me as the benevolent Western dictator. I am that. As the friend of Israel, I am that. But I am more; I am god. Fall down and worship me."

BUILDING TWENTY-FOUR

The next building involves the **Full Manifestation of the Antichrist** (Dan. 7:25; 11:36, 37; 8:23-25; 2 Thess. 2:8-10; Rev. 13:5-8). Second Thessalonians 2 states that the Antichrist will sit (stand) in the holy place, which is the third temple, and declare himself to be god. Many Jewish people and probably some

Gentiles also, will realize that this man is not their friend. He is the enemy.

BUILDING TWENTY-FIVE

Scripture speaks of the **Worldwide Persecution of Israel** (Dan. 12:1; Zech. 11:16; 13:8; Mt. 24:21; Lk. 21:22; Rev. 7:13, 14; 12:13). Matthew 24 and Zechariah also indicate that perhaps as many as 2 out of 3 Jewish people will be killed.

BUILDING TWENTY-SIX

This event is the **Destruction of Religious Babylon** (Rev. 17:15-17). The destruction of religious Babylon should be distinguished from the destruction of economic and political [commercial] Babylon (Building Forty One). I see a need to distinguish between the two. I believe that both are religious systems coming from the city of Babylon, but it is interesting that the religious system is destroyed not by Billy Graham, not by the Father, Son, or Holy Spirit, not by the angel Gabriel or the archangel Michael, but by the Antichrist himself.

Apparently, religious Babylon tries to control the Antichrist. What follows is that there are some harlots so ugly and repulsive that even the Antichrist will not be able to stomach them. The destruction of religious Babylon will occur in the middle of the Tribulation, but the destruction of economic and political Babylon will occur at the end of the Tribulation immediately before the coming of Christ. God himself will destroy that system; when He does, the entire world will lament, in contrast to the world rejoicing at the destruction of religious Babylon.

The next prophetic events are the seven trumpet judgments that are poured out of the last seal judgment. They follow each other (some believe these are synonymous), but for our purposes these judgments will be listed in the way that they chronologically seem to appear in the Bible.

BUILDING TWENTY-SEVEN

The **First Trumpet Judgment** results in one-third of the earth being destroyed (Rev. 8:7).

BUILDING TWENTY-EIGHT

The **Second Trumpet Judgment** results in one-third of the sea being destroyed (Rev. 8:8, 9).

BUILDING TWENTY-NINE

The **Third Trumpet Judgment** results in one-third of the waters being destroyed (Rev. 8:10, 11).

BUILDING THIRTY

The **Fourth Trumpet Judgment** results in one-third of celestial bodies being destroyed (Rev. 8:12).

BUILDING THIRTY-ONE

The **Fifth Trumpet Judgment** is the "first woe" and will bring about the torment of humanity (Rev. 9:1-12).

BUILDING THIRTY-TWO

The **Sixth Trumpet Judgment** is the "second woe" and results in one-third of humanity being destroyed (Rev. 9:13-19).

BUILDING THIRTY-THREE

The **Seventh Trumpet Judgment** is the "third woe" and announces the glorious news that Jesus Christ will be returning soon to the earth as the rightful Ruler of humanity (Rev. 11:15-19). The seven trumpet judgments are then followed by the bowl ("vial") judgments (Buildings Thirty-Four through Forty).

BUILDING THIRTY-FOUR

The **First Bowl Judgment** brings grievous sores upon humanity who received the mark of the beast (Rev. 16:2).

BUILDING THIRTY-FIVE

The **Second Bowl Judgment** results in the destruction of the sea (Rev. 16:3).

BUILDING THIRTY-SIX

The **Third Bowl Judgment** is an answer to the prayers of the martyrs under the fifth seal (Rev. 16:4-7). It is this third bowl judgment that results in the destruction of the rivers and fountains of waters.

BUILDING THIRTY-SEVEN

The **Fourth Bowl Judgment** will bring scorching heat upon those who blasphemed the name of God (Rev. 16:8, 9). The attitude of the world toward God's judgment in the Tribulation here, and in Revelation 9:20, 21, certainly indicates the total depravity of man.

BUILDING THIRTY-EIGHT

The **Fifth Bowl Judgment** results in the kingdom of Antichrist being filled with darkness (Rev. 16:10, 11).

BUILDING THIRTY-NINE

The **Sixth Bowl Judgment** will prepare humanity for the Battle of Armageddon (Rev. 16:12-14).

BUILDING FORTY

The **Seventh Bowl Judgment** will result in worldwide destruction as humanity faces the greatest earthquake and shower of hailstones in earth's history (Rev. 16:17-21).

BUILDING FORTY-ONE

The next building is the **Destruction of Economic and Political Babylon** (Isa. 13:19, 20; Jer. 51:8; Rev. 14:8; 18:1-21). We already viewed this destruction from Building Twenty Six. At this point, we are now at the end of the Tribulation.

BUILDING FORTY-TWO

This building is **The Battle of Armageddon** (Ps. 2:1-5; Isa. 13:6-13; 24:1, 19, 20; 26:21; 34:1-4; 42:13, 14; 63:6; 66:15, 16, 24; Joel 3:2, 9-16; Mic. 5:15; Zeph. 1:14-17; 3:8; Zech. 12:2-4, 9, 14:1-3, 12; Mt. 24:28, 40, 41; Lk. 17:34-37; Rev. 14:14, 20; 16:16; 19:17-21). The biggest, boldest, and most brazen, and bloodiest of all battles up to this time period is the Battle of Armageddon. This is to be contrasted with Building Fifty-Two. The reason for the contrast is that, in one sense of the word (of course) it is not the final battle.

The final battle will be fought at the end of the Millennium, which is Satan's final revolt (Building Fifty-Two).

The dimensions of this battle are incredible. It starts in Megiddo, in Galilee, and goes all the way down to Edom, which is the Sinai; the numbers total 200 miles north and south. The western boundary is the Mediterranean Sea and the eastern boundaries are ancient Moab and modern Jordan (totaling 100 miles). If you multiply 200 by 100, you find that this battle will occur in 200,000 square miles.

BUILDING FORTY-THREE

This building is **The Second Coming of Christ** (Isa. 25:9; 11:12; 40:5, 10; 59:20; Ezek. 43:2, 4; Dan. 7:13, 14; Hab. 3:3-6, 10, 11; Hag. 2:6, 7; Zech. 8:3; 14:4, 8; Mal. 3:1; 4:2; Mt. 24:29, 30; 26:64; Mk. 13:26; 14:62; Lk. 21:27; 22:69; Acts 1:11; 3:20, 21; 15:16; Rom. 11:26; 1 Cor. 15:24; 2 Thess. 1:7, 8; Rev. 1:7; 2:25; 19:11-14). John writes in Revelation 19, and also in Revelation 11, that at the sounding of the seventh trumpet the kingdoms of this world will become the kingdoms of God and of His Christ and the saints of God shall reign forever.

BUILDING FORTY-FOUR

Following the Second Coming is **The Regathering and Regenerating of Faithful Israel** (Isa. 10:20-23; 11:12; 25:8, 9; 35:10; 40:5; 43:5, 6; Jer. 16:14, 15; 23:3; 24:6; 29:14; 31:8, 33; 32:37, 39, 40; 46:27; Ezek. 11:16, 17, 19-20; 34:11-13; 36:25-28; 37:12-14; Hos. 1:10, 11; 3:5; Amos 9:14, 15; Mic. 7:18, 19; Zech. 12:10; 13:1; Mt. 24:31; Mk. 13:27). These Jewish believers will be the ones who did not follow the Antichrist during the Great Tribulation.

BUILDING FORTY-FIVE

The next building is **The Judgment and Punishment of Faithless Israel** (Ezek. 11:21; 20:38; Amos 9:9, 10; Zech. 13:8; Mal. 4:1; Mt. 24:48-51; 25:7-10, 24-30; Lk. 21:34, 35; Rom. 9:6; 1 Thess. 2:14-16; Rev. 3:9). These are the ones who did follow the Antichrist.

BUILDING FORTY-SIX

The Judgment of the Nations is to separate the sheep and goat nations (Mt. 13:40, 41, 47-49; 25:31-46). It is important to note that this judgment is not the same as the Great White Throne Judgment that occurs at the end of Millennium (Building Fifty-Three).

BUILDING FORTY-SEVEN

Next, is **The Judgment of Angels** (Mk. 1:23, 24; 1 Cor. 6:3; 2 Pet. 2:4; Jude 6). I would assume these are the bad guys because the good guys do not need to be judged. All fallen angels will be included in this judgment.

BUILDING FORTY-EIGHT

The Resurrection of Old Testament and Tribulational Saints will occur prior to the establishment of the Millennium (Job 19:25, 26; Ps. 49:15; Isa. 25:8; 26:19; Dan. 12:2, 3; Hos. 13:14; Jn. 5:28, 29; 11:23-27; Heb. 11:35; Rev. 6:9, 11; 20:4-6). The Rapture of the church will have only included all the saved from Pentecost until the Rapture that takes place prior to the Tribulation.

BUILDING FORTY-NINE

The next building testifies of the **Casting of Satan into the Bottomless Pit** (Rom. 16:20; Rev. 20:1-3). Satan will be bound during the Millennial Kingdom so that man cannot say, "the devil made me do it."

BUILDING FIFTY

The Marriage Supper of the Lamb (Isa. 61:10; 22:2; 25:1; Lk. 12:35, 36; Rev. 19:6-9) will take place during the Millennium. This is in contrast to the marriage service of the Lamb, which will happen sometime after the Rapture of the church.

BUILDING FIFTY-ONE

This majestic building is **The Millennial Reign of Christ** (Ps. 2:6-8; 98:4, 9; Isa. 2:2-4; 9:6, 7; 11:6-9; 25:8; 29:18, 19; 30:23-26; 35:5-10; 40:4, 5, 10, 11; 42:16; 45:6; 49:10, 11; 55:13; 60:1, 3, 11, 19, 20, 22; 65:19, 20, 25; Jer. 23:5, 6; Ezek. 34:23, 24; Dan. 2:44; 7:13, 14; Joel 3:18; Amos 9:11, 13; Mic. 4:1-6; Hab. 2:14; Zeph. 3:9, 15, 17; Zech. 6:12, 13; 8:3-5; 14:8, 9, 16, 20; Mt. 19:28; 25:31; Lk. 1:31-33; 22:30; Acts 2:30; Rom. 8:21; 1 Cor. 15:24-28; Phil. 2:10, 11; 2 Tim. 2:12; Heb. 1:8; Rev. 3:21; 5:13; 11:15; 19:15; 20:4-6). Someone has said that there is more information on the Millennial Reign of Christ than any other subject in the Bible.

BUILDING FIFTY-TWO

Satan's Final Revolt will occur at the end of the Millennial Reign of Christ (Rev. 20:7-10). The purpose of this loosing is to demonstrate that even under the best conditions, unregenerate man will still rebel against God.

BUILDING FIFTY-THREE

The Great White Throne Judgment will be the resurrection of all the wicked in order to stand before Christ Jesus as their Judge (Ps. 9:17; Eccl. 12:14; Dan. 7:9, 10; Mt. 7:21-23; 12:36, 37; Jn. 5:22, 27; 12:48; Acts 10:42; 17:31; 2 Tim. 4:1; Heb. 9:27; Rev. 20:11-15). They will be judged for their wickedness. After the judgment, they will be confined to the Lake of Fire for all eternity.

BUILDING FIFTY-FOUR

The Destruction of this Present Earth and Heaven will occur just prior to the establishment of the eternal kingdom of God (Isa. 51:6; Mt. 24:35; Heb. 1:10-12; 2 Pet. 3:10-12; 1 Jn. 2:17). The reason for the destruction is to rid the world of the stain of sin that has contaminated the perfect creation of God.

BUILDING FIFTY-FIVE

The last event on the prophetic outline is **The Creation of a New Earth and Heaven** (Isa. 65:17; 66:22; 2 Pet. 3:13; Rev. 21:1).

WRAPPING IT UP

With the passing by of Building Fifty-Five, we will now land the plane as it were. As I think of the Fifty-Five Buildings, I think the most exciting and perhaps the most important is Building Forty-Three, which is the Second Coming of Christ.

On 20 July 1969, the President of the United States, Richard Millhouse Nixon, made a statement in which no Christian could agree. He said, "Today, 20 July 1969, is the greatest day in human history." The President was wrong! Certainly, 20 July 1969 was a great day in human history and a great day in American history, because Neil Armstrong had just set foot on the moon. However, it was not the greatest day. In fact, according to my reckoning, it was not even the second, third, or fourth greatest day (if I had to count them down).

I would say the fifth greatest day in human history took place some 2,000 years ago when a young virgin girl, Mary, gave birth to her firstborn son, wrapped Him in swaddling clothes, and laid Him in a manger. Perhaps, the fourth most important day in human history took place some 34 years later when this little baby grew up to be a Spirit-anointed servant of God that was put to death between two thieves on an old rugged cross and He cried out, "It is finished."

The third greatest day took place a few days later when some angels in an empty tomb told some women, "Why are you seeking the living among the dead? He is not here. He is risen." I would surmise that the second greatest day in history took place some 40 days later when a group of 11 men stood on a windswept hill outside the city of Jerusalem and watched the Savior ascend into the heavenlies. The greatest day in human history is yet to take place. It will take place at the sounding of the seventh trumpet when the kingdoms of this world will become the kingdoms of our God and of His Christ.

Two hundred fifty years ago, there was a songwriter by the name of Isaac Watts who was studying the Psalms (especially Psalm 98) about the Second Coming of Christ; this study was not about the Bethlehem coming, but concerning Christ ruling the world. He was so impressed with that Psalm that he wrote a song about it that we sing normally at Christmas time even though it really is not a song about the First Coming. The name of the song is *Joy to the World*. Examine his words:

> Joy to the World! The Lord is come!
> Let earth receive her King.
> Let every heart prepare Him room,
> And heaven and nature sing.
> No more let sins and sorrows grow,
> Nor thorns infest the ground;
> He comes to make His blessings flow,

Far as the curse is found.
He rules the world with truth and grace,
And makes the nations prove,
The glories of His righteousness,
And wonders of His love.

Chapter 4

CONSISTENCY FROM GENESIS TO REVELATION

ROBERT LIGHTNER

Though they all embrace its inspiration and authority, evangelicals who defend a particular view of events to come do not all understand Scripture in the same way. They understand it differently because they use different methods of interpreting some of the unfulfilled prophecies of Scripture. This is the most basic reason for the differences over *pre-*, *a-*, and *post-*millennialism. It also has much to do with the differences over the relation of the church to the coming Great Tribulation.

The science and art of biblical interpretation is called is called "hermeneutics," and it is easy to see that a method of interpretation, a system of hermeneutics, is most important to the understanding of God's Word.[1] Without it, the Bible is a closed book, which is true of all literature. Whenever we read anything, we unconsciously follow certain rules of interpretation so that we may understand the material. "What does this mean?" is the question every reader often

95

asks without even thinking about it.

The interpretation of Scripture is one of several crucial matters related to the total doctrine of Scripture. A brief review of these related matters will help us put things in focus before we discuss the bearing that interpretation has upon the differences over things to come.

The meaning of the interpretation of Scripture is related to the revelation, inspiration, authority, canonicity, and illumination of the same Scriptures. The following chart illustrates the order and relation of these aspects of Scripture to each other and emphasizes the divine and human elements in each.

INTERPRETING SCRIPTURE	
REVELATION Hebrews 1:1	God revealing Humanity listening
INSPIRATION 2 Timothy 3:16	God controlling Humanity recording
AUTHORITY John 10:35	God enforcing Humanity obeying
CANONICITY Jude 1:3	God preserving Humanity recognizing
ILLUMINATION 1 Corinthians 2: 10-12	God clarifying Humanity understanding
INTERPRETATION 1 Corinthians 2:12	God enabling Humanity declaring

Revelation, in reference to Scripture, means the act of God whereby He made Himself and His will known to man. God gave the revelation; man received it. God has revealed His Word to many human penmen over about 1,500 years of time. The earliest and simplest revelation is just as true, just as inspired, as the later revelation. It is the amount of information about Himself and about all He has made known which has progressed. Therefore, in order to know what God has said about Himself, or any subject, the whole needs to be examined. The later revelation never changes or corrects the earlier recipients or locations as, for example, from Israel to Israel and the church or from earth to earth and heaven.

Inspiration has to do with the recording of the revelation. When we speak of the inspiration of the Bible like Paul did in 2 Timothy 3:16, 17, we are referring to God's work of guiding and controlling the human writers of Scripture in the very choice of the words used in the original manuscripts. The result of this divine work upon the fallible, human writer was the recording of God's message without error or omission in all its parts.

Because the revelation recorded without error in the Bible came from God, it is of course divinely authoritative. It bears the very authority of the One who gave it.

The God who gave His Word also preserved it for us. From the very time the revelation was given and recorded, it was accepted by God's people as His Word. We call the human recognition of God's Word by His people the *canonization* of Scripture.

The Holy Spirit, who was used in the giving, receiving, and acknowledging of God's Word, is the one who enables the child of God to understand it. This we call the *illumination* of Scripture.

My purpose in presenting this brief background in the doctrine of Scripture has been to distinguish the science of biblical interpretation from the other facets of the doctrine and to show its relation to them. Historically, evangelicals have had little difference over the revelation, inspiration, authority, canonicity, and illumination of Scripture,[2] but they have not ever agreed on a method of interpretation to be followed uniformly throughout the Bible. Nor is there agreement on how the doctrine of progressive revelation affects one's hermeneutics. There is also considerable difference among evangelicals over the relation of the Old Testament to the New and how the use of the Old in the New relates to the question of biblical interpretation.[3]

Is there a single method of interpretation to be used throughout Scripture, or do some parts of the Bible require a difference method? How does the way the New Testament uses the Old affect one's eschatology, his view of things to come? Such issues greatly divide evangelicals and the result is much fighting.

IMPORTANCE OF THE ISSUE

When it comes to the understanding of prophecy or events to come, the most important questions are: "how is it to be interpreted?" and "what does this prophetic Scripture mean?" Representative spokesmen of each of the various evangelical views of things to come candidly admit that, indeed, this is the important issue. All must agree – although some are more reluctant to admit it than others – that they disagree about events to come because they interpret the prophecies differently.

Here are a few admissions which illustrate my point.

Oswald T. Allis put the issue bluntly. His book, *Prophecy and the Church*, was intended to show what he felt was error in premillenial dispensationalism and to defend his own view of amillennialism. He said:

> Old Testament prophecies if literally interpreted cannot be regarded as having been yet fulfilled or as being capable of fulfillment in the present age. It is consequently assumed by premillennialists that they will be so fulfilled during the Millennium when Satan will be bound and the saints will reign with Christ.[4]

A more contemporary amillennial writer reflected the same view in these words:

> One very basic conflict between different millennial groups is their hermeneutics – the manner in which they interpret the Bible. In fact, this difference is what divides equally conservative men into different camps

with reference to the Millennium. This fact is acknowledged frequently by all millennial schools of thought. Each of the millennial views has been held by conservative, scholarly men who were devoted to the correct interpretation of the Bible and all have looked on the Scriptures as being divinely inspired and as the Christian's only rule of faith and life.[5]

In his recent book, *The Time Is at Hand*, Jay Adams also revealed the importance of the interpretation of unfulfilled prophecy:

> In this transition from pre to posttribulationalism, some have gone further and are beginning to test the foundations of premillennialism itself. In the process, doubts about fundamental presuppositions have arisen. Having rejected the unbiblical principle of exclusively literal interpretation of Old Testament prophecy, many no longer look upon the so-called "nation Israel" as God's chosen people. They cannot agree to a "Jewish millennium" fully equipped with rebuilt Temple and restored sacrificial system. They find no indication of a utopian-type millennium anywhere upon the pages of the New Testament.[6]

Loraine Boettner, evangelical postmillennial theologian, expressed his awareness of the crucial importance of one's method of interpretation. He agrees the basic reason for different views of things to come has to do with principles of biblical interpretation:

> That believing Christians through the ages using the same Bible and acknowledging it to be authoritative, have arrived at quite different conclusions appears to be due to different methods of interpretation. Premillennialists place strong emphasis on literal interpretation and pride themselves on taking Scripture just as it is written. Post and amillennialists, on the other hand,

mindful of the fact that much of both the Old and New Testament unquestionably is given in figurative or symbolic language, have no objection on principle against figurative interpretation and readily accept that if the evidence indicates that it is preferable.[7]

But amillennialists and postmillennialists are not alone in acknowledging the importance of biblical interpretation for the understanding of things to come; premillennialists also agree wholeheartedly. Their writings on the future are filled with emphatic statements on this point.

The Theocratic Kingdom of Our Lord Jesus the Christ is a classic three-volume set in defense of premillennialism. In it, George N. H. Peters states his view of the importance of a proper method of interpretation:

> The literal, grammatical interpretation of the Scriptures must (connected with the figurative topical [sic] or rhetorical) be absorbed in order to attain a correct understanding of this kingdom. Its import is of such weight and the consequences of its adoption of such moment, the tendency it possesses of leading to the truth and the vindicating Scriptures of such value that we cannot pass it by without some explanations and reflections.[8]

A contemporary spokesman for premillennialism voiced the same understanding of the importance of the interpretation of prophecy:

> There is a growing realization in the theological world that the crux of the Millennial issue is the question of method of interpreting Scripture. Premillenarians follow the so-called "grammatical historical" literal interpretation while amilleniarians use a spiritualizing method.[9]

It is an accepted fact; nobody debates the issue. The method of interpretation one uses is crucial to the understanding of what is read. This is no less true of prophetic Scripture than of any other literature.

THE METHODS OF INTERPRETATION

Two methods of interpreting the Bible are prominent today. Other methods have been suggested in the history of the church[10] but the literal, or normal, and the spiritualizing, or allegorical method, have been and still are the two most prominent and important methods.

The Literal or Normal Method

Premillennial Christians usually pride themselves on their belief in the literal interpretation of all of the Scripture. They are frequently described by friends and foes as "literalists." They are sometimes called "wooden literalists," which implies they do not allow for types and symbols in their understanding of Scripture. That criticism does not seem to square, however, with the fact that premillenial writers have contributed much to the understanding of these areas of biblical study.

By a literal interpretation of Scripture, premillennialists mean a straight interpretation. To them, the Bible is to be interpreted just like all other literature. "The literal interpretation as applied to any document is that view which adopts as the sense of a sentence, the meaning of that sentence in usual, or normal conversation or writing."[11] "To interpret literally means nothing more or less than to interpret in terms of normal usual designation."[12]

Premillennialists are agreed in accepting the above as an accurate definition and description of their method of interpreting the whole Bible.

The literal method of interpreting Scripture is also called the grammatical-historical method. This designation emphasizes that the meaning of Scripture is determined both by the grammatical and the historical considerations.

Premillennialists, especially dispensational premillennialists, have not failed to support their use of the literal, normal, or grammatical-historical interpretation of Scripture. Many reasons are often given by them in defense of their position,[13] but there seem to be three crucial reasons:

> Philosophically, the purpose of language itself seems to require literal interpretation. Language was given by God for the purpose of being able to communicate with man...If God be the originator of language and if the chief purpose of originating it was to convey His message to man, then it must follow that He, being all wise and all loving, originated sufficient language to convey all that was in His heart to tell men... The second reason why dispensationalists believe in the literal principle is a Biblical one. It is simply this: The prophecies of the Old Testament concerning the first coming of Christ–His birth, His rearing, His ministry, His death, resurrection– were *all* fulfilled literally. There is no nonliteral fulfillment of these prophecies in the New Testament... A third reason is a logical one. If one does not use the plain, normal, or literal method of interpretation, all objectivity is lost. What check would there be in the variety of interpretations which man's imagination could produce if there was not an objective standard which the literal principle provides?[14]

Premillennialists insist the New Testament's use of the Old Testament substantiates the literal method. In support of this, reference is often made to the many Old Testament prophecies that were fulfilled literally in the New Testament. Why, premillennialists argue, should we expect unfulfilled prophecies to be fulfilled any differently?

Appeal is also made to Jesus' method of interpreting the Old Testament. It seems clear from His example that He used a normal, literal, historical-grammatical method. His interpretation of Scripture was always in harmony with the grammatical and historical meaning. Jesus frequently interpreted one passage of Scripture by appealing to another passage to add further clarification to the meaning (i.e., Mt. 19:3-8 and Deut. 24:1; cf. Mt. 12:3-7 and Hos. 6:6).

The Spiritualizing or Allegorizing Method

According to proponents of this view it is simply impossible to apply the literal method of interpretation to all of Scripture. Amillennialists and postmillennialists insist on this and, especially in prophetic portions, employ a less than literal method at times.

Oswald T. Allis, for example, believes a thoroughly literal interpretation of Scripture is impossible.[15] He gives three reasons for his belief:

> (1) The language of the Bible often contains figures of speech. This is especially true of its poetry...(2) The great theme of the Bible is God and His redemptive dealing with mankind. God is a spirit; the most precious teachings of the Bible are spiritual and these spiritual and heavenly realities are often set forth under the form of earthly objects and human relationships... We should remember the saying of the apostle that spiritual things are "spiritually discerned"...(3) The fact that the Old Testament is both preliminary and preparatory to the New Testament is too obvious to require proof.[16]

Premillennialists have not failed to respond to these objections.[17]

No matter which view one takes, however, it must be admitted that not until the third century AD and the Alexandrian school of theology was there any serious opposition to the literal method. Teachers in the school – Clement of Alexandria and Origen – used a method of interpretation that made all Scripture an allegory. In the fifth century, Augustine led a rejection of this movement. He did not completely reject the allegorical method, but taught only prophecy needs to be allegorized or spiritualized. Much of biblical truth was salvaged by Augustine's efforts. Yet, he and many of his followers, including the great Reformers, continued to use the allegorical method in their interpretation of some unfulfilled prophecy.

Luther, Calvin, and others of the Reformers stressed the need for the literal sense of Scripture and a grammatical-historical approach and they stressed the literal meanings in arriving at their view of salvation by faith alone and the inspiration and sole authority of the Bible. But they did not apply those principles to their interpretation of *all* unfulfilled prophecy.

In addition, those who reject the spiritualizing approach argue further that the spiritualizing or allegorizing method of biblical interpretation did not arise out of a desire to understand Scripture. Instead, it owes its birth to heathen philosophy. "The allegorical system that arose among the pagan Greeks was copied by the Alexandrian Jews and was next adopted by the Christian church, and dominated the church to the Reformation."[18] The allegorical or spiritualizing method of interpretation may be defined as "the method of interpreting the literary text that regards the literal sense as the vehicle for a secondary, more spiritual and more profound sense."[19]

Premillennialists believe such a method for seeking to understand the meaning of any part of Scripture has very serious dangers. They question such a method: What is the basic authority in interpretation – the Scriptures or the mind of the interpreter? They do not feel that the allegorical method really involves interpretation of Scripture. How can the conclusions of the interpreter who uses this method be tested?

Do not all evangelical expositors of the Bible use the literal, historical-grammatical method? Could anybody possibly be evangelical if he did not apply this method to the biblical teaching about Christ, salvation, and sin? These are questions literalists ask of allegoricalists. They believe evangelicalism results only by following the literal method. Premillennialists are convinced that the system of hermeneutics they use is a tremendous safeguard against liberal theology.

All evangelicals do use the literal method for their understanding of most of the Bible, but some, namely those of amillennial and postmillennial persuasion, think it best to use a less than literal hermeneutic with much unfulfilled prophecy. It is at this point that the evangelical world is divided over things to come and this is what puts prophecy in the middle of the debate. Premillennialists cannot understand why their Christian brothers and sisters insist on using a different method in interpretation with some unfulfilled prophecy but not with all of it. They wonder on what grounds is the less-than-literal approach to be restricted to only some themes of unfulfilled prophecy?

To summarize the differences between the two schools of thought, this may be said. All evangelicals use the literal method in their interpretation of the Bible. Some evangelicals believe this same method is to be used with *all* Scripture; these are the premillennialists. Other evangelicals believe that while the literal method is to be used of Scripture in general, it is not necessarily to be used with all unfulfilled prophetic portions. Some of the biblical prophecies (i.e., those concerning the first advent of Christ) are to be understood literally and in fact were fulfilled literally,[20] but many prophecies related to the future coming again of Christ must be understood in a less-than-literal way.

Chapter 5

THE BENEFIT OF STUDYING BIBLE PROPHECY

DAVID BREESE

Even in this world, manufacturers provide an owner's manual with their products, so that consumers can learn how to operate and maintain the item they have purchased. It is, therefore, of little surprise to anyone that the Creator of the Universe would provide instructions for His creation as well.

So it is that long ago, the Almighty God inspired faithful men of old to write a Book. That Book was to serve as an instruction manual for life, containing all that man would need to know to enjoy a happy and triumphant journey through this life, and to obtain an abundant entry into the next.

But in the writing of the Bible, God did an amazing thing. He decided to devote almost one third of Scripture to the foretelling of future events, so that man would know that the Word of God was, indeed, Divinely inspired. And the benefits of studying Bible prophecy would not stop there. God ordained that Bible prophecy would have a unique ability to inspire man as to the marvelous possibilities that come as a result of living a life committed to God.

IT BRINGS THE PROMISE OF A BLESSING

Among the many exceptional benefits of studying Bible prophecy is the promise of a spiritual blessing. In the Book of the Revelation, the Apostle John records that promise: *Blessed is he that readeth, and they that hear the words of this prophecy, and keep those things which are written in it; for the time is at hand* (Rev. 1:3). And we would suggest that the promise of a blessing is not limited to the study of the Revelation, but rather, applies in a myriad of ways to the study of any passage of Bible prophecy.

You've been wanting a blessing from God, have you not? You've been saying, "I sure wish God could be closer to me, and I could learn more about Him." Well, that's exactly what will be made available to you, if you commit to the study of the prophetic Word.

Time would fail to tell why I think it is a blessing to study Bible prophecy. But let me suggest that as we read these golden pages of Scripture, we will be constantly reminded that the program of God is so awesome, and the rewards for allegiance to Him so tremendous, as to be almost beyond description.

In contrast, Bible prophecy reveals the awful fate of the wicked to be so horrible, that our little problems, such as a lost toothbrush, or a hangnail, or a slight financial shortage this week, pale in comparison. Our troubles can easily be put into perspective, when compared to what is happening in the broad sweep of history.

IT REVEALS THE PURPOSE OF GOD IN HISTORY

Now, I would not be critical, but I would say that each of us succumbs too often to the temptation of getting narrow-minded: a little wisp of theology here, a short verse of a poem there, and that becomes the whole thing for us spiritually. That ought not to be!

God never intended for us to take one tiny pebble of truth and turn it into a great big mountain of theology. That's how false doctrines and apostasies creep in. That's how even a formerly good church can lose its bearings and wind up on the list of cults, promoting destructive heresies.

How then, shall we, study Bible prophecy? Is there some secret formula that we can apply to the study of prophecy that will make its meaning clear, or is Bible prophecy only for a select group of prophets and teachers who have been given a special gift of discernment? Never believe it! Bible prophecy was written for all of us, so that we can share in the blessing of its study.

But there are some simple, commonsense keys to the study of Bible prophecy that, when applied, will help us understand the Word of God more fully. First, be sure that you *truly study*. There are millions of people in the world, who think they are studying something, but really, they only give it a look and a promise – a very superficial amount of attention – and as a result, their supposed "deep study" amounts to nothing.

Alexander Pope said, "Drink deep, or touch not the Pyorrhean spring, for shallow drafts intoxicate the brain, but drinking deeply sobers one again." So it is that the Scripture instructs us to *study to show thyself approved unto God, a workman that needeth not to be ashamed, rightly dividing the word of truth* (2 Tim. 2:15).

Take some time every day to read what the Scripture has to say. Then compare Scripture with Scripture, because the Bible explains itself. God does not contradict Himself. If you happen to come upon something that seems to be new and startling, be sure that it does not conflict with the rest of Scripture. If it appears to do so, then, look again, to see what might be wrong in your initial interpretation.

Second, *take it seriously*. You are dealing with real things, when you look into the Word of God. With most other elements of thought in this world – philosophy, engineering, science, or anything else – you are dealing primarily with theory. You can take it, or leave it alone. But you had better take the Bible seriously, because what you read in Scripture is a matter of life and death!

Third, *remember the dispensations*. Yes, believe it or not, there are such things as dispensations. God has dealt differently with man in different periods of time. For instance, Adam and Eve were created in total innocence. Everything was permissible for them except one thing: to eat of the tree of the knowledge of good and evil. It was an age of innocence. But when they sinned and ate of the tree, their innocence was lost. They knew that they were naked. And so innocence gave way to conscience.

Conscience dictated what man would do until man hardened his heart and became terribly corrupt. The Great Flood put an end to the Dispensation of Conscience, which was followed by the Dispensation of Human Government. Human Government was followed by the giving of the Law, which was followed by the era of Grace, and so forth.

Be sure that you learn the dispensations, so that when studying Bible prophecy, you will be able to identify the manner in which God was dealing with the people to whom the prophecy was given. The promise of God to Israel under the Law was that they would inherit the world. The promise of God to believers under Grace is that we will inherit the universe. The Christians who want so desperately to claim the promises that God made to Israel to the extent that they are willing to overlook the greater promises that God has made to the Church constantly amaze me! Israel and the Church are not the same thing, and so the promises of God to each of them are different. Remember the dispensations when studying Bible prophecy.

Fourth, *watch the times* in the midst of which we live. When Christ talked about the things that would happen as we move to the end of time, He said there would be signs in the heavens above and the earth beneath (Mt. 24-25). Christ spoke to the Pharisees and said, *...O ye hypocrites, ye can discern the face of the sky; but can ye not discern the signs of the times?* (Mt. 16:3).

There are things happening in our lifetimes that have never happened before since the time of Christ. For instance, the Bible says that Israel would be dispersed, which it was back in Roman times. It also says that Israel would be regathered, brought back to the land, and reborn as a nation, which happened in 1948. That's a political miracle on an international scale. How did it happen? God did it! And it is an amazing sign that we are living in the Last Days.

The Apostle Paul wrote to Timothy and said, *Meditate upon these things; give thyself wholly to them, that thy profiting may appear to all* (1 Tim. 4:15). There is a marvelous profit to be found in studying the prophetic Word of God.

Fifth, *allow Bible prophecy to motivate you.* What does that mean? Well, the Bible talks about the return of Christ, and then it says: *And every man that hath this hope in him purifieth himself even as he is pure* (1 Jn. 3:3). Studying anything from a sterile point of view, not taking to heart what it has to teach, not allowing it to motivate you to greater service, is an inferior way to study. The Word of God was not given to us solely for intellectual stimulation, although it does provide that. It was given to us so that our lives would be challenged and changed – conformed to the will of God.

When we study the Bible with these things in mind, we discover that Bible prophecy works in concert with the rest of the Bible to paint a vivid picture of the plan of God, revealing the great purpose of God in history. And it is so important for us to take those overarching lessons seriously, looking for the main point before we become entrapped by the temptation to focus first on the details.

Take, for instance, the book of Jonah. There are many fascinating things to be learned from Jonah, from the importance of obedience to the protection of God. But without question, the greatest lesson we can learn from Jonah (the prophet who made only one prophecy: a prophecy that, in human terms, did not even come to pass exactly as foretold!) is the truth that the first will of God is not judgment, but revival and repentance. When Jonah told the people of Nineveh that the judgment of God was coming, they repented in sackcloth and ashes, all the way from the king on down to the lowest of servants. So, instead of bringing the destruction He had warned would take place in 40 days, God withheld judgment for an entire generation. Why? Because the first will of God is not judgment, but repentance!

You see, understanding great principles like these, found so many times in the pages of the prophetic Word, helps us get a glimpse of the larger picture: the purpose of God in history. Such grand perspective will help us steer clear of tangents and pitfalls, both in our theology and in our personal lives.

There are those who would dwell on the question of whether Jonah was swallowed by a fish or a whale. Others would focus on the storm and Jonah's efforts to escape the call of God. And so on the four corners of a single intersection, you might find the "Great Fish Congregational Church," the "Jesus Said It Was a Whale Baptist Church," the "You Can't Run from God Methodists," and the "Throw Him Overboard Brethren" churches. If only we took the time to discover the overarching plan of God for man, through the study of Bible prophecy, so much confusion would be averted!

IT UNRAVELS THE MYSTERIES OF THE AGES

Another benefit of studying Bible prophecy is, that nothing does a better job of unraveling life's greatest mysteries, than does the prophetic Word of God. There are many things that the Bible identifies as great mysteries:

- The mystery of iniquity
- The mystery of human nature
- The mystery of divine love
- The mystery of salvation
- The mystery of godliness
- The mystery of the Church
- The mystery of the Rapture
- The mystery of the Antichrist
- The mystery of ultimate reality and more

In this life, people run to and fro asking, "Why am I here? Where am I going? What is truth? Where can I turn to find the answer to life's most perplexing problems?" And the answer to all of those questions can be obtained through the study of Bible prophecy.

As a young man, I loved to read mysteries. The mystery challenged my mind, the twists of plot kept me alert, and the exhilaration of discovering the truth behind the mystery brought immense satisfaction. Yet that was only a small foretaste of the fulfillment that I found when I began to understand the great mysteries of life through the study of the prophetic Word.

IT LETS US KNOW WHAT THE FUTURE HOLDS

Who among us wouldn't like to know what the future holds? We would know whether or not to put the top up on the car at night, what kind of clothes to wear to work or school, whether to save for tomorrow or invest in survival supplies to help us survive terrorist attacks. Come on - admit it! You want to know what the future holds, as much as do I!

In fact, millions upon millions of dollars are made every year by charlatans who deceive fragile people with weak minds into believing that they can learn about the future through the reading of tarot cards, gazing into crystal balls, visiting groaning mediums and the like. Yet the Bible is the only true and reliable source of future prophecy in the world.

We all have seen the tabloids at the turn of each new year, listing 10 or 20 predictions for the year to come. And those cheesy prognosticators do well to get even one of those predictions right. Yet the Bible remains the only 100% reliable source of future information in the world today.

So, what does the future hold? Here are just a few things that we do know, not presented in chronological order:

- The growth of a global economic system
- A great economic crash
- The invasion of the Middle East by a great power from the north, presumably Russia and her allies
- The rise of a powerful and evil world leader named the Antichrist
- The establishment of a world government
- Both marvelous growth and opportunity for the Church, and apostasy that will lead to a Satanic world religion
- Wars and plagues that, along with the supernatural judgment of God, will claim the lives of at least half the people on Planet Earth
- The Rapture of the Church
- The Glorious Return of Jesus Christ

That's just part of what the prophetic Word tells us is in store for the people of Earth. Can you imagine the benefits of knowing what lies ahead? Why, if we learned nothing more than the fact that the Jesus could come at any moment…that the signs of the times point to His soon return…we would be blessed beyond measure because we would be motivated to make the most of the time that remains. The study of Bible prophecy is valuable, really, beyond description!

IT EXPLAINS HOW TO BE A REAL CHRISTIAN

There are many theories circulating today about what it means to be a real Christian. But there is some confusion over the difference between **becoming** a Christian and **being** a Christian. Some say that, "If Jesus isn't Lord **of all,** He isn't Lord **at all!**" And while that is a clever little saying, it brings with it the bondage of a thing called "lordship salvation." That is the idea that we must do something extra, perhaps even something extraordinary, beyond believing on Jesus Christ, in order to prove our salvation. It is the doctrine of salvation by perfection and by works. And while some preachers use that line of teaching to "keep their congregation in line," it simply is not true.

The Bible says, *Believe on the Lord Jesus Christ, and thou shalt be saved* (Acts 16:31). It does not say, "Believe on the Lord Jesus Christ, and thou shalt be put on probation!" Lordship salvation is simply another form of salvation by works, a philosophy that is common to all of the non-Christian religions and cults of the world.

Thank God, "lordship salvation" is not true. If it were true, one could never go to bed at night without wondering, "Have I done enough to be saved? Have I served enough? Have I confessed enough? Have I committed any unknown sin that will keep me from receiving the benefit of the saving grace of God?" Those who believe such things will never know if they have done enough to be saved, but rather will be a quivering mass of doubt and insecurity until they finally stand before God, face-to-face.

That having been said, once the issue of becoming a Christian has been settled, Bible prophecy provides wonderful insights into what it means to be a real Christian in these exciting Last Days. It challenges us to be *the salt of the earth...the light of the world...a city that is set on a hill* (Mt. 5:13, 14). It demolishes the "hunker-down" mentality by giving us a foretaste of the exciting activities of the Church in the End-Times. It turns quiescent, passive Christians into valiant and courageous soldiers in the Armies of Christ. By learning to view life from the prophetic perspective, the Christian gains new appreciation of what it means to live and fight back, in the midst of spiritual warfare.

IT HELPS US REDEEM THE TIME AND FULFILL OUR END-TIME MISSION

Finally, the study of Bible prophecy not only motivates the Christian, but also provides stunning details about End-Time events that will help the Christian avoid the ambush of the Devil in his life so that he can be successful in fulfilling his End-Time mission. As we said before, the prophetic Word foretells the advent of false teachers, the spreading of apostasy, the rise of a world government, world economy, and world religion, and much more.

But lest these warnings should produce too much fear, it also makes the promise that the door of opportunity would remain open (Rev. 3:7, 8) until the Church is caught up in the clouds to meet the Lord in the air (1 Thess. 4 and 5). It promises that the Church will be triumphant in battle against the gates of Hell (Mt. 16:18) and that believers will reign with Christ over the universe throughout the wideness of eternity (1 Cor. 3:22, 23).

So Bible prophecy reveals the true nature of the universe, and the nature of our sojourn as Christians here on Earth. It tells us that we live in the midst of a great spiritual war, and we are soldiers in that eternal battle. The Scripture says that *No man that warreth entangleth himself with the affairs of this life, that he may please him who hath chosen him to be a soldier* (2 Tim. 2:4).

In fact, we are not just soldiers, but we are an army of occupation. Jesus told a parable about a nobleman who was called out of town. When he went away, he left instructions with the people he had appointed to look after his holdings. He commissioned them to *occupy till I come* (Lk. 19:13). When Christ told His disciples this parable, it was not just a story about some strangers, it was about them, and it was about us. With these brief words, He revealed their future, providing a glimpse of His commission to them, and informing them of their great responsibility. "Occupy till I come," that is what we are to do in the period of time, however long or short that may be, between this moment and the moment that Christ returns for us. So, as members of the army of occupation, what are we to do?

First, *hold forth the Word.* I mention this first, because it is the primary obligation of the Church. The Church is not here to do second or third or fourth things, before it does the first things. Yes, we may build buildings. Yes, we may put together interesting and complicated organizations. We may even feed the hungry and clothe the poor. But those things are without significance unless we first hold forth the Word of life. Paul said...*holding forth the word of life, that I may rejoice in the day of Christ that I have not run in vain, neither labored in vain* (Phil. 2:16).

When we do this, the Bible says we accomplish a result *in the midst of a crooked and perverse nation, among whom ye shine as lights in the world* (Phil. 2:15). Really, that "holding forth the word of life" is a blessed secret that many church organizations have long forgotten. They wonder, "Why aren't we succeeding? Why aren't we accomplishing many things in today's world? Why are finances behind? Why are the employees leaving? Why is it all coming apart?"

Let me tell you something! The Gospel is *the power of God unto salvation* (Rom. 1:16). If we remember that, if we do the first things first, if we commit to preaching the Gospel and leave ourselves out of it for a while, it is terrific what God will do!

Second, *be the salt of the Earth.* Jesus said, *Ye are the salt of the earth, but if the salt have lost its savor, with what shall it be salted?* (Mt. 5:13). The "salt of the earth" means that you are the flavor. You are the preservative. You are the ingredient that keeps it all from going to rack and ruin. Be the salt of the Earth. Even though ours is a terribly corrupt society, it will be sustained in those areas where the salt is functioning properly.

Third, *be the light of the world*. Jesus, during the days of His earthly ministry, said, *I am the light of the world* (Jn 8:12). But when He prepared to leave the world, He spoke to His disciples and told them it was their turn: *Ye are the light of the world* (Mt. 5:14). What does that mean? It means that we are to give the world direction. We illuminate the pathway. We tell people the way to go. It is my opinion that the Church should conduct itself in such a fashion that the world, including politicians, will come to us for advice on how to operate. They used to do it in early America and in some other places. That is what should take place, when "the light of the world" is functioning properly.

Fourth, *fight the good fight*. We lose something essential to our identity, when we abandon the concept of Christian life being a battle, and of the Church being an army. *Fight the good fight of faith* (1 Tim. 6:12) is what the Bible says to every Christian. The Apostle Paul spoke about himself at the end of his life and said *I have fought a good fight* (2 Tim. 4:7).

Can you see it? The Apostle Paul, approaching martyrdom, was being asked the questions as though he might crumble: "Was it worth it? How do you feel about your life now?" And this man, with eyes still gleaming, still valiant in combat for Christ, says, "I have fought the good fight of faith. I have not run away from the enemy. I have lifted a voice for Christ."

Fifth, *finish the course*. We are all very good at starting, but not as many are good at finishing. It is well known in dealing with people that many folks make a flashy start, but they run out of enthusiasm along the way. They often say about pilots, "It's a bad thing to run out of ideas and altitude at the same time." Finish the course. Pursue it to the end.

Finally, *expect a crown of righteousness*. Paul said, if you do these things, you can expect... *a crown of righteousness, which the Lord, the righteousness judge, shall give me at that day; and not only to me, but unto all them also that love his appearing* (2 Tim. 4:8). There is a crown of righteousness awaiting those who study Bible prophecy, who live in anticipation of Christ's return, who love His appearing!

So you see, the promises and advantages of studying Bible prophecy are valuable beyond description. Its application to our lives will bring us blessing, and power, and perspective. May we therefore challenge you to look into the golden pages of the Bible, and discover the light that our "more sure word of prophecy" (2 Pet. 1:19) can shed on your life? I pray that you will. I promise, it will be worth it!

Chapter 6

THE MIND WHICH HAS WISDOM

WILLIAM T. JAMES

These are times that delude as perhaps no other times in history.

Signs of biblically prophesied troubles surround this generation and threaten to storm upon us at any moment. The supernatural storm grows ominously on the horizon, flickering against the darkening skies in jagged, lightning-like wickedness that increases by the hour. And yet, very few among us seem to see the coming tempest.

Accounts from our local newscasts and from national and world news reports tell the foreboding truth. The world–mankind–is not getting better and better, as the evolutionists believe. The human race is not progressing toward some ultimately evolved godhood. Indeed, the print and broadcast news media present a far different story. Their stories prove that the Apostle Paul's prophecies are unscrolling before our eyes.

...in the last days perilous times shall come...(2 Tim. 3:1) and *...evil men and seducers shall wax worse and worse, deceiving and being deceived...*(2 Tim. 3:13).

We should not be surprised, then, that people are blinded to what is happening all around us. Paul, under divine inspiration, prophesied that this is how it would be as the end of the age approaches. Blindness to coming dangers of apocalyptic troubles is plainly predicted in God's Word. Why, then, should we find what is happening in that regard something about which to be overly concerned? Why get too worried, since there is really nothing we can do to change it?

The key thing to consider is that Paul used the word "evil" to describe those who will be seduced. "Evil men and seducers will wax [grow] worse and worse, deceiving and being deceived." This indicates that the lost–those who do not know the Lord Jesus as Savior–will be the ones seducing with deceit and being deceived in their turn. No wonder God's prophetic Word has no meaning to them. The Bible says, ...*But the natural man receiveth not the things of the Spirit of God: for they are foolishness unto him: neither can he know them, because they are spiritually discerned*...(1 Cor. 2:14).

SLEEPING CHRISTIANS

Christians are asleep in the pews. Pastors are speaking soothing "don't worry do-goodism and feel-goodism" words from the pulpits. Therein lies the real tragedy of this last-time generation. The very people of god who are charged with presenting God's Word and the salvation message to a lost and dying world are being anesthetized by lifeless, secular-based, sermonizing. This is why we must concern ourselves to such a high degree about what is happening all around us.

America's Christians, in particular, have fallen victim to the seducers, the evil men who preach "another gospel" than the one Paul preached. False teachers and preachers abound, in effect saying: ...*Where is the promise of His coming? For since the fathers fell asleep, all things continue as they were from the beginning of the creation*...(2 Pet. 3:4). Prophecy, these wolves in sheep's clothing say, is all symbolic "gobbledygook," not meant to be understood. Or they proclaim that all prophecy has already been fulfilled.

Revelation, they say, should not have even been put in the canon of Scripture in the first place.

I must say, here, that I am referring both to lost men and women who call themselves preachers and teachers of God's Holy Word, and to those liberal-minded, fuzzy-headed preachers and teachers who might genuinely know Christ as Savior, but who have been deluded into believing that prophecy is all but irrelevant for this generation. Tragically, whether taught by those who are lost, or by those who are saved, the effects on the average Christian who sits under their false notions is the same. The whole purpose of the Christian's understanding God's foretelling things to come is missed.

...Seeing then that all these things shall be dissolved, what manner of persons ought ye to be in all holy conversation and godliness, Looking for and hasting unto the coming of the day of God, wherein the heavens being on fire shall be dissolved, and the elements shall melt with fervent heat? (2 Pet. 3:11, 12).

Preaching, teaching and especially learning God's true prophetic Word edifies the body (the church) of Christ. It lifts us to a higher plane of awareness that Jesus can return at any moment. The study of prophecy can and will make us better, more fervent Christians. It will, if studied with heartfelt conviction, make us dedicated sowers of the Gospel message that Jesus saves!

To disregard prophecy, that is, to say that the Bible does not really mean what it says when it tells of things such as the Rapture, Antichrist, the Tribulation, etc., is to tell Jesus "We think you were not telling us the truth."

Jesus said in Mark 13:37: *What I say unto one, I say unto all. Watch.*

The Lord had, immediately prior to that command to Christians of all the Church Age and beyond, given a list of end-time prophecies that would impact the world. He was warning each of us who is called by His name today to be watchful for prophetic signals. These signals will show us how very near is His Second Coming to earth. But, these signals will also indicate how even nearer is His coming for us in the Rapture. He meant those words for us, as surely as He meant them for the group to whom He was then speaking.

A pastor or teacher who truly is a child of God in Christ's church, but who flings aside God's words of prophecy as unimportant, faces the prospects of answering serious failings when looking into Christ's piercing eyes of perfect knowledge at the *Bema* (judgment seat). Those who are not saved by and through the shed blood of Jesus Christ, and deceive God's flock of believers with such heresy, face a much greater condemnation at the Great White Throne judgment.

INDIVIDUAL CHRISTIAN RESPONSIBILITY

We see, then, how crucial it is for God's teachers and preachers to preach and teach the whole Word of the living God. So it is incumbent upon each one of us who is God's child, through Christ's shed blood at Calvary, to seek earnestly to understand God's love letter to each of us. We must each study and seek the whole counsel of God's Word, the Bible.

Unfortunately, today pastors choose the path of least resistance. They strive to preach only the love of God, preferring to avoid addressing subjects like death, Hell, and the wrath of God to come in the Tribulation era. These things frighten the preachers, apparently, so it will frighten the flock, the ministers obviously conclude.

The Bible says, *My people are destroyed for lack of knowledge...* (Hos. 4:6). God's Word, the Bible, is fully 28% prophetic. Half of that 28% has been fulfilled. That means that half is yet to be fulfilled.

God tells those pastors—and all others who refuse to accept His whole Word—*For I testify unto every man that heareth the words of the prophecy of this book, If any man shall add unto these things, God shall add unto him the plagues that are written in this book: And if any man shall take away from the words of the book of this prophecy, God shall take away his part out of the book of life, and out of the holy city, and from the things which are written in this book...* (Rev. 22:18-19).

Revelation 19:10 says emphatically that the testimony of Jesus is the spirit of prophecy. To ignore or take away the prophetic Word from the Bible is to evict the Lord of Heaven! No wonder God takes so seriously anyone's tampering with His prophetic Word.

UNDERSTANDING PROPHECY

Although the Old Testament contains a tremendous amount of prophecy yet future, it is the New Testament and the book of Revelation that brings all prophecy, past, present, and future, into focus.

To begin with, the book is called "Revelation," not the book of "Mystery" or the book of "Puzzles." Its very name indicates that it is a book meant to be understood. It is, in fact, the Revelation of Jesus Christ in all His glory!

And its words in the earliest part of the book go further with regard to its understandability. Revelation tells us: ...*Blessed is he that readeth, and they that hear the words of this prophecy, and keep those things which are written therein: for the time is at hand...* (Rev. 1:3). God would not use such strong terminology if understanding His Word were too difficult. Why, then, do most of His children–including most preachers and teachers–fear prophecy, and the book of Revelation in particular? What is the answer to breaking down that fear, and to beginning the joyous experience God intends the study and understanding of prophecy to be for each of us?

THE FEAR FACTOR

For God hath not given us the spirit of fear; but of power, and of love, and of a sound mind... (2 Tim.1:7).

We know from this truth that God does not give fear to His children. That fear comes from within ourselves. It also come from our lack of faith and lack of faithfulness.

The fear we experience, in regard to prophecy, comes from the fact that we do not take God at His Word. We are afraid that He will drop us. If we cannot hold on to Him tightly enough, we will slip from His grasp. Therefore, Christians choose to, like the ostrich, stick their spiritual sensibilities into the sand to avoid thoughts of Bible prophecy.

We say we believe in eternal security, but our lack of faith in the matter of Bible prophecy, sometimes indicates otherwise. Our lack of faithfulness is another factor that engenders fear regarding Bible prophecy. We simply refuse to engage in faithful activities like reading of the prophetic Scripture, studying the prophetic Scripture and praying over the prophetic Scripture. Too often we depend on our pastors and teachers to teach us all we need to know about Bible prophecy.

But, as we know, today preachers are preaching less and less about prophecy. Teachers are teaching less and less on prophetic topics. Far too many Christians are therefore ignorant of all-important prophetic truth from the Word of God.

The other source of fear regarding the study of God's prophetic Word is that constant enemy who stalks about like a roaring lion, seeking whom he might devour. Satan never ceases telling us in our faithless, unfaithful minds that prophecy is much too complex, or is no longer important. The devil uses faithless, unfaithful pastors and teachers, through their sins of omission, to get across his deadly message that a loving God would never be so cruel as to bring wrath and judgment. Prophecy, the devil whispers, is gloom and doom. And, it should not even be in a loving God's Bible.

God, in 1 Timothy 1:7, tells us that He has not given us the spirit of fear, but of power, love, and a sound mind. So let us think on these things, using the sound mind with which our Lord has equipped us.

God's wrath and judgment are in fact proof that He is a God of righteousness and love. His Word tells us exactly why sin must be judged, and how it will be judged. The ultimate result of that judgment, God's Word tells us, will be the complete eradication of sin, and a magnificent life for each of us. That life will last forever!

He provided the way for every human being who has ever lived to escape the time of His wrath upon and judgment for sin and rebellion. He gave His only Son, Jesus Christ, upon that bloody cross nearly 2,000 years ago so we will not have to pay the price for our sins.

Prophecy, then, is a large part of the bright effulgence of God's love for His creature called man, not darkness and death. It is up to the individual whether to reach out in belief and accept Christ's offered redemption.

PROPHECY SEEN THROUGH SPIRITUAL VISION

Although Christians, while living in the flesh, do not yet see perfectly, for *...now we see through a glass, darkly...*(1 Cor. 13:12), we nonetheless have within us, because of being born again, the ability to spiritually discern God's truth. Once again, the Bible tells us that people who are without the rebirth that comes with knowing Christ personally as Savior and Lord do not have such perception.

But the natural man receiveth not the things of the Spirit of God: for they are foolishness unto him: neither can he know [them], *because they are spiritually discerned* (1 Cor. 2:14).

Spiritual discernment is a wonderful gift, indeed. But the Christian must, individually, prayerfully and carefully seek to exercise that gift. All who belong to Christ can obtain understanding in every aspect of God's Holy Word. That includes His prophetic Word.

While it is good to read and study things written in books, such as this one, and to listen to the God-impressed words of men and women who preach and teach God's prophetic truth, there is no substitute for reading the Bible, itself. You as an individual Christian, one-on-one with the Word of God, is not only the best way to discern Bible prophecy. It is the way God commands!

Study to shew thyself approved unto God, a workman that needeth not to be ashamed, rightly dividing the word of truth (2 Tim. 2:15).

Also, we must study all of the prophecies God has put in His Word. Together they form the basis for an accurate prophetic picture. In other words, we must not take one or several prophecies, which have no other validating Scripture, and form our own view based upon these limited verses. We must check our conclusions against what the vast body of prophecy has to say.

This truth is found in 2 Peter 1:20: *Knowing this first, that no prophecy of the scripture is of any private interpretation.*

GOD-GIVEN WISDOM

True wisdom comes from God. Solomon is the most in-depth study of God's conferring wisdom on one of His children. Still, Solomon, as we learn from Ecclesiastes, had many, many shortcomings that made him sometimes appear less than a wise man.

The gift and privilege of godly wisdom –and there is in truth no other kind than that from the heavenly Father—can be applied in prophetic matters. That is, in some instances, Christians attuned to the mind and will of God can know much regarding prophetic signals they see being given off around them.

A quite good example of such wisdom that will one day be employed by a specific generation of saints of God is the familiar prophecy found in the book of Revelation. *Here is wisdom. Let him that hath understanding count the number of the beast: for it is the number of a man; and his number is six hundred threescore and six* (Rev. 13:18).

Christians who will receive wisdom for knowing Antichrist's identity will be saints of the Tribulation era. Christians today will not know who the beast of Revelation is, because God has determined that we do not need this wisdom or understanding at the present time. Antichrist has not yet appeared, and will not be fully revealed, until he stands in the Jewish Temple on Mount Moriah during the Tribulation Period, proclaiming himself God. This truth is found in 2 Thessalonians 2:2-6: *That ye be not soon shaken in mind, or be troubled, neither by spirit, nor by word, nor by letter as from us, as that the day of Christ is at hand. Let no man deceive you by any means: for that day shall not come, except there come a falling away first, and that man of sin be revealed, the son of perdition; Who opposeth and exalteth himself above all that is called God, or that is worshipped; so that he as God sitteth in the temple of God, shewing himself that he is God. Remember ye not, that, when I was yet with you, I told you these things? And now ye know what withholdeth that he might be revealed in his time.*

Why are we not privy to that wisdom during this, the Church Age? Probably because we are to be looking not for Antichrist, but for Jesus Christ: *Looking for that blessed hope, and the glorious appearing of the great God and our Saviour Jesus Christ...*(Tit. 2:13).

The Holy Scriptures are clear. Christians this side of the Rapture will not know who Antichrist will be. That is wisdom God has reserved for another group of His beloved saints.

But, through God's permissive will, Christians of this present era are, I believe, being given many prophetic signals of things to come. That is, I am convinced that we who are spiritually attuned to the prophetic Word that God wants us to study, pray about and meditate over can obtain wisdom which provides significant insights into where this generation stands on God's prophetic timeline. This is because we are, I am convinced, very near the prophesied "time of the end."

The proof text for substantiating my belief in this regard is found in the book of Daniel: *And I heard, but I understood not: then said I, O my Lord, what shall be the end of these things? And he said, Go thy way, Daniel: for the words are closed up and sealed till the time of the end* (Dan. 12:9).

END-TIME INDICATORS

No other generation has seen so many indicators of Christ's coming again as this generation of which you and I are a part.

Jesus, in His Olivet Discourse (see Mt. 24; Mk. 13; Lk. 21), foretold a series of issues and events that would point toward and/or prove that the world was in the Seventieth Week of Daniel, or Tribulation Period. This will be, according to Jesus, a time when many troubling signals will assault planet Earth in birth-pang fashion. That is, there will be a tremendous increase in frequency and intensity of very specific symptoms, the closer human history gets to his Second Coming.

The Lord gave the signals to watch for, then commanded all who believe in Him to watch carefully as they unfold (Mk. 13:37). Jesus said these end-time signals will indicate that His coming is very near, even right at the door:

So likewise ye, when ye shall see all these things, know that it is near, even at the doors. Verily I say unto you, this generation shall not pass, till all these things be fulfilled (Mt. 24:33, 34).

The exciting thing to consider here is that the Lord was talking about His Second Coming to this planet. This will be His triumphant return to put an end to the murderous violence and war that will at that time be on the verge of destroying all human life.

At least seven years before that happens, Christ will first come in the clouds, above the earth, for those believers of the Church Age (the time since Pentecost until the present). This will be the Rapture of the Church, the sudden snatching up of all people who have died believing in Him and those who are alive at the time.

Dead Christians will be resurrected. Living Christians will be translated, or supernaturally changed. Both groups of believers will be given bodies and minds made for inhabiting the heavenlies. Millions upon millions of people will vanish before the astonished eyes of those who are left behind. It will happen in a fraction of a second! (Read 1 Thess. 4:13-18 and 2 Cor. 15:51-55)

So many signals similar to those prophesied by Jesus and Bible prophets are taking place at the present time that space here is too limited to fully explain them all. This means that since we are seeing these prophetic indicators impacting our generation with such frequency and intensity that they are hard to keep pace with (Jesus predicted these signals for a seven-year period that cannot begin until Christians of today have disappeared), the Rapture must be very close, indeed!

Jesus, himself, said as recorded in Luke 21:28, ...*When these things begin to come to pass, then look up and lift up your head, for your redemption draweth nigh [near]....*

Our newspaper headlines and television newscasts seem to shout prophetic warnings with each passing hour. Still, most Christians haven't a clue to what is happening all around them.

It is past time for those who call Christ their Lord to get their spiritual eyes and ears attuned to the nearness of Jesus coming again for them. It is high time to lift up our heads and look up!

SOME SPECIFIC PROPHETIC SIGNALS

Jesus said there will be wars and rumors of wars. There will be famine, pestilence and earthquakes in various places. There will be signs in the sun moon and stars.

To show the stark reality of Jesus' prophetic words coming true in our time, consider the Lord's statement about strife among the nations. He said...*nation shall rise against nation, and kingdom against kingdom...* (Mt. 24:7).

The word "nation" in the original manuscripts comes from the Greek word *ethnos*, from which we get the word "ethnic."

Think now about the many conflicts between countries that have taken place in the recent past, and those fightings going on at present. Do we not constantly hear the words "ethnic conflict" and/or "ethnic cleansing" used within the news reports of these raging conflicts?

Again, the Lord gave these signals specifically for the time He called "the Great Tribulation." Actually, that refers to the last three and one-half years of the seven-year Tribulation Period, also called Daniel's Seventieth Week or the Apocalypse.

However, God, in His perfect will, has seen fit to let Christians of our time – that is, the time just before we are called into the presence of Jesus—see a preview of things to come. He is letting us see the prophesied Tribulation storm approaching. Perhaps He is doing so to show us proof, through prophecy, of the veracity of His character and to urge us to be true Ambassadors for Him in these closing days of human history. Again, 2 Peter 3:12, 13 should be ringing in our ears, individually and collectively:

> Seeing then that all these things shall be dissolved, what manner of persons ought ye to be in all holy conversation and godliness, looking for and hasting unto

the coming of the day of God, wherein the heavens being on fire shall be dissolved, and the elements shall melt with fervent heat? (2 Pet. 3:12, 13)

Prophesied scenarios are setting up everywhere on the planet. Here are a few, as I view them.

- *One-world socio-economics*
  Economic Babylon (read Rev. 18) is shaping up before our eyes. The love of money is indeed the root of all evil, just as God's Word says. The world is being enslaved through computers and credit card debt. Antichrist's system of control cannot be far off (Rev. 13).

- *One-world government*
  The United Nations, and many Non-Governmental Organizations (NGOs), along with a nucleus group of elitist New World Order builders, are determined to again mount a one world building project as did Nimrod and the Babel builders (Gen. 11). More and more they insist on intervening into the sovereign affairs of nations. They seek world-unified laws, military, economy and total control of every aspect of human life.

  The on-going Earth Summits promoted by these tower builders are annual testaments to their determination to build their own Tower of Babel. It will not stand (Again, read Dan. 2).

- *One-world religion*
  The call for "unity" is really a call for "One World." This is the beginning of the apostate church, the woman who rides the beast of Revelation 17, in my view.

  The false prophet of Revelation 13 will one day use such an amalgamation of religious organizations and churches to cause all to worship Antichrist or die.

Ecumenism (bringing diverse religious beliefs together) is on the march across the globe. This godless call for unity is the exact opposite of Christ's prayer for unity (Read Jn. 17).

- *Antichrist's control technology*
Eschalon, Carnivore, and other surveillance technologies are growing at a phenomenal pace. The biochip is very near the point that it can be implanted in humans, as is already being done in animals. Internet/satellite/virtual reality and all other cyberspace capabilities are creating addictions to rival the many legal and illicit drugs that can create a robot-like people who will one day follow Antichrist's deluding commandments.

- *Reviving Roman Empire*
The euro's introduction in January 2002, puts the European Union (EU) on the road to becoming the center of geopolitical end-time power, just as Daniel foresaw when he interpreted Nebuchadnezzar's dream (See Dan. 2).

   The EU looks to be the reviving Roman Empire that will produce the "Prince that shall come" of Daniel 9:24-27: the Antichrist.

- *Russia and the Gog-Magog Factor*
Much study has been done on who is Gog and Magog of Ezekiel, chapters 38 and 39. Hal Lindsey, Tim LaHaye, and many other excellent scholars have studied the ancient lands north of Israel and have determined that Russia will be the chief nation that comes against Israel in "the latter days." Russia will bring many of its neighboring peoples with it in the invasion.

   Russia is presently courting the western nations in order to secure technology and money. But, there remains a visceral hunger for hegemony over her neighbors. The Middle East and the oil fields look more and more inviting to an economically depressed Russia, no doubt.

- *King of the East*

  Revelation, chapters 9 and 16, indicate that 200 million troops will invade across a dried up Euphrates River during the Tribulation Period. China has been able to raise such a land army for years! China continues to threaten to overwhelm its Asian neighbors. It threatens Taiwan on a daily basis.

  China has stolen, or has been given, American computer, nuclear, missile and satellite technologies. It is just a matter of time until this great dragon moves aggressively somewhere in the world.

- *Israel*

  The Temple Mount in Jerusalem is the most important spot on earth to God. So, it is the most important place on earth to Satan, who still seeks to usurp the throne of God.

  Although Arab Islamic terrorists have been the main culprits in terror attacks around the world, the tiny nation of Israel is more and more being blamed for the murderous violence. Israel is falsely accused of causing the terrorist actions by oppressing the Palestinian people. In reality, Israel opposes Arafat's deadly designs to get rid of Israel.

  Israel will continue to become more and more the center of all problems for a world worried about keeping petroleum flowing, and fearful of nuclear Armageddon. Zechariah, chapter 12, seems to be fulfilling before our eyes today. Jerusalem is indeed a burdensome stone and a cup of trembling to all nations round about.

SEEK THE MIND OF GOD

Pray that God will give you a mind that has wisdom for this crucial hour. Get into His Word –His WHOLE Word. In other words, begin reading and studying God's prophetic Word along with all other of His marvelous truth.

Then, prayerfully and carefully, look and listen to the issues and events bombarding us every minute of every day. Don't look and listen to these things with fear and trembling. These are but predictors of the birth of a brilliant, magnificent world ruled by the King of Kings and Lord of Lords! It is a birth that, indeed, looks to be on the very brink of taking place.

SECTION 2

THE NATIONS IN PROPHECY

Chapter 7

GOD'S JUDGMENT UPON INDIVIDUALS

PAUL N. BENWARE

Television programs abound that deal with crime, criminals and the law. A number of popular shows take the viewer into the courtroom setting and reveal the tactics of both prosecuting and defense attorneys as well as the biases of the judges. The television viewer is often left with the impression that judgment can be manipulated with many offenders dealing their way out of harsh sentences or, perhaps, avoiding any penalty at all for their crimes. It does appear sometimes that people do "get away with murder." If these programs do, in fact, reflect reality, then we are rightly disturbed by the lack of consistency, fairness and justice in our judicial system.

What can be said with certainty, however, is that even if these television programs do reflect the reality of our culture, they do not reflect ultimate reality. Ultimate reality is that all created beings are accountable to their Creator and will be judged by Him. They will not get away with bad behavior. He cannot be manipulated or coerced and His judgments will be unbiased. With complete understanding and with absolute fairness the Judge of the universe will do what is right. And no man will try and contradict His verdict, for His absolute righteousness and justice will certainly overwhelm all men.

The Bible is quite clear that all men, without exception, face coming judgment. There is no doubt that after death comes judgment (Heb. 9:27). However, when the Bible talks about coming judgment, it does not speak in terms of one general, end time judgment. Rather, the Bible reveals that there are a number of different judgments that take place at different times and involve different groups. The context of any particular biblical text usually determines the time of the judgment and the people involved in that judgment of God. The subject of this study is "God's Judgment upon Individuals." This is not some universal judgment but involves a special group of people at a particular time in God's prophetic calendar. Joel 3:1-3 and Matthew 25:31-46 are the two primary sources of information about this end time judgment.

> For behold, in those days and at that time, when I restore the fortunes of Judah and Jerusalem, I will gather all the nations, and bring them down to the valley of Jehoshaphat. Then I will enter into judgment with them there... (Joel 3:1, 2a)

> But when the Son of Man comes in His glory, and all the angels with Him, then He will sit on His glorious throne. And all the nations will be gathered before Him; and He will separate them from one another, as the shepherd separates the sheep from the goats. (Mt. 25:31, 32)

THE PARTICIPANTS IN THE JUDGMENT

The One Who Judges
The Judge who carries out all judgments in the end times is the Lord Jesus Christ. In His powerful message of self-revelation, the Lord declared that the Father had committed all judgment to the Son (cf.

Jn. 5:21-23, 27). In the capacity of Judge, Jesus will judge fairly and according to the will of the Father. In the Book of Revelation, there is an awesome scene of the heavenly throne and it is at that time that the Lord Jesus is seen receiving this authority to judge and rule (Rev. 4 and 5). The Lord Jesus Christ will be the judge at the "judgment of nations" as well as all other judgments.

During His earthly ministry, Jesus was not impressed nor influenced by the wealth, power or status of anyone. Even Christ's enemies acknowledged this about Him. And this will be true of His judgments in the future (cf. Isa. 11:4, 5). When the nations gather before Him, status, power, reputation and wealth will have no bearing. These who stand before Him can be sure that they come before One who sees all, knows all and cannot be fooled, deceived or bribed (cf. Rev. 1:14; 2:18; 3:7). He will make no mistakes and there will be no miscarriage of justice when He invites some to enter His kingdom and prohibits others from doing so.

The Ones Being Judged

Both of the primary passages of scripture concerning this judgment (Joel 3; Mt. 25) state that the "nations" are gathered before the Lord. The word translated "nations" also means "gentiles" and it is translated that way a majority of times in the New Testament.[1] It is mainly used as a category of those people who do not belong to the chosen nation of Israel. So it would probably be clearer to speak of this judgment as the "judgment of Gentiles" as these are set in contrast to the covenant people of Israel in both of the primary texts.

This judgment, however, does not include all Gentiles who have ever lived on the earth. Rather, it deals with those Gentiles who are living on the earth when Jesus Christ returns at His Second Coming. It should be noted that the term "Gentile" is not used of those who have died, but only of living people. It should also be observed that there is no mention of the dead or of a resurrection from the dead in these passages that discuss the judgment of the Gentiles. Those being brought before the Lord at this judgment are seen as those gathered from the various parts of the earth; the same nations out of which Israel has been regathered (cf. Joel 3:2). And according to Matthew 25:35-40 and Joel 3:2, 3, these Gentiles will be judged for their deeds which were done immediately before Christ's return. All these facts lead to the conclusion that this judgment is of Gentiles who are physically alive when Christ returns at His Second Coming.

A careful investigation of the Scriptures reveals that literally billions of Gentiles will perish during the terrible days of the Tribulation (cf. Rev. 6, 8, 9, 16). Many will die as a result of God's wrath being poured out on the earth. The wrath of God is revealed in three series of judgments commonly referred to as the Seals, the Trumpets and the Bowls. Many others on the earth will perish as a result of the activities of Satan and the Antichrist. As one surveys the seven years of tribulation, it is probably safe to say that the vast majority of Gentiles who enter this seven-year tribulation period will not live through that entire period of time. But in spite of the multiplied millions who die during this time, when the Lord Jesus Christ returns, there will still be millions alive and these are the ones who will stand before Him at the "judgment of the nations."

It should also be noted that this is a judgment of individual Gentiles and not a group activity. Because this judgment has been referred to as the "judgment of nations," some have assumed that national groups will be judged at this time. But that view would not be accurate. This is a judgment of individual Gentiles who are alive at the Second Coming of Christ.

> If this were a judgment of national entities, it is obvious that some unsaved would be included in an accepted nation; on the other hand, some saved would be excluded because they were in a rejected nation. Therefore, it must be concluded that this will be a judgment of individuals, not of nations.[2]

THE TIME OF THE JUDGMENT OF THE NATIONS

The two primary passages of Matthew 25 and Joel 3, along with Daniel 12, give information that enables us to pinpoint the time when this particular judgment takes place. The judgment of the living Gentiles is seen in relationship to the Second Coming of Christ and to His great Millennial kingdom and this makes it possible to establish the time when this judgment will take place.

In Relationship to the Second Coming

According to the prophet Joel, this judgment of living Gentiles generally takes place in connection with the *great and awesome day of the Lord* (Joel 2:31). This makes it clear that the prophet places this judgment in the end times of the Tribulation and coming Messianic Kingdom (the millennium). But he is more specific, stating that this judgment will take place *when I restore the fortunes of Judah and Jerusalem* (Joel 3:1). The restoring of the fortunes of Israel is used often in reference to the wonderful change in Israel's status and prosperity in the Millennial kingdom which is established after the Lord Jesus Christ returns to this present earth in power and great glory (e.g. Ezek. 39:25; Amos 9:14, 15).[3] This places the judgment of living Gentiles after the Second Coming since it is only after that event that Israel will receive the blessings spoken of here.

In His prophetic discourse given on the Mount of Olives, the Lord Jesus also connected this judgment with His Second Coming. He stated that the gathering of the nations for judgment would take place after He comes in glory with the holy angels and is seated on His throne (cf. Mt. 25:31, 32). Therefore, it is after His Second Coming to earth that He judges the living Gentiles.

In Relationship to the Millennial Kingdom

The judgment of the Gentiles must take place prior to the start of Christ's Millennial Kingdom. This must be the case because the purpose of the judgment of the Gentiles is to determine who will enter into and participate in that great Messianic Kingdom. Some Gentiles will be allowed by King Jesus to enter His kingdom while others will be excluded from it.

Daniel 12:11, 12 presents a most interesting idea that may pinpoint this judgment with great precision. In these verses, the prophet Daniel seems to be saying that there will be a period of seventy-five days between the Second Coming and the actual start of the

Millennial kingdom. These verses declare that the one who makes it to the 1,335th day is a blessed person. It would seem that this blessing is a reference to the privilege of entering into the Messianic kingdom, which begins at that point in time. In Daniel 12, the starting point of the 1335 days is at the midpoint of the Tribulation period with 1,260 of those days covering the last half of the Tribulation. The Tribulation, of course, comes to an end with the Second Coming. The remaining seventy-five day period appears to be an interval of time that exists between the Second Coming and the actual start of the 1,000-year reign of the Messiah. It is during this interval that the judgment of the living Gentiles apparently takes place. We can conclude, therefore, that this particular judgment occurs after the Second Coming but before the Millennial Kingdom.

Since the judgment of the Gentiles takes place before the Millennial Kingdom, it should not be confused with the "Great White Throne" judgment that takes place after the Millennial Kingdom is over (cf. Rev. 20:11-15). Unfortunately these two judgments are sometimes confused and equated. It must be remembered that there is a one thousand year period between them, and there are some significant differences in the judgments themselves.

THE PLACE OF THE JUDGMENT

The judgment of the living Gentiles takes place after the Second Coming, which places it on the earth. Christ returns to the earth and then the Gentiles are brought before Him. The earth is where the Lord Jesus places it (cf. Mt. 24:27-31; 25:31, 32). The prophet Joel eliminates Washington D.C., Moscow and all other centers of political power by specifically saying that the Gentiles would be gathered for judgment into the *valley of Jehoshaphat* (Joel 3:2, 12). And while this statement is helpful in eliminating every other place on the planet, Joel's reference is not exactly clear. Some have identified the "valley of Jehoshaphat" with the Kidron valley next to Jerusalem while others see it as the location where God brought a great deliverance to King Jehoshaphat by defeating a coalition of his enemies (cf. 2 Chron. 20). The location of God's great deliverance of King Jehoshaphat was in a valley southwest of Bethlehem.[4] But the exact geographic location is difficult to determine because this name historically is not attached to any specific place.

The name, "valley of Jehoshaphat" meaning "Jehovah judges," may be symbolic in nature. Most likely this will be the place in Israel where the recently returned King of kings will gather the Gentiles in order to judge them. It probably refers to a future site in Israel that will come into existence in connection with the topographical changes that will take place in Israel at the Second Coming. The evidence of Scripture is that tremendous changes in the topography of the earth, including the land of Israel, will occur in the final days of the Tribulation as great earthquakes and other events reshape the land (cf. Zech. 14:4; Rev. 16:18-20). It is most likely that this newly formed valley of Jehoshaphat ("Jehovah judges") will be near to the city of Jerusalem, the city of King Jesus.[5]

THE BASIS OF THE JUDGMENT

The Scriptures consistently testify to the fact that when a person stands before the Lord Jesus Christ, it will not be to determine that person's eternal destiny. The eternal destiny of a person is settled in this life prior to the person's death. In the case of the judgment of these living Gentiles, their destiny is determined in their lifetime prior to Christ's Second Coming and their appearance before Judge Jesus. Their presence or absence from the Kingdom of Messiah is settled during their earthly life and not at the moment of judgment before Christ. Jesus Himself clearly communicated that point to Nicodemus when He told him that entrance into the kingdom comes by the new birth (Jn. 3:5). Entering the kingdom (salvation) is never by means of good works (Tit. 3:5; Eph. 2:8, 9) but is always by faith alone in Christ alone (Rom. 3:20-30; Jn. 3:16; Gal. 2:16-3:14). Salvation is always seen as a gift from God that is received by trusting in Christ.

It is very important to remember that during the 7 years of the Tribulation, everyone on this earth will hear the truth of the gospel of Christ (Mt. 24:14). Unlike this age where some never do hear the message of salvation, in that age all will hear the truth of salvation. While the 144,000 will probably be the main preachers of the gospel message, millions of believers will give testimony of their faith in Christ and be martyred because of it (cf. Rev. 7:4-17). So when the living Gentiles appear before the Lord Jesus at the time of this judgment, we can be confident that they have already heard the gospel and have either already received or rejected God's gracious offer of salvation.

Salvation is not based on works, but there is a great emphasis in this judgment on the deeds that these Gentiles have done. It seems as though their works are a prerequisite for entering the Messiah's kingdom (cf. Mt. 25:35ff; Joel 3:2, 3). Why is there a clear focus on the deeds done by these Gentiles? The answer has to do with the times in which they lived. The setting of the terrible days of the Great Tribulation is the key to understanding this judgment. During the last 3 1/2 years of the Tribulation there will be an active, satanically-energized anti-Semitism over the entire earth (cf. Rev. 12:13-16). The Antichrist, empowered by the Devil, will attempt to the thwart the plan and purpose of God by annihilating the covenant people of Israel. "During the Tribulation the Jews will become the dividing line for those who are believers and for those who are not."[6] The internal spiritual condition of the Gentiles is revealed externally by the way in which they treat Israel during the Great Tribulation. Because of the horrible conditions of the day and the extreme hatred of the Jew, no one but a true believer in Jesus Christ will protect and provide for the people of Israel. This is the valid, unmistakable proof of true righteousness because of the incredible persecution that Israel will endure during the second half of the Tribulation period. Jews forced to flee death and destruction will have no means of caring for themselves. The righteous Gentiles (the "sheep" in Jesus' teaching), at great risk to themselves, will provide food, shelter and comfort for the covenant people and will show many acts of kindness.

144

> Under the widespread anti-Semitism that will prevail in
> the Great Tribulation, anyone who befriends a Jew in
> trouble will be distinguished as a person who has trust
> in the Bible and trust in Jesus Christ. Accordingly,
> while their works do not save them, their works are the
> basis of distinguishing them from the unsaved...[7]

Judge Jesus refers to these Gentiles as righteous (Mt. 25:37). The
good deeds, which are said to be done to Jesus Himself, validate
that designation of "righteous." However, these righteous Gentiles
(the sheep) are confused because they do not recall doing any good
deeds to Jesus. The Lord instructs them that when they did good
deeds to "these brothers of mine" they did them to Jesus Himself
(Mt. 25:40). It must be carefully noted that Jesus' "brothers" is not
a reference to mankind in general as is often declared. Rather it is a
reference to the believing Jews who have come into the New
Covenant during the Tribulation period and are the subjects of the
satanically inspired persecution. Jesus referred to His followers in
this way during His earthly ministry (e.g. Mt. 12:46-50). He is
speaking about the believing Jews who lived during the time of persecution in the Great Tribulation. The righteous Gentiles who did so
much for these "brothers of Jesus" will be welcomed into the
Messianic Kingdom by the King. They are righteous because they
were saved by grace, but the manifestation of their righteousness
was seen in their care for Jesus' "brothers" during those very terrible days.

In like manner, the deeds of the unrighteous (the "goats" in
Jesus' teaching) reveal their true spiritual condition. Their lack of
faith in the message of the "gospel of the kingdom" (Mt. 24:14) is
seen in their anti-Semitism. These will be condemned because of
their aggressive, evil treatment of Israel.

> The sins committed against Israel listed in this indict-
> ment (Joel 3:2b, 3) are: first, scattering the Jews (in the
> middle of the Tribulation); secondly, parting the
> land...and thirdly, selling the Jews into slavery...Each
> Gentile living at that time will be judged on the basis of

his participation or his refusal to participate in these deeds.[8]

Jesus will also indict them on their refusal to give aid and assistance to His "brothers" during the Great Tribulation (Mt. 25:45). Their negative treatment of Jesus' "brothers" is proof positive that they are not righteous and, therefore, are to be excluded from entrance into the Millennial Kingdom. The evidence against them will be clear and incontrovertible.

THE PURPOSES FOR THE JUDGMENT

To Demonstrate the Character of God

It is essential for man to see and acknowledge that God is God. The judgments recorded in Scripture reveal that all creatures eventually will bow the knee and accept their rightful place of submission to their Creator God (cf. Phil. 2:9-11; Jn. 5:22, 23). When the judgments are completed, no creature will challenge or speak against the character of the one and only God. Along with the rest of the judgments, the judgment of the Gentiles will contribute to that significant end.

It is also important for man to see that God is truth and that He speaks the truth. When He says He will do something, it will be done. The judgment of the Gentiles, with its focus on their treatment of Israel, brings to light the ancient but relevant word from God to Abraham in Genesis 12:3. In that initial giving of the Abrahamic covenant, God said that He would bless those who would bless Abraham's descendants but would curse those who would curse his descendants. The judgment of the Gentiles is as clear an application of this truth as one can find in the Bible or in history. The word of God is true and trustworthy and all of creation will acknowledge this.

To Grant Participation in the Kingdom to the Righteous

The righteous Gentiles will be welcomed into the Kingdom of Jesus the Messiah when He tells them to *inherit the kingdom* (Mt. 25:34).

These saved Gentiles are received with joy into Messiah's kingdom. The emphasis of the Lord's teaching in this passage is on their entrance into His kingdom. It should also be observed that these righteous Gentiles are also being honored (rewarded) by the King. The passage suggests that Jesus is speaking of more than entering His kingdom, but of rewards and blessedness in the Kingdom for these righteous ones. These will experience a fullness of life in His kingdom as a reward for their caring for the persecuted covenant people.

To Deny the Unrighteous Entrance Into the Kingdom

As with the righteous "sheep", the deeds of the unrighteous "goats" reveal their true spiritual condition (Mt. 25:41-46; Joel 3:2, 3). These are refused entrance into the Messiah's glorious kingdom. Instead they are sent away to eternal punishment. These will enter a punishment of unending duration, which is said to be the eternal fire that has been made for Satan and his angels (Mt. 25:41). It should be noted that the same word that is used for "eternal" life in this passage is used for "eternal" punishment. If eternal life applies to the never-ending future of blessedness for the believer, it must follow that the wicked face future punishment that is equal in duration. This passage certainly does not allow for the idea of the annihilation of the wicked. X *PUNISHING & PUNISHMENT NOT SAME* ✳

The "goats" reveal their rejection of the gospel message by their refusal to give aid and comfort to Jesus' "brothers" during the Great Tribulation. Joel emphasizes the fact that these Gentiles were not passive in their dealings with the people of Israel. They were responsible for bringing great distress to the Jews as they drove them out of their land, divided up the land and brutalized the people. These unrighteous Gentiles committed the terrible crimes of taking the Lord's portion for themselves. "The nations will have to answer directly to God for having treated His own personal possession, the 'apple of His eye' so lightly."[9] These unrighteous Gentiles will have to bow the knee to the One that they have rejected and treated with contempt.

PUNISHING WOULD BE ONGOING
PUNISHMENT AN END RESULT

147

CONCLUDING THOUGHTS

All men are accountable to the Lord God for what they do with His truth and with His people. And while some might think that God is not watching or does not really care, the Scriptures reveal that everything man does and says is known to Him and will be evaluated by Him. Men might well avoid the judgment of human judges and courts. They might appear to "get away with murder." But they will not do so before the righteous Judge of the universe. Man will be rewarded or punished in accordance with the standard of God's truth. This holds true for all of us, and it holds true with those Gentiles who will live in the days of the Great Tribulation.

Chapter 8

THE GLOBAL
ISLAMIC PERIL

RON J. BIGALKE, JR.

The world's youngest, major world religion is Islam. Its adherents claim the restoration of original monotheism and truth; therefore, Muslims believe Islam supplants both Judaism and Christianity. In addition to Buddhism and Hinduism, Islam is a missionary religion that spread rapidly. After just 100 years of its formation by an Arabian visionary named Muhammad, Islam multiplied throughout the Middle East, the majority of North Africa, and even to the East in India, often spreading through military force.

The most evident and noteworthy present-day religious renewal is occurring in Islam. It is evident that our world is economically interdependent. This has been demonstrated by the increased exposure of oil-producing nations in the press and daily TV news reports on the price of oil. All of this oil is under the Arabian sand, which obviously is a great concern to nations worldwide, even to the point of determining their foreign policies. The late Dr. Walvoord has an excellent book on this subject: *Armageddon, Oil and the Middle East Crisis* (Zondervan, 1976).

Arab nations have also publicized the tension between traditional Islamic beliefs and the changes that have been advanced by secular technology. Although the leaders of Islamic countries want their people to have the latest technology, as a whole, Islam believes the United States is the "Great Satan" because it leads the world in technology. Many Muslims fear that the secularization that accompanies new technology will erode Islamic beliefs and destroy the so-called purity of Islam.

It is because of the above tensions, and an orthodox interpretation of the Qur'ān, that a significant number of Muslim leaders have revived a new religious fervor throughout the world, which often leads to both social activism and even terrorism. Rather than simply affirming what Muslims believe, however, this fervor has brought out an "enemy stance" toward other world religions. Some Muslim sects have endorsed "holy war" or *jihad* as the legitimate "sixth pillar" of Islam (see "The Teachings of Islam" for the other five pillars).

Jihad does hold a variety of meanings, such as the battle over individual sin or martyrdom. It is because there is no concept of a gracious and forgiving God in Islam that Muslims are convinced death by the sword or death on a pilgrimage to Mecca is the only sure means of salvation. Since they have no hope of forgiveness unless dying as a martyr, it helps to explain why Muslims are willing to be suicide bombers. The most common meaning of *jihad* today among Westerners is "shooting wars" such as the war fought in Afghanistan. It cannot be denied that Islam encourages its growth by the sword. This is obvious in the first 100 years of the religion's history.

THE BEGINNING OF ISLAM

Officially, Islam began about 630 in Arabia. By 640, Islam had conquered the Middle East extending its influence to the borders of India. By the 700s, all of North Africa and Spain were in the hand of Islam. The first attempt to conquer the Western world occurred in 710 AD when Islamic armies crossed the Straits of Gibraltar and nearly conquered all of Spain and Portugal. In 732, Charles Martel of France stopped the Arab invasion of his country in the Battle of Tours.

The Ottoman Turks had conquered the Arab world from the 1300s to the 1500s. Another attempt of Islam to conquer the Western world occurred during the Ottoman (Turkish) Empire in the 17th century. The Ottoman Turks wanted to expand their empire but were stopped before they could reach the gates of Vienna in 1683. Nevertheless, they continued to rule the Middle East up until the time of World War I, choosing to fight on the side of the Central Powers (Austria-Hungary and Germany). Due to the Allied victory, the Turks lost their empire.

Today, it appears that a third attempt to conquer the Western world is underway. Islam spreads by force in the Middle East, but it appears that in the Western world Islam desires to employ a false "peace" in its multiplying victories for Allah. It is not uncommon to hear statements that Islam is the world's fasting growing religion. Many researchers of comparative religions believe that if Islam continues at its current growth rate, Muslims will eventually outnumber the world population, thereby, becoming a global threat.

THE GROWTH OF ISLAM

Since Muslims are a minority in America, they make every effort to appear "peaceful" to Americans. Muslims will be employed in the United States and eat the American food, yet the orthodox still denounce America as the "Great Satan" sometimes openly, but usually behind closed doors. For an example of this hypocrisy, see Steve Emerson's excellent PBS documentary, *Jihad in America* (1994).

However, situations are different in other countries such as Egypt. There the clerics persecute the Coptic Christians in the open. In the mosques, they denounce Christianity, Americans and Jews, and the West. The clerics make every attempt to convince the people of these things. Essentially, there is no difference between the current Muslim propaganda and that which Hitler used to seize power among the German people.[1] In fact, it could be said that Islam is the current Nazi movement. Hitler believed that it was perfectly acceptable to kill unbelievers of the Nazi regime, just as Muslims believe it is acceptable to exterminate unbelievers. This is obvious when they approve of their own children dying in the flames of *jihad*. World War II stopped the plans of world domination from the Axis powers. At that point in history, there was no room for tolerance.

Muslims who attempt to say that Islam is innocent from terrorism are not speaking the truth. Islam has spread by employing terrorism in the name of Allah. When the Arabs entered Egypt, they used force to convert the people to Islam, even forcing them to speak the Arabic language by threat of cutting out the tongues of any who would continue to speak the Coptic language. Now Muslims appear "peaceful" in Western countries. However, the goal for world domination and rule according to Islamic law has not changed. Islam demands the complete military subjugation of the earth as mandated by Allah. It may be just a matter of time before Islam attempts to convert all Americans by the use of any means. They attempt to marry Americans in order to convert them and force their children to be Muslim. It is in this manner that Muslims believe Islam will dominate and gain control over the Western countries.

It must be said that Christianity's growth rate is near the growth rate of the world's population, which means that the professing Christians throughout the world's population are a steady number. The birth rate in the United States, Canada, and Europe is lower than in third world countries. Therefore, Islam is not the fastest growing religion in these regions. However, it is true that Islam's growth rate is still higher than that of the world's population. *[Although this author feels the following information is significant, the subsequent paragraphs of this section may appear too technical for those not familiar with comparative religious statistics so that the reader may want to advance to the next section on Islam's history.]*

In a 1997 article, Jay Gary, senior associate of the World Network of Religious Futurists, wrote that Islam is the fastest growing of the major world religions. The reason for the high growth rate is due to demographic issues since the birth rates are higher in the third world countries; therefore, the increase is not by conversions. Religious researchers have projected that Islam will grow to roughly 2 billion devotees by 2025, whereas Christianity is projected to increase to 3 billion by the same year.[2] The above numbers are based on projections of the world's population reaching 8 billion. Gary concludes, "It is unlikely that Islam will overtake Christianity in sheer numbers in the mid-range future. In no probable statistical scenario reaching out to the year 2200, does Islam surpass Christianity in absolute number of adherents."[3]

Barrett and Johnson list the growth rate of Christians "(all kinds)" from 2000 to 2025 as 2.051 to 2.617 billion and the growth rate of Muslims from the same time period as 1.239 to 1.785 billion.[4] Dr. Johnson, the world's leading authority on the quantitative future of religion shares, calculates the growth rate of Christians from 2000 to 2025 as 2.090 to 3.023 billion (33.4% to 35.5%) and the growth rate of Muslims from 2000 to 2025 as 1.16 to 1.72 billion (18.5% to 20.2%). After giving several scenarios (such as Muslim revivals), Johnson charts the most likely scenario for the year 2200 for Muslims at 2.625 billion (22.6%) and Christians at 4.40 billion of the world's population (37.9%).[5]

Samuel Huntington, a well respected political scientist, predicts that "the proportion of Muslims in the world will continue to increase dramatically, amounting to 20% of the world's population about the turn of the century, surpassing the number of Christians some years later, and probably accounting for about 30% of the world's population by 2025."[6] Again, this is driven by the high birth rates. Huntington's prediction is that Islam will surpass Christianity in the beginning of the 21st century. According to his statistics, Islam will possess 5% more devotees than Christianity by the year 2025.

In Europe, the population of Muslims grew over 100% between 1989 and 1998, or 14 million, (according to statistics by the United Nations, this is roughly 2% of the world's population). Writing for *Christianity Today*, Wendy Murray Zoba notes, "During the same period, the Muslim population in the United States grew by 25%." Her conclusion is "Islam is the second-largest religious group in the world, with more than a billion members worldwide (some estimates put it closer to two billion)." Population estimates range from 4 to 6 million Muslims currently residing in the United States with ever increasing numbers. Murray Zoba writes, "Islam could be the second-largest religion in America by 2015, surpassing Judaism, according to some estimates. By other estimates, Islam has achieved that rank already."[7]

The above statistics cause us to often ask whether such growth rates render Islam a global threat. In order to provide an answer to that question it will be important to first understand the history and teaching of Islam, in addition to the present-day relations between Jews and Arabs in the Middle East.

THE HISTORY OF ISLAM

Around 570 AD, Muhammad was born in Mecca of the tribe of Quraish, guardians of the Ka'bah (although Muhammad destroyed all the idols in this pagan temple, he kept the name of the chief idol, Allah, and kept an ancient black meteorite of the pagans that is venerated today by many devout Muslims). Muhammad's father died before he was born and his mother died six years later. He then lived with his grandfather, Abd al-Muttalib, for two years. In 578, he went to live with his uncle Abu Talib.

In 595, Muhammad married a wealthy widow, Khadijah, who was fifteen years older than he. Together they had six children; two sons died in childhood. Fatima, one of his four daughters, married 'Ali (Muhammad's cousin). 'Ali is recognized as the founder of the Shi'ah branch of Islam and the legitimate successor of Muhammad.

Occasionally, Muhammad would spend his nights in a cave near Mecca thinking about the social evils of the city. In 610 AD, at the age of 40, he received his first revelation, which Muhammad believed to be delivered by the angel Gabriel. The alleged revelation began with the word "recite" (Surah 96:1) meaning "recitation." It was with this experience of a divine calling that led Muhammad to begin leading people to the worship of one god. In the Qur'ān, the words and revelations of Muhammad are distinguished. His teachings are called the *sunnah* (path) of the prophet. Numerous collections of Hadiths (traditions) contain these teachings.

It was not long before Muhammad was able to find disciples who regarded him as the prophet of God. In 613, he began preaching publicly in Mecca. His messages called for the worship of one god in contrast to the Arab practice of worshipping many gods. Muhammad achieved success in creating an uncompromising monotheism. This new religion eventually was called Islam meaning "submission to God." Today, Islam is the largest of the non-Christian world religions.

The majority of the inhabitants of Mecca did not readily accept the new religion of Islam as others did. Those who were polytheistic feared that their shrines would be destroyed. In 622, at the age of 52, Muhammad and his disciples journeyed to Medina. Muslims refer to this flight from Mecca to Medina as the *hijrah*; it is the decisive date for the beginning of Islam. On the Muslim calendar, it marks year one. In Medina, the Muslims set up a community (*umma*). This community no longer followed blood or tribal practices, but rested on faith in one god and the belief that Muhammad is his prophet.

In 624, the Muslims began raiding caravans to Mecca. Muhammad's followers continued numerous battles and caravans until the Meccans eventually surrendered to Islam in 630. Muhammad cleansed the Ka'bah of all the idols except for one, Allah (the moon god). Muslims reject the claim that Allah is the moon god. However, since Muhammad was raised a pagan, he would have worshipped the moon as the highest of the gods. In pre-Islamic times, all the Sabeans in Arabia worshipped the moon god. Therefore, it is contended that he chose the chief pagan god to worship as "The God" (the literal meaning of Allah).

Within only two years, all of Arabia was united under Islam. On 8 June 632, Muhammad died in battle (he was 62). His father-in-law, Abu Bakr, became his successor. Muhammad was buried in Medina. Although the Muslims do not believe Muhammad was divine, they continue to recognize him as "God's prophet."[8] Muslims refer to six eminent prophets: (1) Adam, the chosen of Allah; (2) Noah, the preacher of Allah; (3) Abraham, the friend of

Allah; (4) Moses, the speaker of Allah; (5) Jesus, the word of Allah; and, (6) Muhammad, the apostle of Allah. In other words, Muslims argue that Muhammad did not start a new religion, but he revived the true religion as the "Seal of the Prophets."

THE SECTS OF ISLAM

Although there has been a high degree of cohesiveness within the Islamic community around the central tenets of the faith, differences regarding the question of leadership did arise after Muhammad's death. Muhammad had functioned as both a religious and political leader. Since there was no consensus within the community as to the means of selecting a successor, a major dispute arose among Muhammad's followers over his successor and how the choice would be made.

Ultimately, the leading members of the community chose Abu Bakr as successor. It was this decision that marked the beginning of a division among Muslims between those who approved the election of a successor and those that felt the leadership should reside in the "House of the Prophet." Muhammad's cousin, 'Ali, was the chosen candidate of the latter group. Although he was elected as the fourth Caliph (a title given to the successor of Muhammad), 'Ali was murdered and a rival member of another family assumed his title.

The followers of 'Ali (Shi'ah) argued that 'Ali should have been succeeded by his son Hasan. It was this point of contention that drew the clear lines of demarcation. In 680, 'Ali's second son, Husayan, was killed on the plain of Karbala in present day Iraq. Every year on the tenth of Muharram, Shi'ite Muslims commemorate not only the martyrdom of Husayan, but also the subsequent suffering of the Shi'ite community.

According to the Ithna 'Ashari Shi'ites, the twelfth imam, (or divinely appointed leader of the community) went into seclusion. The twelfth imam is believed to be present in the world and will manifest himself at the end of time as the leader who will unite the Islamic world. Shi'ites have stressed the ability of learned scholars to discern the will of the hidden imam. Among the most eminent of these scholars is the Ayatollah.

For centuries, Shi'ites were regarded as passively fatalistic. The impact of developments in Iran drew out the revolutionary potential from the Shi'ite tradition. Similarly, perceived injustices in other Muslim societies have energized believers to apply Islamic standards of justice and truth to their societies.[9]

THE TEACHINGS OF ISLAM

The Muslim confession of faith, *the shahada*, proclaims, "Muhammad is the prophet of God." Muslims believe that God sent many prophets to the world and gave inspired words of Scripture to prophets like Moses, Jesus, Muhammad, and others. Muslims even call Jews and Christians "people of the Book." Muhammad taught that these Scriptures, including the Qur'ān, all come from the "Mother of the Book" (Surah 13:39). This book is said to have existed from all eternity in heaven as the uncreated words of God. Muhammad taught that the Qur'ān not only verified all previous revelations but also supplanted the other revelations. Muhammad is called the "Seal of the Prophets" (Surah 33:40) meaning he is the last and greatest of all the prophets.

Since Muhammad is believed to be the final prophet, he has the final word on religious matters. The words of Muhammad supersede anything that Jesus had spoken. Furthermore, Muhammad was a prophet to the Gentiles, whereas Jesus was a prophet to the Jews.[10] The Qur'ān only ascribes to Jesus the distinction as the perfect man and sinless one. It does not ascribe these characteristics to Muhammad or to any other prophet.[11] Islam does not believe that Jesus is God's Son based on Surah 23:91 which reads, "Neither has Allah begotten a son, nor is there any other god besides Him."

The slave-like submission of Islam is replicated in five basic beliefs and ritualistic practices. The first belief maintains the unity of God. It was Muhammad's rigid insistence of monotheism that motivated him to completely abolish any trace of polytheism. It is not too much to say Islam is characterized by a radical monotheism.

Secondly, the belief in the existence of angels is necessary. However, angels are not to be worshipped. Thirdly, the books of Allah must be obeyed. Fourthly, the prophets of Allah are special messengers. Lastly, all men are accountable to God and there will be a day of judgment.

There are five ritualistic practices, or five pillars, of Islam. The main tenet of Islam is confessing the faith (*Tashahhud*) by repeating the *Kalima*: "Allah is one and Muhammad is his prophet." Muslims participate in five daily prayer sessions[12] in the direction of Mecca (*Salāt*). Each year devout Muslims will observe a fast during the month of Ramadan (*Saum*). Muslims give a charitable contribution of 2.5 percent of their total income (*Zakāt*). Most Muslims hold to the once-in-a-lifetime dream of going on a pilgrimage (*Hajj*) to Mecca in Saudi Arabia.[13] These five pillars are "obligatory" (*fard*) as they are based on explicit commands in the Qur'ān or in the Traditions. While other "duties" of a faithful Muslim are expected and judged necessary, they are not obligatory as the five pillars.

The Muslims believe that the Qur'ān is a holy book directly dictated by God through the angel Gabriel to Muhammad. Although Muslims respect the Bible, the Qur'ān is valued as the last and the final revelation of God. Muslims declare that the Qur'ān cannot be translated and ought to be studied in Arabic. There is a tradition that Muhammad was uneducated and illiterate, yet able to utter the sayings for the holy book, the Qur'ān; this is often called "the miracle of Muhammad." The Qur'ān is the highest validation of the Islamic faith.

The goal of Islam is to follow the rules and principles laid down in the Qur'ān, which is to bring all of mankind into submission and to kill all infidels, or those who do not worship Allah (Surah 2:190-192; 4:76; 5:33; 9:41; 47:4). The Qur'ān declares, "Believers, take neither Jews nor Christians for your friends...slay the idolaters wherever you find them...Fight against such of those to whom...neither believe in Allah nor the Last Day" (Surah 5:51; 9:5, 29). All Muslims may not believe in this manner, but the above quotes are the lucid commands of the Qur'ān.

According to Islamic tradition, the complete military subjugation of the earth is mandated by Allah...In the

Hadith [Islamic written tradition], Mohammad said: "Hear, O *Muslims*, the meaning of life. Shall I not tell you of the peak of the matter; its pillar, and its topmost part? The peak of the matter is Islam itself. The pillar is ritual *Rakatin* prayer. And the topmost part is *Ji'had*—holy war.[14]

Islam hopes to mature mankind morally, thereby enabling him to live in peace and happiness in this world, which will allow mankind (after death) to reach eternal happiness in the next world. Muslims are commanded in the Qur'ān to "invite [all] to the Way of the Lord with wisdom (Surah 16:125). Various organizations have been organized to fulfill this commandment and to make Islam the dominant faith that brings all people under Islamic law. Muslims should not be regarded as more wicked than any other human being for their beliefs; they are sincerely deceived and believe that they are being faithful to their religion. Understanding Muslim beliefs should cause Christians to become all the more motivated to share the fact of man's total depravity and his need for God's grace that comes through faith in Jesus Christ.

THE JEWS AND MUSLIMS

One question that requires an answer is whether there is there any connection in Islamic acts of terrorism with past and future events. After the 11 September attack on the World Trade Center and Pentagon, *Fox News* was one source that noted there might be a reason for the date of the attack on America. It was 11 September 1922 that a British mandate over territory in Palestine was issued despite the Arab protests. The mandate lasted until 1948 when the United Nations authorized a partition of the territory and the state of Israel was established. The Word of God declares the unconditional promises of God that have to do with Israel. These promises are given to Israel as a nation (2 Chron. 6:6; 7:16; Ps. 137:5, etc.), but the promises will never reach fulfillment until Israel repents and declares, "Blessed is he that cometh in the name of the Lord" (cf.

Mt. 23:37-25:46; Rom. 11). Clearly, the unconditional decrees that God has made in the past are impacting the future.

One of the stipulations of the Abrahamic Covenant is that God *will bless them that bless thee* [Israel], *and curse him that curseth thee* (Gen. 12:3). Even though America has turned her back on God it appears that the only reason that has kept America in existence has not been her military strength or her booming economy, but her support of Israel. Responding to the attack on America, President Bush declares "Make no mistake, the United States will hunt down and punish those responsible for these cowardly acts." Israel faces terrorism on a daily basis, yet America has called Israel's response to terrorist attacks as "extreme." America does give some support to Israel, but she also wants Israel to negotiate land for peace with known terrorists. This would be like America negotiating with bin Laden for peace. The Oslo peace process is not working as countless Israelis are being slaughtered since its inception nearly 8 years ago. Perhaps there is a reason why America is not mentioned in Bible prophecy for the moment she turns her back on Israel, as she has on God, then she will be eradicated. According to Daniel 2 and 7, God causes nations to rise and fall in harmony with His sovereign decrees.

There must be peace in the Middle East! The events of 11 September do not fulfill Bible prophecy; rather they are "signs of the times" that are drawing the world closer to the period of time called the Tribulation, or Daniel's Seventieth Week. The start of that period begins with the Antichrist making a peace treaty with the nation of Israel. Truly, Jerusalem is *a cup of trembling unto all the people round about* (Zech. 12:2). The terrorist attacks taking place in Israel, and now America, are unexplainable apart from the fact that this is a religious war stemming all the way back to the Genesis record.

The Muslim faith is a belief in a false god, Allah. During the State prayer meeting at the National Cathedral in Washington following the attack on America, Bishop Jane Holmes Dixon prayed, "There of us who are gathered here—Muslim, Jew, Christian, Sikh, Buddhist, Hindu—all people of faith." The Methodist minister offered prayer to the "god of Abraham and Muhammad, and the

Father of Jesus Christ." All faiths came together in the name of patriotism. The idea is that God has revealed Himself in Buddha, Confucius, Jesus, Muhammad, and many others. Humanity is encouraged to embrace the lie that mankind is taking different paths, but that they are all leading to the same destination. Quite contrary, the Bible declares, *Neither is there salvation in any other* [except Jesus Christ]: *for there is none other name under heaven given among men, whereby we must be saved* (Acts 4:12).

It is interesting to note that prior to the terrorist attacks, someone would have protested against all the talk concerning God lately. However, America's leaders stood on the Congressional steps in order to sing, "God bless America" in unison following that historical event. This is nothing short of hypocrisy when prayer has been removed from school. It is when times get tough that the American people cry out to God for help. Truly, Jesus' words are appropriate that *this people honoureth me with their lips, but their heart is far from me* (Mk. 7:6). America has been blessed greatly, but *unto whomsoever much is given, of him shall be much required* (Lk. 12:48). This country may need to endure such evil acts in order to lead America to repentance whereby individuals cry out to God with genuine faith in the only Savior of mankind, Jesus Christ.

The greatest tragedy is not the bad things that take place in this earthly life, but that there are many who die in their sins when they could have known Christ as their Savior. It was said of those in Noah's day, *before the Flood they were eating and drinking, marrying and giving in marriage, until the day that Noe entered into the ark and knew not* (Mt. 24:38, 39a). In those days, *God saw the wickedness of man was great in the earth* (Gen. 6:5). The same can be said today. Rather than admit his accountability to the Creator, mankind continues to pursue hedonistic, materialistic, and humanistic endeavors. The terrorist attacks were no doubt a call to the American people that *now is the day of salvation...as it is appointed unto men once to die, but after this the judgment* (2 Cor. 6:2; Heb. 9:27). The good news is *not* that God has delivered mankind from devastating times, but *that Christ died for our sins according to the scriptures; and that he was buried, and that he rose again the third day according to the scriptures* (1 Cor. 15:3). To all who trust in

Christ alone as Savior, and not according to one's presumed good deeds, will there be salvation (Tit. 3:4-7).

ISLAM AND EZEKIEL 38-39

For over fifty years now, the United Nations and Arab states have made continuous demands upon the nation of Israel for her to surrender land in exchange for peace. The Arab PLO (Palestine Liberation Organization) leader, Yasser Arafat, has signed agreements with Israel promising to end the brutal warfare that has characterized the Middle East for the last fifty years. However, the question is whether such agreements will lead to true peace or a false peace that will set the stage for the Battle of Gog and Magog prophesied in Ezekiel 38-39.

Although, the Arab governments and the PLO claim that they are offering Israel "peace for land," in truth, they are not offering Israel peace, but rather an armed truce. As an Islamic organization, the PLO has not relinquished their commitment to conquer all of Israel's land and to destroy the Jewish population.

A major problem for Israel is that the Qur'ān teaches that if Muslims ever occupied a land in the past, then Muslims must recover that land through *jihad*. It is for reasons such as these that the potential for lasting peace in the Middle East is remote. The Islamic rationale of the Arabs is the cause for the wars against Israel. The Arab nations tried to annihilate Israel in three wars (1948, 1956, and 1967) long before the Jews possessed the West Bank, Gaza Strip, and the Golan Heights.

Furthermore, the introduction of Iranian nuclear weapons and the growing possibility of Libya, Syria, and Iraq joining the Islamic ranks have seriously altered the strategic balance of the Middle East. The present leaders of Israel realize that an unstable Arab regime, such as Iraq or Libya, might be tempted to use their nuclear weapons despite the obvious fact that such actions would result in mutual destruction. According to Islamic religious philosophy, Muslims believe they will gain paradise if they die in *jihad* in an effort to cleanse the "infidels" from Jerusalem (Surah, 2:244;

3:195). It may be that following the Battle of Gog and Magog, the defeat of the Islamic states will pave the way for the Antichrist to come forward offering Israel a peace covenant.

Since the time of her rebirth as a nation in 1948, Israel has been forced to live with millions of Arabs who publicly call for her complete destruction. Israel has not been able to "dwell safely." However, if peace negotiations continue between the PLO and Israel this may create a false peace over the next few years. The Jewish state may relax her defenses thinking she can now "dwell safely."

When the northern alliance of Ezekiel 38-39 attack Israel, the prophet Ezekiel declares that God will personally intervene with supernatural earthquakes, hail, and pestilence to defeat the combined armies. It is this deliverance that may allow Israel to build the third Temple as described in Daniel 9:24-27 – a situation that may prepare the earth for the rise of the Antichrist who confirms a seven-year covenant of peace with Israel. It is this peace covenant, of course, that actually results in the persecution of the Jews, the purging out of the remnant among the Jewish nation, and the return of Messiah to deliver Israel at the Battle of Armageddon and establish His millennial reign on earth.

THE TEMPLE MOUNT CONTROVERSY

The controversy concerning the rebuilding of the Jewish Temple is a result of the Arab-Israeli conflict, especially as events relate to the city of Jerusalem. Israel gained recognition as a nation in 1948, and even captured East Jerusalem during the Six-Day War of 1967, but the Israeli government made the detrimental move of allowing the Arabs to possess control over the Temple Mount. Although the goal of the concession was to encourage peace with the Arabs this has not been the case.

Now that the Arabs have control over the Temple Mount they consider any effort of the Israelis to rebuild their Temple as an act of war against the Islamic faith. The ultimate goal of Islam is to bring the world into complete subjugation to Allah and then rule the world according to Islamic law. Despite the Middle East peace talks, the military aggression ("holy war") of Islam will not allow the Jews to rebuild their Temple since this would be the culminating act of Israeli sovereignty. If the Israelis were to rebuild on the Temple Mount, then, the Arabs would have to admit that the religion of Allah had failed since the "infidels" were able to demonstrate their sovereignty over the Jewish land and people.

It has already been noted that the Qur'ān teaches that if Muslims ever occupied a land in the past, then they must recover it through *jihad*. Islam invaded the land of Israel in 638 AD. The city of Jerusalem and the Temple Mount have been under the influence of Islam since that time. Both Jews and Muslims claim spiritual precedence over the Temple Mount. Islam refuses to allow Israel to rebuild their Temple since such an act would demonstrate Israeli sovereignty and would make it impossible for the followers of Islam to gain control over all the land of Israel.

Although Islam began in the Arabian Peninsula, it developed its sacredness over the Temple Mount from Judaism and Christianity since there were apostate Jews and Christians among the followers of Muhammad. Islam also claimed sacredness over the Temple Mount due to its proximity to Damascus, one of the early capitals of the Islamic Empire. Another reason why Islam made a special claim over the Temple Mount was its importance to both Judaism and Christianity. Since Muslims considered Islam to be the final revelation of the two faiths, there were adequate reasons for identifying Islamic beliefs with the Temple Mount. One can understand why the Arabs are so adamant in maintaining control over the Temple Mount since the goal of Islam is to bring all of mankind into submission and to kill all infidels. For Muslims, failure to bring the world into submission to Allah would indicate inferiority of the Islamic faith. It is for this reason that they are steadfast in not relinquishing anything in the peace process.

The delay in rebuilding the Temple is due to many political and theological complications. The political complications stem from the fact that the Wakf, the Supreme Muslim Counsel, controls the Temple Mount which renders it impossible to rebuild the Temple. Furthermore, as long as the Dome of the Rock remains on the

Temple Mount it will impossible to rebuild the Temple. In order for the Temple to be built today, either the Dome of the Rock or the Al Aqsa Mosque would have to be moved or destroyed.[15] Either option is currently impossible given the tense, political situation that exists today.

The theological complications stem from a disagreement among some Jewish people as to whether the third Temple can be built by human hands. Some believe that only the Messiah can build the Temple. The Babylonian Talmud is not clear on the issue, but the Jerusalem Talmud would allow for an intermediate Temple prior to the millennial kingdom.

Any attempt today to rebuild the Temple will be met with fierce political and religious opposition. It is possible that the Antichrist will be the individual who is able to offer a solution and grant the Jewish people the right to rebuild the Temple. He comes as an imposter of the true Christ. The Jewish people will think that the Antichrist is the "Messiah" who has come to bring in the messianic age and the one who will give them right to rebuild their Temple. The Antichrist will certainly be capable of solving the political situation; for that reason, the world will adore him. Unless one has lived in a shell for the majority of his life, everyone is aware of the explosive Middle East conflict. It is amazing that some people believe peace will result from current negations among Middle Eastern leaders. However, the witness of history and the prophetic Word demonstrate that the current events of today are pointing toward the time of the Great Tribulation.

Israel has repeatedly been forced to surrender land for peace. Former Prime Minister Yitzhak Rabin was assassinated by one of his own people for giving land in return for promised peace. His "peace plan" gave the PLO control over the Gaza Strip and Jericho. Rabin believed that Joshua (6:26) cursed Jericho; therefore it would not matter to the Jews to give up the land. However, the curse by Joshua only related to fortifying and rebuilding the city of Jericho. The exchange by Rabin disregarded the Land Covenant given to Israel, which included the Gaza Strip and Jericho. God promised the nation of Israel that He would preserve this land on their behalf in fulfillment of His covenant (Deut. 11:21).

The loss of Jericho to the Arabs is devastating in light of Israel's history. Not only were the areas under the control of Israel, but also Jericho was the "gateway" to the land of Israel. For instance, when Israel was to enter the Promised Land they had to first conquer Jericho. The Arab League Charter of 1948 did not request for liberation of the Gaza Strip and Jericho, but the entire area of Palestine (including all that is west of the Jordan River).

The giving of land to the Arabs will never result in peace that is long lasting. The faith of a nation is directly connected to the politics of that nation (2 Kgs. 21:11-15; Prov. 14:34). This is true regarding the nation of Israel in the future. The political kingdom and the Promised Land to Israel are inseparably linked (Ezek. 37:24, 25). Therefore, this nation's lack of faith is the cause of political unrest.

The city of Jerusalem is of tremendous importance to the Jew. Every prayer, Sabbath, wedding ceremony, death, and holy day recalls the sacredness of the city in the heart of the people. The holiness of the city is due to the belief that Jerusalem bears the name of God. Furthermore, the Jewish people know that Jerusalem is the site of the Temple where the divine presence of God was manifested upon the mercy seat of the Ark. Tension in the Middle East is high because the Jews are restricted from the Temple Mount located in this sacred city.

The struggle to possess the Promised Land naturally includes Jerusalem. Yet Jerusalem is a major objective to the Arabs. The Declaration of Principles, which was signed on 13 September 1993, set a date of three years for resolving the issue of Jerusalem. Even though there was the unification of Jerusalem in 1967, the Temple Mount is still controlled by the Muslim Wakf.

The establishment of the PLO was to exercise control of "Palestinian Lands Only." Originally, the West Bank and the Gaza Strip belonged to the Arabs, and the goal of the PLO was to gain control over the remainder of the land of Israel. The real intent of the PLO is not to liberate any land, but to accept land grants from Israel with the goal of liberating all parts of Palestine. Therefore, the commitment of the PLO is to establish a Palestinian state, which will include all the land of Israel.

The ultimate goal of the Palestinians is gain complete control over Jerusalem. The majority of Palestinians today regard East Jerusalem as the future capital of the Palestinian state. Any efforts to re-divide Jerusalem would be catastrophic for the nation of Israel. The fate of the city of Jerusalem will be the deathblow to any plan for peace in the Middle East.

In March 1994 there was a temporary restriction of the Jews to the Western Wall in response to an Arab stoning that took place there. This closing of the Western Wall was the first time that there was a restriction of the religious rights of the Jews. Religious Jews saw the action as symbolic of the attitude of Israeli government toward the Temple Mount in the future. The Muslim Wakf may bear some responsibility for the decision.

The Muslim authorities now view any usurpation of Islamic control of the Temple Mount to be the responsibility of the Israeli government. Whenever a Jewish group asserts just cause over the Temple Mount, the Muslim Wakf will react in aggression against Israel. Although the Israeli government views such concessions as examples of peace, the Islamic world interprets such gestures as moving the Muslims closer to war against the Jews.

The tension between Arabs and Israelis is irreconcilable. In fact, the Muslim faith understands the murder of Jews as consistent with faith in Allah. It is for such reasons that government demands for settlers to abandon their homes in the West Bank and Gaza Strip are viewed as ludicrous.

Another major objective of the PLO is to establish an autonomous police force for avenging fellow Palestinians which they claim have been wronged by Israelis. This, of course, would be with complete knowledge of Arab murders in 1929 within Jewish synagogues, murder of the 1972 Israeli Olympic team, murder in 1974 of the schoolchildren at Ma'alot, murder of the Jewish passengers on the *Achille Lauro*, and the murder of many others. It should be clear that one of the last things the PLO needs is an autonomous police force.

It is true that Yasser Arafat appears to have delayed the declaration of statehood of Palestine. However, most Arabs would argue that the declaration of Palestinian statehood, today or tomorrow, is not as important as the complete removal of Israeli occupation and the establishment of an Islamic state. Yasser Arafat is in the forefront of the attacks. On 1 July 1998, at a special session of the Palestinian Legislative Council in Ramallah, Arafat declared, "There will be no peace, no security, no stability without the return of liberated Jerusalem, the eternal capital for an independent Palestinian state, whether they like it or not."[16] Al-Muhajiroun, "the voice, the eyes, the ears of the Muslims," states in a similar fashion:

> There can be no peace until all of the stolen area is returned back to the   rightful owners. It is inconceivable for any Muslim to agree to take back the garden shed of his illegally occupied house, with the illegal occupant keeping the rest. Not only is it against logic, and all laws known to a civilized world but more importantly, it is not permitted from the Legislator, Allah (SWT). The ONLY solution is JIHAD and we must support it physically, financially and verbally.[17]

It is clear from the above quotes that Islam will never share sovereignty over land or property. What is also evident is the call for *jihad* as the only legitimate means of regaining occupied territories from non-Muslims. Therefore, in Islam both religion and politics are inseparable. Despite all the media hype regarding Islamic fundamentalists not representing true Islam, it is evident that the Qur'ān and Islam endorse and even command violence against unbelievers (Surah 2:89, 98, 191, 216; 4:74-76; 5:33, 51; 9:5, 14, 29, 88, 123; 47:4; 61:4; 61:9). Muhammad made *jihad* a command for Muslims. Certainly, there are some Muslims that are peaceful and either ignore the above verses or do not take them seriously. There are professing Christians who do not take Scripture seriously. The major difference between Christianity and Islam is that when Christians take the Word of God seriously, they are commanded to demonstrate the love of God (Mt. 5:44; 6:14; Lk. 6:27, 28). When Muslims take the Qur'ān seriously, it is evident that the Muslim suicide bombers and terrorists are acting as fundamental evangelicals of the Islamic faith. If a Muslim is sincere about the words of the Qur'ān, he is required to "fight for the cause of Allah; whether they die or conquer" (Surah 4:74).

CONCLUSION

Islam appeals to the human nature of man, promising numerous sensual delights in an afterlife. History bears record that Islam always spread by force—through *jihad*—and many times in history, it seemed as if there was no power to check it since the sword is considered the key to heaven. If one died fighting on behalf of Allah, immediate access to heaven would be granted. Those who attempt to equate peace and tolerance with Islam are simply meagerly informed. All of the suicide bombers in the attack on America on 11 September were devout Muslims acting "in the name of Allah." It is confounding that during the interfaith ceremony at Yankee Stadium on 23 September 2001, Imam Izak-El M. Pasha implored, "Do not allow the ignorance of people to have you attack your good neighbors. We are Muslims, but we are Americans." It is staggering to think that more than 34,000 Americans have converted to Islam since 11 September.[18]

There is yet another view of terrorist attacks, such as 11 September. This view holds that the attacks represent genuine Islam. Individuals like Osama bin Laden and his many followers were acting in accordance with the consistency of their faith. The revolutionary fervor of bin Laden is not ambiguous in light of the Qur'ān. The command to kill all Americans and their allies, both civilian and military, is a required duty of every Muslim no matter what country he is in and to do so whenever possible. Writing for *Christianity Today*, James A. Beverley cautions those who will believe the lie that Islam is a peaceful religion.

> In 1999 I had lunch with an American whose identity I must conceal lest I place his life in renewed danger. Over our meal, he told me of a simple but life-altering fact. A few years earlier, he realized that he no longer believed in Islam, and he abandoned his faith. As a

result, he received death threats—not in Sudan, or Libya, or Iraq, but in the United States.[19]

The Islamic threat is not the first time that the world's eyes have been fixed on the Middle East. Furthermore, it will not be the last time, for history will reach its climax in the Middle East. The end of the age will end will the Battle of Armageddon between *the way of the kings of the east...unto the kings of the earth and of the whole world*, as the nations united under Antichrist will gather *to the battle of that great day of God Almighty* (Rev. 16:12-16). Neither side will win, for Jesus Christ will return with His *armies which were in heaven* (Rev. 19:14). Christ alone will be the Victor as *his feet shall stand in that day upon the Mount of Olives, which is before Jerusalem on the east* (Zech. 14:4). History began in the Middle East (the traditional site of the Garden of Eden), and it will reach its climax in the Middle East when Jesus Christ returns.

Although God is in control of prophetic events, this does not mean that He is the cause of evil dictators and nations. In fact, one of the reasons for Christ's return is that the world becomes so desperately wicked. However, even though world situations are serious and will eventually escalate to unprecedented proportions, the most important concern today is not whether you will experience the Battle of Armageddon; rather, it is whether you will be *cast into the lake of fire* forever (Rev. 20:11-15). It is important to understand world events, but it is more important to know where you will go when you die. *And as it is appointed unto men once to die, but after this the judgment* (Heb. 9:27). *Behold, now is the accepted time; behold, now is the day of salvation* (2 Cor. 6:2). As a warrior (Surah 2:216), Muhammad was quick to shed blood (Surah 2:191). In contrast, as the Deliverer (Col. 1:13), Jesus Christ shed His blood for the redemption of mankind, *the forgiveness of sins, according to the riches of his grace* (Eph. 1:7).

Chapter 9

ISLAM AND TERRORISM

DAVE HUNT

oday, everyone wants to know if there is significance to
the attack of September 11. In other words, could it be a
step toward the false peace that must be in place prior to
Armageddon and could it be moving history in the direction of both
the one-world religion and government of the end times? In the discussion of terrorism by the United Nations General Assembly on
October 4, 2001, the ambassador to the United Nations from
Tajikistan said that no imaginable tragedy or disaster could unite the
world as the events of September 11 had done. There was a tremendous unity that was expressed by all in their determination to track
down all terrorists, and to place outside the pale of civilization, and
treat as such, any country that harbors terrorists. Of course, many
countries expressing such sentiments have promoted terrorism. So
far the world seems to have been shaken out of its dream to take
action that could lead to a new era of "peace and safety" that will,
of course, eventually be shattered, but must prevail for a time following the Rapture of the church.

Today, we are hearing that "Judaism, Islam and Christianity share the same values and have a common spiritual heritage," as the ambassador for the Northern Alliance opposing the Taliban declared. Of course, this is false, but being brainwashed with this delusion could add impetus to the lie which Roman Catholic popes and Rome's official documents have been declaring for years: that Allah is the same God whom Christians and Jews also worship. Certainly huge strides are being made in the direction of the world religion over which Antichrist will preside, leading to his worship by all except those who refuse to take his mark.

SEPTEMBER 11 AND BIBLE PROPHECY

Therefore, even though there are no specific prophecies that could be directly tied to the events of September 11, these events do have prophetic significance. Christians must be careful to base any opinion as thoroughly as possible upon the inerrant Word of God. Clearly, this recent event has nothing to do with Revelation 18. Chapters 17 and 18 of Revelation both speak of Babylon revived and then destroyed. In Chapter 17 we are told that the woman riding the beast is mystery babylon.

Is "mystery Babylon" America? Certainly not. She is not a country, but a city built on seven hills (Rev. 17:9, 18). Could that be New York? No. The angel gives John at least 14 descriptive characteristics that identify this woman beyond question. This is a city that existed in John's day, ruling over the kings of the earth, was drunk with the blood of the saints, and would continue until destroyed. That this city was guilty of fornication with the kings of the earth could apply only if it was a spiritual entity which claimed fidelity to God – certainly not true of either New York or the United States. In both the book and the video, *A Woman Rides the Beast*, this woman is identified beyond question as the Vatican in its ultimate role as head of the false world church, bride of Antichrist.

Yes, billions of dollars were lost when the World Trade Center fell, but this was nothing compared to what lies ahead. Furthermore, "Babylon" was not destroyed. New York will recover, the stock market will recover, and America will recover. That must be because of the *peace and safety* that will dominate during the end times just prior to the Rapture leading to *sudden destruction* that Christ will bring when He returns to earth in judgment (1 Thess. 5:3).

THE RELATION OF ISLAM TO SEPTEMBER 11

It needs to be stated unequivocally that Islam is not a religion of peace. Islam not only condones terrorism but also considers it the legitimate means by which it operates. Certainly some Islamic scholars on radio and TV say that Islam opposes suicide so that these terrorists could not have been Muslims at all; and that the Qur'ān condemns taking innocent lives. In fact, the Qur'ān does state that there is "no compulsion in religion" (Surah 2:256). Does that statement contradict the charge that Islam is not a peace-loving religion? Muslim leaders, American government, and church leaders as well deny that charge. Should we apologize publicly to all Muslims for claiming that Islam is not a religion of peace? It is only when we examine the history of Islam and its official teaching and practice that we will be able to ascertain the truth.

THE "PEACE" OF ISLAM

The town of Yathrib (later renamed Medina, "home of the Prophet"), in which Muhammad (570-632 AD) lived for some years (and where he is buried), had been founded by Jews. He killed every male Jew and sold the women and children into slavery. In Saudi Arabia, to this day, no Jew is allowed. Muhammad planned 65 campaigns of plunder and death against fellow Arabs and personally led 27 of them, forcing all of Arabia to submit to Islam in the name of Allah.

Islam's prophet commanded, "He who relinquishes his faith, kill him!" That penalty is still the rule in Islam (though not always enforced). Executions are announced on Saudi radio and TV in advance and carried out before cheering crowds in Riyadh's "chop-chop" square. In October 1993, for example, a father and son were publicly beheaded for having believed in Jesus Christ. There can be no non-Muslim place of worship built, and while it is technically legal to have a prayer meeting or Bible study in the privacy of one's home, participants could be jailed or deported. Such is the "freedom" and "peace" Muslims intend to force upon the entire world. Yet Muslim nations who, in the name of Allah, have supported terrorism, now claim to be against it as America's coalition partners.

Muslims point to the Crusades and argue that Muslim conquests have been no worse than these "Christian" soldiers. The Crusaders, however, acted in disobedience of Christ's commands and example. Muslim terrorists act in obedience to the Qur'ān, Muhammad, and Muhammad's example. Only one of Christ's disciples, Peter, swung a sword. He ineptly cut off an ear. Christ rebuked him, healed the man's ear, declared that His kingdom is not of this world, and that His servants do not fight in the cause of the gospel (Jn. 18:36). Popes and crusaders, proving they were not Christ's servants and not of His kingdom, fought wars to establish a vast kingdom that was very much of this world, killing Jews, Muslims and true Christians in the process.

Islam is an Arab religion. Muhammad conquered Arabia for Allah. Upon Muhammad's death, Arabians abandoned Islam *en masse*. Abu Bak'r, Muhammad's successor, and his fierce jihad warriors, killed tens of thousands of Arabs, forcing them back into the "peace" of Islam. But Christ's disciples, shunning the sword, preached peace with God by grace through faith in Christ and His sacrifice for sin – and died testifying to His miracles and resurrection as facts they had witnessed and could not deny. Clearly, no one is fool enough to die for what he knows to be a lie.

Islam's "martyrs" kill themselves while spreading terror through murdering innocent women and children. Suicide bombers are heroes whose images look down on admiring throngs throughout the Muslim world. Incredibly, just hours before the attack on America on September 11, *Al-Hayat Al-Jadida*, Arafat's PLO-controlled newspaper, wrote, "The suicide bombers of today are the noble successors of the Lebanese suicide bombers who taught the

U.S. Marines a tough lesson…These suicide bombers are the salt of the earth…the most honorable people among us." And now Arafat supports the war against terrorism?

In fact, Muhammad received contradictory "revelations," depending upon the circumstances. (The Qur'ān contradicts itself many times and on important issues, as documented in my book *A Cup of Trembling: Jerusalem in Bible Prophecy*). Some Muslims cite verses such as Surah 2:25b which were "inspired" when the "prophet's" new religion was just being launched and Islam was too weak to compel anyone to follow it. But later he received other "revelations" about using not only force but also killing in order to bring the whole world into submission to Islam. The sword was the "evangelistic tool" for Islam's fierce evangelists. Islamic scholars offer two differing explanations for this particular contradiction. Some declare that Surah 2:25b (and other verses like it) was "abrogated" by later revelations such as "Whoso desires another religion than Islam, it shall not be accepted of him…" (Surah 3:85); "Slay the idolaters wherever you find them" (9:5); "O Prophet, struggle with the unbelievers and hypocrites and be thou harsh with them" (9:73), etc. Others admit that "no compulsion" was a temporary revelation due to conditions, and that it can apply even today in those places, times and circumstances where Islam is not strong enough to use force. Thus in the United States, Islam presents a face of peace, but when it is strong enough it will be imposed harshly. The terrorists are the advance troops.

As for the claim that those who hijacked and crashed the passenger planes could not have been Muslims because Islam condemns suicide, common sense should have immediately unmasked that piece of misinformation to every viewer and listener. To sacrifice one's own life in the process of striking at Allah's enemies was nothing new. This kind of "suicide" has long been an honorable Islamic practice.

In the war between the followers of Islam's two major sects (Iraq's Sunnis and Iran's Shi'ites) young schoolboys were sent to walk ahead of troops to clear minefields. In one battlefield alone, about 5,000 children were torn to bits so the army could move across the cleared path.[1] The Ayatollah Khomeini assured these innocent children that if they were killed in battle they would go directly to Paradise.[2] It is this teaching of Islam which provides the unusual courage to sacrifice one's life in the destruction of infidels.

Hundreds of suicide bombers, *all* of them devout Muslims and *none* who were not, have died in Israel and elsewhere during the past ten years. All were promised Paradise for killing themselves to murder "infidels" (i.e., those who will not repeat the formula, "There is no god but Allah, and Muhammad is his prophet"), and all have been celebrated as heroes. Their families are extremely proud of them and are often handsomely rewarded financially. Never has a word of protest been raised in all of these years by the leading Islamic scholars in Afghanistan, Egypt, Saudi Arabia or other Muslim countries. Yes, suicide is forbidden as self-murder. But to sacrifice one's life in the process of killing infidels gains a Muslim the highest reward.

To become a Muslim one need only repeat the *shahada* (creed): "There is no god but Allah and Muhammad is his prophet." Millions have done so under threat of death. How can Muslims imagine that sincere "faith" is produced under such intimidation? Common decency and common sense recoil. Like Herod, who sought to kill the baby Jesus, so Muslims today are killing those who believe in Him. Here, reported by International Christian Concern (ICC), are a few recent accounts from one small part of Indonesia:

> The day the Jihad warriors attacked, we ran toward the jungles. My father quickly tired...the attackers...took his own machete and cut him to pieces...it was my Muslim neighbor who did this...!
>
> The Islamist group Laskar Jihad...proclaimed over loudspeakers its goal to exterminate all Christians [and] have posted this on their website.
>
> To avoid being slaughtered we agreed to be circumcised to become Muslims. We still held Christ in our hearts....
>
> Because of the help the Jihad received from the military...more than 400 people were slain and another 120 drowned while trying to escape in a boat.[3]

Just as the Allies turned a blind eye and deaf ear to the Nazi holocaust (until it was too late), so we have forsaken today's victims of the holocaust which Muslims have perpetrated for nearly 1,400 years ever since Muhammad. If we had acted in defense of the victims in Indonesia, Iran, Nigeria, Pakistan, Saudi Arabia, Sudan and elsewhere, we might have preempted the September 11 attacks. Will our response continue to be selfishly selective or will we diligently pursue Islamic terrorism until we have stopped it everywhere?

Peace through Islam!? The Muslim world has more unrest, uprisings, riots, and assassinations than all the rest of the world together. Muslims betray and kill not only non-Muslims but also fellow believers in bloody coups and brutal civil wars (the current fighting in Algeria has taken 100,000 lives).

In Nigeria and the Philippines, as in Indonesia, mobs screaming *"Allahu Akbar!"* (Allah is great!) attack Christians, killing and maiming thousands while burning down hundreds of churches and homes. *This is happening today!* In the Sudan, the Muslims from the north have brutalized and slaughtered about 2 million of non-Muslims in the south and sold thousands into slavery. There is an active slave trade today in many Muslim countries. Kadafi buys slaves for $15 each.

Not only the terrorists who attacked America on September 11 but also the vast majority of terrorists around the world are Muslims. Lest anyone suspect that fact to be more than coincidence, there is a rush to insist that Islam is "peace." Shakespeare would reply, "Me thinkest thou protesteth too loudly." Nor can the whitewashers offer *one* example of when, where or how Islam has ever brought peace into this world. There are none – but there are hundreds of examples of wars and violence caused by this "peaceful" religion.

Israel is blamed for the violence in the Middle East. Yet the Arab world was full of hatred and violence long before modern Israel came to birth. Former UN Secretary General Boutros Boutros-Ghali admitted that in three decades "more than 30 conflicts between Arab states have erupted."[4] In the first 25 years following Israel's independence, there were "30 successful revolutions in the Arab world and at least 50 unsuccessful ones [and] 22 heads of state and prime ministers were murdered."[5] None of this violence among Muslims could be blamed upon the "existence of Israel."

REJECTING CHRIST THE SAVIOR

Islam firmly rejects Christ, the One whom God gave to the world to bring peace. The Qur'ān calls Jesus "Isa," probably from Muhammad hearing Jews contemptuously refer to Him as Esau. Islam's central teachings in the Qur'ān and Hadith (tradition of equal authority to the Qur'ān) directly oppose Christ and His salvation.

Islamic scholars all agree that Isa is not the Son of God and was not crucified for our sins. There is general consent that Allah put a likeness of Isa upon one of His disciples, probably Judas, who died in Isa's place. Taken alive to heaven (in one version), Isa is covered with feathers and flies with angels around Allah's throne until the time he returns to marry, have children and die a natural death!

Islam makes it clear that Isa is not divine and certainly not the Son of Allah (that Allah could have a son is denied sixteen times in the Qur'ān). Though in the Qur'ān he was born of a virgin, did miracles including raising the dead (Surah 3:45-49), was sinless and is called the word of God, Isa is clearly not the Jesus Christ of the Bible. And yet some Christians imagine they can win Muslims to Christ by presenting Islam's Isa.

Bethlehem is where Israel's greatest king of the past, David, was born, as was the Messiah who will reign on David's throne forever. Bethlehem has nothing to do with the Muslims or Arabs, yet they lay claim to it just as they do to all of the land that was promised to Israel and in which the Jews have lived for the last 3,000 years. And today, in pursuit of Islam's false claims, has taken over Bethlehem and turned to such violence that most tour groups no longer visit the place of Christ's birth. The Israeli army has even had to bring tanks into Bethlehem to quell the violence.

MOVING TOWARD A ONE-WORLD RELIGION

The September 11 terrorist attack exposed a shocking hypocrisy. Suddenly millions of people (who for years had no time for God) began talking and singing about Him – of course, any god would do – and attending or tuning in to prayer services. There was little recognition that God has moral standards, is grieved with our behavior and wants something more from us than just crying out for Him to "bless America" on our terms. Few seem concerned that America pollutes its youth and the world with R-rated movies, immoral videos and TV programs, slaughters millions of unborn babies (some murdered with only a few inches of the head barely held inside the birth canal) and mocks God with homosexual parades flaunting in His face the grossest perversion. Clearly, in these areas there is some truth in Muslim complaints against our immorality. It seems to have been taken for granted that, as soon as disaster struck, God would answer our prayers at our convenience. Such impertinence should be an embarrassment before the whole world and send a collective shudder through all Americans.

We are deeply grieved for the victims and survivors who have suffered such great loss. We love our country and are loyal to it. That is why we are concerned that America, which has long forgotten God, repeatedly broken His laws and flaunted its immorality in His face, imagines that without true repentance it can so easily merit His blessing by repeating its new mantra, "God bless America." Should we not ask who this God is to whom we cry in deep distress, and what He expects of us if we are to receive His help?

Recent memorial services have featured representatives of many different gods. *Imams* praying in Arabic praise "Allah, the only true god" (he is demonstrated to *not* be the god of the Bible), joined by Buddhists for whom there is no God, Hindus for whom there are millions of gods (take your pick), and "Christians" who have forsaken God and His Word. The assumption is that God does not care how He is addressed or what caricature of Him forms the basis of one's "faith." But the biblical God does not answer to any but His own name and is not pleased to be identified with false deities which represent demons: *the things which the Gentiles sacrifice, they sacrifice to devils, and not to God* (1 Cor. 10:20).

YAHWEH

179

Christ said, *If any man thirst, let him come unto me, and drink* (Jn. 7:37). The Ethiopian who *asked* to be baptized was told the only condition: *if thou believest* [in Christ] *with all thine heart* (Acts 8:37). God does not force anyone to believe in and serve Him because faith and love are not aroused by fear. God pleaded with His people Israel to repent, wept when they did not, and urged, *Come now, and let us reason together* (Isa. 1:18).

But there is no reasoning in Islam, only a blind submission under threat of death which breeds the fanaticism of raging mobs out of control wreaking mayhem almost daily in Muslim areas around the world. Who can forget the television images of mobs in Pakistan chanting their support of Osama bin Laden, or the school children in Gaza chanting death to Israel? Peace necessarily involves freedom. Not one Muslim country offers the freedom we hold dear in America (of the press, of vote, of religion, etc.) because Islam cannot survive where men are free to choose. Israel is the only democracy in the Middle East.

Paul said, *we persuade men* (2 Cor. 5:11), not with a sword but with irrefutable evidence. Paul confounded the Jews which dwelt at Damascus, proving that this is very Christ (Acts 9:22). Apollos *mightily convinced the Jews...publicly, shewing* [proving] *by the Scriptures that Jesus was Christ* (Acts 18:28). Lacking such proof, Islam resorts to violence.

By employing intimidation and threats, Muslims prove that Islam cannot persuade with love and truth and dare not engage in serious discussion. That fact is the best reason for them to abandon terror and force. That the death penalty is required to keep Muslims in the fold proves Islam's inability to win hearts and minds. The joyful liberation of Afghanistan has demonstrated that multitudes who were forced to submit did so only out of fear. Hearts and minds had never changed. Muslims need to recognize that Islam presents itself as a big bully without any valid claim upon the hearts, minds and souls of its followers or would-be converts.

CAN THERE BE COMMON GROUND?

Clearly, Islam is not a peace-loving religion. Nevertheless, Robert Schuller has preached in several mosques and has had a Muslim *imam* in his pulpit and on his worldwide program, "The Hour of Power." Schuller exemplifies the lack of discernment among some Christian leaders when claiming that Muslims worship the same God and have a common faith with Christianity. Despite all evidence to the contrary, some individuals seem to think it is wrong to hold Muslims accountable for the violence Islam has spread, as though Muslims only fought wars in defense of Islam and Allah.

Islam's fierce warriors did not merely fight defensive wars. They carried Islam with the sword outside Arabia by conquering Iran, Iraq, Syria, *et al,* all the way to the border of China, and in the other direction across North Africa, took Spain and were turned back in France as they tried to take over all of Europe. Was this series of aggressive, expansionist invasions with force of arms *an act of defense*? If this is believed then there is simply nothing else to discuss.

Israel did not try to convert with the sword anyone to faith in Yahweh. "Faith" forced upon anyone is not faith. Nor were they commissioned by God to take over the world. They were given a "promised land" of limited area with defined borders (Gen. 15:18-21) and this was only because the wickedness of its inhabitants was so great that God in His righteousness had to wipe them out, as He had done to all mankind except Noah and his family with the flood.

The Crusaders were not Christians but Roman Catholics who fought to take for Rome the land God gave to the Jews. They did so believing the unbiblical promise of Pope Urban II, who organized the first Crusade – similar to the promise of Paradise for *jihad's* martyrs – that if they died in that venture they would go straight to heaven. This was the only real assurance of eternal life they could have as Catholics. The Crusades were carried out in direct *disobedience* to the Bible, to Christ's commands and to His example and that of the Apostles. But Muslims employ violence to spread Islam in *obedience* to the Qur'ān, to Muhammad and to Allah and following Muhammad's example. The Crusades were the very antithesis of Christianity, whereas *jihad* is the very heart of true Islam and its long established method for making "converts" – a huge difference!

WHAT CAN CHRISTIANS DO?

Let us pray that, in the wake of the September 11 attacks, the world will recognize the obvious dishonesty of Islamic countries suddenly claiming they are against terrorism, whereas, the day before, they supported and praised it. Let us pray that millions of Muslims will have their minds and hearts opened to the gospel of Jesus Christ. Let us pray, too, that Islamic countries will at last allow their citizens – so long held in the bondage of fear – freedom of conscience and of faith, and that many will receive Christ. And let us do our part to bring this to pass.

I am still praying, as I have for years, that the true nature of Islam will be exposed to the world. Islamic nations are now declaring vehemently that Islam is a peaceful religion that does not condone terrorism and stands for freedom. Perhaps that will embarrass Islamic countries such as Saudi Arabia to open their borders, to allow some freedom, to relax their cruel hold on citizens – at least to the extent that the gospel may enter and those people who have been held in the iron grip of Islam will be allowed to come to a decision concerning faith and God which is not imposed upon them under the threat of death.

Chapter 10

THE DESTINY OF AMERICA

LARRY SPARGIMINO

WITH SWC

The rosy optimism that characterized many evangelicals with the election of George W. Bush as President and acceptance of John Ashcroft as Attorney General – both professing Christians – has slowly waned in the aftermath of the 9/11 terrorist attacks. New invasive measures to deal with terrorism along with the flood of illegal aliens, has raised some eyebrows. Where is America headed?

Good question, but like many good questions good answers are hard to come by. Complicating the issue is the fact that there are no *direct* references in Scripture to America. But are there *indirect* references?

IS AMERICA IN PROPHECY?

It is hard to believe that there is not some mention of America in prophecy. After all, a nation of 200 million people that has become the financial center of the world, with the most powerful military forces in the history of the mankind, must fit into the end-time scenario somewhere.

In the 1960s S. Franklin Logsdon wrote a book suggesting that the real Babylon of end-time prophecy is the United States. He had noticed two things: (1) All of the Old and New Testament prophecies concerning Babylon have not yet been fulfilled. For example, Jeremiah 50:39-40 states that Babylon will be so completely overthrown that it will remain desolate for ever. Its destruction will be so complete that it is likened to the overthrow of Sodom and Gomorrah. Yet, when the Medes and the Persians invaded Babylon in 539 BC and brought about its historical fall, the city and nation continued to exist. (2) There are several parallels between the Babylon of prophecy and the United States of the present day. The commercialism, the large cities on the seacoast with towers (New York City?), the pornography that is being consumed by the entire world coming from studios in Southern California – all fit Babylon so well that it appears that the prophecies of final doom for Babylon are in reality prophecies of final doom for America. "Going back to 1968, we might wonder why a scholar like Dr. Logsdon," asks Noah Hutchings, "would go off on a tangent and present the unpopular opinion that the U.S. was Babylon?" Hutchings continues with the following observations:

> ...the 1960s were the decade of the 'flower children'— the hippies; the dropout generation; free love; if it feels good, do it; flag burners; Jane Fonda in Hanoi and Bill Clinton in Moscow; and hundreds like them trying to bring down our government while aiding and abetting our enemies. Theologians were preaching that God is dead, and so-called Christian leaders like James Pike were searching for the bones of Jesus in the Judean desert. In the meantime there was the U.S. military war in Vietnam, and the Russians threatening to nuke the U.S. into oblivion. All of this was happening while our courts were pushing God out of education and our music and art both looked and sounded like a thousand

cats fighting, or worse. It is small wonder that a man of God after the heart of Jeremiah would conclude that this must be the Babylon of Revelation.[1]

In his new book *101 Answers To The Most Asked Questions About The End Times*, Mark Hitchcock presents the different views that have arisen because America is not specifically mentioned in Bible prophecy. The one that Hitchcock favors is the view that America will become a third-rate nation because, at the Rapture, millions of productive Americans will no longer be here. "If the Rapture were to happen today," writes Hitchcock, "the United States would probably lose more people per capita than any other nation in the world. At the Rapture the Islamic nations in the Middle East would feel almost no effect at all. But the U.S. could become a third-world nation overnight. Millions of home mortgages would go unpaid, the stock market would crash, and millions of productive workers would be suddenly removed from the workforce."[2]

This is a possible explanation as to why we do not find America in prophecy. The Rapture removes such a large portion of the population that America is no longer a viable national entity. This explanation, however, is based on the Rapture occurring today, or at least pretty soon. If there is a delay, however, and the Christian population of America dies out and is replaced by an overwhelming influx of immigrants who are not Christians, America would lose no more of its citizens at the Rapture than any other nation. While the Judeo-Christian Scriptures have played a determinative factor in molding the values of the West, that situation is quickly changing. On the back cover of Patrick J. Buchanan's book, *The Death of the West* (St. Martin's Press) we read: "America is losing the cultural war. Militant paganism is crowding out the old faiths. Separatism is triumphing over integration. The melting pot has become the salad bowl. And the impact upon American society, politics, and culture will be devastating." At the current rate of things, America could lose hardly anyone at the Rapture.

With the vast array of views regarding the destiny of America, and America in prophecy, one is almost reluctant to even deal with the topic. Yet I believe much can be gleaned from Scripture, history and current events. The study of biblical prophecy is intensely rewarding, not simply as a predictor of future events, but as a source of understanding concerning the significance and meaning of contemporary events. Prophecy provides insights not normally presented in the secular media. What, then, can we learn about the destiny of America?

GOD'S SOVEREIGN WILL AND THE DESTINY OF AMERICA

America's destiny is ultimately tied in with the sovereign will and purpose of God. That God is sovereign means that He consults with no one in determining how to administer the affairs of His creation. The rising and falling of nations is certainly no exception (Dan. 2:21; 4:35). Because God is sovereign, He must be honored, and His determinative role in the destinies of nations must be acknowledged.

America's history shows that this is clearly what was intended by our Founding Fathers. They wanted to honor the God of the Bible. That is why certain groups want to change the telling of our history. "Because the portrayal of history so affects current policy," writes David Barton, "some groups have found it advantageous to their political agenda to distort historical facts intentionally. Those particularly adept at this are termed 'revisionists.'"[3]

America was not intended by our Founding Fathers to be a secular nation, nor was it intended to be anti-religious. To again quote Barton: "The records are succinct. They clearly document that the Founders' purpose for the First Amendment is *not* compatible with the interpretation given it by contemporary courts. The Founders intended only to prevent the establishment of a single national denomination, not to restrain public religious expressions."[4]

GOD'S REVEALED WILL AND THE DESTINY OF AMERICA

While the Founders did not want to prohibit or restrain "public religion expressions," certain religious groups are tied to ecclesiastical authorities and national governments in ways that violate the spirit of the Constitution in that absolute power is granted to a foreign body that is not accountable to the American public. This was one of the issues of concern that some of the Founders had with Roman Catholicism. The Founders were quite happy with Catholics as individual citizens of America. Catholics had signed the Declaration of Independence and the Constitution, and there were several Catholic patriots and leaders in America's struggle for liberty. What concerned the Founders, however, was an aspect of Catholic doctrine that they viewed as contrary to the spirit of the American form of government. "Specifically, they opposed the vesting of total, absolute, and irrevocable power in a single body (the Papal authority) without recourse to the people – and they were able to point to specific examples to bolster their argument."[5]

In our contemporary setting, this concern can be raised regarding Islam, the fastest-growing religion in the world and one that is quickly outstripping Judaism as the religion with the second largest constituency in the United States. By its nature, Islam does not coexist with other religions. On the basis of its authoritative writings, the Qur'ān and Hadith, and in accordance with the example of its founder, Muhammad, Muslims are on a *jihad* to conquer the world for Allah.[6]

At the present time Islam is making tremendous gains in American education and government, as I document in the March 2002 *Prophetic Observer* of Southwest Radio Church Ministry. While national leaders, security experts and many ordinary citizens around the world were stunned by the suddenness and savagery of the events of 9/11, the strangest aspect of 9/11 and its aftershocks is that many are converting – to Islam! According to Marina Jimenez, in an article appearing in the *National Post* (1/19/02) "The Sept. 11 terrorist attacks have served as a catalyst to conversion for some Americans attracted to Islam's 'mysticism and clear theology.'" Jimenez quotes Imam Siraj Wahaz of the al-Takwah Mosque in

Brooklyn, New York, who stated: "Americans have bought more flags since 9/11, but they have also bought more Qur'āns...I've had more converts since 9/11 and I've spoken in so many different forums and inter-faith meetings."

Despite the natural animosity that is felt by many against them following 9/11, American Muslims sense a new political opportunity. Writing for the Russian news outlet *Pravda On-Line*, Chris Deliso reports: "American Muslims are seeking to capitalize on the current anti-Islamic sentiment by proclaiming the need for education about Islam and by announcing their political goals – including the possibility of a Muslim-American president by the year 2020." On October 13, 2001 a national Muslim convention was held in San Jose, California. The nearby city of Fremont has one of the largest Afghan populations in America, with a section of the city known as "Little Kabul." At the convention, speakers called on Muslims to take charge of their future and to strive for a greater political presence in the United States. But is it possible for Muslims to take charge of their future in the United States? Deliso feels that this is a distinct possibility because of the American system of government.

> Muslims would like to use the political freedom inherent to the American governmental structures to push their own foreign policy agenda, one which they feel has been ignored for too long in a country dominated by pro-Jewish political power...And so America's great tolerance and freedom, if it can survive the 'war on terrorism,' may eventually provide its undoing...minority religions are protected to the extent that overwhelmingly Christian small towns in America have been prevented even from putting up a Christmas tree on the town common. Even as the continued threat of terrorism in America has led Congress towards endorsing right-wing conservative measures that would curtail Americans' civil liberties, it is also possible that the 'political correctness' of deferential sensitivity to other cultures which comes from the Left, will erode the country's freedom from within.[7]

Does this rise of Islamic influence in what started as a Christian nation have anything to do with God's revealed will? I believe it does. There are several statements in Scripture that show that God has moral expectations for nations governments. *Righteousness exalteth a nation*, we read in Proverbs 14:34, *but sin is a reproach to any people*. God's moral nature has not changed. But we must ask, "Does God bring judgment on nations?" Does He raise up an evil enemy who, acting freely out of the evil nature of his own heart, is an agent of Divine judgment?

In 2 Chronicles 36 we read how God, because of His great compassion for His people, sent them messengers to warn them. Verse 16 relates their tragic response: *But they mocked the messengers of God, and despised his words, and misused his prophets, until the wrath of the Lord arose against his people, till there was no remedy.* God's response to the mocking of His people is revealed in verse 17: *Therefore he brought upon them the king of the Chaldees, who slew their young men with the sword in the house of their sanctuary, and had no compassion upon young man or maiden, old man, or him that stooped for age: he gave them all into his hand.*

Following the 9/11 attacks some expressed the view that America was simply reaping the wages of its own rebellion against God. Others, however, were outraged that anyone would even dare to think that maybe, somehow, God was responding to the evils of America. NewsMax.com (9/29/01) reported: "Cronkite Calls Falwell A Terrorist." According to the report "The Rev. Jerry Falwell is in the same league as the terrorists who downed the World Trade Center and devastated the Pentagon, according to Walter Cronkite," who was outraged by Falwell's initial statements on the *700 Club* that 9/11 was Divine retribution on America for tolerating "pagans, abortionists, feminists, homosexuals, the American Civil Liberties Union and the People for the American way." Cronkite stated that Falwell's statements about the terrorist attacks "were the most abominable thing I've ever heard."

Though I can understand Cronkite's reaction, the fact remains that America's destiny – as is true of every other nation – is tied in with America's response to God. America has been richly blessed with the Word of God. Yet, Scripture reminds us that the greater the privilege, the greater the responsibility. It has often been said that if God does not judge America He would have to apologize to Sodom and Gomorrah.

MAN'S DELEGATED AUTHORITY AND THE DESTINY OF AMERICA

While God's sovereign will ultimately determines all things, human decision, be it right or wrong, is not without significance. God alone determines the plan, but the Scripture reveals that the free acts of man are part of that plan. Theologians speak of God as "The First Cause," but they also speak of the "reality of second causes." God was free to make man free in some measure, and to delegate to him authority and influence.

Jeremiah 18, for example, records the Parable of the Potter and Clay. Verses 7, 8 state: *At what instant I shall speak concerning a* nation, *and concerning a* kingdom [emphasis mine], *to pluck up, and to pull down, and to destroy it; If that nation, against whom I have pronounced, turn from their evil, I will repent of the evil that I thought to do unto them.* Does God change His mind? According to fixed principles that originated in His sovereign will – "if that nation…I will repent." Just as a thermometer changes in a pre-dictable fashion, so does God. In His sovereignty God has chosen to change His promises of doom, or blessing, in accordance to man's response to His offer of forgiveness or to His threat of judgment. Human response can affect the destiny of a nation. God made it that way. Because of the importance of man's delegated authority, we have to ask: "What is man doing that could influence the destiny of America?"

SECRET SOCIETIES

In his best-selling book, *Brotherhood of Darkness,* Stan Monteith expands on important concepts that help the reader understand some of the forces that are at work in the human arena influencing the destiny of America. One of the important concepts is: "An under-standing of the forces that have shaped the events of the twentieth century is predicated not on facts to be learned, but rather on secrets to be discovered." Monteith observes: "I have studied history for over fifty years, and the longer I live the more convinced I have become that it is impossible to grasp what is taking place today without an understanding of the secret societies."[8]

Monteith refers to Alfred Lord Tennyson, best known for his "The Charge of the Light Brigade," but whose 1842 poem "Locksley Hall" has had far greater influence on world history. Initially written to popularize Tennyson's belief that Great Britain has a moral obligation to consolidate the world under British rule, "Locksley Hall" grew out of a heart that anticipated peace through a league of nations. The relevant lines follow:

> For I dipt into the future.
> > far as human eye could see,
> Saw the Vision of the world,
> > and all the wonder that would be;
> Heard the heavens fill with shouting,
> > and there rained a ghastly dew
> From the nations' airy navies
> > grappling in the central blue;
> Till the war-drum throbb'd no longer,
> > and the battle-flags were furl'd
> In the Parliament of man,
> > the Federation of the world.
> There the common sense of most
> > shall hold a fretful realm in awe,
> And the kindly earth shall slumber,
> > lapt in universal law.[9]

Some of Tennyson's contemporaries shared his globalist/utopia vision. John Ruskin, professor at Oxford University, used the class-room lectern to convince his students that they had the moral obli-gation to bring the world together under British rule. Upon their graduation many of these students became government officials, serving in the early 1900's and holding positions of influence in British government. "These were the men who were responsible for creating, and then prolonging World War I. Why would rational men want a long and bloody conflict?" asks Monteith. "Because they realized that countries would never relinquish their national sovereignty unless they recognized the futility of war, and World War I convinced most people that war was futile…and when the war finally ended, most people and most nations were ready to cede their sovereignty to the League of Nations."[10]

Edward Bellamy who, in 1888, wrote a provocative and amazingly up-to-date manifesto for world government and socialism entitled *Looking Backward: 2000-1887* picked up the vision. Bellamy begins his story in Boston in 1887 with a young man who falls asleep after taking a potion and awakens in the year 2000 to find that the world had become a socialist utopia. Bellamy describes all of the benefits of this utopia in language that is truly remarkable considering that it was written more than a century ago. He writes of "an American credit card…[that] is just as good in Europe as American gold used to be, and on precisely the same condition, namely, that it be exchanged into the currency of the country you are traveling in. An American in Berlin takes his credit card to the local office of the international council…the amount being charged against the United States in favor of Germany on the international account."[11]

America is currently in the throes of a culture war, a war that is ultimately about who will exercise control and final authority. Who will be Lord – God or man? The new world order is not about international peace and security. It is about international control on a magnitude never before imagined. The ultimate security system would not only be one that can instantaneously access everything about an individual's life, but also one that could probe the depths of the heart and the intents of the will. Even the mere thought of conceiving a terrorist plot would be revealed. In this way any possible terrorist attacks could ultimately be averted. Such technology is not far off. Will it be used?

TERRORISM

Christopher Cox, Republican Congressman from California and Chairman of the House Policy Committee, recently spoke on the implications of 9/11 and stated: "The first attack on America in 60 years is also an assault on our nation's freedoms – political, religious and economic. Our free society is what those who attack us hate most. That's why the defense of that freedom must be our central objective as we race these terrorists in war." Cox says that this war against terrorism will be fought in our own country, and then asks, "Will our civil liberties be a victim of friendly fire?"[12]

In the past, America has responded to threats on national security by extending the reach of federal authority. President Lincoln's suspension of *habeas corpus* during the Civil War; the World War I Espionage and Sedition Acts; the Internment of Japanese-Americans following Pearl Harbor, along with the McCarthyism of the Cold War era, all demonstrate that in reacting to a threat we must be careful that we do not over-react. Such over-reaction is dangerous since once liberties are lost they can only be gained back with great difficulty, if at all.

The threat of further terrorist attacks on a far greater scale than what occurred on 9/11, plus the many convenience options that have been developed, has made the surveillance microchip a friend in the eyes of many. Some are even standing in line to have a chip implanted in their bodies. *Inc—The Magazine for Growing Companies* (2/6/02) reports on a phenomenon that promises to sweep the world. Jeffrey and Leslie Jacobs, and their son Derek, are a fairly typical American family. They are middle class and ambitious. Dad is a dentist and mom is an account executive for an interior design magazine. Fourteen-year old Derek plays jazz and tinkers with computers. However, there is one thing that may soon make the Jacobses unique: They could become the first family on planet earth to be voluntarily implanted with microchips that contain personal information about them. The chip that is to be used is known as the VeriChip. Made by Applied Digital Solutions (ADS), the VeriChip stores six lines of text and is slightly larger than a grain of rice. It emits a radio signal that can be picked up by a scanner four feet away. ADS plans to market the chip in the U.S. as a medical device that would allow hospital workers to simply scan a patient's body in an emergency situation to access their health records and to give them the kind of medical help they may need – all in a moment's notice.

The Jacobs family, who live in Boca Raton, Florida, first heard about the chip in a television report. Derek jumped up and said, "I want to be the first kid implanted with the chip!" Jeffrey Jacobs, who is severely disabled, was interested in the device for medical reasons. So Mrs. Jacobs telephoned Palm Beach-based ADS and offered her family as guinea pigs once the microchip is approved for testing by the FDA. Since the VeriChip was announced in December of 2001, ADS has been bombarded with queries from people interested in the device. "Right now we have over 2,000 kids who have e-mailed wanting to have the chip implanted," said Keith Bolton, ADS chief technology officer. "They think it's cool."

There are many advertised advantages to having an implanted chip in your body. Derek, with teenage exuberance, says that he dreams of a day when he will be able to log onto his computers or unlock his house and turn on the lights without lifting a finger. He was inspired by Richard Seelig, the company's director of medical applications, who injected two VeriChips into himself after hearing stories of rescue workers at the World Trade Center scrawling their names and Social Security numbers on their bodies in case they did not make it out of the rubble alive. Indeed, the desire to feel safe in the face of future terrorist attacks and the convenience of having an implanted microchip are natural human inclinations, but these inclinations are fast moving us to the fulfillment of the one-world scenario described in Revelation 13.

America is but one step away from total control by one central authority. This is the new world order that we hear so much about. Terrorists are doing more than blowing up buildings and crashing jetliners into skyscrapers. Though they think that they are furthering the cause of Islam, they are in reality hindering it by creating conditions that are ripe for a surveillance society in which there is no freedom for anyone and certainly no room for the aggressive religion that they follow.

AMERICA AND ISRAEL

Like every other nation that has something to do with Israel, America has a destiny that is connected to her treatment of Israel. Recently two authors – John McTernan, co-founder of International Cops for Christ, and Bill Koenig, a White House correspondent of Koenig's International News Service (*World Watch Daily*) – completed a book entitled *Israel: The Blessing or the Curse.* In this volume the authors document the impact Israel is having on world affairs and how God is making good His promise to curse those who curse Abraham and his descendants (Gen. 12:3). Though we may not be sure of how to explain the absence of specific references in Bible prophecy to America, there seems to be much evidence showing that America's destiny is inextricably related to America's treatment of the Jew and her respect for God's covenant land-grant. "On March 23 [of 1999]," write McTernan and Koenig, "Yasser Arafat met with President Clinton in Washington, D.C. to discuss a Palestinian state with Jerusalem as its capital. On March 24 Arafat went to the United Nations to discuss Palestinian statehood. On March 23 the stock market took the biggest fall in months. The market fell two hundred nineteen points while Arafat was meeting with Clinton to carve up the nation of Israel."[13]

In the spring of 1999 I did several "Bible in the News" reports for our nationwide radio broadcasts on the massive Russian military buildup and the Russian mock bombing attack on America. It was also in the spring of 1999 that unbelievably vicious tornadic weather ripped into central Oklahoma, and devastated areas near where I live. On Monday evening, May 3, I decided not to go for my regular jog because of the severe weather alerts and the visible churning in the sky. McTernan and Koenig explain how the Russian build-up and bad weather all fits:

> On March 24 President Clinton authorized the attack on Serbia. Top military leaders in Russia made statements that World War III had begun. Viktor Chechevatov, a three-star general and commander of ground forces in Russia's Far East region said this

attack 'was the beginning of World War III.'...During the maneuvers, Russia actually sent bombers on a mock attack mission against America. The bombers were intercepted near Iceland and turned away...The backdrop of the attack of Serbia was massive homosexual political activity across the entire fifty states and Arafat meeting with Clinton to carve up Israel...On May 3, 1999...the most powerful...storms to ever hit the United States fell on Oklahoma and Kansas. The wind of one tornado was officially measured at three hundred sixteen miles per hour, making it the fastest wind ever recorded...One F-5 tornado was over a mile wide and traveled four hours, covering eighty miles on the ground...Tornadoes are usually a couple of hundred yards wide at the most, not over a mile; they seldom last for more than ten to fifteen minutes, not for hours; and they only stay on the ground for a couple of minutes, not for four hours...The damage of this storm was incredible. The head-lines of the newspapers stated: 'Everything was gone—At least 43 dead in monstrous Plains tornados;' '20 hours of terror'...[14]

The specific time of these storms bears noting. The storm warnings began at 4:47 PM (CST) which would be approximately 1AM on May 4, 1999. That was the day that Arafat was to announce a Palestinian state with Jerusalem as its capital. Clinton, however, requested a postponement in this declaration. "On May 4, President Clinton declared parts of Oklahoma and Kansas disaster areas. On this very same day, the President sent a letter to Arafat. In the letter, Clinton encouraged Arafat's aspirations for his 'own land,' said the Palestinians had a right to 'determine their own future on their own land,' and that the Palestinians deserved 'to live free, today, tomorrow, and forever.'"[15]

It is hard to imagine that all of this is merely a string of coincidences. "The most powerful tornadoes to ever hit the United States fell on the same day (May 4, Israeli time) that Arafat was to proclaim a Palestinian state with Jerusalem as its capital. The United States has forced Israel into this 'peace process,' and pressured Israel to give away some of the covenant land...the very same day Clinton encourages Arafat about the Palestinian state, he declares parts of America a disaster area from the worst tornados in history."[16]

Will America turn against Israel? The destiny of America is inextricably tied in with this very issue. The demands of our military strategy could influence America's position with regard to Israel. Harsh rhetoric has come from the White House concerning Israel's response to Palestinian terrorism. America's close ties with Israel have always been a stumbling block to building a coalition to back America's war on terrorism. American military strategists believe that if America's war on terrorism is to be effectively pursued beyond the mountains of Afghanistan, America will need the help and support of Middle Eastern countries – and that help will not be given until the Palestinian issue is settled, possibly in the form of backing the Palestinian demands for statehood. American military strategists are not concerned about who really owns the West Bank. They are concerned with being able to defeat state-sponsored terrorism.

MEDIA BIAS

Bernard Goldberg, who has spent nearly thirty years with CBS news, has recently written a book entitled *Bias: A CBS Insider Exposes How the Media Distort the News*, published by Regnery. Conservatives have been claiming for years that the media is biased in favor of liberal causes, a claim that the liberals have tried to refute and have repeatedly stated, "We want proof!" Goldberg has come forward with irrefutable proof. Chapter 6—"Epidemic of Fear" reveals how the media has distorted the facts about AIDS to suit its liberal agenda.

Shortly after AIDS became a big news item scientists discovered that AIDS was basically restricted to gay men who engaged in high-risk sexual behaviors, and junkies who shot drugs into their veins and shared "dirty" needles. This, however, did not arouse the concern of too many Americans – most of whom are not gay and who do not engage in high-risk activities. AIDS activists feared that there would never be a national outcry in support of AIDS victims as long as AIDS was confined to a small segment of the population. Neither Congress nor the President would spend whatever it takes to combat a disease that affects only a small portion of the taxpaying public.

Media pundits worked feverishly, therefore, to give the truth their desired "spin." While AIDS was virtually leaving "straight" America untouched, the media created another reality. Goldberg cites several headlines that were carefully crafted to create this new reality. *US News & World Report* stated: "The disease of THEM is suddenly the disease of US." *USA Today* ran a headline that few could ignore: "Cases Rising Fastest Among Heterosexuals." *Time* wrote: "The proportion of heterosexual cases...is increasing at a worrisome rate...The numbers as yet are small, but AIDS is a growing threat to the heterosexual population." *Ladies Home Journal* had these words on the cover: "AIDS & Marriage: What Every Wife Must Know." Even Oprah Winfrey put in her two cents and joined the Federal Government's Campaign that advertised: "AIDS Doesn't Discriminate." Through media hype a disease that is very restricted in scope was gradually presented as one that is a national threat. The Center for Disease Control (CDC) monitored the reports coming over the TV networks and concluded: "TV's visual portrait of AIDS victims has little in common with real life." The CDC reported that during the period studied, 6 percent of the people with AIDS shown on the evening news were gay men, but in real life 58 percent were gay men. The CDC also reported that on the TV, 2 percent of the AIDS sufferers were IV drug users, whereas in life 23% were IV drug users. The CDC concluded the report by saying: "The high risk groups the news audiences sees are very different from the real-world counterparts."[17]

EROSION OF MORAL VALUES

America is changing. Not too many years ago, men and women swimming in the same area would cause its own rip tide. Today, mixed bathing is accepted in most public beaches. But will mixed wrestling become commonplace, too?

According to the Minnesota *Education Reporter* for May 2001, a Minnesota high school wrestler in a private Christian institution had to wrestle a young lady in order to qualify for the state wrestling tournament. The young man initially refused, but after talking to his father and coach, he decided to do so:

> As the embarrassed boy walked out on the mat, spectators began to laugh. He quickly flipped the girl to her back, but couldn't bring himself to pin her, which required pushing directly on her chest. For about 40 seconds the boy remained frozen. Finally his coach, in frustration, shouted 'Just do it!' The boy made his move, pinning the girl to the mat. But walking off, he looked defeated, not victorious. With hanging head, he strode—angry and humiliated—straight to the locker room.

Katherine Kersten, the author of the article, voiced her disapproval of mixed wrestling. "...the primary objection to boys wrestling girls is this: A civilized society should teach men that they must not use their superior strength to overpower and control women. If the sexes are to live in harmony, they must ground their relations in a kind of compact, centered in mutual dignity and regard."

America provides us with a conspiracy of evil. It is not evil that is simply a coincidence – like the flip of a coin that sometimes produces "heads" and sometimes "tails" – but it is evil that is a giving of oneself over to the forces of evil, as explained in the Book of Revelation: *These have one mind, and shall give their power and strength unto the beast* (17:13).

Though we are not in the Tribulation, the present conspiracy of evil is certainly foreshadows it. Nowhere is this more obvious than in the vile productions of popular culture which are often sheltered from censure under the banner of "freedom of expression" and "freedom of speech." A prime example is the Brooklyn Museum's

2001 presentation of Renee Cox's *Yo Mama's Last Supper*. Highly controversial, to say the least, this photo of a naked Ms. Cox portraying Jesus, with eleven black friends as apostles and a white man as Judas, led New York City's Mayor Giuliani to denounce the work and announce a commission to set "decency standards." Bronx borough president Fernando Ferrer, however, said the Mayor's proposal "sounds like Berlin in 1939."[18]

THE CHRISTIAN'S MORAL RESPONSIBILITY AND THE DESTINY OF AMERICA

Monteith writes "men and women become accomplices to those evils they fail to oppose."[19] In whatever direction America is moving, Christians have the moral responsibility to be salt and light. If we choose to do nothing we become co-conspirators of evil.

In view of the overwhelming flood of evil we must ask: "How then are we to live?" Are we to surrender and wait for the Rapture? Are we to hate America, and hate the liberals who control the media, and the globalists who are in high places? Are we to lay down our spiritual weapons and to grudgingly raise the white flag of surrender?

Some evangelicals believe that we should. "America is gone. It's over," is their lament. Some would point to the 9/11 tragedy and see it as indicating that we are now in the Tribulation. The terrorist attack on New York City is given as proof that Babylon is judged. Did not the whole world, via satellite TV "see the smoke of her burning," and is it not true that given the sequence of events, from the initial impact of the jetliners and the collapse of the buildings, that *in one hour is thy judgment come* as prophesied in the Book of Revelation? (18:9, 10). Yet as Hutchings point out, how could we be in the Tribulation since there are still musicians, weddings and parties, many of them celebrating with the *light of a candle* (Rev. 18:23).[20]

Frankly, America can be confusing. At times it can be seen as a place of great evil, but at other times one must thank God for the great good that is being carried on. Great opportunities for witness and Christian service still remain. It would show ingratitude to God, and to those who have fought long and hard in the past and present, to deny that. This author serves in a small mission located next to a large university and has a ministry to students whose opportunity to hear the Gospel in their homeland is severely restricted. I believe that surrender is totally inappropriate. In the closing pages of his book *The Death of the West*, Patrick J. Buchanan writes:

> America is a paradox. She remains the greatest nation on earth...We are the most blessed people on earth. Our science, technology and medicine are the envy of mankind. Some of us are alive today only because of surgical procedures, medical devices, and miracle drugs that did not exist when we were young...And while no one can deny the coarseness of her manners, the decadence of her culture, or the sickness of her soul, America is still a country worthy fighting for...[21]

While America is often maligned for its Viet Nams and the rampant racism that has unfortunately marred our history, nations like Russia and China would have been over-run by the Axis powers of WW II if it had not been for American involvement. American blood was spilled on many a foreign battlefield fighting for the rights of human beings thousands of miles from home. "The United States has fought in two World Wars to save the world from cruel dictatorships, and hundreds of thousands of our citizens have suffered and died in these wars."[22] After these wars were over American money poured into devastated nations to help them rebuild.

America has also had a special role in the work of Christian ministry and evangelism. Great revivals have been poured forth from God that have left a legacy of schools, institutions and mission organizations in America that have left an indelible mark on the world. Premillennial institutions, authors and pastors have reminded their audiences of God's unconditional covenant with Israel. And though most local churches are not all that they can be, faithful pastors and congregations are doing the Lord's work through worship services, the Sunday School, Vacation Bible Schools and other church-related organizations.

There is still much work for Christians in America. The nation is clearly moving in a dangerous direction but we need not share its coming end that it will undoubtedly share with all the nations of the world. Many prophetic teachers, including this author, believe that Christians living in the present dispensation will not experience the judgments of the Tribulation period. Though 9/11 was a terrible disaster it is not to be equated with Armageddon. America's contemporary war against God is a sad spectacle and no one knows how much longer we may have.

What is the destiny of America? It will have the same destiny as any nation that has been richly blessed by God but has turned its back on the One who gave those blessings. What is different about America, however, is the continuing work of those who have not bowed the knee to Baal.

Chapter 11

THE AXIS OF EVIL: BABYLON

JOSEPH CHAMBERS

The ultimate name or type for evil is Babylon. Not only is it a name or type; but the actual location, the very geographic location of evil and the center of its activity. Just as Jerusalem is central to God's revelation, Babylon is central to Satan's design of evil. They are the antithetic/opposite cities of the world. It is amazing to watch Bible scholars and prophecy teachers in their pursuit of Babylon's meaning to name other cities as the fulfillment of this center of evil. As we get closer and closet to the end, Babylon and the country of Iraq become more and more central to the world's attention. The Heavenly Father Himself is both guiding and allowing this axis of evil to be the focus of the world in preparation for judgment. May I say, "You have not seen anything yet." The grand finale of darkness will spring from this earthly location.

God has assigned a major and powerful angel in directing the fulfillment of Revelation chapter 18. I believe that angel has already begun his activities, although the ultimate fulfillment is during the seven years of final judgment. When I was in Babylon in 1988, the atmosphere was pregnant with evil. At the same time, there was a sense of the Divine hand of God absolutely in control. Satan and all his hordes of fallen angels are never free to act beyond the Divine hands of the Father of all. One day, while in Iraq, as we were racing toward the ancient cities of Ur and Erech, the taxi radio was blaring music. The music sounded like demons rejoicing over their prey. I asked the guide that had been assigned to me by the Iraqi government what the lyrics of the song were saying. He would not answer, but quickly turned the radio off. I could sense the battle of the ages in progress. I still remember that event with a sense of foreboding, but also a great feeling of impending victory. The world's best days are soon to begin.

Just as every action of the church, good or bad, cannot be disconnected from the center of all Revelation, which is Jerusalem, neither can any action of evil be separated from the city of Babylon, where it all began. The world's kingdoms, its commerce, political powers and all its designs of control are Babylon in spirit. That is why it is easy for Bible teachers to see the Babylonian nature or spirit in New York, Paris, London, and even Rome. The diabolical forces of fallen angels all have a bent towards Babylon. It is their inspiration. This spirit of the false religions and all evil actions will show a semblance to Babylon.

The eighteenth chapter of Revelation is the prophetic record of the final events of literal Babylon. Do not confuse Chapter 17 with Chapter 18. Chapter 17 is "Mystery Babylon," the religious counterpart of the literal city. There is a clear break between the two chapters that moves from the pagan religion to the political and literal city. Many good Bible teachers appear to lose sight of this distinction at this point. The word "mystery" in Chapter 17 is a prefix before the word "Babylon" and shows this to be a *type* of the literal, not the literal itself. Let's look at the introduction of the eighteenth chapter.

> And after these things I saw another angel come down from heaven, having great power; and the earth was lightened with his glory. And he cried mightily with a strong voice, saying, Babylon the great is fallen, is

fallen, and is become the habitation of devils, and the hold of every foul spirit, and a cage of every unclean and hateful bird. For all nations have drunk of the wine of the wrath of her fornication, and the kings of the earth have committed fornication with her, and the merchants of the earth are waxed rich through the abundance of her delicacies. And I heard another voice from heaven, saying, Come out of her, my people, that ye be not partakers of her sins, and that ye receive not of her plagues. For her sins have reached unto heaven, and God hath remembered her iniquities. Reward her even as she rewarded you, and double unto her double according to her works: in the cup which she hath filled fill to her double (Rev. 18:1-6).

This great picture reveals a lengthy process, which has already begun. The key words are, "Babylon the great is fallen, is fallen." Of course, the final judgment is not completed at the utterance of these words, nor was it completed when Isaiah or Jeremiah spoke these almost exact words (cf. Isa. 21:9; Jer. 51:8). It is a process that began its descent into judgment when these prophets declared their prophecies. Throughout the Scripture, God's prophets have declared the end from the beginning and spoke of many events with a language filled with finality. We do not try to say that Jesus had already been born when the Psalmist David wrote the forty-fifth Psalm or that Jesus had been crucified when Isaiah penned Isaiah 53. Neither should we say that Babylon had been forever destroyed when Isaiah and Jeremiah prophesied of the final judgment for this pagan city. Our God was simply declaring what the end would be, and we are living in the preparation for this fulfillment.

The fact that twice in Revelation we see the Holy Ghost using precise language to unite the prophecies of Isaiah and Jeremiah with the world of John the Revelator shows the perfection of Scripture. How could anyone deny such precision? Let's look at these prophecies together.

And, behold, here cometh a chariot of men, with a couple of horsemen. And he answered and said, Babylon is fallen, is fallen;

and all the graven images of her gods he hath broken unto the ground (Isa. 21:9).

Babylon is suddenly fallen and destroyed: howl for her; take balm for her pain, if so be she may be healed (Jer. 51:8).

And there followed another angel, saying, Babylon is fallen, is fallen, that great city, because she made all nations drink of the wine of the wrath of her fornication (Rev. 14:8).

And he cried mightily with a strong voice, saying, Babylon the great is fallen, is fallen, and is become the habitation of devils, and the hold of every foul spirit, and a cage of every unclean and hateful bird (Rev. 18:2).

The prophecy world is filled with ministers and Bible teachers that refuse to take Revelation chapter 18 literally. That is why I stress this point, because this will soon be a great frontier in fresh Bible prophecy fulfillment and hopefully new understanding. The entire history of Saddam Hussein is a picture of Bible prophecy in perfect expression. Just as God used the ancient character of Nebuchadnezzar to build the ancient city of Babylon, God has used Saddam Hussein to resurrect the name and location of this city and to begin the process of its reconstruction. The whole city foundations lay beneath the dust until this man began to dream that he was the modern day Nebuchadnezzar. He seeks Jerusalem's destruction exactly as did his ancient counterpart. He also finds himself just as frustrated with Israel as did Nebuchadnezzar and just as helpless to eliminate the memory of these chosen people. Remember, it was Israel's God that finally won the day with this evil despot of the past. Hallelujah, it will surely happen again!

When the angel descended from Heaven in Revelation chapter 18, he came with great power and his glory lightened the earth. His message was judgment of the earthly kingdoms that have been birthed from Babylon and Babylon itself as the source of all these kingdoms. This chapter may look foreboding and absolutely horrible, but the message is clearly one of hope. All the pagan ideas and human sorrows that the kingdoms of this world have championed are soon to pass beneath the purifying powers of His holiness. This chapter is a picture of the redemption of this earth from the effects of Babylon.

Babylon is declared to be the "habitation of devils and the hold of every foul spirit and a cage of every unclean and hateful bird." Evil spirits (fallen angels) have an earthly center for their activities and Babylon has been that center since the very fall of Lucifer. Revelation 9 records activities that spring from Babylon. *And the sixth angel sounded, and I heard a voice from the four horns of the golden altar which is before God, Saying to the sixth angel which had the trumpet, Loose the four angels which are bound in the great river Euphrates. And the four angels were loosed, which were prepared for an hour, and a day, and a month, and a year, for to slay the third part of men. And the number of the army of the horsemen were two hundred thousand: and I heard the number of them* (Rev. 9:13-16).

The Euphrates River is intimately connected with the city of Babylon. It actually flowed through the city and beneath the walls in Nebuchadnezzar's days of earthly glory. Babylon has always been a name synonymous with evil. It originated as Satan's capitol when Nimrod sought to build a gate to Heaven and to rip God Himself off His throne. There is no other proper description of Babel and the evil intent of this first expression of false religion.

Remember, before Satan sinned, he also shared the Garden of Eden with the Father, Adam and Eve, as an anointed cherub that covereth. There is a possibility that he was the "covering" that allowed Adam to walk with God in the evening shadows. Note this incredible passage. *Son of man, take up a lamentation upon the king of Tyrus, and say unto him, Thus saith the Lord GOD; Thou sealest up the sum, full of wisdom, and perfect in beauty. Thou hast been in Eden the garden of God; every precious stone was thy covering, the sardius, topaz, and the diamond, the beryl, the onyx, and the jasper, the sapphire, the emerald, and the carbuncle, and gold: the workmanship of thy tabrets and of thy pipes was prepared in thee in the day that thou wast created. Thou art the anointed cherub that covereth; and I have set thee so: thou wast upon the holy mountain of God; thou hast walked up and down in the midst of the stones of fire. Thou wast perfect in thy ways from the day that thou wast created, till iniquity was found in thee* (Ezek. 28:12-15).

The Garden of Eden was in Southern Iraq, not far from where Nimrod, under Satan's motivation, built Babel, which was the beginning of Babylon. No wonder God forsook this area and directed His newfound friend Abraham to travel to the Middle East, where the Father would choose the City of Jerusalem to be His earthly Zion. History is replete with the contrast of Babylon and Jerusalem. After thousands of years, the focus of the world has returned to Babylon and Jerusalem. That is how it will be from now until the end.

Babylon is intimately connected to the cities of the world in this great text of Revelation 18. *For all nations have drunk of the wine of the wrath of her fornication, and the kings of the earth have committed fornication with her, and the merchants of the earth are waxed rich through the abundance of her delicacies* (Rev. 18:3). No one dares deny that the new shift in the Western world is back toward Eastern religions and ideas. Millions of Americans are involved with gurus, Islamic religion, pagan-type New Age ideas, etc. The elitist educators are almost totally given to Eastern thinking and the trashing of the Western culture. Psychology is not anything but Eastern humanism. The liberals in our political parties are actually being mentally baptized into Eastern thinking. The homosexual and lesbian culture is Eastern and pagan at heart. The cultural war in America is a war between the supernatural revelations of God our Creator and the paganistic ideas of Eastern cultures. The world is under the final sway of fallen Babylon.

I do not dare suggest that anyone can know all that will happen between now and the great final moment of Babylon's judgment. Let's consider a couple of possibilities.

UNITED NATIONS MOVING TO BABYLON

The present United Nations is absolutely opposed to the Western culture. Everything we stand for, they hate. Israel has been condemned so many times that it has all become a joke. Biblical Christianity and Orthodox Judaism are considered by the majority of the United Nations personnel to be the plague of the earth. Nothing could be more fitting to their mindset than to move to Baghdad or Babylon. When Saddam Hussein is removed, the United Nations will be the proper entity to establish a new government. Americans are becoming more and more hostile to the United Nations and we would be blessed to have them off of our shores. I believe America will be a sheep nation right through the seven years of tribulation.

IRAQ – AN ARCHAEOLOGICAL TREASURE

Almost every ancient civilization was connected to Iraq. When a world friendly government is established, this country could become the most visited country on the earth. If they will exploit their treasures of art, ancient history, archaeology and anthropology, it will become a world treasure. It may even be possible to identify the ancient location of the Garden of Eden. If the wealth of oil was used to rebuild Iraq and to promote the cultural and historic beauty, the cities would soon become the envy of the world. These are the kinds of possibilities in the fulfilling of Revelation chapter 18.

Regardless of what may occur, Babylon and the country of Iraq have a destiny with the Creator. The final judgment is a picture of horror. While this country must become a world center, it will be judged and left to be an ash heap. Jeremiah declared her final end. *Babylon is suddenly fallen and destroyed: howl for her; take balm for her pain, if so be she may be healed. We would have healed Babylon, but she is not healed: forsake her, and let us go every one into his own country: for her judgment reacheth unto heaven, and is lifted up even to the skies. The LORD hath brought forth our righteousness: come, and let us declare in Zion the work of the LORD our God* (Jer. 51:8-10).

It is breathtaking to see that this city, whose builders and defenders have hated Jerusalem, will have the first announcement of her judgment announced and declared in Jerusalem. "Come, and let us declare in Zion (Jerusalem) the work of the LORD our God." When you consider the oil deposits that lay beneath this country and the fact that this oil is mixed with gas, which creates great pressure, you have all God's needs to do exactly what Revelation chapter 18 declares. I just heard discussed on the news the possibility of Saddam Hussein igniting the oil wells as he did in Kuwait.

Before this destruction occurs, the Antichrist will be defeated in Israel's Valley of Megiddo, and will flee back to his capitol in Babylon. It will be in the gates of Nimrod (Babylon) that the Antichrist will be killed and cast into the Lake of Fire. A minor prophet, Micah, declared this long ago. He said, *And they shall waste the land of Assyria with the sword, and the land of Nimrod in the entrances thereof: thus shall he deliver us from the Assyrian, when he cometh into our land, and when he treadeth within our borders* (Mic. 5:6).

How clever of the Holy Ghost to connect the Ancient Nimrod that founded this center of fallen angels and demons with the day of its judgment. The Gate of Nimrod is clearly the City of Babylon.

CONCLUSION

Anything that represents the spirit of Babylon, its pagan nature, or its demonic activities must be off-limits to the saints of the Living God. There is a war occurring between the culture of absolute Biblical truth and the revealed ideas of the Babylonian world. The church world is quickly adapting to Babylonian thinking. The new theology says that the Bible is open and new revelations are occurring. The church world is calling it a paradigm shift. They are right, there is a paradigm shift. It is the spirit of Babylon preparing the world for the masterstroke of Satan. Remember, *And I heard another voice from heaven, saying, Come out of her, my people, that ye be not partakers of her sins, and that ye receive not of her plagues* (Rev. 18:4).

Flee every idea that is not rooted in clear Biblical revelation. The Babylonian spirit is invading the world. Even though the city's reconstruction may be far from complete, its influence is breathtaking. The fallen angels that find their center of activity in this region are spreading its ideas to the entire world. Every Eastern thought, the religion of Islam, the spirit of terrorism, and even the New Age philosophies are all Babylonian in nature. The world is under her sway to prepare for the invasion of that final manifestation of the Antichrist. It is exciting to be filled with the eternal revelations of the true God and to have the joy of soon beholding the end of all things that offend. Keep a pure heart and a pure mind saturated with the life of the Lord Jesus Christ.

Chapter 12

DEMOCRACY IN WORLD GOVERNMENT

ARNO FROESE

T his image's head was of fine gold, his breast and his arms *of silver, his belly and his thighs of brass, His legs of iron, his feet part of iron and part of clay* (Dan. 2:32, 33). In the Old Testament book of Daniel we learn that the prophet interpreted a dream for King Nebuchadnezzar, the first Gentile world ruler. The gold, silver, brass and iron in the dream represent the four Gentile superpowers:

1. Babylon
2. Medo-Persia
3. Greece
4. Rome

However, the last part of the Iron Empire is a combination of iron and clay. It is part of the fourth world Empire, but it is different.

As we begin our analysis of democracy in world government, we must keep the following principles in mind. Four Empires will be in charge of planet Earth. These Empires will be destroyed by a Stone and replaced by an everlasting kingdom that is set up by the God of heaven.

A study of history tells us that great things transpired between Rome (the last Empire), and the final kingdom established by a Stone. However, the Bible ignores these great events and simply mentions only these four categories of world rulership followed by the emergence of the Stone kingdom which is the cause of the destruction of these four systems. Most scholars agree that we are living in the age of the fourth kingdom. How do we know that?

IRON EMPIRE: ROME

When Jesus was born in Bethlehem, He was subject to the rules, laws and regulations of the Roman Empire. Scripture is quite clear that the same Empire will rule the world when Jesus returns. Furthermore, we must understand that the Stone that is cut out of the mountain will destroy the iron, brass, clay, silver and gold. Thus, it stands to reason that these four Empires must exist in some form at the coming of the Stone.

Current events in Persia (Iran) and Babylon (Iraq) should not surprise or confuse us. The key to endtime development is still the Iron Empire. It is significant that when Daniel interpreted Nebuchadnezzar's dream, he only described the first three kingdoms briefly: *...Thou art this head of gold. And after thee shall arise another kingdom inferior to thee, and another third kingdom of brass, which shall bear rule over all the earth* (vv. 38, 39). But when he comes to the fourth Empire, he goes into much greater detail. This is also the case in Chapter 7, in which Daniel received the vision of the four beasts. The first beast was a lion (Babylon); the second, a bear (Medo-Persia); the third, a leopard (Greece). Daniel does not offer any description regarding the likeness of an animal of the fourth beast. We simply read: *...and it was diverse from all the beasts that were before it; and it had ten horns* (Dan.

ENG/RUSSIA/GERMANY

7:7). The word diverse appears several times in Chapter 7 in reference to the fourth beast.

THREE GROUPS OF PEOPLE

Fundamentally speaking, there are only three groups of people: Gentiles, Jews and Christians. Up until Abraham, everyone was a Gentile. Therefore, the Jewish race has Gentile roots. Through one Jew, Jesus Christ, salvation was brought forth and gave birth to the Church, which is the third group of people. Although God creates all people, the Jews and the Church are two special groups of people known as the "elect." We read the Jew's position from God's perspective in Deuteronomy 14:2: *For thou art an holy people unto the LORD thy God, and the LORD hath chosen thee to be a peculiar people unto himself, above all the nations that are upon the earth.*

First Peter 2:9 identifies the Christian: *But ye are a chosen generation, a royal priesthood, an holy nation, a peculiar people; that ye should shew forth the praises of him who hath called you out of darkness into his marvelous light.* Notice how both groups of people are described as "peculiar."

The Jews are destined to be "above all the nations that are upon the earth" and the Church is to "shew forth the praises of him who hath called you out of darkness into his marvelous light." A countless number of promises throughout the Bible indicate that the Jews will become the leaders of the world. For example, prior to His death, Moses proclaimed, *Happy art thou, O Israel: who is like unto thee, O people saved by the LORD, the shield of thy help, and who is the sword of thy excellency and thine enemies shall be found liars unto thee; and thou shalt tread upon their high places* (Deut. 33:29). The Jewish people have an earthy calling, among which is a country with defined borders. But Christians have been given no such promise. We live within the nations of the world; we have no country to call our own. In fact, Christians do not even possess an organization that officially represents the Church of Jesus Christ.

Although many groups have tried to develop an earthly representation of the Church, all have and will continue to fail because the Bible does not allow for such a development. In any event, the Church is real and it is alive and well on planet Earth. The Bible refers to the Church as a "mystery." This mystery remains hidden from the eyes of the world. Only a genuine Christian knows what this "mystery" entails. Even though every individual Christian has his or her own nationality, is educated differently, speaks multiple languages, is culturally diverse and differs in appearance, particularly from continent to continent, this diverse group of people is nevertheless one.

The Bible says, *There is neither Jew nor Greek, there is neither bond nor free, there is neither male nor female: for ye are all one in Christ Jesus* (Gal. 3:28). That is the true Church. Her members have been born again of His Spirit. They may belong to different denominations and local churches, giving the appearance of diversity, but we are united as one in Christ. The Church, however, is part of Israel. We are organically one because we have been grafted into the olive tree: *For if thou wert cut out of the olive tree which is wild by nature, and wert grafted contrary to nature into a good olive tree: how much more shall these, which be the natural branches, be grafted into their own olive tree?* (Rom. 11:24). The Church is a global entity and can be found all over the world.

Reports have indicated that the largest number of evangelical Christians can be found in communist China. This should not surprise us because God does not depend on any political circumstances or western civilization's sophisticated ability to propagate the Gospel. He continues to build His Church and He does it His way.

DEMOCRACY RULES

Now that we have identified the world's four superpowers and the three categories of people on earth, we must answer one question: "how is it possible for such a diverse group of people to become solidly united?" This is a one-word answer: Democracy. The great English statesman, Winston Churchill, made this profound statement: "Democracy is the worst form of government but it is the best we have." Many were shocked when I wrote *How Democracy Will Elect the Antichrist* in 1997. Why? Because we have been taught that there is some kind of relationship between democracy and Christianity.

So, then, what is democracy? Democracy originates with the Greek word *demos*, meaning "the community," and *kratos*, meaning "sovereign power." In short, it is a government elected by the people, for the people. The Romans practiced a certain degree of democracy and are credited with the laws that govern today's world. History books record that Iceland practiced a form of democracy in the 10th century. The British practiced an upper-class form of democracy in the 13th century. However, modern democracy was initiated by the French and American Revolutions. Although they are different types of democracies, they are all based on a "let the people govern" philosophy. For example, Swiss citizens are directly involved in the decision-making process; subsequently, they enjoy more rights than other democracies. The United States has a representative democracy in which elected officials are supposed to present the people's interest. Needless to say, some do; others do not.

ROMAN ORIGINS

Let's take a comparative look at Roman democracy as illustrated in the prestigious monthly magazine, *National Geographic*:

> We know that early on, the Romans were ruled by the Etruscans, a powerful nation of central Italy. Chafing under an often brutal monarchy, the leading families of Rome finally overthrew the Etruscan kings—a revolution that would influence, some 2,200 years later, the thinking of Thomas Jefferson and George Washington. In the year 244 AUC (that is, 509 BC) the patrician families of Rome set up a quasi-representative form of government, with a pair of ruling consuls elected for a one-year term. This marked the beginning of the Roman Republic, a form of government that would

continue until Julius Caesar crossed the Rubicon 460 years later. Those five centuries were marked by increasing prosperity and increasing democracy.[1]

This early democratic system was barely different than our system today. The article continues:

Fat Cat Contributors? By the second century BC the right to vote was so firmly established among the plebeians that Rome developed a vigorous political system—one that would not be unfamiliar to citizens of a modern democracy. There were parties and factions, fat-cat contributors, banners and billboards, negative advertising, and a pundit class to castigate the pols.[2]

Just as in a modern democracy, the Romans granted rights, which required duties.

Rights And Duties of Citizens

Within the broad sweep of uniformity, Roman administration at the local level was flexible, tolerant, and open. When Rome conquered a new province, the defeated general and his army were carted away in chains; almost everyone else came out ahead. The local elite were given positions in the Roman hierarchy. Local businesses gained the benefit of Roman roads, water systems, the laws of commerce and the courts. Roman soldiers guarded the town against pirates and marauders. And within a fairly short period, many of the provincial residents would be made *cives Romani*—citizens of Rome—with all the commensurate rights and duties.[3]

No one less than Augustus ardently supported the Roman pro-life movement.

Anti-Abortion

Augustus used all the tools of governing. Concerned about a decline in the birthrate, he employed both the stick (a crackdown on abortion), and the carrot (tax incentives for big families). To see if his policies were effective he took a census of his empire now and then. Thus it did in fact come to pass in those days that there went out a decree from Caesar Augustus that all the world should be registered. And just as St. Luke's Gospel tells us, this happened 'when Quirinius was governor of Syria,' in 6 AD. Under Roman rule, "world citizenship" was real and prosperity greatest.

Citizens of the World

History recalls Marcus Aurelius (161-180), the philosopher-king who maintained perspective in the midst of imperial splendor: 'As the Emperor, Rome is my homeland; but as a man, I am a citizen of the world...Asia and Europe are mere dots on the map, the ocean is a drop of water, mighty Mount Athos is a grain of sand in the universe.' Even the cynical Gibbon had to tip his hat: 'If a man were called to fix the period in the history of the world, during which the condition of the human race was most happy and prosperous, he would, without hesitation, name that which elapsed from [96 to 180 AD]'— That is, the era of those 'Five Good Emperors.'[4]

Today's democracies would not be capable of functioning without Roman law.

Literacy and Law

The English historian Peter Salway notes that England under Roman rule had a higher rate of literacy than any

British government was able to achieve for the next 14 centuries. One of the most important documentary legacies the Romans left behind was the law—the comprehensive body of statute and case law that some scholars consider our greatest inheritance from ancient Rome. The ideal of written law as a shield—to protect individuals against one another and against the awesome power of the state—was a concept the Romans took from the Greeks. But it was Rome that put this abstract notion into daily practice, and the practice is today honored around the world.[5]

Ancient Rome was concerned with a citizen's liberty.

Innocent Until Proven Guilty

The emperor Justinian's monumental compilation of the Digests, the Institutes, and the Revised Code, completed in 534 AD, has served as the foundation of Western law ever since. Two millennia before the Miranda warnings, the Romans also established safeguards to assure the rights of accused criminals. We can see this process at work in the case against the Christian pioneer St. Paul, as set forth in the New Testament in the Acts of the Apostles. In chapter 22 of Acts, Paul is brought before a Roman magistrate on criminal charges—apparently for something like 'provoking a riot.' The police are just about to beat and jail him when Paul pipes up that he is a Roman citizen. That changes everything, and he is permitted to remain free pending a trial. Festus responds in chapter 25, with a lecture on legal rights: 'It is not the Roman custom to hand over any man before he has faced his accusers and has had an opportunity to defend himself against their charges?'[6]

America's democratic system is clearly modeled after the Roman Republic.

Rome—U.S.A.

The Roman process of making laws also had a deep influence on the American system. During the era of the Roman Republic (509 to 49 BC) lawmaking was a bicameral activity. Legislation was first passed by the comitia, the assembly of the citizens, then approved by the representative of the upper class, the senate, and issued in the name of the senate and the people of Rome. Centuries later, when the American Founding Fathers launched their bold experiment in democratic government, they took republican Rome as their model. Our laws, too, must go through two legislative bodies. The House of Representatives is our assembly of citizens, and, like its counterpart in ancient Rome, the U.S. Senate was originally designed as a chamber for the elite (it was not until the 17th Amendment, in 1913, that ordinary people were allowed to vote for their senators).

Impressed by the checks and balances of the Roman system, the authors of American government also made sure that an official who violated the law could be 'impeached,' a word we take from the Roman practice of putting wayward magistrates *in pedica*. The reliance on Roman structures at the birth of the United States was reflected in early American popular culture, which delighted in drawing parallels between U.S. leaders and the noble Romans. There was a great vogue for marble statues depicting George Washington, Alexander Hamilton, even Andrew Jackson in Roman attire. A larger-than-life statue of Washington in a toga and sandals is still on exhibit at the National Museum of American History in Washington, D.C.[7]

These historical researched quotations offer overwhelming evidence that Rome has never really stopped ruling the world. Rome will continue to guide the world until the masses are captivated by the peace, success, and prosperity found under the democracy banner upheld by the Antichrist. The only entity that can fill these shoes is unmistakably Rome, or, in modern language, the European Union.

WHY EUROPE MUST RULE THE WORLD

Virtually all European nations can identify that their greatest glory occurred during the Roman Empire. The power, wisdom, glory and culture of the Empire had a major impact on European history, but also could be felt around the world. Rome (Europe) must be credited as the founders of the world's westernized civilization and the birth of democracy. Today, democracy is an indisputable global ideology in virtually all political systems. But Europe is the major influence on Western civilization:

- It is the center of the world, located between the east and the west.
- It is the center of philosophy that has shaped the progressive civilization of the world.
- It is the center of trade, commerce and finance.
- It is the center and leader of religion. No religious leader has as much of a dramatic impact on the political world than the Pope of Rome.

When the Pope travels anywhere in the world, he attracts multitudes. The audiences that even top political leaders draw pale in comparison with the Pope's. His listeners hang on every word he speaks. Church doctrine proclaims his infallibility when speaking ex cathedra. The Catholic Church claims that he is the apostle Peter's successor and he, and each successor of his, is Christ's earthly representative. Millions long to be touched and have their babies blessed by this adored spiritual icon clothed in a long white flowing robe.

EUROPE WANTS TO REPLACE ISRAEL

The prophetic shadow that is being cast shows that Europe (the new Roman Empire), attempts to imitate Israel. Therefore, it is not surprising that the European flag contains twelve stars, not fifteen, or whatever the final number of nations belonging to the European Union will eventually be. Europe's constitution requires that only twelve stars represent the nations that are brought into the Union. We do not need much of an imagination to see that the twelve stars imitate Israel in two ways: first, it is a representation of the twelve tribes of the children of Israel; and second, it represents the twelve apostles of the Lamb! As I have already mentioned, the spirit of Europe is not limited to the geographical continent. Let me explain:

THE WEST

Over 500 years ago, Christopher Columbus, a Roman Catholic Jew, discovered America. The entire continent (both north and south) was claimed by Spain in the name of the Roman church. The populations of the United States, Canada, and South American countries are largely made up of European descendants. Our governments are based on Roman principles. The supreme council of ancient Rome was called the Senate. This identical system is used today in the United States and Canada. This form of government is also practiced in Italy, France, Ireland, South Africa, and Australia, just to name a few.

Also obvious is the striking similarity between United States and Roman architecture of the Vatican. Virtually all major government buildings are crowned with the cupola, or dome, just like St. Peter's Basilica in Rome. Our history has obvious ties to the Roman Empire. Although a time of apparent separation has taken place, sooner or later, the West will return to its roots under the revived Roman Empire.

THE EAST

Australia is also rooted in European civilization. Ninety-two percent of the continent's population is of European descent. If we analyzed the governments of Japan, Korea, Singapore, Hong Kong, India, Taiwan, and any other progressive Asian country, we would also notice an obvious trend in the countries' use of Western European principles. Infrastructures such as government, education, transportation, communication, business transactions, and law are clearly based on European fundamentals.

India, the world's largest democracy, is a British creation. Although it has vigorously tried to implement Hindi as its national language for decades, English remains the language of communication in business and government. Those people whose mother tongue is not Hindi, but Bengali, Gujarat, Kashmiri, Telugu, Sanskrit, and an additional 1652 dialects, refuse to accept Hindi as India's national language. Therefore, they have no other choice but to communicate in English, a Roman-based language!

THE SOUTH

The African continent is located to the south of Rome. Fifty percent of the continent speak French, while forty percent speak English. Africa is also saturated with European civilization; therefore, it, too, comes under the jurisdiction of the spirit of Rome. Southern European countries view Africa as a neglected continent. European Union members would like nothing more than to see such African nations somehow brought into the fold. Mediterranean nations have long complained that the Union is facing the wrong direction. They claim that while the Union focuses its attention on Eastern Europe, a much greater threat is looming in the south. They argue that unless Europe does something, Islamic fundamentalists will seize power in North African countries and unleash a wave of emigration.

In its March 9, 1995 issue, *The European* printed the following article:

Will the southern governments succeed in persuading their northern E.U. partners to allocate more E.U. resources to the troubled Muslim nations of the Maghreb—Algeria, Morocco, Libya and Tunisia—across the new fault line that has replaced the Iron Curtain?

Their goal is to persuade the E.U. to provide aid for developing industries in the Maghreb countries so that prosperity will reduce both emigration to Europe and support for fundamentalism.

An increasing number of Europeans recognize their responsibility and the dangers involved in neglecting northern African nations. Islamic fundamentalism has become one of the world's major security risks, especially since the fall of the Soviet Union. But Muslims will not adhere to any dictate. A religious compromise must be found. This compromise can only be achieved through the Vatican, the leader of the world's largest religion. Again we see Rome's worldwide influence.

FOREIGN AID

What comes as a shock to most Americans is that Europe is by far the most generous foreign aid contributor in the world. The United States is ranked as the least generous. According to the Organization for Economic Cooperation and Development (OECD), the percentage of foreign aid for each countries' Gross National Product (GNP), was recorded in 1997:

OFFICIAL DEVELOPMENT ASSISTANCE FLOWS IN 1997[8]

EU DAC members		Non – EU DAC members	
Country	**ODA/GNP%**	**Country**	**ODA/GNP%**
Denmark	0.97	Norway	0.86
Netherlands	0.81	Canada	0.36
Sweden	0.76	Switzerland	0.32
Luxembourg	0.50	Australia	0.28
France	0.45	New Zealand	0.25
Finland	0.33	USA	0.08
Belgium	0.31		
Ireland	0.31		
Germany	0.28		
Austria	0.26		
United Kingdom	0.26		
Portugal	0.25		
Spain	0.23		
Italy	0.11		
Greece	N/A		

The most generous country in the world, Denmark, contributes almost 1%, followed by the Netherlands with 0.81%. Needless to say, not being as generous as most other rich countries, American moral influence decreases drastically. Recognizing this deficit, President Bush is urging Congress to double the amount of foreign aid in the coming years. What is interesting about this revelation is Europe's relative silence about their generosity. Yet because of it, they are building tremendous global support for the New World system headed by Europe: A democracy ruled by diversity. In the United States, it is almost overemphasized: "United we stand." Europe's philosophy is just the opposite: "Diversified we stand."

The European Union Constitution urges individual member-nations to protect and defend each nation's uniqueness, its culture, tradition and language. It stands to reason that in such a case, virtually all of the nations can participate. Not surprising is that Turkey, a Muslim nation, is desperately seeking membership into the Union. Therefore, this new European democratic system is potentially the only one that can accommodate the entire world.

ISRAEL: THE CHOSEN

Israel is different and she should remain so. However, the great tragedy lies in the fact that she does not want to be separated from the other nations. Israel's real sentiment, which is expressed by both intellectuals and politicians, clearly seems to be that she is the same as any other nation. Subsequently, the first steps for the clay to be mixed with the iron are being undertaken and will result in a Gentile-Israel democracy. Israel is the only Middle Eastern country that adheres to a true Roman democracy.

A "We the people" philosophy rules Israel. Governments and laws are installed by the people, for the people. Because of Israel's initial success, I believe that democracy will also be implemented throughout the Middle East and the rest of the world in the near future. If Israel is in fact being integrated into the Gentile iron nations, then we can safely assume that the time of the end is drawing near, and the fulfillment of Daniel 2:45 is just on the horizon: *Forasmuch as thou sawest that the stone was cut out of the mountain without hands, and that it brake in pieces the iron, the brass, the clay, the silver, and the gold; the great God hath made known to the king what shall come to pass hereafter: and the dream is certain, and the interpretation thereof sure.*

EUROPE TO REPLACE ISRAEL

God chose Israel to rule the world; however, Europe has led the world for over 2,000 years. As it looks today, Europe will continue as the world's primary leader. But God has ordained only one country and that is Israel. Therefore, events must conclude in the near future. Someone may object and say: "How can you say Europe ruled the world when only America and Russia have attained status as superpowers?" The term "superpower" was coined by the United States to identify the Soviet Union as a communist country and the United States as a capitalist country. Since the Soviet Union no longer exists, it is natural to assume that the United States is the only remaining superpower. However, I believe that a superpower cannot exist within the framework of democracy unless the world becomes a mass democracy led by the United Nations. As a result, the first true world superpower will be created. It will be a global nation that will undoubtedly exist in the future.

When the Bible speaks of world rulership, it identifies only four powers: Babylon, Medo-Persia, Greece, and Rome. However, the fourth will merge into the fifth and final Gentile "superpower." Based on Bible prophecy, the European "Iron Empire" must spread around the world and unify the nations to form a global society. Europe is already the wealthiest and most sophisticated continent at this time.

PANTHEISTIC DEMOCRACY

Webster's Dictionary defines the word "Pantheism" as 1) a doctrine that equates God with the forces and laws of the universe; 2) the worship of all gods of different creeds, cults, or peoples indifferently; also: toleration of worship of all gods (as at certain periods of the Roman Empire). When the Soviet Union fell, the doors were opened wide to a Pantheistic world revolution. Communism was America's number one enemy. The United States did everything in its power to oppose communism. One of the most insulting words in the American culture is to be labeled a "communist." But when we analyze communism and capitalism we notice that to a certain extent, communism exists in all societies. True capitalism, on the other hand, does not exist other than in dictatorial countries.

BIBLICAL RIGHTEOUSNESS

From a biblical perspective, we see that democracy (where the majority decides) sold Joseph into slavery. Democracy rejected the God of Israel and chose a king. Democracy condemned Jesus and nailed Him to the cross. In essence, democracy must fail because it is not the majority, but all people on the face of the earth who have been judged unworthy by God. The book of Romans says, *There is none righteous, no not one.* The Old Testament book of Isaiah says: *All of our righteousness are as filthy rags.* So it stands to reason that "filthy rags righteousness" can only produce a "filthy rags peace." In Matthew 7:18 Jesus said: *A good tree cannot bring forth evil fruit, neither can a corrupt tree bring forth good fruit.* This is very simple: Our corrupt nature cannot bring forth good fruit. Sooner or later, the democratic philosophy built on a man's sinful imagination will collapse.

When will that happen? When Jesus, the Light of the world appears, darkness will be exposed and defeated. Nevertheless, virtually the entire world loves democracy, cherishes it, and realizes that we have more freedom, civil rights and a degree of prosperity than we do without it. Therefore, democracy is okay, it is the best system, and it is a global winner.

THE CHURCH AND DEMOCRACY

Can we correctly say that the Church is reaching the world, or is it safer to say that the world is reaching the church? Samuel J. Andrews wrote a book entitled, *Christianity And Anti-Christianity In Their Final Conflict,* copyright © 1898 (out of print). Under the subhead, "The Pantheistic Revolution," he wrote the following on page 254 in reference to Pantheism and democracy:

> The multitude is made familiar with its principles through magazines and newspapers, through lectures and the church. Its prevalence is shown in the rapidity with which such systems as those of Christian Science, Mental Science, Theosophy, and others kindred to them have spread in Christian communities, for all have a Pantheistic basis. The moral atmosphere is full of its spirit, and many are affected by it unawares. What shall we say of its diffusion in the future? To judge of this we must look upon its spread from another point of view, and consider its affinity with Democracy.
>
> It is not to be questioned that social and political

conditions have much influence in molding religious opinions, and we assume that the democratic spirit will rule the future. What kind of religious influence is Democracy adapted to exert? In what direction does the democratic current run? According to De Tocqueville, it runs in the direction of very general ideas, and therefore to Pantheism. The idea of the unity of the people as a whole, as one, preponderates, and this extends itself to the world, and to the universe. God and the universe make one whole. This unity has charms for men living in democracies, and prepares them for Pantheistic beliefs. Among the different systems, by whose aid philosophy endeavors to explain the universe, I believe Pantheism to be one of those most fitted to seduce the human mind in democratic ages; and against it all who abide in their attachment to the true greatness of man, should struggle and combine.

If these remarks of this very acute Christian observer are true, we may expect to see Pantheism enlarging its influence in Christendom as democracy extends. What prophetic insight this man possessed at the end of the 1800s.

In this connection, I am reminded of an article, in which Midnight Call Ministry founder, Wim Malgo wrote, in 1967 entitled: "Communism Doomed To Fail." At that time it seemed virtually impossible for anyone to oppose communism. They took one country after another, crushing any uprisings with brute military force and thereby threatening the West. The reason for Dr. Malgo writing such an article about communism was its rejection of religious value. The Bible clearly states that the religious power of the endtimes is intertwined with politics and economy. Thus, it is plainly written: *For all nations have drunk of the wine of the wrath of her fornication, and the kings of the earth have committed fornication with her, and the merchants of the earth are waxed rich through the abundance of her delicacies* (Rev. 18:3).

Aren't the nations of the world, with few exceptions, intoxicated by commercial success? Doesn't every politician court religious groups in order to win votes? Haven't the world's economies grown rich during the last hundred years when compared with the previous 2,000 years? Isn't there an "abundance of delicacies" offered to us in our warehouses and supermarkets on a daily basis? We do not need much of an imagination to see that the world has indeed become rich. Just try to compare today's standard of living, degree of human rights and the material goods an average person enjoys with those enjoyed a hundred years ago.

If you are not sure that a gaping difference exists, take a look at some of the houses located in the downtown or suburb districts that existed (if they are still standing), 100 years ago. Our forefathers literally lived in shacks. Not everyone had running water, and the bathroom was located outside of the house. The temperature of the house was cold in the winter and hot in the summer. Wood or coal was the available fuel used to cook meals. Think about the dirt, dust and filth. The breadwinner of the home had to work 60-80 hours a week just to make ends meet! Children, as young as 10-years-old, were part of the work force. Basic human rights applied only to the rich. Many were considered disposable servants. Women were considered second-class citizens who had no right to vote, much less utter an opinion. In some states, they could not even own property. If you worked in a factory, you were under the total authority of your boss. In some cases, you were required to rent a house from the company and buy your food from the company store. In essence, the company owned you. The title of the late Tennessee Ernie Ford's song, "I Owe My Soul To the Company Store," is completely relevant. The progress and development of modern democracy has given us riches our forefathers would never have even dreamed possible.

Under the subhead, "The Church of the Beast and the False Prophet," Samuel J. Andrews continued:

> How then in an age which denies a personal God can we find an object of worship? Such an object modern Pantheism gives us. As God is in all men, and becomes self-conscious only in man, he in whom the Divine is most manifested may be an object of worship. This unity of the Divine and human in man lies at the foundation of

the many antichristian movements for unity which we see in all regions of human thought and life, political, social, religious. In the Christian Church many are weary of its divisions and crying aloud for unity; and in the non-Christian bodies many are manifesting the desire to have only one religion, one church, one worship. Accepting as an incontestable fact that the human race is making continual progress, and that though religions may die, religion will live and develop forever, they affirm that the future must bring with it in time a universal Church. It is said by one of this school: 'Instead of religion passing away, we are in the time of its rebirth. There is to be a more magnificent religion, a grander church, than the past has ever dreamed of...We are getting ready to build the new temple in which God shall manifest Himself as He has not in the past, and that shall be full of light and love and peace for all mankind.'

But a more significant sign is seen in the recent Chicago assembly of "The World's Parliament of Religions," the first of its kind ever held. It contained many men of great learning and ability, and of high ecclesiastical positions. A Roman Cardinal commended it as "worthy of all encouragement and praise." And an Archbishop said: "The conception of such a religious assembly seems almost like an inspiration." A Protestant Bishop spoke of the movement as "a grand one, and unexampled in the history of the world." Other Bishops and Protestant clergymen spoke in the same way. It was said by one: "It has been left to the mightier spirit of this day to throw the gates of the Divine Kingdom wide open, and bid every sincere worshipper in all the world, of whatever name or form, 'welcome.'" And by another: "A Pentecostal day is come again, for here are gathered devout men from every country under heaven, and we do hear them speak the wonderful works of God." And so is fulfilled in a sense more august than on Pentecost itself, the memorable prophecy in Joel 2:28 of the one coming, universal religion. And yet another clergyman states: "This Parliament marks the first step in the sacred path that shall one day bring the truly humanitarian and universal religion." Thus Christianity appears before the world as one of many religions – having, it may be, more truth – but still without the element of universality.

What do today's churches and Christian ministries look like? The overwhelming majority of evangelical Christianity worships Pantheistic democracy! In view of these facts, we may not expect, as so many schools of thought try to convey, a coming dictatorial Antichrist who will brutally force his New World Order upon the citizens of the world. In fact, just the opposite is true, and it is happening today. Citizens of the so-called "free world," including biblical Christianity, are enthusiastically headed toward the goal of a universal church. The spirit of this non-existent church has such overwhelming support that any negative mention would be considered blasphemy.

Brother Samuel J. Andrews saw this coming over a hundred years ago. The church is becoming worldly and the world is becoming religious. As the days go by, it becomes increasingly difficult to make a distinction between the real Jesus and a false one, between the spirit of God and a false spirit, between the Gospel of salvation and a gospel of imitation. The Bible warns: *And no marvel, for Satan himself is transformed into an angel of light* (2 Cor. 11:14).

Dear reader, this may be your final warning to come out from among them. Continue to ...*press toward the mark for the prize of the high calling of God in Christ Jesus* (Phil. 3:14) because it is much later than we may think.

TRANS: CALLING FROM ON HIGH
— NAME AT "R"

THE MOVEMENT OF PROPHECY

Chapter 13

THE EMERGING WORLD RELIGION

MIKE GENDRON

S ince the dawn of the new millennium, we have been witnessing the greatest push toward ecumenical unity the
world has ever seen. Nearly every religion is in a dialogue together, seeking to find common threads of truth as a basis
for unity. Professing Christians, under the banner of AD 2000, are
joining hands in a unified effort to fulfill the Great Commission.
The Roman Catholic Church is building bridges to all Christian
denominations and non-Christian religions to seek unity under the
papacy. The tragedy of September 11, 2001 has brought religious
leaders from every religious persuasion together to petition a "common god" for world peace. Yet as diverse as some of the religious
beliefs appear, there is a common bond among all the religions of
the world. It is the denial of salvation by grace, the unmerited favor
of God. All religions, with the exception of biblical Christianity,
teach salvation by works – a salvation based on what men must do
for God, instead of what God has already done for man through
Jesus Christ.

This ecumenical unity, which is the worldwide gathering of all people into one faith, should not surprise students of biblical prophecy. Throughout the New Testament we see warnings about a growing apostasy and the formation of a one-world religion. The end times will be marked by the universal worship of the Antichrist (Rev. 13:12). So as we see professing Christians falling away from the true faith of the apostles, it is both discouraging as well as encouraging. The apostasy from the pure Gospel of grace is discouraging because many professing Christians, who have never been born of the Spirit, are following the broad road to destruction (Mt. 7:13-23). However, we can also be encouraged because Jesus and His Word declare these things must happen before He returns to set up His earthly kingdom.

The United Religions Initiative (URI) Charter, *A Document Designed To Lay The Groundwork For The Unification Of The World's Religions*, was officially signed 26 June 2000, at Carnegie Mellon University in Pittsburgh, PA, during a six-day URI Global Summit. The signing of the Charter officially launched the United Religions Initiative, an "international grassroots organization" which purposes to "bring religions and spiritual traditions to a common table, a permanent, daily, global assembly." An Associated Press report stated that 225 URI Global Summit participants who "want to establish a global group that could speak for the religions of the world" were involved in the signing of the Charter.[1] Faiths represented at the Global Summit included Hindus, Zoroastrians, Christians, Jews, Muslims, Hoa Haos, Buddhists, Taoists, Wiccans, Cao Dais, Baha'is, Sikhs and Indigenous Peoples. Episcopal Bishop William Swing founded the URI and has served as its president.

A few months later, the first ever, religious summit sponsored by the United Nations was held in New York City on Aug. 28-31, 2000. In the name of world peace, the United Nations pronounced a religious universalism that views all religions as equals. However, that view was met with strict opposition from the Vatican, which opposes the notion that all religions are equal. According to Francis Cardinal Arinze, president for interreligious dialogue at the Vatican and a speaker at the summit, the Catholic Church also would favor one religion in the world – if it were Roman Catholicism. Less than a week after the summit the Vatican released a 36-page declaration rejecting what it said are growing attempts to depict all religions as equally true.[2] The Pope has said he wants his brand of Christianity to be the cement that reunites Europe.

The emerging world religion will be widely accepted and embraced by the multitudes. They will be lovers of pleasure rather than lovers of God and have a form of godliness but deny its power (2 Tim. 3:4, 5). All beliefs will be tolerated. Spirituality without truth will be the rule. A false love and peace will prevail for a time. People will follow deceitful spirits and doctrines of demons (1 Tim. 4:1-3). The way of truth will be maligned and false teachers will revel in their deception (2 Pet. 2:2, 13). People will be lukewarm towards Christ, wealthy and in need of nothing, but unaware of their wretched and miserable condition (Rev. 3:16, 17). Those who expose "wrong" teachings will be persecuted.

The quest for peace in a world brutalized by terrorism has provided fertile ground for rebuilding the religious tower of Babel. God's smashing of man's first attempt at ecumenical unity around the original Tower of Babel was a blessing for mankind. The potential for satanic influence is infinite whenever religious unity is man-ordained. Therefore, it should come as no surprise that the Vatican is the driving force behind the emerging world religion. In May 2001, John Paul II addressed 300 participants on the phenomenon of globalization. The Pope encouraged the members as they strive towards a "well-articulated reflection on globalization, based on solid ethical and spiritual values." He said that globalization is "no doubt a phenomenon which allows for great possibilities for growth and producing riches but the wealth produced often remains in the hands of only a few."[3] In January of 2002, Pope John Paul II sponsored a "Day of Prayer for Peace" in Assisi, Italy for leaders from the world religions, including the Catholic and Orthodox churches, the World Council of Churches (WCC), the Sikhs, the Muslims, the Buddhists, the Confucians, and a variety of African religions. A joint declaration of commitment, issued by the Assisi participants, called for universal peace and justice, along with openness, diversity, and "mutual trust." The Name of Jesus Christ was omitted entirely. Wherever the participants gathered, including the famous Basilica of St. Francis, all crosses and other "Christian objects" were removed in order to make everyone feel "more comfortable."[4]

Throughout history, the Roman Catholic Church has sought to bring all religions under the power and influence of the papacy. No longer able to openly force people to submit to its Popes under the threat of death and persecution, the Vatican has changed its strategy for world dominion. Seduction, rather than force, is the new strategy. At the 15th International Meeting of Prayer, Pope John Paul II addressed the 1500 religious leaders who signed a "Proclamation of Peace Appeal" with these words: "We can no more bear the scandal of division...dear representatives of the great world religions."[5]

Since the close of the Second Vatican Council in 1965, the Roman Catholic Church has developed a softer, gentler approach to establishing one church for the whole world. She is now urging all "separated brethren," whom she once called "heretics," to come back home to the "one true church." This ecumenical movement has captured the hearts and minds of many professing Christians. The guiding principle is to "tolerate everyone's beliefs as long as they love Jesus." By seeking common ground and overlooking doctrinal differences the movement has gained popularity in a world weary from religious strife. However, the call for Christians to overlook their differences and unite, for the purpose of peace and evangelizing the world, is not biblically based. It completely ignores the fact that Roman Catholic, Orthodox and many Protestant churches preach another gospel. The Jesus of the Bible brings division, not unity (Mt. 10:32-39). He separates those who deny Him by rejecting His finished work of redemption from those who receive Him by faith alone. He divides those who merely profess Christ from those who have been born-again (Mt. 7:21-23; Jn. 12:48).

Jesus and His disciples never tolerated ecumenical evangelism. Time after time zealous religious leaders, with their own agendas for building the kingdom, were strongly rebuked. They all had one thing in common – a refusal to submit to the authority of the Lord Jesus Christ and His Word.

- Jesus brought division, not unity with Jewish leaders for their religious pride and spiritual blindness (Mt. 23).

- Paul did not unite with the Judaizers who loved Jesus but preached another gospel (Gal. 1:6-9).
- Jude refused to unify with those who crept into the church to pervert the grace of God (Jude 4).
- John did not seek unity with those who went out from us because they were never really of us (1 Jn. 2:19).
- Peter never joined hands with the false teachers who had forsaken the right way to follow the way of Balaam (2 Pet. 2:15).
- The writer to the Hebrews did not pursue unity with those who ignored such a great salvation (Heb. 2:3).

In light of these witnesses set before us, one must wonder how evangelicals can be so easily seduced by the Vatican's push for ecumenical unity. Surely they are not ignorant of the additional requirements Rome has added to the gospel of salvation. Surely they are not ignorant of the 100 anathemas the Roman Catholic Church uses to condemn those who do not believe their false gospel! How can Christians join hands with a church that condemns them? Could they be so easily persuaded by the Catholic Church's worldly influence, incredible wealth, one billion followers and a leader that is so loved by the world?

THE VATICAN'S CALL FOR UNITY

The Catholic Church has long taught that there is no salvation outside the Roman Catholic Church. Consider the following quotes of Catholic Popes throughout history...

> "We declare, say, define, and pronounce that it is absolutely necessary for the salvation of every human creature to be subject to the Roman Pontiff"
> —Pope Boniface VIII, *Unam Sanctam*, 1302.[6]

"Those who are obstinate toward the Roman Pontiff cannot obtain eternal salvation"

—Pope Pius IX, 1864.[7]

"The Catholic Church alone is the Body of Christ."

—Pope Paul VI.[8]

"It is a sin to believe there is salvation outside the Catholic Church"

—Pope Pius IX.[9]

It is indeed disturbing to see so many evangelicals unaware of the Vatican's attempt to bring the world under the dominion of the papacy. In his 1995 encyclical *Et Unum Sint,* Pope John Paul II said he intends "...to promote every suitable initiative...to increase the unity of all Christians until they reach full communion" and "to encourage the efforts of all who work for the cause of unity." The Pope's stated desire is "to gather all people and all things into Christ, so as to be for all—an inseparable sacrament of unity... expressed in the common celebration of the Eucharist."

During a week of prayer for Christian unity Pope John Paul II said:

I gladly take this opportunity to call the attention of all believers to the ecumenical commitment that marked Vatican Council II. The council rightly defined the division among Christians as a scandal. The council Fathers felt the need to beg pardon of God and of their brethren for the sins committed against unity. He asked Catholics 'to cultivate an authentic spiritual ecumenism' through the Virgin Mary [not through the Lord Jesus]. (*Et Unum Sint*)

An indication of the success of the Pope's push for unity is noted by an announcement made by the Archbishop of Canterbury. He urged all Christians to recognize the Pope as the supreme authority of a new global church. In a document called *The Gift of Authority,* he describes the Pope as a "gift to be received by all the churches."

The Vatican's ecumenical movement goes beyond the call for unity of all professing Christians. Their strategy is to bring *all* religions under the power and influence of the papacy. Pope John Paul II has been actively courting the world's one billion Muslims. In a 1998 address he said:

> Christians and Muslims, we meet one another in faith in the one God...and strive to put into practice...the teaching of our respective holy books. Today, dialogue between our two religions [Roman Catholicism and Islam] is more necessary than ever. There remains a spiritual bond which unites us and which we must strive to recognize and develop.

Mother Theresa also contributed to the ecumenical spirit as noted in her book *Servants of Love*. She stated:

> ...we went every day to pray in some temple or church. The Archbishop gave us permission to do so. We prayed with the Jews, the Armenians, the Anglicans, the Jains, the Sikhs, the Buddhists, and the Hindus. It was extraordinary. All hearts united in prayer to the one true God.

THE VATICAN'S STRATEGY FOR CHRISTIAN UNITY

The Vatican's strategy for uniting all of Christianity can be summarized by the following five points:

1. Promote the concept that Catholics, Orthodox and Protestants are all already brothers in Christ. Urge "separated brethren" to come home to "Holy Mother, the Church" to enjoy the fullness of salvation. The Vatican's Cardinal Cassidy proclaims that baptism is what causes the unity of all Christians. He said, "One

of the most important achievements of the ecumenical movement has been the recognition that through baptism members of the various Christian denominations become brothers and sisters in Christ."[10]

2. Redefine evangelical terms. They masterfully and deliberately redefine biblical terms to make them more vague, ambiguous and acceptable to both Catholics and Protestants. An example of this is the 1999 Lutheran-Roman Catholic *Joint Declaration on the Doctrine of Justification*. In the document, equivocal and indefinite words are used to affirm the doctrine of "justification by faith alone." However, the Vatican continues to affirm the anathema's that condemn all who believe this doctrine. The *Joint Declaration* is just a smoke screen because the Roman Catholic Church cannot change its position on dogmas pronounced by so-called infallible Popes and Church Councils!

3. Take advantage of biblical ignorance and poor discernment. The fact that the Roman Catholic Church covers its false gospel with a veneer of truth has convinced many professing Christians that it is a genuine Christian denomination. Many who are ignorant about the true Gospel are easily deceived. Biblical commands to expose false teachers are either not known or are being ignored.

4. Seek unity under the guise of brotherly love, world peace, tolerance, morality and social reform. One of the basic ideas of religious philosophy is that love is more important than doctrinal truth. This is because love unifies, while doctrine divides. However true love rejoices in the truth (1 Cor. 13:6). Why? Because without truth, it is impossible to define love. Love is the servant of Truth. We are to speak the truth in love (Gal. 4:15). Love is doing for a person whatever is best for him in the light of

eternity, no matter what the cost may be. Love is confronting someone in doctrinal error that leads people to a Christ-less eternity. World peace, morality and social reform are important issues but they all pale in comparison to the eternal destiny of souls. Pope John Paul II would have us to believe otherwise. He said, "It is clear that disunity has impaired our mission in the world, in these troubled times, the world needs, more than ever, the common witness of Christians in every area, from the defense of human life and dignity to the promotion of justice and peace."[11] The ultimate mission of Jesus was to save souls not to bring peace. He said *I did not come to bring peace, but a sword. For I came to set a man against his father and a daughter against her mother...*(Mt. 10:34, 35). Tolerance is a virtue only when dealing with people and their personalities. There is no room for tolerance when dealing with the message of Jesus Christ. Biblical unity is not found in uniformity of religious faith, but in the ministry of the Holy Spirit and the clear teaching of Scripture. C.H. Spurgeon framed the issue well. He said:

> Charity by all means: but honesty also. Love of course, but love to God as well as love to men, and love of truth as well as love of union. It is exceedingly difficult in these times to preserve one's fidelity before God and one's fraternity among men. Should not the former be preferred to the latter if both cannot be maintained? We think so.[12]

5. Suppress doctrines that cause division. The Vatican attempts to remove the walls of separation between denominations and religions by minimizing the essential doctrines of the Gospel. One example of this is the 1994 *Evangelicals and Catholics Together Accord*. In a follow-up document, known as *The Gift of Salvation*,

we see Rome's strategy to suppress doctrinal truth for the sake of unity with this statement. "All who truly believe in Jesus Christ are brothers and sisters in the Lord and must not allow their differences, however important to undermine this great truth, or to deflect them from bearing witness to God's gift of salvation in Christ." According to the document, these differences are said to "require further and urgent exploration": baptismal regeneration, the Eucharist, sacramental grace, justification, purgatory, indulgences, Marian devotion, the assistance of the saints in salvation, and the possibility of salvation for those who have not been evangelized. These differences should be significant for all Christians because they nullify or oppose the essential doctrines of the Gospel. Each one denies the sufficiency, efficacy or necessity of Jesus Christ and His finished work of redemption! Each one opposes, contradicts or nullifies the glorious gospel of grace! Evangelicals and Catholics are divided on: how one is born again, how one is justified, how one is preserved in grace, how one is purified of sin, who mediates between God and man, what Christ's atonement accomplished and who is part of God's plan of salvation. We can summarize this discussion in eight words…

KNOW DOCTRINE - KNOW DIVISION

NO DOCTRINE - NO DIVISION

The Apostle Paul wrote about men who *will not endure sound doctrine; but wanting to have their ears tickled, they will accumulate for themselves teachers in accordance to their own desires; and will turn away their ears from the truth, and will turn aside to myths* (2 Tim. 4:3, 4). When doctrinal truth is suppressed there can be no distinction between believers and unbelievers. Doctrine is what divides the true church from the emerging world religion. While unity and brotherhood sound wonderful to a hostile world full of fighting and killing, the Bible condemns unity that is not founded in God's Word. False unity is based upon man's ambitions and is independent of God (Gen. 11:1-9). This type of unity will be a tool of the Antichrist (Rev. 17, 18). Biblical unity is based on apostolic truth (Eph. 4:3, 13). It is a work of the Holy Spirit, not of man (1 Cor. 12:13). There can be no spiritual unity whatsoever between those who believe the Gospel and those who do not.

One of the greatest dangers to Christianity today is the deliberate suppression of biblical truth for the sake of unity. The danger intensifies as we see many highly visible and influential Christians jumping on the Vatican's ecumenical bandwagon. Instead of warning believers that this false unity is the emergence of the "last days" apostate church, evangelicals are embracing and applauding those who are engineering it. Instead of obeying biblical exhortations to keep the gospel pure, they are tolerating those who preach another gospel (Gal. 1:6-9). Rather than being sanctified by the truth, they are joining hands with unbelievers (Jn. 17:17). Rather than hating everything false, they are tolerating doctrines of demons and counterfeit gospels (Ps. 119:104, 128). Instead of exposing and naming the agents of compromise, they are enduring them (Eph. 5:11; 2 Tim. 1-4). Following are several examples...

"It's time for Protestants to go to the shepherd [the Pope] and say, 'What do we have to do to come home?'"[13]

—Robert Schuller, televangelist

"I'm eradicating the word Protestant even out of my vocabulary...[it's] time for Catholics and non-Catholics to come together as one in the Spirit and one in the Lord."[14]

—Paul Crouch, president of TBN

In 1995, religious broadcaster Pat Robertson said his meeting with His Holiness Pope John Paul II was 'very warm' and, through a personal letter hand-delivered to the Pontiff, pledged to work for Christian unity between Evangelicals and Catholics.

SAME STORY, DIFFERENT VERSE

When Rome attempted to re-unite Catholics and Protestants in Germany in 1541, Martin Luther warned the believers. "Popish writers pretend that they have always taught, what we now teach, concerning faith and good works, and that they are unjustly accused of the contrary, thus the wolf puts on the sheep skin till he gains admission in the fold."

We must heed the warning of another great preacher, C. H. Spurgeon in April 1868, concerning unity with the Roman Catholic Church. "There is a deep and indelible sentence of damnation written upon the apostate church...the curse is registered in heaven...its infamy is engraven in the rock for ever...followers of Jesus, for their own sake as well as for their Lord's, should oppose it with all their might."

WHAT ARE CHRISTIANS TO DO?

The Bible exhorts us search the Word of God for wisdom, understanding, and discernment (Prov. 2). We are to test every teaching. *Examine everything carefully; hold fast to that which is good* (1 Thes. 5:21). We are warned not to believe every spirit because many false prophets have gone out into the world. Only by using God's Word can we discern the Spirit of Truth from the spirit of error (1 Jn. 4:1, 6). We are to be like the Bereans who examined the Scriptures daily to verify the truthfulness of the Apostle Paul's teachings (Acts 17:11). Since an apostle who wrote over half the New Testament was tested, it stands to reason everyone's teaching must be examined in the light of God's Holy Word.

What are we to do with the false teachers within Christendom? We are to expose their false teachings and refrain from participating in their endeavors (Eph. 5:6, 11). With gentleness, we are to correct those who are in error in hopes that God may grant them repentance leading to the truth (2 Tim. 2:25). Those who *profess to know God but by their deeds they deny Him* must be exposed and silenced so others will not be deceived (Tit. 1:9-16). We are commanded to separate from those who persist in false teaching (Rom. 16:17; Tit. 3:10). For some, this may mean finding another church. For others, it may mean withholding support from ministries that continue to compromise the Gospel. The apostles warned us that if we do not separate from false teachers we could be disqualified for service, become identified with them and their error, and risk being partakers of their fate (2 Tim. 2:20; 2 Jn. 10, 11; Jude 11-13).

As end time deception increases and more people are led into apostasy, we must contend fervently for the faith that was once delivered to the saints (Jude 3). As more Christian leaders seek the approval of men rather than the approval of God, the way of truth will become more narrow and less traveled. Those who remain on it will face persecution for refusing to compromise the Gospel (2 Tim. 2:12). They will be accused of being intolerant, unloving and narrow-minded.

As the ecumenical movement grows in popularity within the church, maintaining doctrinal purity will be an unpopular position to pursue. Yet it is indeed what we are called to do! By pointing out false doctrine and practices, we will be good servants of Christ Jesus as we are nourished by His Word and sound doctrine (1 Tim. 4:6). Upholding truth can, and will be divisive within the church, but division is not always bad. Sometimes it is necessary to show which ones are approved of God (1 Cor. 11:19). When we "know doctrine" we will "know division" but when there is "no doctrine" there will be "no division."

Often times those who contend for the purity of the Gospel are criticized for quibbling over things that do not appear to be significant. However, contenders for the faith realize that the most dangerous lie is the lie that most closely resembles the truth. Conversely, ecumenists consider anything that appears close to the truth as an opportunity for unity. Thus they embrace the false gospel of Roman Catholicism because it is the cleverest of all Christian counterfeits.

The church today is suffering from a lack of discernment because many of its leaders are teaching partial truths and tolerating doctrinal error. Paul rebuked those who tolerated this is the first century church. In these days of apostasy, the church needs Christians who will boldly and courageously proclaim the whole counsel of God and expose as error everything that opposes it. Christians need to seek God for the grace, power, discernment and courage to be contenders for the faith.

THE CHURCH MUST BE WARNED

Amazingly, we seldom hear warnings against apostasy from our churches. Rarely are false teachers exposed who lead people away from the true faith. These apostates are appearing as ministers of righteousness and are facing very little opposition. They successfully deceive the undiscerning because pastors and church leaders are not speaking out against them. Very few Christians are warning the church of these ferocious wolves dressed in sheep's clothing. The twenty-first century church needs strong leaders like the apostle Paul. He warned the early church, "even from your own number men will arise and distort the truth in order to draw away disciples after them. So be on your guard! Remember that for three years I never stopped warning each of you night and day with tears" (Acts 20:30, 31). Throughout the Scriptures we are exhorted to test every spirit, every teacher and every doctrine because men are so easily deceived.

As the ecumenical unity movement gathers momentum, we must be strong and continue to contend for the faith, no matter what others might do or say. Let us pray for our evangelical leaders to return to the authority of Scripture for every issue of faith. Let us use God's Word to lovingly admonish any church leader who encourages unity with apostates or unbelievers. And finally, let us resist the pressure to participate in any activity or event that will deliberately suppress or compromise biblical truth for the sake of unity. We must return to the infallible, inerrant and inspired Word of God to heed its warnings and obey its commands.

Chapter 14

THE KINGDOM OF ANTICHRIST

DAVID BENOIT

In this chapter, I will address the characteristics of the kingdom of the Antichrist when he comes forward upon the world scene. Whereas Jesus taught His disciples to pray, "Thy kingdom come, thy will be done on earth as it is in Heaven," the Satanic version of that prayer may state, "Satan's kingdom come, his will be done on earth totally contrary to heaven." This prayer will be answered during the Tribulation period. We will now examine the kingdom of Antichrist that will come.

THE NATURE OF THE ANTICHRIST

He will be a humanist: *And the king shall do according to his will; and he shall exalt himself, and magnify himself above every god, and shall speak marvelous things against the God of gods* (Dan. 11:36a).

He will prosper for a while: *...and shall prosper till the indignation be accomplished: for that that is determined shall be done* (Dan. 11:36b). Some prophecy teachers believe the Antichrist will be Jewish, since the following verse reads, *neither shall he regard the God of his fathers* (Dan. 11:37a).

He will probably be a homosexual: *neither shall he regard...the desire of women* (Dan. 11:37b). One version of the Bible translates this verse to read that he is not desired of women. I have never known a powerful man to have problems attracting women. There are millions of women who could overlook the outward appearance of a man solely for the power they may gain from him.

He will be a blasphemer: *neither shall he...regard any god: for he shall magnify himself above all* (Dan. 11:37c).

He will honor the forces of witchcraft: *But in his estate shall he honor the God of forces: and a god whom his fathers knew not shall he honor with gold, and silver, and with precious stones, and pleasant things* (Dan. 11:38). Witches and occultists do not pray to the devil. The Devil is a biblical term and witches and occultists do not adhere to the teachings of the Bible. They pray to the forces of earth, air, water, fire, and spirit (the elementals).

He will be a divider, yet he will receive great approval ratings: *Thus shall he do in the most strong holds with a strange god, whom he shall acknowledge and increase with glory: and he shall cause them to rule over many, and shall divide the land for gain* (Dan. 11:39).

He will tax people universally under his plan: *Then shall stand up in his estate a raiser of taxes in the glory of the kingdom: but within few days he shall be destroyed, neither in anger, nor in battle* (Dan. 11:20).

He will win his battles as a great negotiator: *And in his estate shall stand up a vile person, to whom they shall not give the honor of the kingdom: but he shall come in peaceably, and obtain the kingdom by flatteries* (Dan. 11:21). *And I saw, and behold a white horse: and he that sat on him had a bow; and a crown was given unto him: and he went forth conquering, and to conquer* (Rev. 6:2).

THE NATURE OF THE FALSE PROPHET

The second most important person in the kingdom of the Antichrist will be the false prophet. It will now be important to examine the nature of this coming religious leader and his part in the kingdom of the Antichrist.

Although it has been said, "Religion and politics do not mix," we will see that such a statement is misinformed. Throughout the Bible, we find examples of religion and politics walking hand in hand. In certain circumstances, kings followed God and were led by prophets of God. In other circumstances, the wicked kings surrounded themselves with false prophets. For example, the Pharaohs of Egypt had spiritual leaders (Gen. 41:8; Exod. 7:11), Nebuchadnezzar had his spiritual advisors (Dan. 2:2, 27; 4:7), King Ahab surrounded himself with the prophets of Baal and even married Jezebel, whose name means, "Baal exalts," (cf. 1 Kgs. 18:19, 20), King Saul had Samuel as an advisor, King David had Nathan as an advisor, the high priest Caiaphas placed pressure on the government to crucify Jesus, former President Clinton listened to Jessie Jackson and Tony Campola, President Bush has Billy Graham and other Christian leaders around him for spiritual advice, and even Osama bin Laden surrounded himself with spiritual advisors. In like manner, the Antichrist will have a spiritual sidekick who is simply called False Prophet. Therefore, another purpose for this chapter is to expose the coming religious organization, its leader, and the groundwork for this system that is now in operation.

During the Tribulation period there will be an unholy trinity established; the Devil will create this unholy force. This satanic trinity will be in accordance to the manner in which Satan does things since he is a counterfeiter.

The Dragon, Satan

The Beast, or Antichrist   **The False Prophet**

The workings of the satanic trinity are quite simple. Satan will empower the Antichrist. The Antichrist will engulf the people. The False Prophet will enlighten the people to worship the beast. Revelation 16:13, 14 reveals the unity of these three entities: *And I saw three unclean spirits like frogs come out of the mouth of the dragon, and out of the mouth of the beast, and out of the mouth of the false prophet. For they are the spirits of devils, working miracles, which go forth unto the kings of the earth and of the whole world, to gather them to the battle of that great day of God Almighty.*

In order to be faithful to the interpretation of the Word of God, we understand that these are three unclean spirits likened to frogs. To understand this passage, you must understand the relationship of the frog to pagan worship.

The frog goddess, Hekt, was worshipped in Egypt (the only species of frog existing in Palestine is the green frog, *Rana esculenta*, the well-known edible frog of the continent). Every September, the Nile River would overflow its banks and this would produce an overabundance of frogs. The Egyptians loved to hear the sounds of the frogs; we might call them the 'praise and worship team' for the gods and goddesses who would bless them with the water they would need to produce a harvest for the following year. The Egyptians believed that the frog was a symbol of life. The second plague God unleashed on the Egyptians was against the goddess, Hekt (cf. Exod. 8:1-14). The frogs may be a revealing factor of understanding the unholy trinity.

Frogs were unclean. (the Hebrew word, *tsepharde'a*, simply means a "marsh-leaper"). The frogs would emerge from the mud and mire of the river. They would emerge, as the banks of the Nile would overflow. The influence of the unholy trinity will emerge from the mire of the decadency of man. They will emerge from the overflowing boundaries of sin. They will come to power by the total depravity of man. It is from the mud you find diseases and sickness. The world will be diseased by the sins of humanity.

Frogs represented life. The goddess, Hekt, was said to be the giver of life. She was allegedly responsible for breathing the breath of life into man. Christians understand the truth of the breath of life as follows: *And the LORD God formed man of the dust of the ground, and breathed into his nostrils the breath of life; and man became a living soul* (Gen. 2:7).

Have you ever wondered why people die? The doctor's report may reveal that the cause of death is a heart attack, brain tumor, etc. But why do people die? There are life support machines that imitate all of the body's functions, yet the person is still dead. The answer to the question is quite simple—a person dies because the breath of life has departed. Again, we find that Satan is the great impostor. *And I saw one of his heads as it were wounded to death; and his deadly wound was healed: and all the world wondered after the beast. And they worshipped the dragon which gave power unto the beast: and they worshipped the beast, saying, Who is like unto the beast? Who is able to make war with him?* (Rev. 13:3, 4). This false resurrection produces what Satan has always desired – to be worshipped. It will be refreshing for a world filled with death, since it will be during this time the world will find a life giver. The irony of this is that during the Tribulation period there will be a five-month period when those desiring to die will be unable. *And in those days shall men seek death, and shall not find it; and shall desire to die, and death shall flee from them* (Rev. 9:6). As a child, I watched the *Night of the Living Dead* and had nightmares for weeks. This will not be a bad dream, or a Hollywood production; rather it will be reality for those who dwell upon the earth.

Frogs undergo a unique transformation. They begin as tadpoles and metamorphosis into frogs. Their change is a noticeable transformation. They start with a tail and no legs appearing perfectly adapted to the water in which they live. Later, the tail shortens and legs appear giving them the appearance of a land animal. This gradual process is readily observed. In like manner, there will be a noticeable transformation of the Antichrist.

The Antichrist will begin his reign as a peacemaker, but later comes the transformation into a warrior. He will begin as a provider and transform into a destroyer. He will appear as one loved by all prior to his metamorphosis but afterward, he will be someone who is greatly feared. The transformation will be slow yet noticeable, just as is the tadpole's alteration. He will transform right before the people's eyes. Transformation is not a new trick for the devil since he has used this technique throughout the centuries. Second Corinthians 11:13-15 make a clear statement of this fact: *For such are false apostles, deceitful workers, transforming themselves into the apostles of Christ. And no marvel; for Satan himself is transformed into an angel of light. Therefore it is no great thing if his ministers also be transformed as the ministers of righteousness; whose end shall be according to their works.*

Frogs represented praise and worship. The singing of these frogs was like a mass choir who sang praises to the gods and goddesses. They would all sing in perfect unison. This will again happen during the Tribulation period. The False Prophet will lead the entire world into praise and worship of the coming ruler who will proclaim himself as god. This brings us to the heart of this chapter, as we key into the life and ministry of the third part of the unholy trinity, that is, the False Prophet. He will impersonate the Holy Spirit whose restraining ministry through the church will have ceased at this point (2 Thess. 2:6, 7).

IDENTIFYING CHARACTERISTICS OF FALSE PROPHETS

Jeremiah 23:14 gives a basic description of false prophets. *I have seen also in the prophets of Jerusalem an horrible thing: they commit adultery* [they are sexually impure], *and walk in lies: they strengthen also the hands of evildoers* [they work together with the wicked], *that none doth return from his wickedness* [they lead people into a lack of repentance], *they are all of them unto me as Sodom, and the inhabitants thereof as Gomorrah.*

We can also deduce eleven characteristics for identifying false prophets. First, they will promote self-gratification instead of God-glorification. *Thus saith the LORD of hosts, Hearken not unto the words of the prophets that prophesy unto you: they make you vain* (Jer. 23:16a). Second, their message is out of their own heart and not from God. *They speak a vision of their own heart, and not out of the mouth of the LORD* (Jer. 16b). Third, their message is always that God will not judge sin. *They say still unto them that despise me, The LORD hath said, Ye shall have peace; and they say unto every one that walketh after the imagination of his own heart, No evil shall come upon you.* The Devil in the garden told Eve that God would not punish her for her disobedience (Jer. 23:17). *And the serpent said unto the woman, Ye shall not surely die* (Gen. 3:4).

Fourth, their message is *for* profit not *by a* prophet. *The heads thereof judge for reward, and the priests thereof teach for hire, and the prophets thereof divine for money: yet will they lean upon the LORD, and say, Is not the LORD among us? None evil can come upon us* (Mic. 3:11). This does not mean that a true prophet must be poor, but it is to say that a true prophet is not motivated by profit. I am an evangelist who for nearly twenty years has traveled from church to church based on a love offering, and God has always met my needs. This does not mean I find fault with those who charge fees. There are some great men and women of God who have to guard their time; therefore, they must set a fee. The fee is not what motivates them; rather it is a way to protect their time. The rewards of mammon, not the blessing of God, motivate a false prophet.

Fifth, they always work better undercover. *Beware of false prophets, which come to you in sheep's clothing, but inwardly they are ravening wolves* (Mt. 7:15). The wolf is crafty and preys mainly on the helpless. While I was preaching in Alaska, I had a chance to accompany a wolf trapper. He said he had to trap the wolves because they prey on the young helpless moose calves. Wolves have been known to backtrack on a man and attack him. Wolves travel in packs and work together for the kill. In the same manner, the false prophets will network together to make sure they have the power to overcome the weak and spiritually helpless. Wolves have even been known to gnaw their own leg off in order to free themselves. If they show no mercy on themselves, do not expect them to show mercy on their prey.

Sixth, they are foolish foxes faking the fold. *Thus saith the Lord GOD; Woe unto the foolish prophets, that follow their own spirit, and have seen nothing! O Israel, thy prophets are like the foxes in the deserts* (Ezek. 13:3, 4). The fox is a burrowing animal that has the ability to destroy the vineyard. They also desire the taste of the young, vine ripe grapes. The fox can be a genuine pest to a vineyard keeper. It is the same with a false prophet for they will burrow their way into the vineyard of God and try to feast off the tender, ripe fruit.

Seventh, they are like the wind that spread bad seeds. *And the prophets shall become wind, and the word is not in them: thus shall it be done unto them* (Jer. 5:13). You cannot see the wind, but you can certainly feel the effects of the wind. You may not be aware of the origin of its power, but you can see the effects after a storm has passed. Bad seeds of doctrine are today flying here and there on the winds produced by false prophets. *But there were false prophets also among the people, even as there shall be false teachers among you, who privily shall bring in damnable heresies, even denying the Lord that bought them, and bring upon themselves swift destruction* (2 Pet. 2:1).

Eighth, their dreams are from the prophet, not from God. *Behold, I am against them that prophesy false dreams, saith the LORD, and do tell them, and cause my people to err by their lies, and by their lightness; yet I sent them not, nor commanded them: therefore they shall not profit this people at all, saith the LORD* (Jer. 23:32). Some dreams are produced by pepperoni pizza, not the power of God. Joseph Smith was a false prophet of the Mormon Church and his claims of visions from God have led millions into false doctrine.

Ninth, they have a form of godliness. There is a form of godliness that is not godliness whatsoever; it is a cheap imitation. I have often said, "I have never seen a church destroyed by a drunkard."

What I mean is that leadership posing as a godly person who appears to have the best interest of the congregation splits; they lead a rebellion against the pastor or the authority of the church. The Scripture clearly warns us in 2 Timothy 3:5 of this kind of person: *Having a form of godliness, but denying the power thereof: from such turn away.* You must understand that it takes a very dedicated, religious person to deceive truly, godly people.

Tenth, their goal is to cause God's people to forget His name. *How long shall this be in the heart of the prophets that prophesy lies? Yea, they are prophets of the deceit of their own heart; Which think to cause my people to forget my name by their dreams which they tell every man to his neighbor, as their fathers have forgotten my name for Baal* (Jer. 23:26, 27). How many times God led the children of Israel out of bondage only to have false prophets give the victory to false deities. On one occasion, God delivered the Israelites out of the Egyptian bondage only to have the people build a golden calf while Moses was on Mt. Sinai receiving the covenant of God with the Israelites.

Eleventh, false prophets are never 100% accurate. *But the prophet, which shall presume to speak a word in my name, which I have not commanded him to speak, or that shall speak in the name of other gods, even that prophet shall die. And if thou say in thine heart, How shall we know the word which the LORD hath not spoken? When a prophet speaketh in the name of the LORD, if the thing follow not, nor come to pass, that is the thing which the LORD hath not spoken, but the prophet hath spoken it presumptuously: thou shalt not be afraid of him:* (Deut. 18:20-22). There are many so-called "prophets" that make prophecies over people in our churches today. Some of these may be true but some predictions never happen. Under the Mosaic Law, they would be put to death. For someone to say, "thus says the Lord" was a serious matter back then. It carried a stiff penalty for those who spoke presumptuously. The Apostle John reiterates this point: *Beloved, believe not every spirit, but try the spirits whether they are of God: because many false prophets are gone out into the world. Hereby know ye the Spirit of God: Every spirit that confesseth that Jesus Christ is come in the flesh is of God: And every spirit that confesseth not that Jesus*

Christ is come in the flesh is not of God: and this is that spirit of antichrist, whereof ye have heard that it should come; and even now already is it in the world (1 Jn. 4:1-3).

THE IMITATION OF THE FALSE PROPHET

As previously mentioned, the False Prophet is a counterfeiter of the third Person of the trinity. For instance, consider the following five contrasts.

Contrast 1

The Holy Spirit leads the world in truth. Without the influence of the Holy Spirit, there would be no truth. *Howbeit when he, the Spirit of truth, is come, he will guide you into all truth* (Jn. 16: 13a). The Holy Spirit does not guide you in some truth, partial truth, or half-truth. He guides you in all truth.

The False Prophet leads the world by lies. *And deceiveth them that dwell on the earth by the means of those miracles which he had power to do in the sight of the beast; saying to them that dwell on the earth, that they should make an image to the beast, which had the wound by a sword, and did live* (Rev. 13:14). It has been said that George Washington could not tell a lie. This may sound noble but actually, this very statement has no truth. Lying is a part of the make-up of man. *Ye are of your father the devil, and the lusts of your father ye will do. He was a murderer from the beginning, and abode not in the truth, because there is no truth in him. When he speaketh a lie, he speaketh of his own: for he is a liar, and the father of it. And because I tell you the truth, ye believe me not* (Jn. 8:44, 45). God despises lying (Prov. 12:22). Lying hinders your prayer life (Isa. 59:2, 3).

Contrast 2

The Holy Spirit gives glory to Christ. *He shall glorify me: for he shall receive of mine, and shall shew it unto you* (Jn. 16:14). The Holy Spirit's role has never been to bring glory and honor to Himself.

The False Prophet will give glory to the Antichrist. The False Prophet will create a worldwide effort to worship the Antichrist. *And he exerciseth all the power of the first beast before him, and causeth the earth and them which dwell therein to worship the first beast, whose deadly wound was healed* (Rev. 13.12). People naturally associate miracles with God. False messiahs often use miracles to turn people toward false gods. People have a tendency to worship the miracle worker instead of the one true God. If Jesus wanted to gather a following, He could have used miracles to do it; instead, He always used the miracles to draw attention to the Heavenly Father. Clearly, the False Prophet will use miracles to bring glory to the Antichrist. *And deceiveth them that dwell on the earth by the means of those miracles which he had power to do in the sight of the beast; saying to them that dwell on the earth, that they should make an image to the beast, which had the wound by a sword, and did live* (Rev. 13:14).

Contrast 3

The Holy Spirit made fire come down from Heaven at the Day of Pentecost. *And suddenly there came a sound from heaven as of a rushing mighty wind, and it filled all the house where they were sitting. And there appeared unto them cloven tongues like as of fire, and it sat upon each of them* (Acts 2:2, 3).

The False Prophet will call down fire from Heaven. *And he doeth great wonders, so that he maketh fire come down from heaven on the earth in the sight of men* (Rev. 13:13). The False Prophet will make sure that men will see his miracles; however, we know that he will use the miracles for deception.

Contrast 4

The Holy Spirit is the life giver. *For the law of the Spirit of life in Christ Jesus hath made me free from the law of sin and death* (Rom. 8:2).

The False Prophet will be a life taker. *And he had power to give life unto the image of the beast, that the image of the beast should both speak, and cause that as many as would not worship the image of the beast should be killed* (Rev. 13:15).

Contrast 5

Christians are sealed today by the Holy Spirit. *In whom ye also trusted, after that ye heard the word of truth, the gospel of your salvation: in whom also after that ye believed, ye were sealed with that Holy Spirit of promise* (Eph. 1:13). *Who hath also sealed us, and given the earnest of the Spirit in our hearts* (2 Cor. 1:22). *And grieve not the Holy Spirit of God, whereby ye are sealed unto the day of redemption* (Eph. 4:30). *And I saw another angel ascending from the east, having the seal of the living God: and he cried with a loud voice to the four angels, to whom it was given to hurt the earth and the sea, Saying, Hurt not the earth, neither the sea, nor the trees, till we have sealed the servants of our God in their foreheads* (Rev. 7:2, 3). The seal is important because it is a conformation of authenticity. It could also be a proof of ownership.

The False Prophet will demand that his converts are sealed. *And he causeth all, both small and great, rich and poor, free and bond, to receive a mark in their right hand, or in their foreheads: And that no man might buy or sell, save he that had the mark, or the name of the beast, or the number of his name* (Rev. 13:16, 17). The False Prophet will not request that a seal confirm his followers; he will demand it with a penalty of death to those who will not receive the seal.

THE INTERFAITH OF THE FALSE PROPHET

The basic doctrine of the False Prophet needs to be addressed in order for us to see how his influence is already at work today. He will have a universal message to attract a universal audience. Mystery Babylon will be the platform upon which the False Prophet will stand. His religious views will rise from Babylonian paganism. The doctrines will be both seductive and demonic. *Now the Spirit speaketh expressly, that in the latter times some shall depart from the faith, giving heed to seducing spirits, and doctrines of devils* (1 Tim. 4:1).

Identifying doctrines of demons can sometimes be difficult since they are often well camouflaged. Satan is the master of guerilla warfare. In the same manner that terrorists take refuge in highly populated, civilian areas and use innocent people as shields, demonic doctrine always surrounds itself with good doctrine or good intent. Demonic doctrines always start with the perversion of the three basic questions of life. Who am I? Where did I come from? Where am I going? We need to examine these three basic questions in the light of demonic doctrine.

The first basic question is: "Who am I?" It is because man was created in the image of God that Satan seeks to distort that identity. A quick look at Genesis 1:26, 27 provides a perfect example of the distortion of truth. *And God said, Let us make man in our image, after our likeness: and let them have dominion over the fish of the sea, and over the fowl of the air, and over the cattle, and over all the earth, and over every creeping thing that creepeth upon the earth. So God created man in his own image, in the image of God created he him; male and female created he them.*

The demonic view of the above passage would state something like the following: "We are all gods." The New Age Movement has ministers such as Shirley MacLaine who claim they are god. Furthermore, they claim that we are all gods and we only need to realize this truth. The belief that humanity is divine forms the basis for self-realization.

There are those who believe that the Genesis passage refers to the sexuality of God. For example, a man attending a seminar that I was holding in Wisconsin stood up and claimed that the Bible taught God is part male and part female. The man argued this proved that goddess worship was a part of the Christian faith. He even claimed that God created man in his own image, male and female, so that God must not only be a god but part goddess as well. This is a tremendous perversion of Scripture. Genesis 1:26, 27 have nothing to do with gender; it testifies of the holiness of God. Both men and women were created holy in the image of God. In order to understand who we are, we must understand who God is.

The second basic question is: "Where did I come from?" Evolution is not a science; it is a faith. Faith in evolution is taught as a fact worldwide. In his book *Algeny*, Jeremy Rifkin states clearly the necessity of protecting this lie.

> Evolutionary theory has been enshrined as the center-piece of our educational system, and elaborate walls have been erected around it to protect it from unnecessary abuse.[1]
>
> We no longer feel ourselves to be guests in someone else's home and therefore obliged to make our behavior conform with a set of pre-existing cosmic rules. It is our creation now. We make the rules. We establish the parameters of reality. We create the world, and because we do, we no longer feel beholden to outside forces. We no longer have to justify our behavior, for we are now the architects of the universe. We are responsible to nothing outside ourselves, for we are the kingdom, the power, and the glory forever and ever.[2]

Evolution has a twofold purpose: to confuse people about their origin and to deny the existence of a Creator. This confusion will lead to lawlessness, which will be the standard of life in the Antichrist's kingdom.

The third basic question is: "Where do I go when I die?" Without a God in their system of belief, the Antichrist and the False Prophet will have to produce an eternal lie. The New Age Movement explains death by reincarnation. The atheist explains death by ceasing to exist. The religionist will explain to the masses that God is a loving God only and will never punish sin.

The above three lies will be sufficient to deceive billions who will be lost for eternity. It will be so intoxicating that the whole world will be drunken by its influence. The universality of Babylon's influence is something that even astounded the prophet Jeremiah. *How is Sheshach taken! And how is the praise of the whole earth surprised! How is Babylon become an astonishment among the nations!* (Jer. 51:41).

Sheshach is another name for Babylon. It means "thy fine linen." Apparently, it is derived from the goddess "Shach." The counsel of Scripture follows:

Flee out of the midst of Babylon, and deliver every man his soul: be not cut off in her iniquity; for this is the time of the LORD's vengeance; he will render unto her a recompense. Babylon hath been a golden cup in the LORD's hand, that made all the earth drunken: the nations have drunken of her wine; therefore the nations are mad. Babylon is suddenly fallen and destroyed: howl for her; take balm for her pain, if so be she may be healed. We would have healed Babylon, but she is not healed: forsake her, and let us go every one into his own country: for her judgment reacheth unto heaven, and is lifted up even to the skies (Jer. 51:6-9).

Chapter 15

STORIES GIVEN FROM THE KING

MIKE STALLARD

When one reads the parables of the mystery of the kingdom of heaven given by Jesus in the thirteenth chapter of the Gospel of Matthew, one immediately senses a majestic air to this teaching of Christ.[1] However, the Bible student also discerns that a mere casual reading of theses stories from the King will not uncover all there is to know. In fact, it is tempting to believe that the disciples lied when they told Jesus that they understood all that He had said (13:51, 52)![2] Nonetheless, a proper awareness of background issues of interpretation along with a rather straightforward reading of the text will yield a comprehension of the passage that is available, not just to the technical experts in biblical studies, but also to the average Christian in the world who contemplates these remarkable words of Jesus.[3]

THE INTERPRETATION OF PARABLES IN GENERAL

A parable can be defined as "a figurative narrative that is true to life and is designed to convey through analogy some specific spiritual truth(s) usually relative to God's kingdom program."[4] The most significant issue in the interpretation of parables in general is the analysis of the structure and details of the parable and the identification of the central truth of the parable and its relationship to the kingdom. The pendulum swings between the view that says the details of the parable are unimportant (so we must focus on the big idea of the parable) and the position that the minutest details are significant. The last opinion has been rejected largely because of those who, following the historical example of the early Church Fathers, have used the details as a launching pad to do subjective allegorical interpretation based upon the interpreter's whim.[5] The first view, however, has the unfortunate plight of being contrary to the way that Jesus interpreted parables whenever they were interpreted (e.g., the parable of the sower, parable of the tares). In all cases, he attaches specific meaning to the details. This is in fact the historic approach of the Church in interpreting the parables.[6] The real mistake in using the details to interpret a parable has not been the attempt to understand the minutiae but to divorce the enterprise from the whole of the parable or from the whole of the context, whether with respect to a cluster of parables or to the biblical theology of the book in which the parable exists. The interpreter should seek to do justice to *both* the details *and* the big idea of the parable.[7]

THE STRUCTURE OF MATTHEW 13:3-52

What Matthew 13 provides is a cluster of eight parables with some (the first two) interpreted by Jesus and some stated without interpretation. Furthermore, the *first* and *last* parables, the parable of the sower and the parable of the householder, respectively, serve as **bookends** to identify the general ideas of the entire cluster and to tie the cluster to the ongoing argument of the entire book of

Matthew.[8] The two main points here are the rejection of Jesus by the leaders of Israel and the subsequent development of something new in the transition from the focus on the Jews to the focus on Gentiles. The other parables flesh out more details with respect to these general themes. The following diagram serves as a visual aid to understanding the structure of these parables:

1	The Sower (vv. 3-23)			
2		The Tares (vv. 24-30)		*Spoken to the Multitudes*
3			The Mustard Seed (vv. 31-32)	
4			The Leaven (v. 33)	
Interpretation of the Parable of the Tares Given to the Disciples (vv. 36-43)				
5			The Hidden Treasure (v. 44)	
6			The Costly Pearl (vv. 45-46)	*Spoken to the Disciples*
7		The Dragnet (vv. 47-50)		
8	The Householder (vv. 51-52)			

One issue of structure involves the grouping of the parables within the cluster. It has already been suggested that the first and eighth parables go together as bookends to the entire sequence. How should the structure of the middle six parables be understood? Parables two, three, and four are all prefaced with a statement that Jesus was speaking another parable (vv. 24, 31, 33). Parables four, five, and six are not introduced in such a manner. More significantly, the first three in this sequence are spoken to the multitudes (v. 34). The last three are declared to the disciples.

Another issue of structure is whether the second and seventh parables in the cluster (tares along with the dragnet) are to be grouped together. What makes the possibility attractive is the mention of the "end of the age" with respect to both of those parables and nowhere else in the cluster (v. 40—interpretation of the tares, v. 49). The imagery of fire is also present in both (vv. 30, 42, 50) as is the end-time picture of angels harvesting the wicked out from among the righteous (vv. 39-41, 49). This does not mean that there are no differences. The wheat-and-tares parable does not seem to emphasize in any direct way the gathering of "every kind" as does the dragnet parable. However, both make essentially the same point, although in one the primary image used is tares while in the other the analogy is fish.

Perhaps the most important fact about structure is that in the middle of all of the parables stands the interpretation of the parable of the wheat and the tares (vv. 36-43). In light of the presence of some chiastic elements in the cluster of parables and that often the centrally located element of any chiasm is what is being highlighted, the central location of the interpretation of the parable of the tares within Matthew 13:3-52 takes on added weight. If this analysis is correct, what features in the wheat-and-tares parable would be the chief focus of Jesus in Matthew's presentation?

First, it highlights the transition from the multitudes to the disciples in Jesus' explanations. What Jesus had explained earlier in the parable of the sower as a general principle now is the direct experience of the disciples as they alone hear the interpretation of the wheat-and-tares parable and the remaining parables in the cluster. This is in keeping with the larger development in Matthew's narrative concerning the shift away from ministry specifically centered on Israel (e.g., Mt. 10:5, 6) to a different focal point.

Second, the centrality of the interpretation of the wheat-and-tares parable in Matthew 13 causes one to focus on God's judgment of the wicked and the rewarding of the righteous at the end of the age. What may be essential in this is the message that the Pharisees and rulers of the Jews had rejected Christ and were among the tares or weeds similar to wheat in appearance. Yet they would not make it while other "sons of the kingdom," genuine followers of Christ, would enter into the rewards of the kingdom. That is, this parable gives continued explanation to the theme of surprise that is current throughout the book of Matthew.[9]

THE PARABLE OF THE SOWER

At the outset Jesus is speaking to the multitudes when he teaches about the sower of seed (v. 2). The text also states at the beginning that Jesus was speaking in parables (v. 3). Although in comparison to other Gospels, Jesus had used the parabolic form earlier in his ministry, this is the first occasion that Matthew mentions this form of teaching.[10] Throughout the chapter, the reason for Jesus' use of this style of presentation is clear. With respect to the interpretation of the parable of the sower, Jesus states plainly that its design was two-fold: to reveal new understanding to His true followers and to hide truth from those who rejected Him (vv. 10-17).

The fact that Christ is giving new understanding to His disciples is based upon two lines of thought. First, Jesus says that the disciples are allowed to know "the mysteries of the kingdom of heaven." Although there is a great deal of variance concerning the exact content of the mystery Jesus speaks of, most scholars agree that the word is "not necessarily a reference to a truth difficult to understand, but rather to truths that can be understood only on the basis of divine revelation."[11]

The second line of evidence, which suggests that Jesus is revealing new truth and understanding to the disciples, comes from two occasions later in the passage. Jesus, after announcing the three parables of the tares, mustard seed, and leaven, quotes Psalm 78:2: *I will utter things hidden since the foundation of the world.* Immediately, he leaves the multitudes and "explains" the parable of the tares to the disciples only. The overall structure of the chapter seems to reinforce the notion that this is a shift that is part of the overall message of the parables of the kingdom. The second confirmation of this parabolic purpose to reveal new truth to the disciples comes when, right before the last parable (householder), Jesus' question about the disciples' understanding, along with their conscious affirmation of it, leads to the summary statement about the scribe who apparently possesses both the old and new (vv. 51, 52). It is hard to escape the conclusion that such a scribe understands the new revelation that Jesus is giving. In summary, the following progression may be seen: (1) Jesus begins by using a parable to hide the truth from those who reject Him and to reveal something new to His followers (part of the interpretation of the parable of the sower); (2) Jesus uses parables to provide opportunity to explain new truth to the disciples (part of the interpretation of the parable of the wheat and the tares given mid-way through the cluster of parables); (3) Jesus ends by using a parable to demonstrate the kind of person who understands both the old truth and the new truth (parable of the householder).

The actual content of the parable of the sower is the well-known picture of a man sowing seed in four diverse situations: by the side of the road, on rocky places, among thorns, and on the good soil. Much debate has occurred about which ones of these four occasions bring genuine eternal life. For example, while most would agree that the first category probably refers to those who never respond at all to God's message (i.e., the "lost"), there would be quite a range of opinions concerning whether the other occasions refer to "saved" followers of Jesus. However important such a determination is, it does not seem to be the case that this debate is what Jesus really had in mind as the main point of this section.

Jesus' interpretation of this parable affirms that the sown seed is the *word of the kingdom proclaimed* (v. 19). One can certainly say that a man or woman must respond to the gospel of eternal life with faith in Jesus to be part of God's kingdom. However, that is not the precise intent of Jesus' statement in this context. The kingdom must be clearly understood from the context of Matthew's entire Gospel. John the Baptist had preached it (Mt. 3:2). Jesus had declared that it was at hand (Mt. 4:17). The disciples had been sent out to proclaim its message (Mt. 10:7). The notion of kingdom that prevails throughout Matthew is that which occupied the Old Testament prophets – the literal, political, ethnic, national kingdom promised to the nation of Israel (e.g., Dan. 2, 7).[12] This eschatological kingdom is the one anticipated by Christ even after the shift that takes place in Matthew 13. The kingdom in view in all of Matthew, including chapter 13, is the eschatological kingdom of blessing when the nation will be restored.[13] Consequently, what is in view are the responses to the proclamation of that kingdom.

Jesus never identifies the sower in this parable. Since John the Baptist, Jesus, and the disciples had all proclaimed the message of the kingdom prior to this point in Matthew's Gospel, he probably means for it to be generalized. *Anyone* who sows the seed will get different responses. In light of the ongoing sowing that takes place in the following parable of the tares (vv. 24ff), a sowing that seemingly takes place until the "end of the age" (vv. 40, 41), it may be best to see direct application of the sowing in the present age until, and including, the events which mark the end-time tribulation events.

However, at this point, it is not entirely clear what it is that is *new* revelation to the disciples. Proclamation of the message of God's coming kingdom was an integral part of Old Testament teaching (e.g., Dan. 7-12; Amos 9:11ff). How can it be said to be new? The parameters for the answer are fleshed out in the other parables. What can be said at this point is that the flow of the narrative of Matthew has already provided the preliminary elements of an old/new dichotomy. On the one hand are many Jews (not all) who reject Christ, especially the national leaders. On the other hand are Gentiles who surprisingly gain acceptance into God's favor and/or kingdom. Such teachings in Matthew precede chapter 13 (8:5-13; 11:20-24; 12:21-41) as well as follow it (15:1-28; 21:23-32). Matthew 13 and its initial parable of the sower simply formalize God's intention to do some new work relative to the eschatological kingdom in light of the rejection of Christ by the nation of Israel.

In correlation to these factors, one must remember the nationalistic context that may be behind the parable, which is often obscured by the individualistic focus that is sometimes brought to the text. One example will suffice: "Therefore I say to you, the kingdom of God will be taken away from you, and be given to a nation producing the fruit of it. And he who falls on this stone will be broken to pieces; but on whomever it falls, it will scatter him like dust" (Mt. 21:43, 44). Here Jesus talks to Pharisees and chief priests as individuals. They get quite mad when they realize that He is talking about them in all of the parables (vv. 45, 46). Notice, however, that Jesus in pronouncing judgment upon them talks in a "nationalistic" way. His reference to the removal of the *kingdom* from them means that they would not be privileged to be part of it since they had rejected Him. That kingdom would be given to another nation.[14] Notice that this means that the kingdom would not be established for the entire current generation of Jews. What is the significance for the understanding of Matthew 13? In light of the fact that Matthew intertwines throughout his Gospel both individualistic and national truths with respect to the producing of fruit, the interpreter should not focus entirely on individual salvation in the text while ignoring the larger national ones also present in the context. Thus, the parable of the sower can be seen, in its possible connections to these other themes in Matthew, to highlight the fact that those who should have accepted the Messiah, i.e., the Jewish leaders, had denied Him, while many Gentiles would surprisingly accept Him and produce the fruit demonstrating their citizenship in the coming eschatological kingdom.

THE PARABLE OF THE TARES

The parable of the tares (Mt. 13:24-30) along with its interpretation (Mt. 13:36-43) is crucial to the overall theme of the chapter as the discussion about the structure of the cluster of parables showed. The phrase "the kingdom of heaven is like" is first used in this parable and introduces the next five parables in the sequence (vv. 24, 31, 33, 44, 45, 47). In each of these opening statements, there is a basic analogy in which a "kingdom" comparison is made to certain images and the statements made about them. It is important to realize that the language of the comparisons in the parables of the kingdom does not automatically force one to view the kingdom as co-extensive with the present Church Age.

First, one must understand that the entire parable, not just the introductory statement of comparison, is a description relative to the kingdom. As Toussaint notes, "these formulas do not mean that the kingdom of heaven is symbolized by the man, or the mustard seed, or leaven, or any other single object in the parables. It is simply used to introduce narrative which represents truth relative to the kingdom."[15] Thus, it is not necessary to take the image as, in fact, the picture of the kingdom itself.

Second, it is instructive that the first and eighth parables (sower and householder) do not use the comparison language in the same way, but do highlight the kingdom (see verses 19 & 52). This lends support to the idea that the focus is on facts that relate to the kingdom and that it is not essential to view the actions described in the parables as occurring during the time of the kingdom. Such a conclusion is strengthened if the chiastic structure presented in this chapter is accurate, since the unity of the parables would be heightened under such a scheme.

Most importantly, however, the actual details of the wheat-and-tares parable support the idea that the events described in the parable occur during a preparatory time to the kingdom and not the actual time of the kingdom itself. This is best seen in its correlation to the Olivet Discourse. According to the details of the parable, the Son of Man (Jesus) sows good seed (wheat) while the devil sows the tares or the wicked (vv. 37, 38). The "end of the age" marks the harvest performed by the angels, which results in the fiery judgment of the wicked and the reward of the righteous (vv. 39-43). The similarity of such language to the Olivet Discourse has already been noted. Yet the "end of the age" question of the Olivet Discourse (Mt. 24:3) seems tied to Jesus' responsive teaching about his own Second Coming (24:29-31) that also involves the use of angels in judgment. The judgment language, furthermore, uses the same descriptive elements including fire (25:30, 41; cp. 25:46). There is also the similar teaching on rewards in the Olivet Discourse (25:14-30).

Consequently, the similarities of the imagery in the wheat-and-tares parable of Matthew 13 to the Olivet Discourse are so clear that one is compelled to believe the time frame of the events which are described are also the same. Yet, the Second Coming is described in Matthew 24:29-31 using the language of Daniel 7:13, 14. That means that Matthew's understanding of the kingdom in the Olivet Discourse is the same as the Old Testament understanding of a restored national kingdom for Israel. Therefore, it is difficult to imagine the kingdom as understood in Matthew 13 to be any different. The parable of the tares explains to the disciples that, in spite of the rejection of Christ by the current leaders of Israel, the promises and expectations about the coming kingdom would be fulfilled as God had said. However, before that time comes, some other events will take place relative to and in preparation for that kingdom. It is these events and the time frame associated with it that is the mystery unknown in the past and now being revealed in the kingdom parables. The actual nature of the kingdom is not in view.

Another interpretive issue in the parable of the tares is the identification of the *sons of the kingdom.* Christ classifies these sons as the *good seed,* which are sown by the Son of Man or Christ Himself (Mt. 13:37, 38). However, in light of the scope of the entire parable, which extends to the end of the age, it is unlikely that this sowing should be limited to something that only Jesus has done. More likely, the message of Jesus, the *word* of the kingdom in the previous parable, produces followers who also sow the message. They in turn would produce followers who would continue the chain throughout the entire age as an extension of Christ's work.[16] This is in keeping with the previous missionary thrust the immediate disciples had been assigned (see Mt. 10) although it is being expanded. As Blomberg notes, "He [Christ] specifically identifies the farmer with himself...This suggests that a similar equation would be legitimate in the parable of the sower. But, derivatively, the farmers in both passages can stand for all who sow God's Word."[17] The message is similar to the parable of the sower although the imagery is slightly different (seed refers to the message rather than to people).

The use of the term *sons of the kingdom* occurs only one other place in Matthew although the word *son* is used almost eighty times.[18] The immediate sense that comes to mind is that the phrase refers to those "who belong to something," in this case, the kingdom.[19] However, to belong to the kingdom is to belong to the King. This seems to be in the foreground since the bad seed are referred to as sons of the devil (vv. 38, 39). Again, this should remind the interpreter of the context of the King's rejection so that His kingdom is taken away from the contemporary generation of Jews.

In summary, the parable of the tares suggests that Jesus, in light of the rejection of Him by the leaders of the nation of Israel, is teaching that the kingdom will not happen immediately. Instead, there will be a time of sowing in preparation for the future kingdom. Furthermore, the kingdom will be preceded by a pronouncement of judgment upon unbelievers and the rewards for the followers of

Christ, which takes place at the end of the present age. In the end, many kingdom citizens will be produced, who the Jews were not expecting.

THE PARABLES OF THE MUSTARD SEED AND LEAVEN

The lengthy discussions above for the parable of the sower and the parable of the tares are justified due to the significant role each plays as prologue and centerpiece, respectively, of the cluster of parables in Matthew 13:3-52. The remaining parables, though shorter and less complicated, are significant in their own right. However, since neither Christ nor Matthew interprets these parables (with the exception of the terse interpretation in vv. 49, 50), the interpreter has less information with which to base his understanding.

In particular, the two parables (mustard seed, 13:31, 32; and leaven, 13:33) are grouped together with the parable of the tares in the structure of the chapter and precede the explanation of that parable. They are spoken to the multitudes, which would also include the disciples.

The essential meaning of the parable of the mustard seed is that the period of preparation leading up to the kingdom will be one in which many would come to accept Christ as the Messiah. Even though the work during this time starts small, as a mustard seed, it ends up becoming large or having an impact upon the entire world. One must be careful here not to accept the postmillennial understanding that these verses suggest the success of the Church in ushering in the kingdom.[20] The disciples could hardly have missed the rejection that Christ was experiencing. It was surely disheartening for them to notice the leaders of the nation not following the King. Jesus' words serve the dual purpose as a warning to the multitudes and an encouragement to the disciples that their (or any follower's) work for Him will not be in vain.

The parable of the leaven has generated more controversy due to the debate over the word *leaven* itself. One main view would be that the parable gives a positive picture that is identical to the parable of the mustard seed. A small pinch of leaven or yeast ends up expanding and producing much that is good. This can then be associated with the producing of sons of the kingdom that is crucial to the parable of the tares in the context. Such a view ignores the use of leaven elsewhere in Scripture as a picture of sin and evil (Mt. 16:6-12). Blomberg suggests that the immediate context (the close association of the two parables) overrides these associations.[21]

However, the immediate context supports an understanding of the parable of the leaven as distinct from the parable of the mustard seed and in harmony with Matthew's association of the term *leaven* with the evil of the scribes and Pharisees (Mt. 16:6-12). The controlling factor here is the parable of the tares, whose presentation introduces the group of three parables and whose interpretation concludes them. That parable has two key elements with respect to the activities of the present time, one good and one evil. It is not a stretch exegetically to see that Jesus gives these two parables (mustard seed and leaven) to illustrate the two elements of good and evil.[22] In this light, the period leading up to the kingdom will see many come to Christ, but will also see many reject Him as well. Each of the two parables illustrates one-half of the description given by the parable of the tares. The disciples would need to be cautious as well as encouraged.

THE PARABLES OF THE HIDDEN TREASURE, PEARL, AND DRAGNET

These three parables are also grouped together following the interpretation of the parable of the tares. They are spoken only to the disciples. There is also some question as to whether the first two parables (treasure, pearl) go together. However, the details of each show too many differences for the two parables to be merely varying ways of describing the same idea.

One common dispensational approach is to view the hidden treasure as referring to the nation of Israel and the pearl merchant as Christ who dies for the Church. In this view, the parable of the hidden treasure focuses on Israel, the pearl on the Church.[23] While it is not possible to interact with all views on these parables, one should notice that the overall flow of Matthew's narrative does lend itself to the above interpretation. This is especially true in light of the fact that the parable cluster is moving toward its wrap-up with the mentioning of the new and old together (see below). One of the transitions taking place in the text is that Israel, due to its rejection of Christ through its leaders, is being rejected for a time while Christ does some work that is unexpected, namely the calling out of many unanticipated sons of the kingdom throughout the world. It is not a stretch to see the language of "hiding" refer to this temporary rejection by Christ. However, the focus of joy by the man in the parable (Christ) shows that He has a heart for the world (the field) in light of the treasure itself. This is in keeping with the theological understanding of the mission of Israel as a light to the world (e.g., Isa. 49:6) and the Pauline portrait of Israel's judicial blindness as a boon to the Gentile mission (Rom. 11). This interpretation harmonizes well with Matthew's own comprehension of the shift from the focus on Israel to the Gentiles. In fact, Jesus' teaching would be timely with respect to the experience of the disciples themselves at this time.

The parable of the dragnet, third in this group, must somehow make sense within such a scheme as well. This parable of the dragnet repeats the core message of the parable of the tares concerning a judgment to come as seen by its appeal to the "end of the age," the angels who reap, the fiery furnace, and the "weeping and gnashing of teeth" (vv. 49, 50). The good fish and bad fish are separated in the same way that the wheat is to be separated from the tares.

THE PARABLE OF THE HOUSEHOLDER

Although the parable of the householder (Mt. 13:51, 52) has been discussed above in its connections to the parable of the sower and the rest of the parables, there are some other issues that need to be resolved. First, the Bible student must take note of the fact that the old as well as the new things are considered part of the treasure. The old is not something that has been done away with in any complete sense. What is old in the context of Matthew's narrative is the traditional understanding of the kingdom relative to its Jewishness in light of the nation's expectations. Jesus seems to be saying that Israel's place in the coming kingdom is assured and that the straightforward understanding of its kingdom hopes as offered to them by Christ earlier in the Gospel has not been set aside in any permanent way. Israel continues to be and will always be a part of God's kingdom treasure (cp. Mt. 19:28). The old understanding of the kingdom should be reinforced. However, the new understanding concerning the kingdom is that which the preceding parables have introduced and outlined, namely, that kingdom citizens are going to be produced which the Jewish leaders of Christ's day did not anticipate as part of the kingdom. This new element of the treasure anticipates God's work in and through the Church. This entails the fact that there is a time period that will exist before the kingdom begins when the new aspect of treasure is brought to light.[24]

In other words, the parable of the householder, like the other parables in the chapter, does not require an understanding that the kingdom has already been inaugurated with the advent of the new treasure. The parable describes a scribe who follows Christ as having a correct understanding of both the old and new things relative to the kingdom. That the issue of understanding is in the forefront is seen by the preceding question of Christ about the disciples' understanding of the previous parables (v. 51). Thus, the main question is not the timing of the kingdom. The issue is facts about the kingdom, especially who will be entering it.

CONCLUSION

In the context of Christian ministry, we often hear preachers speak and pray about "advancing the kingdom" or similar church lingo. Such language is virtually synonymous with the phrase "cause of Christ." What is usually meant is that the kingdom is now and that we are adding to it by winning souls to Christ. While God's sovereign kingship and Jesus' headship over the church continue today, the focus of Matthew's Gospel is the Messianic Davidic kingdom ruled by Christ which is promised throughout the Old Testament to the nation of Israel. Thus, we judge such language as "advancing the kingdom" to be potentially misleading. Christians do indeed advance the kingdom by winning souls to Christ. However, they do not do so because Christ is ruling on the throne of David today. The parables of the kingdom in Matthew 13 give positional truth. Christian ministry today (the sowing of the seed), during the time we wait for the coming kingdom, produces numerous citizens of the coming kingdom. Their citizenship is a present reality, although their experience of the kingdom itself awaits the end of this preparation time for that coming kingdom. What will be surprising about all of this to the unfortunate Jewish leaders of Jesus' day is that they will not take part in that kingdom. In the end, the preparation time for the coming kingdom leads to the harvest of a largely Gentile ingathering into the coming kingdom.

Chapter 16

STAGE-SETTING OF THE LAST DAYS

Thomas Ice

I s there any relationship between the events of which we read, hear, and see in the daily news and biblical prophecy? You better believe there is a relationship! Just as when we are traveling and see signs beside the highway to tell us what to expect on the road ahead; so also, does the Bible speak about signs of the times to point to events of the future.

As we integrate God's Word into every area of life, we need to include the relationship between biblical prophecy and world events. God's prophetic plan for humanity is on track and on schedule. History and current events are moving toward a final end in which God's program will be fully realized. With the return of a significant portion of world Jewry to the Promised Land and the subsequent establishment of Israel as a nation in 1948, God's plan is moving closer and closer to fruition. Hardly a day goes by without the media reporting on news from that tiny country in the Middle East—Israel. Such focus is as God's Word said it would be. Israel is God's super-sign of the times that makes significant many other developments and world events.

The Gulf War that ushered in the 90s caused many Americans to wonder how current events relate to Bible prophecy. The late Dr. John Walvoord noted that "these events were not precisely the fulfillment of what the Bible predicts for the future. Instead they could be a setting of the stage for the final drama leading to the Second Coming."[1] Even though not a specific fulfillment of prophecy, this does not mean that current events are not significant in relation to God's fixed plan for history. "Although the events sparked some premature conclusions that the world is already in the end time, they had a beneficial effect on the study of prophecy," contends Dr. Walvoord. "Many people searched the Scripture, some perhaps for the first time, to learn what the Bible says about the end of the age."[2]

The next event on the prophetic timetable is the Rapture of the church, which will give rise to the seven-year tribulation or countdown to the return of Jesus Christ to planet earth. The signs of the times are passing by—do you see them and recognize them? Are you equipped to interpret them in terms of God's prophetic template for history? As we see the direct hand of God at work in history we know that our day is a great and opportune time to be alive!

A CONSISTENT APPROACH

How does the interpreter of biblical prophecy insure that he properly understands the timing of prophetic events? A good interpreter keeps the future in the future. If an event in a passage is to occur during the Tribulation, then it cannot happen during the current church age. It is wrong to say that something is being fulfilled in our day when in fact, the biblical context sets it within the future time of Tribulation.

In the early 1970's, during my college days, I recall reading Isaiah 24:4, 5, which speaks of the earth as "polluted by its inhabitants." I had the thought enter my mind that this was a prediction of the pollution of our day, because I had been hearing so much about pollution in the news. Therefore, I approached a number of my friends with the notion that Isaiah 24:5 was being fulfilled in our day. Needless to say, they were not as excited about my interpretive find as was I. Later I found out that I was wrong because the context of the passage refers to the judgments that will take place during the future Tribulation period. Thus, whatever was happening in 1970 with regard to pollution was not related to Isaiah 24:5. I had used a historicist approach to the passage by relating a future event to the present church age.

Having emphasized the point that we are not to commingle the future with the present, it does not mean that current events have no future meaning in the present. The issue is how they relate and have meaning. After all, as a futurist, I do expect that God will one day fulfill His plan for the last days. But what is a consistent approach to this matter?

I believe that it is valid to realize that God is *setting the stage* for His great end-time program. What does that mean? The Rapture and the end of the current church age are related to a signless event, thus making it impossible to identify any signs that indicate the nearness of the Rapture. This is why all attempts to date the Rapture have had to wrongly resort to an application of passages relating to God's plan for Israel to the church. However, since the Bible outlines a clear scenario of players, events and nations involved in the end-time Tribulation, we can see God's preparation for the final seven-years of Daniel's seventy weeks for Israel.

STAGE SETTING FOR THE TRIBULATION

I think it is consistent with futurism to develop a scenario of players and events, which will be in place when God's plan for Israel resumes in the Tribulation, after the Rapture. This scenario views current events as increasingly setting the stage for end-time events, even though they will not commence during the current church age. Such a model allows a pretribulational futurist to see the Rapture as imminent, but at the same time believe that we could be the last generation of the church age. John Walvoord has noted:

> In the present world scene there are many indications pointing to the conclusion that the end of the age may soon be upon us. These prophecies relating to Israel's coming day of suffering and ultimate restoration may be destined for fulfillment in the present generation. Never before in the history of the world has there been a confluence of major evidences of preparation for the end.[3]

The present church age is generally not a time in which Bible prophecy is being fulfilled. Most Bible prophecy relates to a time after the Rapture (the seven-year tribulation period). However, this does not mean that God is not preparing the world for that future time during the present church age—in fact, He is. But this is not "fulfillment" of Bible prophecy. So while prophecy is not being fulfilled in our day, it follows that we can track "general trends" in current preparation for the coming tribulation, especially since it immediately follows the Rapture. We call this approach "stage-setting." Just as many people set their clothes out the night before they wear them the following day, so in the same sense is God preparing the world for the certain fulfillment of prophecy in a future time.

Dr. John Walvoord explains:

> But if there are no signs for the Rapture itself, what are the legitimate grounds for believing that the Rapture could be especially near of this generation?
>
> The answer is not found in any prophetic events predicted before the Rapture but in understanding the events that will follow the Rapture. Just as history was prepared for Christ's first coming, in a similar way history is preparing for the events leading up to His Second Coming...If this is the case, it leads to the inevitable conclusion that the Rapture may be excitingly near.[4]

The Bible provides detailed prophecy about the seven-year Tribulation. In fact, Revelation 4-19 gives a detailed, sequential outline of the major players and events. Using Revelation as a framework, a Bible student is able to harmonize the hundreds of other biblical passages that speak of the seven-year Tribulation into a clear model of the next time period for planet earth. With such a template to guide us, we can see that already God is preparing or setting the stage of the world in which the great drama of the tribulation will unfold. Thus, this future time casts shadows of expectation in our own day so that current events provide discernible signs of the times.

A point to remember is that just as there was a transition in the early church away from God dealing with Israel as a nation, so it appears that there will be a transition at the end of the church age as God sets the stage to resume His unfinished plan with Israel after the Rapture. The church age clearly began on the Day of Pentecost; however, about 40 years later with the destruction of Jerusalem in 70 AD a specific prophecy relating to God's plan for Israel was historically fulfilled. This was the final fulfillment relating to the transition from Israel to the church. During the last 100 years we have seen events occur which are setting the stage for the players to be in place when the Rapture brings to an end the church age and God resumes His plan for Israel during the Tribulation.

In addition, there are general predictions about the course of the church age such as a trend toward apostasy (1 Tim. 4:1-16; 2 Tim. 3:1-17). These do not relate to the timing of the Rapture, but are instead general trends about the church age. It is important to realize that when speaking of a general characteristic like apostasy, no matter how bad something may be it can always get a little worse or progress a little further. Thus, it is tenuous to cite general characteristics, apart from clear historical indicators, as signs of the last days. Regardless of how much our own time may look like it fits that trend, we can never be certain that there is not more development yet to come.

Some pretribulational futurists understand Matthew 24:3-8 as referring to the end of the church age leading up to the Tribulation (Mt. 14:9-28). They see contemporary significance to recent world wars, famines, and earthquakes (Mt. 24:7, 8). Other pretribulational futurists interpret Matthew 24:3-8 as descriptive of events that will take place during the first half of the Tribulation and thus do not see contemporary significance to wars, famines, and earthquakes. However, this is a legitimate difference in interpretation, not application.

GUIDELINES FOR UNDERSTANDING THE SIGNS OF THE TIMES

Just because there may be legitimate signs in our day pointing to the return of Christ, it does not mean that every thought and speculation being brought forth is legitimate. In fact, there is entirely too much wild speculation that some current event is related to Bible prophecy. For some, virtually everything that happens is an indication that the Lord's return is near. Wild speculations are all too common today and too often they are not grounded in a proper biblical approach to the issues. This is why we need to spell out some guidelines to discipline our thoughts so that we can guard against extreme and unfounded speculation.

There are at least three key steps that must be processed before developing a proper approach to understanding the signs of the times. Prophecy expert, Dr. Ed Hindson calls these three items facts, assumptions, and speculations.[5] Dr. Hindson says:

> In our effort to make sense of all this, let me suggest a simple paradigm:
> *Facts.* There are the clearly stated facts of prophetic revelation: Christ will return for His own; He will judge the world; there will be a time of great trouble on the earth at the end of the age; the final conflict will be won by Christ; and so on. These basic facts are clearly stated in Scripture.
> *Assumptions.* Factual prophecy only tells us so much and no more. Beyond that we must make certain assumptions. If these are correct, they will lead to valid conclusions, but if not, they may lead to ridiculous speculations. For example, it is an assumption that

Russia will invade Israel in the last days. Whether or not that is factual depends on the legitimacy of one's interpretation of Ezekiel's Magog prophecy (Ezek. 38-39)....

Speculations. These are purely calculated guesses based on assumptions. In many cases they have no basis in prophetic fact at all. For example, the Bible says the number of the Antichrist is "666" (Rev. 13:18). We must try to assume what this means. It is an assumption that it is a literal number that will appear on things in the last days. When one prominent evangelist saw the number 666 prefixed on automobile license plates in Israel a few years ago, he speculated the "mark of the Beast" had already arrived in the Holy Land.

The greatest danger of all in trying to interpret biblical prophecy is to assume that our speculations are true and preach them as facts. This has often caused great embarrassment and confusion. For example, when Benito Mussolini rose to power in Rome in the 1920s, many Christians assumed he might be the Antichrist, who would rule the world from the city of seven hills in the last days. Some even speculated that Adolph Hitler, who rose to power later in Germany, was the False Prophet. Others were sure the False Prophet was the pope, who was also in Rome.

The time has come when serious students of biblical prophecy must be clear about what is fact, what is assumption, and what is speculation.[6]

Thus when we are approaching the study of biblical prophecy and attempting to relate it to events in our own day we must first make sure that we start with a proper interpretation of the biblical text before we can draw conclusions upon which to speculate. It stands to reason that if we have an incorrect interpretation of a passage then the conclusion or assumptions we draw will of necessity be wrong (unless we are illogical and inconsistently stumble onto a right conclusion).

For example, if we are studying the area of the world from which the Antichrist will come, we must start with a correct interpretation of biblical passages that bear on the subject. Having properly gathered the biblical data, we then draw conclusions, or as Dr. Hindson called it: *assumptions*. Thus, we might conclude that the Antichrist will arise out of the Revived Roman Empire. Since 2 Thessalonians 2:6-9 indicates that he will not be revealed until after the Rapture, we would not be able to legitimately speculate as to who he might be within the community of present day possibilities. We could use such an interpretation and assumption to exclude a suggested candidate from somewhere like Japan, if one were to bring forth such a speculation.

Legitimate views about the signs of the times must start with (1) sound biblical interpretation, (2) proper assumptions or conclusions drawn from the interpretation, and (3) speculation consistent with the previous two factors. Only after following such an approach can we conclude that any contemporary development is a sign of Christ's return.

ISRAEL: GOD'S SUPER SIGN OF THE END TIMES

The study of Bible prophecy is divided into three major areas: the nations (Gentiles), Israel, and the church. More detail is given prophetically concerning God's future plans for His nation—Israel. When the church takes these prophecies that relate to Israel literally, as we do, then we see a great prophetic agenda that lies ahead for Israel as a people and nation. When the church spiritualizes these promises, as she has done too often in history, then Israel's prophetic uniqueness is subsumed and merged unrealistically in the church. God has an amazing and blessed future for elect individual Jews and national Israel. Israel is God's super sign of the end times.

God's promises to Abraham and Israel are unconditional and guaranteed through the various covenants. A definite pattern for Israel's future history was prophesied in Deuteronomy before the Jews set even one foot into the land (Deut. 4:28-31). The predicted pattern for God's program with Israel was to be as follows: they would enter the land under Joshua, they would eventually turn away from the Lord and be expelled from the land and scattered among the Gentile nations. From there the Lord would regather them during the latter days and they would pass through the Tribulation. Toward the end of the Tribulation they would be regenerated and recognize their Messiah. Christ then returns to earth and rescues the Israel from the Nations who have gathered at Armageddon in order to exterminate the Jews. A second regathering of the nation occurs in preparation for their millennial reign with Christ during which time all of Israel's unfulfilled promises will be realized. This pattern is developed by the Prophets and reinforced by the New Testament.

As with the church and the nations, God is moving His chosen people—Israel—into place for the future fulfillment of His program involving them after the Rapture in the direct fulfillment of prophecy relating to the nation. He has already brought them back to their ancient land (1948) and has given them Jerusalem (1967). However, the current situation in Israel is one of constant turmoil and crisis, especially surrounding the old city of Jerusalem. But this is preparation by God for Israel's signing of the covenant with the European Antichrist that will kick off the seven-year Tribulation.

That ethnic Israel has been reestablished as a nation and now controls Jerusalem is a strong indicator that we are near the end of the church age. This can only be a general indication, since no timetable is specifically given for current preparation. Therefore, we cannot know for certain that we are the last generation before the Rapture since God may choose to "stage set" for another 100 years or longer. Dr. John F. Walvoord correctly says, "There is no scriptural ground for setting dates for the Lord's return or the end of the world...As students of the Bible observe proper interpretation principles, they are becoming increasingly aware of a remarkable correspondence between the obvious trend of world events and what the Bible predicted centuries ago."[7] While probably all of the Old Testament passages that predict the restoration and return of Israel to the land in the last days relate to future tribulation or millennial events and thus, in a precise, technical sense are not fulfilling Bible prophecy (Ezek. 37 is the exception), this does not mean that today's events are unrelated to the fulfillment of Bible prophecy.

The many reasons that constitute specific signs indicating that God's end-time program is on the verge of springing into full gear, but, the fact that all three streams of prophecy (Nations, Israel, and the church) are converging for the first time in history at the same time constitute a sign itself. This is why many students of prophecy believe that we are on the edge of history. If you want to know where history is headed, keep you eye on what God is doing with Israel.

Israel's Dispersion

The Latin word *Diaspora* has been coined to refer to Israel's dispersion throughout the Gentile nations. Christ speaks of the current 2,000 year dispersion of Israel in His prophecy about the destruction of Jerusalem in 70 AD when He said, *and they will fall by the edge of the sword, and will be led captive into all the nations; and Jerusalem will be trampled underfoot by the Gentiles until the times of the Gentiles be fulfilled* (Lk. 21:24). As usual within biblical prophecy, the pronouncement of judgment also contains an ultimate hope of restoration. In this passage Christ said, "until," which means the dispersion will not last forever, it will soon come to an end.

As early as the Mosaic Law, the threat of dispersion throughout the nations was discussed (Lev. 26:33; Deut. 4:27; 28:64; 29:28). Nehemiah said, *Remember the word which Thou didst command Thy servant Moses saying, 'If you are unfaithful I will scatter you among the peoples'* (Neh. 1:8). This cycle is repeated many times throughout the prophets.

Israel's capture of the Northern Kingdom by the Assyrians in the 8th century BC and the trip to Babylon in the 6th century BC did not constitute a worldwide scattering as prophesied. This did not occur until the nation's rejection of Christ and God's subsequent judgment in 70 AD.

We rejoice that God is currently in the process of ending the Diaspora. May it happen soon!

The Regathering and Conversion of Israel

There are dozens of biblical passages that predict an end-time regathering of Israel back to her land. However, it is a common mistake to lump all of these passages into one fulfillment time frame, especially in relation to the modern state of Israel. Modern Israel is prophetically significant and is fulfilling Bible prophecy. But readers of God's Word need to be careful to distinguish which verses are being fulfilled in our day and which references await future fulfillment. In short there will be two end-time regatherings: One before the Tribulation and one after the Tribulation.

Hebrew Christian scholar Dr. Arnold Fruchtenbaum explains:

> The re-establishment of the Jewish state in 1948 has not only thrown a wrench in amillennial thinking, but it has also thrown a chink in much of premillennial thinking. Amazingly, some premillennialists have concluded that the present state of Israel has nothing to do with the fulfillment of prophecy. For some reason the present state some how does not fit their scheme of things, and so the present state becomes merely an accident of history. On what grounds is the present state of Israel so dismissed? The issue that bothers so many premillennialists is the fact that not only have the Jews returned in unbelief with regard to the person of Jesus, but the majority of the ones who have returned are not even Orthodox Jews. In fact the majority are atheists or agnostics. Certainly, then, Israel does not fit in with all those biblical passages dealing with the return. For it is a regenerated nation that the Bible speaks of, and the present state of Israel hardly fits that picture. So on these grounds, the present state is dismissed as not being a fulfillment of prophecy.
>
> However, the real problem is the failure to see that the prophets spoke of two international returns. First, there was to be a regathering in unbelief in preparation for judgment, namely the judgment of the Tribulation. This was to be followed by a second world-wide regathering in faith in preparation for blessing, namely the blessings of the messianic age. Once it is recognized that the Bible speaks of two such regatherings, it

is easy to see how the present state of Israel fits into prophecy.[8]

First World-Wide Gathering in Unbelief

In 1948 when the modern state of Israel was born, it not only became an important stage setting development but also, it began an actual fulfillment of specific Bible prophecies about an international regathering of the Jews in unbelief before the judgment of the Tribulation. Such a prediction is found in the following Old Testament passages: Ezek. 20:33-38; 22:17-22; 36:22-24; Isa. 11:11, 12; Zeph. 2:1, 2 and Ezek. 38–39 presupposes such a setting.

Zephaniah 1:14-18 is one of the most colorful descriptions of "The Day of the Lord," which we commonly call the Tribulation period. Zephaniah 2:1, 2 says that there will be a worldwide regathering of Israel before the day of the Lord. "Gather yourselves together, yes, gather, O nation without shame, before the decree takes effect—the day passes like the chaff—before the burning anger of the Lord comes upon you, before the day of the Lord's anger comes upon you."

Ezekiel 37 teaches that Israel will be restored to the land in phases. These stages are the reverse of what happens in the decaying process of a dead body—in this instance, a collection of dead bodies. Thus, Ezekiel 37:6-8 pictures a valley of dry bones in which the sinews connect the bones; the flesh grows back on the bones; skin recovers the flesh and bones; and then the last stage occurs when breath is restored to the body and life will have been restored to national Israel. Even though the completed, end product, will be finished at some point in the future Tribulation, it is clear that Israel is currently being regathered in unbelief for preparation of that future point in time when she will be spiritually reconstituted.

Futurist prophecy scholars have long taught that on the basis of Ezekiel 37 Israel will be regathered to the land in unbelief and will then be converted to Jesus her Messiah. For example, in 1918, the Philadelphia Prophetic Conference adopted a statement of prophetic faith. The fifth article read: "We believe that there will be a gathering of Israel to her land in unbelief, and she will be afterward converted by the appearing of Christ on her behalf."[9] The modern state of Israel is in the process of fulfilling Bible prophecy because of her current existence and regathering, and because the context of Ezekiel 37 allows for the fulfillment of part of that passage before the Tribulation, in the current church age. Thus, the fact that national Israel exists and is being regathered does give meaning to other current "stage-setting" events.

Second World-Wide Gathering in Belief

Many passages in the Bible speak of Israel's regathering, in belief, at the end of the Tribulation, in conjunction with Christ's Second Coming, to prepare for the commencement of the millennium. These references are not being fulfilled by the modern state of Israel. Some of the citations include: Deut. 4:29-31; 30:1-10; Isa. 27:12, 13; 43:5-7; Jer. 16:14, 15; 31:7-10; Ezek. 11:14-18; Amos 9:14, 15; Zech. 10:8-12; Mt. 24:31 and many more.

The fact that the last fifty years has seen a world-wide regathering and reestablishment of the nation of Israel, which is now poised in just the setting required for the revealing of the Antichrist and the start of the Tribulation, is God's grand indicator that all of the other areas of world development are prophetically significant. Dr. Walvoord says,

> Of the many peculiar phenomena which characterize the present generation, few events can claim equal significance as far as Biblical prophecy is concerned with that of the return of Israel to their land. It constitutes a preparation for the end of the age, the setting for the coming of the Lord for His church, and the fulfillment of Israel's prophetic destiny.[10]

Israel, God's "super sign" of the end times, is a clear indicator that time is growing shorter with each passing hour. God is preparing the world for the final events leading up to Israel's national regeneration.

SOME OTHER AREAS OF STAGE SETTING IN OUR DAY

The Revived Roman Empire and The European Union

Scripture teaches that the Antichrist will rise to power out of a federation of nations that correlate in some way with the Roman Empire of two thousand years ago. Dr. J. Dwight Pentecost explains:

> Now, when we turn to the prophecies of Daniel 2 and 7 and to Revelation 13 and 17 and other parallel passages, we find that at the end time, during the Tribulation period, the final form of Gentile world power is a federation of ten separate nations, the ten toes or ten horns. It seems as though Europe's leaders are advocating that which Daniel prophesied hundreds of years before Christ, when he said that the final form of Roman world power would be a federation of independent states who elect one man to take authority over them while maintaining their own sovereign authority. The more movement we see in Europe for a common market and a federation of nations, the closer the coming of our Lord must be.[11]

One would have to be totally ignorant of developments within the world of our day to not admit that, through the efforts of the European Union, "Humpty Dumpty" is finally being put back together again. This is occurring, like all of the other needed developments of prophecy, at just the right time to be in place for the coming Tribulation period. Prophecy popularizer, Hal Lindsey tells us:

> A generation ago, no one could have dreamed that an empire formed of the nations that were part of old Rome could possibly be revived. But today, as Europe is on the advent of real unity, we see the potential fulfillment of another vital prophecy leading to the return of our Lord Jesus Christ.[12]

Russia

In conjunction with tribulation events, Ezekiel 38-39 teaches that there will be an invasion into Israel by a coalition lead by "Gog of the land of Magog, the prince of Rosh, Meshech, and Tubal" (Ezek. 38:2). Gog appears to be modern Russia. Coalition partners in the invasion are Persia (modern Iran), Cush (Ethiopia), Put (Libya), and Gomer and Beth-togarmah (likely modern Turkey) (Ezek. 38:5, 6). Chuck Missler concludes, "All the allies of Magog (Russia) are reasonably well identified and all of them are Muslim."[13]

The 20th century rise of Russia as a military power and her alignment with those nations who will invade Israel under Gog's leadership, once again, in concert with all of the other prophetically significant factors, are a sign that the stage is set indicating the nearness of our Lord's return. The modern Russian bear is a player in end-time prophecy and thus should be watched as a sign of the times. Mark Hitchcock, a specialist on the Gog invasion agrees:

> Russia is a wounded, starving bear and is more dangerous than ever before. Vladimir Zhirinovsky is gaining power in Russia, and the entire focus of his political plan is a massive military campaign into the Middle East.
>
> The stage is being set. The events of Ezekiel 38—39 are more imminent than ever before. The consummation of history could begin at any time. All that remains is for the curtain to be raised.[14]

Political, Economic, and Religious Globalism

As never before current events are working in concert with one another, preparing the way for the rise of Globalism and the infamous character historically known as the Antichrist. The Bible indicates (Rev. 13:12-17) that the Beast (another name for the Antichrist) will expand his rule from his European base to the world during the first 3 1/2 years of the Tribulation. Today preparation is well under way for the coming Globalism and the rule of Antichrist.

Only in the last fifty years has Globalism become a realistic option for mankind at the practical level. Revelation 17-18 indicates

that Antichrist's global empire will revolve around political, economic, and religious issues. Many who reject the Bible and God's
plan for history believe that the ultimate solution to this world's
political, economic, and religious problems have only global
answers. They are right...if the Bible is *not* true. But of course,
Scripture is true, so that ultimately they are wrong. Dr. Ed Hindson
comments on the motives behind the rise of the modern global
thrust:

> All previous attempts at structuring a world order have,
> without fail, fallen on the harsh realities of man's pride,
> arrogance, greed, avarice, and self-destruction.
> Woodrow Wilson's League of Nations failed to stop
> World War II, and the present United Nations has strug-
> gled since its very inception. Yet there seems to be
> something within the international community pro-
> pelling us toward a unified world system. Many fear
> that driving force is Satan himself.[15]

The thrust toward global religious unity has never been stronger
than in our day. The flames have been fanned the last few decades
by the rising popularity of New Age thought that has invaded every
aspect of North American society, including the Evangelical
Church. Dr. Charles Ryrie speaks:

> The Superchurch of World Religions is on its way:
> powerful, worldwide, and invincible—for three and
> one-half years.
>   The progress toward organizational unity waxes and
> wanes, but the movement is steadily going forward.
> Whatever happens to ecumenical organizations, how-
> ever, do not overlook what is happening on the theo-
> logical scene. Universalism and revolution in the name
> of the church are sweeping the theological world.
> Organizational unity and theological heresy may be
> compared to two runners. One may pass the other tem-
> porarily, causing the lead to seesaw back and forth

between them. But as they approach the finish line they will join hands, and from their combined forces will emerge Superchurch.

The stage is set. The script has been written. The props are in place. The actors are in the wings. Soon we shall hear, "Curtain!"[16]

The world is clearly being prepared for the rise of the Antichrist out of Europe, as the Bible demands. While many items could be cited as evidence of such preparation, none is more striking than the rise of an electronic, cashless society, which will facilitate fulfillment of the "mark of the beast" during the Tribulation (Rev. 13:16-18).

At what other time in history, other than our own, could such a prophecy be successfully implemented?

It is becoming increasingly apparent that today's developing cashless system will become the instrument through which the Antichrist will seek to control all who buy or sell, based upon whether they are a follower of Jesus Christ or a follower of the European ruler, and thus, Satan. It is obvious that any leader wanting to control the world's economy would avail themselves of the power that an electronic cashless system holds as a tool for implementing total control...But surely the coming cashless society is one of the signs that prophecy is being fulfilled.[17]

Babylon

Babylon is depicted throughout the Bible as the focus of the kingdom of man that is set in opposition to God, Israel, and His plan for history. It is not surprising to realize that many biblical passages speak of an end-time role for Babylon as God's enemy (Rev. 14:8; 17-18). "What are the specific signposts that can serve as indicators of God's end-time program for the world?" asks Dr. Charles Dyer. "The third sure signpost is the rebuilding of Babylon."[18] Is Babylon being rebuilt in our day? Yes it is!

Dr. Joseph Chambers traveled to Iraq, shortly before the Gulf War, and witnessed firsthand Saddam Hussein's rebuilding of Babylon. "I have walked through those ruins and have seen repeatedly the ancient bricks of Nebuchadnezzar with the bricks of Saddam Hussein laid on top and workers proceeding to erect wall after wall and building after building," declares Dr. Chambers. "Every nuance of God's infallible Word is being fulfilled."[19]

God's prophetic plan includes His restoration of many of Israel's ancient enemies who will once again, but for the last time, plague God's people. Joseph Chambers says:

> The only biblical fulfillment in our generation that surpassed the rebuilding of ancient Babylon is the regathering of Israel to their God-given homeland. Babylon represents to the world system what Israel represents to biblical ideas and Christianity. The climax of all the ages is at hand.[20]

The resurrection of ancient Babylon in our day constitutes another sign of the times, which sets the stage. Once again, this development, after thousands of years, just happens to be happening in conjunction with all the other developments necessary for the fulfillment of the prophecies of the coming Tribulation.

CONCLUSION

There are signs of the time, which indicate that we are likely near the time of the start of the Tribulation. Some stage-setting developments casting a shadow in our day include religious apostasy, preparation for a revived Roman Empire in Europe, Israel's return to the land, revival of Israel's ancient enemies such as Iraq as Babylon, and the rise of Russia as a military power (Gog and Magog invasion), all preparing the way for Tribulation events. But before the curtain rises, the church will rise into the air at the Rapture. In the mean time, let's get back to the future, by keeping the future in the future. Maranatha!

Chapter 17

SEQUENCE OF END-TIME EVENTS

PHILLIP GOODMAN

As I looked at the 15 1/2-foot Wall Chart of World History, I marveled at the obvious imprint of Bible prophecy on the events of mankind. The chart, first published in 1890, was hand drawn and developed over a period of 10 years by Sebastian Cabot Adams and 20 researchers. It has since been updated to the year 1997.[1] In a bird's eye view, you can scan the secular record of the history of the world. As you visually survey the horizontal color-coded timelines concerning the rise and fall of empires, you will note the major characters and episodic events of recorded history. What is so striking is that, in a single moment, you can plainly see the prophecies of Daniel and Revelation unroll as fulfilled history before your eyes. At the 20th century mark on the chart, surrounding the revival of the State of Israel in 1948, it becomes apparent that the stage is being set for the final drama and the return of Christ. There is the rise of the Islamic nations and their alliances with Russia, the founding of the European Union and its spread eastward, the reemergence of sovereign nations in the

Mediterranean realm that are predicted to reappear at the end of history, and the explosion of giant far east populations. They all point to a world primed and ready for the arrival of the Author and King of history, Jesus Christ.

UNBELIEF DISGUISED AS HUMOR

As I contemplated the accuracy of Bible prophecy reflected in the chart, I recalled a rather disconcerting experience. A pastor once visited me while I was teaching a Bible class on prophecy. The pastor knew that, in my class, we did not neglect the one-third of the Bible which deals with prophecy, so he seemed to go out of the way to greet us with this remark, "Some teach premillennialism, some teach postmillennialism, but I believe in panmillennialism— I believe it will all 'pan out.'" There was not as much humor in this worn-out witticism as there was skepticism and unbelief. At that moment I realized why most people, after spending decades in church Bible studies, are still ignorant about Bible prophecy! Bible prophecy is simply ignored in much of the church. Since the Holy Scriptures are replete with prophecy, the bottom line for this mass lack of knowledge has to be unbelief within the church leadership.

The Bible, of course, does teach that the things involving the future will "all pan out." But it also teaches us that the prophecies will "pan out" in a specific way, with a particular order to coming events. Paul said in 1 Thessalonians 4:13, *But we do not want you to be uninformed*, and then went on to tell of the Rapture of the church, and, importantly, the sequence of events involved in that great event. He continues to emphasize a definite sequence to prophetic events in both 1 Thessalonians 5 and 2 Thessalonians 2. It is clear then, that for the meaning of prophetic events to be correctly understood, one must be aware of their proper sequence. How could one ever understand the sequence of kingdoms that were predicted to dominate the earth until Jesus Christ returns if one were to simply brush aside the vision of the great statue in Daniel chapter 2 with the "it will all pan out" mindset predominant in today's church! Bible prophecy was given to encourage us, and that includes the details and sequential order of events. We are to know these things. That is why Paul wrote *I pray that the eyes of your heart may be enlightened* [believe], *so that you may know* [understand] *what is the hope of His calling* [prophecy], *what are the riches of the glory of His inheritance in the saints* [prophecy]...(Eph. 1:18).

AN ORDERLY SEQUENCE TO PROPHECY

God, the creator of all that exists, created time. In doing so, He set history on a past, present, and future time continuum. In Isaiah 46:9-11 God surveys this time continuum. First, He points to the importance of remembering past history when He says *Remember this, and be assured; recall it to mind, you transgressors. Remember the former things long past.* Then, God speaks in the present tense, saying, *For I am God, and there is no other; I am God, and there is no one like Me.* He then refers to the whole span of the time continuum, when He proclaims that only He can declare *the end from the beginning.* Next, He points to future time when He says *Truly I have spoken; truly I will bring it to pass. I have planned it, surely I will do it.* This passage is just one of many which confirms God's intent that the series of events which parade across time must flow in a linear, sequential pattern. The events of Bible prophecy are no different.

There is a divine plan and an orderly process to the events around us. And of course this is also true of the events yet to come— the events of Biblical prophecy. For example, in Genesis 15:13, 14 the Lord tells (Abram) Abraham that *your descendants will be strangers in a land* [Egypt] *that is not theirs, where they will be enslaved and oppressed four hundred years. But I will also judge the nation whom they will serve; and afterward they will come out with many possessions.* Notice that first, the Jews were to be enslaved in the future, and then "afterward" they would be freed. This orderly time progression in Bible prophecy is just one example of how we can expect a sequence, or a chronological pattern, in the events to come.

The fact that there is order and sequence to the events of prophecy is affirmed many times in the Bible. This can be seen clearly in Matthew 24 where Jesus gave an outline of future events leading to His return. Notice how often the Lord uses time or sequence words and phrases, such as *not yet* (v. 6), *beginning* (v. 8), *then* (vv. 9, 14, 16, 21, 23), *at that time* (v. 10), *to the end* (v. 13), and *immediately after* (v. 29). In describing the future Rapture of the Church in 1 Thessalonians 4:13-18, words such as *shall not precede* and *shall rise first* emphasize a definite order to coming events. The same holds true for the passage describing the prophecies of the resurrections where, in 1 Corinthians 15:23, it specifies that each will arise *in his own order*.[2]

We see, then, that the events of the future will unfold in a particular sequence. Though we cannot know with certainty every detail, we can discern a basic timeframe for Bible prophecy. Within this timeframe is a fairly clear schedule of the sequence of coming end time events. After all, it is the Lord Jesus Himself who set the precedent for seeing a chronological order in events yet to come when He said in Revelation 1:19: *Write therefore the things which you have seen and the things which are, and the things which shall take place after these things.*

THE TIMEFRAME FOR END TIME EVENTS

The basic timeframe for Bible prophecy is found in Daniel 9:24-27.[3] That passage defines a 7-year period of time containing the final events leading to the return of Jesus Christ. This 7-year time is called the Tribulation period. Daniel then foresees the end of our current age and the beginning of an everlasting age of righteousness and peace. The rest of Scripture confirms this timeframe.

The 7 year Tribulation period is divided in the middle by an event of such blasphemous proportions that it serves as one of four key time markers for determining the sequence of end time events.[4] The Antichrist will take his seat within the rebuilt Jewish temple and declare himself to be God. This monstrous episode is called the Abomination of Desolation. It divides the final 7 years into two 3 1/2-year periods. The second 3 1/2 years, or the last half of the 7 year Tribulation time, is referred to by three different time terms in the Bible: "time, times and half a time," "1260 days," and "42 months." It is essential to remember that whenever one reads one of these terms, which are found only in Daniel and Revelation, each of them always refers to the second half of the Tribulation period.[5]

In summary, there is a 7 year prophetic timeframe that will close out this age. It is divided at the midpoint into two 3 1/2-year periods by the Abomination of Desolation of the Jewish temple by the Antichrist. The time designations, "time, times and half a time," "1260 days," and "42 months," all of which are initiated by the Abomination, are equivalent time references. They always refer to the second half of the 7 years, the 3 1/2-year period which is called the Great Tribulation.

THE FOUR TIME MARKERS

Within this prophetic timeframe there are four specific events that can be used as time markers for determining the sequence of end time events. One of these time markers, the Abomination of Desolation, has already been shown in Daniel 9:27 to mark the middle of the Tribulation. That passage also reveals another time marker, the false peace covenant. The false peace covenant is an agreement confirmed by the Antichrist with the nation Israel. It will mark the start of the 7 year Tribulation period.[6] The third time-marker is the Great Tribulation itself. It runs the last 3 1/2 years of the final 7 year period, according to Matthew 24:15-21, Daniel 7:25 and Revelation 13:5-7. The entire second half of the 7-year Tribulation, then, is "marked" by the worldwide persecution and martyrdom (the Great Tribulation) of believers in Jesus Christ. Therefore, all events that include the reign of the Antichrist and his war against believers must find their time placement within the second half of the 7 year Tribulation.[7]

With the false peace covenant marking the start of the last 7 years, and the Abomination marking the middle point of that period, and the Great Tribulation marking the last half of that same period, the fourth time marker occurs at the very end of the 7 years. It is what we will call the "sky sign." This is an event so significant and of such catastrophic celestial proportions that it could only happen once. Indeed, it is called a unique day in Zechariah 14:6, 7.

This sky sign encompasses a single event when the sun turns "black as sackcloth", the moon turns "blood red," the stars fall from the sky, and the sky itself "rolls up like a scroll," all of which is accompanied by an earthquake of global proportions. It is mentioned in several Old and New Testament passages.[8] The sky sign serves as a time marker because it is precisely timed. Matthew 24:29, 30 says the sky sign occurs "immediately after" the Great Tribulation and just before the return of Christ. Joel 2:31 says the sky sign occurs before the Day of the Lord. Therefore, the sky sign, with its spectacular celestial phenomena, is the event that turns the earth's attention to the opened heavens and the Second Coming of Jesus Christ.

These four time markers— the false peace covenant to begin the 7 year Tribulation, the Abomination of Desolation to mark its middle, the Great Tribulation spanning its second half, and the sky sign to introduce the return of Christ at its end— now make it possible to insert the other end time events and create a reasonable sequence of coming events.

THE PRE-TRIBULATION EVENTS

The first event on the prophetic calendar is the Rapture, which will include the resurrection of all of the believers who have died since the resurrection of Christ.[9] When we keep in mind exactly what is involved in the Rapture, it becomes apparent that it must occur before the 7 year Tribulation. At the Rapture, the Lord will change the bodies of all believers to spiritual bodies, and instantly remove them from earth to heaven. Therefore, the Rapture cannot occur at the end of the Tribulation period, because there are believers (sheep & goats) in natural bodies on the earth who are survivors of the Great Tribulation and who meet the Lord at His return. Nor can the Rapture take place in the middle of the Tribulation period, because there are believers on the earth who become the victims of the Antichrist throughout the second half of that time.

The Rapture has to occur before the Tribulation because believers are told to *wait for His Son from heaven, who delivers us from the wrath to come* (1 Thess. 1:10). This can only be an expectation that Christ could come at "any-moment" since the Bible says it is evil to say in one's heart that *my master is not coming for a long time* (Mt. 24:48). If one were to say that the Rapture cannot come until certain events in the Tribulation period occur, then one would in fact have to say that my master is not coming for a long time! The next event, then, will be the Rapture of all believers *to meet the Lord in the air* (1 Thess. 4:17).

Another pre-tribulation event is that recorded in Ezekiel 38-39. Since the Jews returned to their ancient homeland and the new state of Israel after a 1900-year absence in 1948, the prophecy of the northern invasion of Israel has been waiting in the wings to happen. It will occur before the 7 year Tribulation because Russia invades when Israel is at peace, not while Israel is in tribulation (Ezek. 38:11). Then, after God directly intervenes in a scathing judgment and destroys Russia on the mountains of Israel, the Jews "go out of the cities" in a survival mode for 7 years (Ezek. 39:9). This is the only 7 year reference in the Bible involving the Jews outside of the tribulation reference in Daniel 9:27. Since both 7 year timeframes involve the final spiritual conversion of the Jews (Dan. 9:24-27; Ezek. 39:7, 22), the two 7 year periods are both describing the final time known as the Tribulation.

At some point, the incessant Mid East violence will drive Israel to accept an internationally brokered peace agreement— one which will set the stage for the northern invasion. Then Russia and a host of Muslim nations will take advantage of this apparent peace (Ezek. 38:1-8). They will invade Israel while they are *living securely, all of them*. God will then intervene and directly cause the destruction of the invading Russian and Islamic forces. The ensuing supernatural destruction of these ungodly forces will be evident to the whole world (Ezek. 39:7). It will inspire such an upsurge of support (both true and false professions of faith) for the God of Israel that the Antichrist will come forward and guarantee the peace covenant spoken of in Daniel 9:27, and set the tone for accomplishing the impossible—the rebuilding of the Jewish temple on its original site!

THE FIRST HALF OF THE TRIBULATION PERIOD: THE BIRTH PAINS

The false peace covenant will be one of the great political coups and will position the Antichrist as a man of peace and worldwide renown. The peace covenant is specified by Daniel 9:27 to inaugurate the 7 year Tribulation time. Its timing is a certainty and thus it serves as one of our time markers.

In all probability this covenant will serve to order the rebuilding of the Jewish temple. It will be rebuilt on its ancient mound. This will necessitate the demolition from the temple mount of the Dome of the Rock, the centuries-old "holy" shrine of the Islamic nations that will be destroyed during the failed Russian invasion. But, like the earlier "peace," Israel will not find true peace until the coming of the Prince of Peace, Jesus Christ. But this second peace treaty will signal the start of the Tribulation period. It is destined to be broken after 3 1/2 years by the one who granted it, the Antichrist.

The beginnings of spiritual rebirth in Israel following the Russian invasion will lead to the emergence of 144,000 messianic Jewish believers.[10] Their ministry apparently bears fruit in the salvation of Gentile believers across the world.[11] The Jewish and Gentile believers fill the void of missing believers taken earlier in the Rapture of the church to Heaven.

But these believers will also become the victims of the Great Tribulation. Both groups are seen in Heaven, the Gentiles in Revelation 7:9-17 and the Jews in Revelation 14:1-5. They will have spilled their blood for the name of Jesus Christ in defiance of the Antichrist.[12]

The "beginning of birth pains" covers the first half of the Tribulation period. It starts with the false peace covenant, seen in the rider on the white horse in Revelation 6:1, 2. It is followed by world war, famine, and the death of one-fourth of the earth's population.[13] During this time the Antichrist and 10 kings of the Revived Roman Empire will gain control of the world.[14] They will share rule with an emergent one-world religion whose headquarters will be in the capital of the Antichrist, the rebuilt city of Babylon, located in present day Iraq (Rev. 17-18). But midway through the Tribulation period the second time marker will trigger a series of events that will initiate the last half of the Tribulation.

THE LAST HALF OF THE TRIBULATION PERIOD: THE 1260 DAYS

After a run of 3 1/2 years, the false peace covenant will be broken by the Antichrist (Dan. 9:27). He will enter the Jewish temple, profane it with a blasphemous display of himself as God, and commence to institute the Great Tribulation against Jews and Christians (Mt. 24:15-21; 2 Thess. 2:3, 4). As previously noted, this event is called the Abomination of Desolation. In the act of the Abomination, the Antichrist will demand the worship of himself by all who desire to stay alive and participate in the new society that he will inherit when Satan and the 10 kings give him rule over the Revived Roman Empire, and for all practical purposes, over the entire world. The immediate fallout will be both the destruction of the rival one-world religion and the apostasy, or "falling away", of millions of pseudo-believers.[15]

As the Great Tribulation initiates the final 3 1/2 years, true believers who refuse to participate in the global identification program required to prove allegiance to the Antichrist will be persecuted and martyred worldwide. In the midst of this demonic campaign, God will provide an umbrella of supernatural protection to a group of believing Israeli Jews who will heed the Scriptures and flee from the Antichrist when he takes up residence in their temple and proclaims himself to be God (Rev. 12). They will be protected for the full 1,260 days of the Great Tribulation. Meanwhile, the Lord will provide that a gospel testimony should remain for the unbelieving Jews left behind in Jerusalem. Two witnesses will be left behind to preach to those Jews who do not flee from the Antichrist. These two witnesses will also be under divine protection for the 1,260-day term of the Great Tribulation.[16]

It is also during the second half of the Tribulation period that God will release the seven trumpet judgments (Rev. 8-9). The timing of these judgments is determined by finding the timing of trumpet 7 and using it as the time-anchor for the whole series. Of trumpet 7 it is stated, in Revelation 11:7, that "the mystery of God is finished." This phrase means that in the outpouring of the 7th trumpet, the program of God's current dispensation over the earth "will reach its completion without delay."[17] That means the 7th trumpet will bring in the Second Coming of Christ and His Kingdom, as Revelation 11:15 says. Therefore, since the 7 trumpets seem to be patterned after the 10 Egyptian plagues during the time of Moses, occurring in rapid succession, the previous 6 must fit within the last 3 1/2 years.

IMMEDIATELY AFTER THE GREAT TRIBULATION: THE 75 DAYS

It is actually "immediately after" (Mt. 24:29) this 3 1/2-year Great Tribulation that quiet a number of significant events occur. This period is said to include 75 days according to Daniel 12:11, 12. Included among those events that occur after the 1,260-day or 42-month period, within the 75-day interval that occurs before the start of the Millennial Kingdom of Christ, are: the death and resurrection of the 2 witnesses, followed by a great earthquake in Jerusalem, followed by public panic, followed by the 7th trumpet and the ensuing 6 bowl judgments,[18] which include the march of the armies of all nations to the valley of Armageddon, followed by the return of Christ and His armies out of heaven. This 75-day interval between the close of the Great Tribulation and the inauguration of the 1,000-year kingdom of Christ is rife with both judgment and seeds of restoration.[19]

The 6th seal also describes this period.[20] The seal judgments of Revelation 6, which only Christ can open because God has *given all judgment to the Son* according to John 5:22, are a panoramic view of the entire Tribulation period through seal 6. Seal 6 describes the sky sign at the end of the Tribulation.[21] Then Christ opens the 7th seal. It flashed back in time to begin the series of judgments that only Jesus Christ can deliver. These Tribulation judgments will flow out of the 7 trumpets and the 7 bowls. The final judgments will occur as

Christ returns from heaven to ascend His "glorious throne" (Mt. 25:31-46). These will include the defeat of the nations' armies at Armageddon, followed by the Antichrist and the False Prophet being cast into Hell (Rev. 19:17-21). Then the nations, or Gentiles, will be judged on the basis of their faith in Christ as borne out in their deeds, including their treatment of Israel during the harsh Tribulation days. There will also be a judgment of the Jews based on each individual's relationship to Christ as personal Savior (Zech. 13:8, 9).

THE KINGDOM OF CHRIST: 1000 YEARS

From the time that Christ returns to ascend His "glorious throne," the chronology of events becomes much clearer. The timeframe for these events, the establishment of Christ kingdom, is stated six times in Revelation 20 to last 1,000 years. At the start of this 1,000-year timeframe, Satan will be bound for the duration of that period (Rev. 20:1-3). The saints who died during the days of the Old Testament and during the Tribulation period will be raised to life as part of the "first resurrection" (Rev. 20: 4, 5; Dan. 12:1, 2, 13).

The Bible records a glorious existence that will predominate during the Millennial Reign of Christ.[22] Except for a residue of sin that will remain among the saved survivors of the Tribulation who enter the Millennial Kingdom in their natural bodies, it will be a type of throwback to the original creation. This sin in the "natural-man" will fester throughout that period. Then, at the end of the Millennium, Satan will be loosed to tempt the nations (Rev. 20:7-10). A contingent of rebellious nations will rise to the occasion, only to be quickly and decisively destroyed by the Lord. Satan will be thrown into Hell. Then all of the lost of all of the ages will take part in what is called the second resurrection (Rev. 20:11-13; cf. 20:5). They will stand in final judgment at the Lord's Great White Throne to face judgment and eternal doom (Rev. 20:14, 15). At this point, after the end of the 1,000 years, sin, death, and the curse will be eradicated forever, and time will merge with the glorious eternal condition of righteousness and peace in the presence of God and His Lamb, Jesus Christ, who made it all possible.

THE WORLD TODAY: THE EXPLOSION IN KNOWLEDGE

This sequence of end-time events could begin to unfold soon, according to the light of Bible prophecy on conditions in today's world. Today there is a real eye-opener happening in our world— one that ought to open the eyes of skeptics of Bible prophecy, especially in today's sleeping church. Since the time of Jesus Christ, the population growth of the world has remained almost flat when plotted on a graph. It resembles the path of an arrow, traveling horizontally for 1,700 years with only a slight incline. Then, around 1850, that population arrow metamorphosed into a moon-bound rocket ship, arching off the launch pad with a rumble, and by 1950 shooting straight up to the 6 billion people we have on the planet today.

This phenomenon of vertical population explosion is unprecedented in world history. Yet it is paralleled in virtually every category of human experience, all driven by an incredible acceleration in human knowledge. The knowledge explosion has spawned rapid transit and telecommunications systems that have, for the first time in history, set mankind within a hairs breath of a one-world political, economic, and religious system. This same acceleration in human progress has led to the development of other "chart busters." There is a corresponding increase in evil, in the development of weapons of apocalyptic destructive power, in environmental deterioration, and the list goes on. We are the "blowout" generation. Population, knowledge, technology—they are all shooting straight up to a single point in history. This is the very scenario Bible prophecy says will exist in the last days.

THE WORLD TODAY: THE EVENT-TIME WARP

A direct result of this rapid growth is the acceleration of time— that is, "event-time." While the timepiece on your wrist still ticks steadily onward at a rate synchronized with the rotation of the earth, the time interval between events has been compressed, yea, even crunched. Imagine traveling 50 mph while watching out your side window as telephone poles spaced 100 yards apart pass by. Suddenly they begin to fly by in a blur, not because your car accelerated, but because the poles are now spaced only 10 feet apart.

Through the acceleration effect of 21st century technology, events are exploding onto our world in the same way. In our lifetime, we are seeing mighty nations rise and fall literally overnight. Iran was transferred from the Shah to the Ayatollah in the space of a single day; the same happened with the breakup of the Soviet Union in 1990. The tragedy at the World Trade Center and the Pentagon on what we now know as 9/11/2001 changed the course of the world within a period of two hours. Time, when measured by events, has increased dramatically. Event-time is at mach speed! And Bible prophecy is tied to event-time.

Jesus, referring to the events of the last days in Luke 21:28 said, *But when these things begin to take place, straighten up and lift up your heads, because your redemption is drawing near.* Today the world is poised to burst forth in rapid-fire fashion with the series of head-spinning events foretold by the prophets.

We are the generation that has seen the rebirth of the nation of Israel, accompanied by a host of stage-setting events budding forth as the leaves on a fig tree. These events will march into our world as an orderly, sequential parade of prophetic fulfillment. And we are called upon to recognize these things as surely as we recognize the signs of nature, for in Mathew 24:32, 33 we read: *Now learn the parable from the fig tree: when its branch has already become tender, and puts forth its leaves, you know that summer is near; even so you too, when you see all these things, recognize that He is near.*

Chapter 18

CONTROVERSY OVER PROPHETIC FULFILLMENT

MAL COUCH

One of the major controversies over prophetic fulfillment has to do with preterism, the belief that most, if not all, of Bible prophecy has already been fulfilled. Some time ago, a friend was in a debate with a preterist pertaining to end-time events. The preterist could not field many good arguments, though he continued to squirm as the conversation intensified. The preterist finally admitted that his biggest problem concerned the Jewish people. He submitted, "I just don't know what to do in my theology about the nation of Israel!"

Preterists are bedfellows with amillennialists when it comes to understanding the Middle East and the miraculous establishment of the Jewish people back in their ancient homeland. They have discarded the Jewish people on the rubbish pile of history. Their view is that God *is* through with the Jews! He has no need for them. His promises have been re-written to put the church in the place of the

Jewish nation. In interpretation, "Israel" now means church; "Jerusalem" means the spiritual people of God presently; any "re-gathering" has to do with the enclosure of the church into God's "only" and final plan of history.

To be fair, it must be noted that a few preterists and amillennial-ists, in a very foggy sense, possibly see some kind of blessing upon the Jewish people in the end-times; however, that blessing simply means that they are individually incorporated into the church as it presently exists. Most have nothing to say about any future re-gath-ering for the Jews, or any literal reign of Christ on the throne of David in Jerusalem at the close of history.

Preterist R. C. Sproul attempted to address the issue of the end-times in his book *The Last Days According to Jesus*.[1] He said that he wrote the book to defend the Scriptures against the skeptics and critics who needed to be answered regarding Christ's eschatological statements in the Gospels, especially in Matthew 24-25. He demon-strates an almost paranoid kind of fear over the attacks made by past atheists and critics Albert Schweitzer and Bertrand Russell. Sproul writes, "We must take seriously the skeptics' critique of the time-frame references of New Testament prophecy, and we must answer them convincingly."[2] To Sproul, the way to answer them convinc-ingly is to re-write the prophetic formula. And that means disre-garding any idea of a literal earthly kingdom, with the Jews re-gath-ered and Christ reigning on a literal throne in Jerusalem.

ANTI-SEMITISM?

Amillennialists and preterists will cry 'foul play' if we label them anti-Semitic, but the facts speak loud and clear. In Sproul's book, he mentions the Jewish people only a few times. If his book is about the end-times, how could he omit discussing, even negatively, the Rapture, the Tribulation, the gathering of national Israel, and the mil-lennial reign of Christ? To Sproul, Christ returned *spiritually* in 70 AD, though there may be "another" more literal return in the future.

Others, in a similar manner as Sproul, do anything to dispose of Israel. The amillennial unbiblical theory of eschatology attempts to abracadabra any biblical teaching on the return of the Jews back to the Holy Land. Oscar Cullmann gives his D-Day analogy of the beginning of the kingdom with the resurrection and ascension of Jesus. "What was left was a mop-up exercise (the Battle of the Bulge notwithstanding). In like manner the decisive work of the kingdom has been accomplished. We are living in the interim awaiting the consummation that will occur at Christ's Parousia."[3] Again, the preterists' sentiment is that the kingdom is really the church age and God is through with the Jews!

While he was a godly Bible teacher, English scholar Martyn Lloyd-Jones (1899-1981) set the pace for modern amillennialism, especially within the Church of England in Great Britain. In his book *The Church and the Last Things* he said regarding Ezekiel 37-48 of the return of the Jews and the establishment of the millennial temple: "A literal interpretation of these chapters involves us in believing that a day is coming when the Jews will again occupy the whole of the land of Palestine with a literal Temple again built in Jerusalem. Not only that, but burnt offerings and sacrifices for sins will again be offered."[4]

He adds that these things are impossible, and then says: "But if you understand Ezekiel's words pictorially and spiritually there is no difficulty."[5] Lloyd-Jones then becomes the judge and juror as to how these verses are to be taken. He would agree that "literal interpretation" is the starting place for understanding Scripture. But then he sets forth a "spiritualized" interpretation since, in his way of thinking, he says these things are simply *impossible*. This is typical amillennialism. This approach to understanding the Bible is to re-write and re-constitute what the Bible is saying. The amillennialist is certain that future events cannot be taken at face value. The church is the end of the line for most of the Old Testament prophetic teaching.

Again, in amillennial fashion, Lloyd-Jones argues that Israel has no special position with God in the future. He quotes Colossians 3:11 that says: *There is no distinction between Greek and Jew, circumcised and uncircumcised, barbarian, Scythian, slave and freeman, but Christ is all, and in all.*

As in all of Paul's letters, Lloyd-Jones fails to remind his reader that the larger context concerns "those *in* Christ." God is accomplishing a unique work in this church dispensation that He has never done before, but He has made promises to Israel that, as a nation, they will be spiritually regenerated and brought back to their own land. For now, in the church age, there is no distinction, but this will change when "those in Christ" are raptured. Lloyd-Jones overlooks these facts and these distinctions.[6]

Here in Colossians Paul says for now, with Jew and Gentile, we have "been raised up with Christ," "hidden with Christ," and now find that "Christ is our life." Lloyd-Jones overlooks this incredible event of the church age—being placed *into the spiritual body of Christ.* He does not face the fact that the church will someday end with the Rapture. He sees the church simply existing until the final judgment, and then, all history just stops cold and eternity begins. He fails to see this Age of Grace as unique and having an ending before the Tribulation and the coming Messianic literal kingdom on earth. He writes that the distinction between Jew and Gentile is "finished, once and for ever."

Lloyd-Jones should have said that this distinction continues through the age of the church but has a distinct end before the other events just mentioned fall into place. He does not see the church being removed with the Rapture in order that the 7 year period of Tribulation might come. Those who are consistent in their hermeneutics, with normal interpretation, understand that the kingdom follows when Israel will be spiritually restored, be finally re-gathered worldwide, with Jesus the Messiah reigning and ruling on earth. Lloyd-Jones in no way speaks to these issues.

Almost with some kind of sense of fear, Lloyd-Jones makes some extreme and dogmatic statements:

> It seems to me, …that there is no special place for the Jews as a nation; it is impossible.[7]
>
> Some think the term 'Israel' means the literal, physical nation of men and women, all of whom are Jews— but it doesn't. Israel, as used in the Scriptures, doesn't mean every single Jew because 'they are not all Israel, which are of Israel.' There is the vital distinction.[8]
>
> How dangerous it is to think in terms of the physical

nation and not to realize that 'they are not all Israel, which are of Israel.'[9]

First, those who believe that Israel will someday be restored to a place of blessing do not think this means every single Jew. It will be a remnant who have survived the Tribulation and have placed their trust in Christ as Savior and King. Lloyd-Jones has set up a straw man argument in order to knock it down.

Secondly, Lloyd-Jones repeatedly refers to and misapplies Paul's statement in Romans 2:28, 29a. The apostle says, *For he is not a Jew who is one outwardly; neither is circumcision that which is outward in the flesh. But he is a Jew who is one inwardly; and circumcision is that which is of the heart, by the Spirit, not by the letter.*

Lloyd-Jones fails to note what Paul said previously in this context. Paul was addressing Jewish people. Lloyd-Jones fails to note this. The apostle then writes, "But if you bear the name 'Jew,' ..." He continues by saying that these to whom he is writing "boast in the Law," practice circumcision, etc. Paul is writing to national Israel, not to Gentiles. Paul's point was that they were displaying certain things outwardly but not from a conviction of the heart. Lloyd-Jones misquotes the thought of these verses. Paul's point is NOT that these are spiritual Gentiles who are then called "spiritual Jews," but instead, they are Jews who are not living like Jews and trusting like Jews are supposed to do. They were legalistic and without faith in their own Messiah. Paul's argument is that outward circumcision does not validate Jewish-ness but *circumcision of the heart, by the Spirit, not by the letter* does (v. 29).

As is the case with many amillennialists, Lloyd-Jones continues to misquote the biblical texts. One of the most common ways he and other amillennialists do this is by re-defining the scriptural passages. For example, at the Jerusalem Council recorded in Acts 15:6-29, the apostle James refers to Amos 9:11, 12 and the rebuilding of the tabernacle (tent) of King David. The order of James' discussion is as follows:

1. Presently, God is *taking from among the Gentiles a people for His name* (Acts 15:14).

2. Before quoting the Amos 9 verses, James adds, *After these things I will return ...* (v. 16). "After these things" has to do with "after" the Lord had taken a people from among the Gentiles—the church!

3. Then comes the literal kingdom that had fallen down, David's tabernacle. *I will rebuild its ruins, and I will restore it, in order that the rest of mankind may seek the Lord, and all the Gentiles who are called by My name* (vv. 16, 17).

It must be observed that, in Amos, this tabernacle is a destination – a restored place. The church is not now something simply restored; it is something completely new and unknown in the Old Testament (Eph. 2-3). The church does not have a location. It is a worldwide body of believers made up of *both* Gentiles and Jews. But in no stretch of the imagination can the church be called "the tabernacle of David."

Lloyd-Jones fails to see this order as set down by James, and, he works hard to allegorize the meaning of this Scripture and so many others. On this Acts 15:14-18 passage he writes, "The 'tabernacle of David' means the Christian Church which has been founded by David's greater Son. So James does not take Amos' prophecy literally but spiritually."[10]

Lloyd-Jones also says "our Lord never spoke about the restoration of the Jews to the Holy Land. Never...He never said that they were going back to Jerusalem."[11] These statements are not completely correct. The Lord spoke of His coming as the King who would judge the nations as He sat "on His glorious throne" following His coming with His angels (Mt. 25:31, 32). All of the Jews knew that this would be in Jerusalem!

Through the prophet Zechariah the Lord said:

> Behold, I am going to make Jerusalem a cup that causes reeling to all the peoples around, and when the siege is against Jerusalem, it will also be against Judah. And it will come about in that day that I will make

Jerusalem a heavy stone for all the peoples. And all the nations of the earth will be gathered against it.

And it will come about in that day that I will set about to destroy all the nations that come against Jerusalem. And I will pour out on the house of David and on the inhabitants of Jerusalem, the Spirit of grace and of supplication, so that they will look on Me whom they have pierced and they will mourn for Him as one mourns for an only son. (Zech. 12:2, 3, 8-10)

Nothing could be clearer then that the Messiah will come from Heaven to Jerusalem in an historic moment in the future. Lloyd-Jones and other amillennialists fail to quote this passage. There is no time in the past that one could say this has happened. History waits for the Lord to come from glory following the terrors of the Tribulation. Tribulation and earthly kingdom events are totally ignored and rejected by the allegorists.

THE "BONE OF CONTENTION"

The issue that stirs the allegorists and amillennialists the most is present Israel. Is present-day Israel a fulfillment of the Old Testament promises of a return to the land? What is the biblical support of dispensationalists, and why do amillennialists resist so strongly?

Reformed theologian and allegorist DeCaro writing about the military conflicts and events in the Holy Land from approximately 1948 to 1970 says:

The current critical political developments in the Middle East—the explosive and convulsive situation in that area threatening world peace; the still unresolved injustice claimed by he Arabs constantly feeding that situation—is causing the perceptive mind to wonder whether the biblical hermeneutics of Christian dispensational interpreters are essentially correct in respect to the state of Israel. It is a growing conviction among these inquiring minds that dispensational teachers are making a faulty correlation of prophetic Scripture with the modern state of Israel.[12]

DeCaro then continues to accuse dispensationalists of indiscriminately relating "Zionist statecraft and Zionist political determination to Old Testament prophecy and conclude that the state of Israel—ipso facto—is a fulfillment of prophecy. Thus, *"in their thinking the state of Israel is assumed to exist by divine decree"* (italics mine).[13] He concludes his book by saying that he does not believe the Israeli state relates to any future divine plan such as the promised return of Jesus Christ.[14]

Notice that DeCaro wonders if the explosive Middle East is "causing the perceptive mind to wonder whether the biblical hermeneutics of Christian dispensational interpreters" are correct with respect to the state of Israel. First of all, dispensationalists realize that almost all of the Jews now in the state of Israel are not bornagain. They are not in the land in belief but in unbelief. But this would not negate the fact of God beginning the process of bringing them back home.

Secondly, it is interesting to note the statement about the Arab claim to injustices. Though no dispensationalist would claim that everything the Jews do in their own land is perfect, the weight of "injustice" is with the Arabs and not the Jewish people. Almost all fair observers have to admit to this. However, at the beginning of the 21st Century, it seems as if more and more Christians are throwing rocks at the Jewish people and appear to be defending the Arab terrorists. This is strange in the light of Arab terror aimed at both America and Israel before and since 11 September 2001. The Arabs have made it clear that their attacks against America are because of its support of Israel. And too, the Arab world has vowed to continue their violence until the Jews have been driven from their land and from the holy city of David—Jerusalem!

Thirdly, it is strange that DeCaro would question whether Israel is back in the land by God's "divine decree." As a good Reformed Calvinist, he has to admit that all things occur through God's divine providence. The Jews are back in their land because God promised they would be! He is the One who has led them home!

The "bone of contention" then is about the present state of Israel and the fact that the Jews have not been restored spiritually. Our Reformed brethren seem to have no patience with the Lord! They refuse to let Him work "progressively" and over a period of time to bring about spiritual conversion for Israel. But too, the Reformed theologians have studied all the Scriptures that tell us their return to the Lord will accelerate during the period of Tribulation that has not yet begun.

What do the prophesies of Scripture say about the Jews' return to the Lord?

THE RETURN OF THE JEWS IN UNBELIEF

Since this seems to be one of the amillennial sticking points, Ezekiel's prophecy describing the end-times re-gathering as a process seems to answer the doubts. In the vision of the "dry bones" of the Jewish people from their "graves," the Lord shows that this coming back together will be gradual:

> Then He said to me, "Son of man, these bones are the whole house of Israel, behold, they say, 'Our bones are dried up, and our hope has perished. We are completely cut off.'" Therefore prophecy, and say to them, "Thus says the Lord God, 'Behold I will open your graves and cause you to come up out of your graves, My people; and I will bring you into the land of Israel'" (Ezek. 37:11, 12)

This coming back together involves the collection of the bones into skeletons, then flesh comes on them and they become cadavers strewn on the desert. At the end, the process of the breath of God comes on the bodies, and they become a Spirit-filled army and nation. This is how the restoration to the land takes place. It happens in stages; the conversion of the Jews is also progressive.

Can anyone deny seeing this "work in progress" going on at the present time? The Jews have been out of the land for almost 2,000 years. They had been persecuted in land after land, unfortunately *in the name of Jesus.* They began returning in the early 1900s, and began to stream back when the Balfour declaration was implemented during World War I. Balfour was the Foreign Minister of Britain who believed earnestly in the return of the Jews back to their Promised Land!

When this return began, amillennialists and covenant theologians had almost nothing to say about the event. Their quietness and lack of support for the Jewish people could be taken as anti-Semitism by silence. While they deny this, the facts speak for themselves. The response of Satan to the dry bones movement would be World War II. Hitler blamed all of Europe's problems on the Jews. From the beginning, he determined to destroy all the Jewish people. Over 6 million Jews died by his hands and by what he called the "final solution of the Jewish question."

Despite the terrible events of the holocaust against God's own people, their persecution started the greater impetus to return to the land. In fact, many Jews say Hitler was the whip that drove them back to the holy land. With the support of the United States, Russia, and the United Nations, the State of Israel was established in 1948. At one time, 20,000 Jews per month were flowing back home to Israel. Against impossible odds, and following 5 wars of aggression against it, the nation survived. One has to call these wars, "miracle wars." God spared His own!

Again, while the nation of Israel was under siege and suffering, the liberal World Council of Churches, with the help of left-leaning groups, were silent. But so were the amillennialists, allegorists, and covenant theological churches and denominations. If support was to be had, it was for the Arabs, who were, time and again, the aggressors. Throughout it all, Israel survived and even prospered. How can this *not* be the hand of the God of Abraham, Isaac, and Jacob?

The amillennialists have proven to be virtually agnostic about the historic development in the Middle East. They do not recognize "the signs of the times" with the Lord progressively working in Israel. They have also gone so far as to accuse the Jews of "mistreating" the

Arabs. In fact, the Arabs have committed 100 times more offenses against the Jews, than the Jews have against the Arabs. Again, no one condones mistreatment. Evangelicals who support the Jewish state would not accept official mistreatment.

Some critics of Israel today say that what is missing in the Israeli-Arab conflict is that Israel should treat the Arabs like strangers in their land, with kindness and love! They even add that the Jews have no claim to the land until they accept Christ as their Savior and Messiah. They forget that the title deed and the covenant to the land are irrevocable. It is still in effect even though the Jews are in the land in unbelief. And of course premillennialists and dispensationalists know that they will not enjoy the land until they turn to the Lord, and even more so, until the Son of Man comes from heaven! The *ownership* to the land is an irrevocable and unconditional grant. However, the *possession* of the land is conditional upon Israel's obedience, as indicated in the Law of Moses.

The prophet Daniel understood this and wrote:

> O my God, incline Thine ear and hear! Open Thine eyes and see our desolations and the city which is called by Thy name; for we are not presenting our supplications before Thee **on account of any merits of our own, but on account of Thy great compassions**. O Lord, hear! O Lord, forgive! O Lord, listen and take action! **For Thine own sake**, O my God, do not delay, because Thy city and Thy people are called by Thy name (Dan. 9:18, 19). [bold mine]

Daniel asks for restoration not on the basis of obedience, but on the basis of God's grace and love for His disobedient covenant people. Therefore, though they may now be disobedient, this does not hinder God's working with them to bring them back to the land. Some argue that we must be careful about getting involved in the political divide in the Middle East. "We just want the Lord's perspective," they argue. But His perspective is already given in Scripture. It could be that those who cry "politics" are really more for the Arabs than the Jews. Current events are clear. The overwhelming aggressions such as car and suicide-bombings are not coming from the Jews but from the Arabs.

The Bible adds ammunition to the support we should give to Israel. When Rahab the harlot hid the spies she said *I know that the Lord has given you the land* (Josh. 2:9, 10). God blessed Rahab and her family on the basis of the fact of the covenant, not on the basis that the Jewish people deserved the land.

When the 70-year captivity of the Jews in Babylon was over, and Persia had miraculously and prophetically had taken over Babylon in an almost bloodless invasion, King Cyrus made a decree (initiated by the Lord) that the Jewish people were to return to Jerusalem to rebuild the temple (Ezra 1:1-4). What if the king had told the Jews that they were removed from Jerusalem because they had displeased their God, and He would not change His judgment by helping them to return? However, this is not the attitude of Cyrus. Instead, he supported their restoration to the land. God returned a blessing to the Gentile King Cyrus by giving him such an easy victory over Babylon, one of the greatest empires of antiquity. Would Rahab or king Cyrus sit on the fence today as the amillennialists? It is certainly doubtful.[15]

CONCLUSION

While not the only cause, basic covenant theology may be very much to blame for the attack against the right of the Jews to their own homeland. Hodge wrote, "This dispensation [of the gospel] is...the last before the restoration of all things."[16] And, "The true Israel is not a political but a spiritual community...a spiritual kingdom."[17] Berkhof teaches that the Old Testament kingdom promises are now invalid. He writes, "The kingdom, that is, the Old Testament theocracy, was predicted and was not restored, and the Church was not predicted but was established."[18]

Reformed writer Reymond says that the apostle James taught "the multiethnic expansion of the church is fulfilling the predicted 'rebuilding of the fallen house of David' (Acts 15:13-17)...[Christ] makes no reference or allusion to a future thousand-year reign of peace on earth."[19] While not all amillennialists align themselves along the same eschatological views, the observations below are fair as to their teaching, in an overall sense, about Israel:

- The church usurps the nation of Israel from her future promises as given by the ancient Old Testament prophets.
- The church then is a replacement for that literal kingdom prophesied for Israel.
- While some Jews may be saved individually and added to the church, there is no national restoration for Israel.
- What is presently happening in the holy land has no eschatological or spiritual meaning.
- Christians must be even-handed with the Jews and the Arabs.
- To support Israel would be a "political" endorsement and therefore must be avoided.
- The militant Arabs in the holy land are simply "strangers" in the land and must be treated with fairness, no matter what they do.
- There should be no consideration of the Jews having the holy land until they accept Christ as Savior.
- Because the Jews are in the land in unbelief, they should not be seen as having the Davidic covenant and the land covenant promises of restoration as a people now providentially being progressively blessed by the Lord!
- It is assumed that the Jews in the Promised Land are, in the present conflict, automatically the most aggressive people rather than the Arabs.

Conclusion

LIVING IN LIGHT OF ETERNITY

RON J. BIGALKE, JR.

The life of a Christian is compared to earthen vessels that are filled with precious metal. However, Christians must be "broken" in order for the treasure to be seen: *So then death worketh in us, but life in you* (2 Cor. 4:12). The reference to death is to the inner death of self that results from a life of self-denial. In other words, the death is *in* the body as opposed to a threat *to* the body. It is only when the self is "broken" that Christ is seen. The comfort is given in verses 17, 18: *For our light affliction, which is but for a moment, worketh for us a far more exceeding and eternal weight of glory; while we look not at the things which are seen, but at the things which are not seen: for the things which are seen are temporal; but the things which are not seen are eternal.*

The life of the Christian must be lived with an eternal perspective for it is only the treasures laid up in heaven that matters (Mt. 5:19-21). C. S. Lewis once said, "There have been times when I think we do not desire heaven but more often I find myself wondering whether, in our heart of hearts, we have ever desired anything else." One day all Christians will stand before the judgment seat of Christ (Rom. 14:10; 2 Cor. 5:10). Daniel Webster, the noted American statesman, once said: "The greatest thought that has ever entered my mind is that one day I will have to stand before a holy God and give an account of my life." It is sobering indeed that all Christians must "appear before the judgment seat of Christ."

The judgment seat (Gr. *bema*) was an elevated chair or platform, which resembled a throne that an official judge would sit upon in the Roman courts of law. In the Grecian world, the bema was the official seat of a judge who would observe the competitions in the theaters and award honor to those who competed well.

When Christians appear before the judgment seat of Christ it will be *that every one may receive the things done in his body, according to that he hath done, whether it be good or bad* (2 Cor. 5:10). This event does not pertain to non-Christians. Furthermore, it is not the recalling of sins for the Christian (Isa. 43:25; Rom. 8:3; 2 Cor. 5:21; Gal. 3:13; Heb. 8:12). This is not a judicial judgment; rather, it is a judgment to determine rewards. Christians will be judged here not in terms of salvation; rather, they will receive a reward for those things done in the body on earth.

It is clear that the sins of Christians will not be recalled to determine salvation since God poured out His wrath for their sins upon Christ (2 Cor. 5:21). Jesus Christ, the sinner's substitute, took the judgment that man deserved (Rom. 8:3; Gal. 3:13). God has forgotten the sins of the Christian in the sense that He will not lay them to their charge (Ps. 103:12; Isa. 43:25; Heb. 8:12; 10:17). Once justified, the Christian will be always justified, because he has been judged for sin by grace through faith at the cross of Christ (Jn. 5:24; Rom. 8:1, 2; 10:4).

THE JUDGMENT OF WORKS

It is often said that the receiving of rewards should not motivate Christians. While this is true, it does not take into account the fact that Jesus Christ is pleased to reward His disciples. It is not wrong to be motivated by rewards if one is longing to be pleasing to Christ.

Furthermore, one may think that they will be happy as long as they are in heaven, even if this means sitting in the back row. However, what if the same individual is in the back row because he did not please God? What if God, in fact, wanted him up front and near to Himself? The rewards one receives are not to sing "glory be to me." By contrast, the rewards are given in order to serve and honor God all the more in the coming kingdom. Forever, Christians will be trophies of God's grace.

God gives gifts to His church in order to fulfill His will (see Rom. 12:3-8; 1 Cor. 12-14; Eph. 4:1-16; 1 Pet. 4:10, 11). Those that use their gifts as good stewards will receive more. There will also be ruling authority with the Lord granted, because of one being faithful to Christ (Lk. 19:11-27).

The quantity of our works, as illustrated in the parable of the pounds, illustrates this point (Lk. 19:11-27; Rom. 2: 6, 7). Indeed, Christians are "[Christ's] *workmanship, created in Christ Jesus unto good works*, (Eph. 2:10) and *peculiar people, zealous of good works* (Tit. 2:14).

At the judgment seat, the quality of our works will be judged (1 Cor. 3:10-14). Scripture makes clear that some will be saved *yet so as by fire*, that is, their soul is saved but their life on earth was one of unfaithfulness so that all is burned up. These individuals will experience shame before God for not being good stewards of the gifts that God has given them (1 Jn. 2:28). Just as the stars differ in glory, so will some of the saints (1 Cor. 15:41, 42). Only those who have built on the correct foundation, Jesus Christ, will not experience loss.

We should pray as David to *search me, O God, and know my heart* (Ps. 139:23). It should be that every motivation to do something "as unto the Lord" might be judged pure. The motivation of each individual's actions will certainly be examined (1 Cor. 4:5). Christians are to use the gifts that God has given to accomplish the work He has set before them and to glorify Him forever. To glorify God and enjoy Him forever is the aim.

THE DEGREES OF REWARD

Many will receive crowns from the Lord at the judgment seat. The verses below should inspire Christians to labor for the Lord. The motivation is gratitude for all that God has done in procuring salvation through His Son, Jesus Christ.

And every man that striveth for the mastery is temperate in all things. Now they do it to obtain a corruptible crown; but we an incorruptible crown (1 Cor. 9:25). This incorruptible crown is the victor's crown.

For what is our hope, or joy, or crown of rejoicing? Are not even ye in the presence of our Lord Jesus Christ at his coming? For ye are our glory and joy (1 Thess. 2:19, 20). This crown of rejoicing is given to the soul winner.

Henceforth there is laid up for me a crown of righteousness, which the Lord, the righteous judge, shall give me at that day: and not to me only, but unto all them that love his appearing (2 Tim. 4:8). This crown of righteousness is given to all who eagerly anticipate the return of Christ.

Feed the flock of God which is among you, taking the oversight thereof, not by constraint, but willingly; not for filthy lucre, but of a ready mind; neither being lords over God's heritage, but being examples to the flock; and when the chief Shepherd shall appear, ye shall receive a crown of glory that fadeth not away (1 Pet. 5:2-4). This crown of glory is given to pastors-teachers.

Fear none of those things which thou shalt suffer: behold, the devil shall cast some of you into prison, that ye may be tried; and ye shall have tribulation ten days: be thou faithful unto death, and I will give thee a crown of life (Rev. 2:10). This crown of life is given to martyrs.

The receiving of these rewards will allow one to join in with the casting of crowns before the throne of the Lord God Almighty in an act of worship (Rev. 4:9-11). How sorrowful it will be that some will have no crowns to cast before the Lord, the only One worthy to be glorified. At that time, it will be made clear that every good and perfect work was for God and through His power so that He alone should be praised. This will not be a time to draw attention to self;

rather it will be a time to worship the Savior who alone is worthy "to receive glory and honor and power."

Christians are also given robes to wear (Rev. 3:14; 19:8). Clearly, this event occurs somewhere between the Rapture and the Second Coming which would only make sense to be the judgment seat of Christ (cf. 1 Cor. 3:10-15; 2 Cor. 5:10). When the church as the "the armies in heaven" follow Christ, they are adorned as Christ's bride "clothed in fine linen" [e.g. imputed righteousness]. Jude 23 exhorts Christians to hate *even the garment spotted by the flesh*. The emphasis is upon motivation and the excellence of things done in the body. The passage here refers not to the righteousness of Jesus Christ with which believers are clothed for salvation (Isa. 61:10). The garments mentioned are those of good works (a fruitful life) in the life of a Christian having persevered with a profitable result. Just as rewards may be gained, there may also be loss of rewards to the Christian's shame when Christ returns for His church (1 Cor. 3:11-16; 4:1-5; 9:24-27; Tit. 3:8; 1 Jn. 2:28; 2 Jn. 1:8).

THE EXPECTATION OF HEAVEN

Thomas Watson (1620-1686) wrote, "Heaven is a kingdom worth praying for; nothing is wanting in that kingdom which may complete the saint's happiness; for, wherein does happiness consist? Is it in knowledge? We 'shall know as we are known.' Is it in dainty fare? We shall be at the 'marriage supper of the Lamb.' Is it in rich apparel? We shall be 'clothed in long white robes.' Is it in delicious music? We shall hear the choir of angels singing. Is it in dominion? We shall reign as kings, and judge angels. Is it in pleasure? We shall enter into the joy of our Lord."

Although the church is often called the bride of Christ, it is never stated in so many words within the Bible. Certainly passages such as 2 Corinthians 11:1-2, Ephesians 5:25-27, and Revelation 21:9 seem to intimate this idea, but the phraseology of the bride of Christ are all future in meaning. Furthermore, the Hebrew meaning of the word bride can have two meanings. The Hebrew word *kallâh* (from the verb *kâlal*) means "to be completed" and "make perfect." The word "bride" then indicates one who is "complete" and "perfected." In this present dispensation, this is not true of the church, but it will be in the future when she is presented "to Christ...as a pure virgin."

In most biblical passages, the New Testament church is a local congregation of believers. Yet, in another sense there is one large, universal church (1 Cor. 12:13). Presently, God is carrying out His decrees through the local congregations of believers. Second Corinthians 11:1, 2, Ephesians 5:25-27, and Revelation 21:9 testify of a future event when the glorified church (assembly) is gathered together and presented to Christ as His bride.

Following the judgment seat of Christ will be the marriage of the Lamb. This event will take place in heaven before the Second Coming of Christ to earth and after the Rapture of the church. This is apparent in Revelation 19:7, 8: *His* [Christ's] *wife hath made herself ready.*" John the Baptist declared, *He that hath the bride is the bridegroom* (Jn. 3:29). Revelation 19:7 states the bride *hath made herself ready* for her soon marriage because of *the fine linen* of good works. The sad truth is that many Christians are not working for Christ (as fruits of salvation) and therefore, they will not be ready to meet the Bridegroom. There will be shame in a lack of readiness (1 Jn. 2:28).

In the last chapter of Revelation, Jesus says, *"And, behold, I come quickly."* The response of the faithful is *"Amen. Even so, come, Lord Jesus!"* It is because Christ may return at any moment that those in Christ are to encourage each other to live godly lives so that each may obtain the prize of the high calling of God in Christ Jesus (1 Cor. 9:24; Phil. 3:10-14; Heb. 12:1, 2). Furthermore, the imminent return of Christ is an impetus to tell the lost of the glorious gospel of grace. Faith in Jesus without the earnest expectation of His return is like a journey leading to nowhere and ending in utter emptiness.

The church is to join that bridal chorus which cries, *"Even so, come, Lord Jesus."* It is certain that the heavenly Bridegroom will be delighted to respond to that cry. It is due to the riches of God's love that He would have Christ Jesus die in the stead of sinful man. By grace through faith, sinful man can be justified through the blood of God's own Son and be saved from the wrath that he rightfully deserves for his rebellion against God (Rom. 5:8-11). The joy of the Christian will be great at Christ's return, yet it will scarcely match the joy of the Redeemer to take His church home to the Father (Jn. 14:1-3). The following poem, "Jesus only," by the great evangelist D. L. Moody furnishes a fitting conclusion.

The light of heaven is the face of Jesus
The joy of heaven is the presence of Jesus
The melody of heaven is the name of Jesus
The harmony of heaven is the praise of Jesus
The theme of heaven is the work of Jesus
The employment of heaven is the service of Jesus
The duration of heaven is the eternity of Jesus
The fullness of heaven is Jesus Himself

BIOGRAPHIES OF CONTRIBUTING AUTHORS

David Benoit

Evangelist David Benoit became a Christian in 1972 after a rebellious teenage life had led him to reform school. In 1978, he graduated from Liberty Baptist College with a B.S. degree in church ministries. In 1984, David was led of the Lord to establish Glory Ministries for the purpose of exposing the damaging effects of rock music on society, and presenting the only solution being regeneration by Jesus Christ. In the past few years, David has used his vast knowledge of the occult and the New Age movement to expose how Satan is subtly gaining entrance into the home and church through seemingly harmless children's cartoons, movies, and toys. He has written two books on this subject: *Fourteen Things Witches Hope Parents Never Find Out* and *Who's Watching the Playpen?*

David has the rare ability to communicate his message to young people, as well as parents. His goal is to strengthen the family and to equip them with the biblical tools that are necessary to survive these troubled times. The goal of his ministry is to assist the fundamental, Bible-believing churches in America and overseas both in evangelism outreach and subsequent church growth.

Paul N. Benware

Paul Benware is currently professor of Bible and doctrine at Philadelphia Biblical University. His former professorships were at Moody Bible Institute and Los Angeles Baptist College (now Master's College). He has served as pastor in California, Indiana, and Illinois. He earned his Th.M. degree from Dallas Theological Seminary and a Th.D. degree from Grace Theological Seminary. Recently, he authored *The Believer's Payday* (concerning the Judgment Seat of Christ). His other publications include *Understanding End Times Prophecy*, *Survey of the Old Testament*, *Survey of the New Testament*, and *The Gospel of Luke*. He and his wife, Anne, have four grown children and four grandchildren.

Ron J. Bigalke, Jr.

Ron Bigalke, Jr. is a author, lecturer, and former pastor. He graduated from Moody Bible Institute and earned his M.Apol. degree from Columbia Evangelical Seminary. He is a scholarship student and Ph.D. candidate (majoring in eschatology) with Tyndale Theological Seminary. He is a professor at the Florida extension of the Moody Bible Institute and mentor for Columbia Evangelical Seminary, in addition to teaching Bible and history at Shepherd's Christian Academy in New Port Richey. He is also an administrative intern with the Association of Christian Schools International (ACSI). He is the founder and director of Eternal Ministries—a discipleship and evangelistic ministry dedicated to teaching and proclaiming the Word of God. He and his wife, Kristin, are recently married.

David Breese

Dave Breese was an internationally known author, lecturer, radio broadcaster, and Christian minister. He was the founder and president of Christian Destiny and publisher of the *Destiny Newsletter*. He ministered in church and area-wide evangelistic crusades, leadership conferences, student gatherings, and related preaching missions. He is a graduate of Judson College and Northern Seminary. Among his most popular books are *Discover Your Destiny*, *His Infernal Majesty*, *Know the Marks of Cults*, *Living for Eternity*, and *Seven Men Who Rule from the Grave*. Dave went to be with the Lord on 3 May 2002.

Joseph R. Chambers

Joseph Chambers, senior minister of Paw Creek Church of God at Charlotte, North Carolina, is president of Paw Creek Christian Academy, which he founded in 1974. He is radio host of a weekly two-hour program, "Open Bible Dialogue," and has been involved in broadcast and writing ministries on the evangelical-political scene for more than twenty-five years. In his commentary, he covers a wide range of topics, but one of his specialties is exposing false teachings in the Body of Christ. Joseph has produced several videotapes that expose the errors of the Word of Faith movement. His publications include: *The Challenge of the Ministry*, *Miracles: My Father's Delight*, and *A Palace for the Antichrist*. In addition, he has written many articles for various publications. He and his wife, Juanita, have three grown children and six grandchildren.

Mal Couch

Mal Couch is founder and president of Tyndale Theological Seminary and Biblical Institute in Ft. Worth, Texas. He earned his Th.M. degree from Dallas Theological Seminary, M.A. degree from Wheaton Graduate School, and a Th.D. degree from Louisiana Baptist Seminary. He has taught at Dallas Theological Seminary, Moody Bible Institute, and Philadelphia College of the Bible. He is a prolific writer and conference speaker. His publications include *A Bible Handbook to the Acts of the Apostles*, *The Coming of the Holy Spirit*, *Dictionary of Premillennial Theology*, *The Fundamentals for the Twenty-First Century*, and *The Hope of Christ's Return*.

Russell S. Doughten, Jr.

Russell Doughten, Jr. is the founder and president of Russ Doughten Films and Mustard Seed International. In 1965, he founded Heartland Productions. Under the Heartland banner, he produced and directed eight dramatic features that present the Gospel of Jesus Christ. He also co-founded Mark IV Pictures in 1972, where he produced 12 feature length, dramatic Christian movies over a 12-year period. The best-known movies of Russ are a series of four films based on biblical end times prophecy: *A Thief In The Night*, *A Distant Thunder*, *Image of the Beast*, and *The Prodigal Planet*. Millions of people around the world have been touched by the Gospel message in this series. It is for these reasons that he has been called the "Father of the Modern Christian Movie."

In 2001, at the WYSIWYG Film Festival (similar to the Academy Awards) held in San Francisco, CA, Russ was awarded the "Lifetime Achievement Award" for lifetime contribution in presenting the gospel through motion pictures. He also received the Milestone Award for 50 years of achievement in communicating the gospel of Jesus Christ through movies recently at the February Annual Meeting of the National Religious Broadcasters in Nashville, Tennessee.

Reg Dunlap

Reg Dunlap is a nationally known speaker, having served the Lord as a pastor, writer, evangelist, and teacher. As founder and director of the *Evangelism for Christ Association*, he directs an interdenominational ministry which functions as a servant to the local church in the area of evangelism, renewal, and revival. He is the author of many books, including *Sound Doctrine May Be Harmful to Your Religious Experience*, *The Next Invasion from Outer Space*, and *Revelation and the End of the World*. As an ordained Baptist minister, he has received invitations to conduct evangelistic crusades and Bible conferences across the country and different parts of the world with thousands of lives being touched by his preaching and teaching ministry. He is also one of the most popular contributors of sermons on the Internet. He and his wife, Eleanor, have two grown children.

Arno Froese

Arno Froese is the executive director of Midnight Call Ministry and editor-in-chief of the critically acclaimed prophetic magazines *News from Israel* and *Midnight Call*, which is internationally distributed in many foreign languages. Arno has sponsored more than fifty national and international prophecy conferences, in addition to leading numerous study tours through Israel. He has authored several prophecy-oriented books including: *The Great Mystery of the Rapture, How Democracy Will Elect the Antichrist, Saddam's Mystery Babylon, The Coming Digital God,* and *Terror over America,* which explains the tragedy of September 11th from a biblical, prophetic perspective.

Mike Gendron

Evangelist Mike Gendron was a devout Roman Catholic for 34 years and a strong defender of the "one true church." In 1981, at an evangelistic seminar, Mike heard for the first time that salvation is not by works or sacraments but by grace through faith in Jesus Christ! He also discovered the Bible must become his authority in all matters of faith. After graduating from Dallas Theological Seminary in 1991, Mike began this ministry to reach the many Catholics who are where he was for most of his life—believing he was heaven-bound but, in reality, destined for a Christ-less eternity.

Phillip Goodman

Phillip Goodman is the founder and former president of The Spiritual Armour Project, which he directed for 10 years. In 2000, he formed a partnership with Dr. Charles Pack of Thy Kingdom Come, where he now serves as a vice president. He is a Vietnam veteran, and was the director of the award-winning adult and community education program for the Tulsa Public Schools for 21 years, and has taught at Tulsa Community College. Phillip has conducted prophecy seminars in both Canada and the United States. He and his wife, Mary, a native of Bethlehem, Israel, have four sons.

Dave Hunt

Dave Hunt is an internationally known best-selling author and lecturer. He is known for making the Bible relevant in this quick and ever changing world. Oftentimes, Dave is considered controversial because of his fearless defense of the biblical faith. Dave is recognized as an impeccable researcher and authority on cults, occult, prophecy, and world religions. His books, which have been translated into more than forty languages, have combined totals of over four million copies. His bestseller, *The Seduction of Christianity*, exposed many false teachings that had crept into the church practically unhindered. His other publications include: *In Defense of the Faith, Occult Invasion, The God Makers*, and *An Urgent Call to a Serious Faith*. He and his wife, Ruth, have four grown children and eleven grandchildren.

Thomas Ice

Thomas Ice is the executive director of The Pre-Trib Research Center in Arlington, Texas, which he founded in 1994 with Dr. Tim LaHaye to research, teach, and defend the pretribulational rapture and related Bible prophecy doctrines. He earned his Th.M. in historical theology from Dallas Theological Seminary and Ph.D. in systematic theology (specializing in eschatology) from Tyndale Theological Seminary. He was the pastor of Trinity Bible Church in Fredricksburg, Virginia. He has co-authored over 20 books, written dozens of articles, spoken at some of the largest churches in the

United States, and is a frequent conference speaker. He lives with his wife Janice, and their three boys in Arlington, Texas.

William T. James

William T. James ("Terry," as he is addressed by those who know him) is frequently interviewed for broadcasts throughout the nation. He has been completely blind since 1993, but says he is "thankful to my Lord for helping me better focus on the things he truly wants me to research, see, and report through my writing." He considers himself an intensely interested observer of historical and contemporary human affairs. He is always attempting to analyze those issues in light of the Holy Bible. He is the author and editor of numerous books on Bible prophecy. His most recent publication is *Prophecy at Ground Zero.*

Robert Lightner

Robert Lightner is a respected theologian and author of numerous books and articles. He is professor emeritus of systematic theology at Dallas Theological Seminary. For over 29 years, he has taught courses in Bible, theology, and eschatology. He graduated from Dallas Theological Seminary with a Th.M. and Th.D., and from Southern Methodist University with a M.L.A. He is listed in *Who's Who in American Education*, *Outstanding Educators of America*, and *Community Leaders of America*. He is a member of the Evangelical Theological Society and served on the executive board of Bible Memory Association International. He is married and has three daughters.

Larry Spargimino

Larry Spargimino is associate pastor and editor of Southwest Radio Church Ministries, the oldest, continuously broadcasting radio ministry in the world. He has a Ph.D. in New Testament and Greek from Southwestern Baptist Theological Seminary in Fort Worth, Texas. His latest book, *Religion of Peace or Refuge For Terror?* shows how the world's fastest growing religion spawns terrorism. He has also authored *The Anti-Prophets: The Challenge of Preterism* and is one of the contributors to the new book on Preterism to be published by the Pre-Trib Research Center. Having served as a pastor in local churches over the last twenty five years, Larry Spargimino has also been a Christian school administrator. He currently has a ministry to Chinese students in Oklahoma City.

Mike Stallard

Mike Stallard is professor of systematic theology at Baptist Bible Seminary in Clarks Summit, Pennsylvania. He is also founder and director of Mission Scranton in Northeast Pennsylvania and interim pastor at Southside Baptist Church in Scranton, Pennsylvania. He maintains the website "Our Hope" taken from the name of one of the most prominent evangelical, dispensational magazines in America from 1894 to 1945. *Our Hope* magazine was edited by Arno C. Gaebelein, a figure Mike studied in his Ph.D. dissertation at Dallas Theological Seminary.

Harold L. Willmington

Harold Willmington was a pastor for over 17 years and currently serves as dean of Liberty Bible Institute. He graduated from Moody Bible Institute, Ashland Theological Seminary, and Trinity Evangelical Divinity School. He has authored numerous books including *Willmington's Complete Guide to Bible Knowledge, Willmington's Guide to the Bible,* and *The King is Coming.* For 17 years, his wife, Sue, appeared on the nationally televised program *Old Time Gospel Hour* as an interpreter for deaf viewers in both America and Canada. He and his wife have one son and two grandchildren.

END NOTES

Introduction—Hoofbeats of the Apocalypse

[1] Charles C. Ryrie, *Dispensationalism* (Chicago: Moody Press, 1995; reprint, Chicago: Moody Press, 1966), 25.

[2] Ibid., 39-41.

[3] Ron Bigalke, Jr., "How Progressive Is Dispensationalism?" *Conservative Theological Society Newsletter* (December 2000).

[4] The covenants of God with Israel are as follows: (1) Abrahamic Covenant—Gen. 12:1-3; 13:14-17; 15:4, 21; 17:1-8; 22:17, 18; (2) Land (Deuteronomic) Covenant—Deut. 30:1-9; Jer. 32:36-44; Ezek. 11:16-21; 36:21-38; (3) Davidic Covenant—Sam. 7:10-16; Ps. 89; Jer. 33:20, 21; and, (4) New Covenant—Isa. 59:20, 21, Jer. 31:31-34; Ezek. 16:60; Hos. 2:14-23.

[5] Gene Edward Veith, "The New Multi-Faith Religion," *World* (15 December 2001), http://www.worldmag.com/world/issue/12-15-01/cultural_1.asp

[6] Thomas L. Friedman, "The Real War," *New York Times* (27 November 2001), http://www.yale.edu/dsj/docs/NYTimes_11-27_TheRealWar.pdf

[7] Ibid.

[8] Ibid.

[9] Frederic W. Baue, *The Spiritual Society* (Wheaton: Crossway Books, 2001).

[10] Veith, *Op Cit.*

[11] John F. Walvoord, *Major Bible Prophecies* (Grand Rapids: Zondervan, 1991), 314-315.

[12] Arnold G. Fruchtenbaum, Class notes in *Highlights of the Book of Matthew*, Ft. Worth: Tyndale Theological Seminary.

[13] John F. Walvoord, *Israel in Prophecy* (Grand Rapids: Zondervan, 1962), 129-131.

[14] While covenant theology is typically deemed synonymous with Calvinism, Reformed, or Puritanism there are similar covenant constructs that can also be found in Catholicism and other Anglo-Catholic denominations. Amongst the Reformed/Calvinists there are numerous variations and sub-groups: Princeton, Dutch Reformed, Southern Reformed, New Covenant, and Reconstructionist to name just a few.

[15] Louis Berkhof, *Systematic Theology* (Grand Rapids: Eerdmans, 1941), 293.

[16] Alva J. McClain, *Law and Grace* (Winona Lake: BMH Books, 1973), 30.

[17] The distinction between Israel and the church is important because God's plan and purpose for the church is different than that of her biblical predecessor. For instance, the New Testament clearly teaches that the church will experience persecution and suffering (Jn. 15:18-25, 16:33; Phil. 1:29; Col. 1:24; 2 Tim. 3:12, *et al*). However, the same New Testament promises a future deliverance from a future time of wrath. Henceforth, it logically follows that there must be different kinds or even periods of persecution that the church will experience and another kind of wrath or persecution that she will be delivered from. The church is promised deliverance from a future coming wrath although she will suffer persecution during the current church age (Rom. 5:9; 1 Thess. 1:10; 5:9; Rev. 3:10).

[18] For instance, the Dallas Theological Seminary doctrinal statement (Article V) reads: "We believe that different administrative responsibilities of this character are manifest in the biblical record, that they span the entire history of mankind, and that each ends in the failure of man under the respective test and in an ensuing judgment from God. We believe that three of these dispensations or rules of life are the subject of extended revelation in the Scripture, viz., the dispensation of the Mosaic Law, the present dispensation of grace, and the future dispensation of the millennial kingdom.

We believe that these are distinct and are not to be intermingled or confused, as they are chronologically successive."

[19] Larry Crutchfield, "Ages and Dispensations in the Ante-Nicene Fathers," *Vital Prophetic Issues*, Roy Zuck, gen. ed. (Grand Rapids: Kregel, 1995), 57-58.

[20] Floyd Elmore, "John Nelson Darby," *Dictionary of Premillennial Theology*, Mal Couch, gen. ed. (Grand Rapids: Kregel, 1996), 83-85.

[21] Ryrie, *Dispensationalism*, 65-69.

[22] See E. R. Campbell, *A Dispensational Panorama of the Bible* (Silverton: Canyonview Press, n.d.).

[23] Ryrie, *Dispensationalism*, 27.

[24] Elmore, "John Nelson Darby," 84.

[25] Os Guinness, *Fit Bodies, Fat Minds* (Grand Rapids: Baker Book House, 1994), 64.

[26] Ibid., 65.

[27] Ryrie, "What is Dispensationalism?" (Dallas Theological Seminary, 1980), 7.

[28] Ryrie, *Dispensationalism*, 212.

Chapter 3—Teaching the Prophetic Word

[1] Editor's Note: For another detailed analysis of this subject by the referenced author, please see Charles H. Dyer, "The Identity of Babylon in Revelation 17-18: Part 1." *Bibliotheca Sacra* 144/#575 (July-September 1987): 305-16; "The Identity of Babylon in Revelation 17-18: Part 2." *Bibliotheca Sacra* 144/#576 (October-December 1987): 433-449. For additional study by other contributors to this book, please see Joseph R. Chambers, *A Palace for the Antichrist* (Green Forest: New Leaf Press, 1996); Arno Froese, *Saddam's Mystery Babylon* (West Columbia: The Olive Press, 1998).

Chapter 4—Consistency from Genesis to Revelation

[1] Bernard Ramm, *Protestant Biblical Interpretation* (Boston: W. A. Wilde Co., 1950), 1.

[2] For a discussion of more recent differences some evangelicals want to make between inspiration and inerrancy, see Harold

Lindsell's *The Battle for the Bible* (Grand Rapids: The Zondervan Corporation, 1976), and his *The Bible in the Balance* (Grand Rapids: The Zondervan Corporation, 1979). Also see *Inerrancy*, edited by Norman L. Geisler (Grand Rapids: Zondervan, 1979).

[3] I recommend the following for study in this area: Roy B. Zuck, *Basic Bible Interpretation* (Wheaton, IL: Victor Books, 1991) and Elliott Johnson, *Expository Hermeneutics: An Introduction* (Grand Rapids: Zondervan, 1990).

[4] Oswald T. Allis, *Prophecy and the Church* (Philadelphia: Presbyterian and Reformed Pub. Co., 1945), 238.

[5] William E. Cox, *Amillennialism Today* (Philadelphia: Presbyterian and Reformed Pub. Co., 1966), 13.

[6] Jay Adams, *The Time Is at Hand* (Nutley, NJ: Presbyterian and Reformed Pub. Co., 1966), 13.

[7] Loraine Boettner, *The Millennium* (Philadelphia: Presbyterian and Reformed Pub. Co., 1964), 82.

[8] George N. H. Peters, *The Theocratic Kingdom of Our Lord Jesus the Christ* (Grand Rapids: Kregel Publications, 1957; reprint, New York: Funk & Wagnalls, 1884), 47.

[9] John F. Walvoord, *The Millennial Kingdom* (Findlay, OH: Dunham Publishing Co., 1959), 59.

[10] For other methods see Milton S. Terry, *Biblical Hermeneutics* (Grand Rapids: Zondervan Publishing House, 1969), 163-174.

[11] Bernard Ramm, *Protestant Biblical Interpretation* (Boston: W. A. Wilde, Co., 1950), 53.

[12] Ibid., 64.

[13] Examples of these may be found in J. Dwight Pentecost, *Things to Come* (Findlay, OH: Dunham Publishing Co., 1958), 9-15, and Paul Lee Tan, *The Interpretation of Prophecy* (Winona Lake, IN: B. M. H. Books, Inc., 1974), 29-39.

[14] Charles C. Ryrie, *Dispensationalism Today* (Chicago: Moody Press, 1965), 87-88.

[15] Allis, *Prophecy*, 17.

[16] Ibid., 17-18.

[17] Pentecost, *Things to Come*, 14-15.

[18] Ramm, *Interpretation*, 23.

[19] Ibid., 21.

[20] See Meno J. Brunk, *Fulfilled Prophecies* (Krockette, KY: Rod & Staff Publications, Inc., 1971).

Chapter 7—God's Judgment Upon Individuals

[1] Geoffrey W. Bromiley, *Theological Dictionary of the New Testament,* ed. by Gerhard Kittel and Gerhard Friedrich (Grand Rapids: Eerdmans, 1992), 201.

[2] J. Dwight Pentecost, *The Words and Works of Jesus Christ* (Grand Rapids: Zondervan, 1981), 409.

[3] Thomas J. Finley, *The Wycliffe Exegetical Commentary: Joel, Amos and Obadiah* (Chicago: Moody Press, 1990), 84.

[4] E. B. Pusey, *The Minor Prophets* (Grand Rapids: Baker Book House, 1965), 1:201.

[5] J. Dwight Pentecost, *Things to Come* (Grand Rapids: Dunham Publishing Co., 1964), 417.

[6] Arnold G. Fruchtenbaum, *The Footsteps of the Messiah* (Tustin, CA: Ariel Ministries Press, 1993), 260.

[7] John F. Walvoord, *Major Bible Prophecies* (Grand Rapids: Zondervan, 1991), 386.

[8] Fruchtenbaum, *Footsteps,* 259.

[9] Finley, *Joel, Amos and Obadiah,* 87.

Chapter 8—The Global Islamic Peril

[1] Martin Gilbert, *The Illustrated Atlas of Jewish Civilization* (New York: Macmillan, 1969), 160-183.

[2] Todd M. Johnson, "Religious Projections for the Next 200 Years," http://www.wnrf.org/cms/next200.shtml

[3] Jay Gray, "Ten Global Trends in Religion," http://www.wnrf.org/cms/tentrends.shtml

[4] David B. Barrett and Todd M. Johnson, "Annual Table of World Religions, 1900-2025," http://www.wnrf.org/cms/statuswr.shtml; World Evangelization Research Center, "Status of Global Mission, 2002," http://www.gem-werc.org/

[5] Todd M. Johnson, "Religious Projections for the Next 200 Years," http://www.wnrf.org/cms/next200.shtml

[6] Samuel P. Huntington, *The Clash of Civilizations: Remaking of World Order* (New York: Touchstone, 1997), 66.

[7] Wendy Murray Zoba, "Islam, U.S.A.," (*Christianity Today*, 3 April 2000), http://www.christianitytoday.com/ct/2000/004/1.40.html

[8] Dale E. Bishop, "Profile of Islam," *New World Outlook* (Nov.-Dec. 1989): 243, 245.

[9] Tariq, "Islam," 14.

[10] See Mufti Afzal Hoosein Elias, "Hadhrat Esa (Alaihis Salaam): The Truth Revealed and Major Signs of Qiyamat," (http://islam.tc/ask-imam/index.php).

[11] Mikail Juma Tariq, "Islam: A Brief Introduction to the Muslim Faith" (Gainesville: Alachua County Dawah Society, n.d.), 19.

[12] These are designated to take place as follows: (1) *Fajr*, at dawn and before sunrise; (2) *Zuhr*, shortly after midday; (3) *'Asr*, at mid-afternoon; (4) *Maghrib*, shortly after sunset; and (5) *'Ishā*, after nightfall.

[13] Tariq, "Islam," 6.

[14] George Grant, *The Blood of the Moon* (Brentwood: Wolgemuth and Hyatt, 1991), 41.

[15] It is possible that the Muslim mosques could be destroyed in one of the early cataclysmic judgments of Revelation, or even in the Battle of Gog and Magog (Ezek. 38-39). Even if the Muslim holy sites were destroyed, it is still not plausible that the Arabs would abandon the site completely.

[16] Boris Shusteff, "Humiliation of Jews and Israelis," http://www.freeman.org/m_online/aug98/shusteff.htm

[17] The Khilafah Movement, "Jihad The Only Solution For Palestine," http://www.geocities.com/al_khilafah2001/Israel.html

[18] Julia Duin, "Anglican Priest Believes West is Underestimating the Zeal of Islam" (*The Washington Times*, 16 January 2002), http://www.washtimes.com/culture/20020116-99672079.htm; Sultan Islamic Links, "A Wave of Conversion to Islam in the U.S. Following September 11," http://sultan.org/articles/convert.html

[19] James A. Beverley, "Is Islam a Religion of Peace?" (*Christianity Today*, 7 January 2002), http://www.christianitytoday.com/ct/2002/001/1.32.html

Chapter 9—Islam and Terrorism

[1] National & International Religion Report (26 December 1994): 2.

[2] David Reed, "The Unholy War Between Iran and Iraq," *Reader's Digest* (August 1984): 39.

[3] International Christian Concern, "Indonesia: Operation Rescue Maluku," http://persecution.org/concern/2001/04/pl.html

[4] *Foreign Affairs*, Spring 1982; cited in Ramon Bennett, *Philistine* (Jerusalem: Arm of Salvation, 1995), 27.

[5] John Laffin, *The Arab Mind* (London: Cassell, 1975), 97-98; cited in Ibid., 28.

Chapter 10—The Destiny of America

[1] Noah W. Hutchings with S. Franklin Logsdon, *The U.S. In Prophecy* (Oklahoma City: Hearthstone, 2002), 11.

[2] Mark Hitchcock, *101 Answers to the Most Asked Questions About the End Times* (Sisters, OR: Multnomah, 2001), 33.

[3] David Barton, *Original Intent: The Courts, The Constitution, And Religion* (Aledo, TX: WallBuilders, 1996), 5.

[4] Ibid., 24.

[5] Ibid., 26.

[6] For documentation, see this author's *Religion of Peace or Refuge for Terror?* (Oklahoma City: Hearthstone, 2002).

[7] News and Analysis, http://English.Pravda.ru.

[8] Stan Monteith, *Brotherhood of Darkness* (Oklahoma City: Hearthstone, 2001), 9.

[9] This poem was held in high esteem by Winston Church (Ibid., 12-13). President Harry Truman carried a copy of it in his wallet (Ibid., 17).

[10] Ibid., 14.

[11] Ibid., 17.

[12] *Forbes* (15 October 2001).

[13] John McTernan and Bill Koenig, *Israel: The Blessing or the Curse* (Oklahoma City: Hearthstone, 2002), 70.

[14] Ibid., 70-71.

[15] Ibid., 72.

[16] Ibid., 72-73.

[17] Bernard Goldberg, *Bias: A CBS Insider Exposes How the Media Distort the News* (Washington, D.C.: Regnery Publishing, Inc., 2001), 188-192.

[18] Patrick J. Buchanan, *The Death of the West* (New York: St. Martin's Press, 2002), 193.

[19] Monteith, *Brotherhood*, 9-10.

[20] Hutchings and Logsdon, *U.S. in Prophecy*, 239-240.

[21] Ibid., 67-268.

[22] Ibid., 229.

Chapter 12—Democracy in World Government

[1] *National Geographic* (July 1997): 15

[2] Ibid, 21

[3] Ibid, 30

[4] Ibid, 35

[5] *National Geographic* (August 1997): 62-63

[6] Ibid, 68

[7] Ibid, 70

[8] *The Courier* (October 1998): 103

Chapter 13—The Emerging World Religion

[1] *Los Angeles Times* (1 July 2000).

[2] http://www.Insightmag.com (2 October 2000).

[3] *Vatican Information Service* (17 May 2001).

[4] *Koenig's International News* (26 January 2002).

[5] The World Seen From Rome (4 September 2001), http://www.Zenit.org.

[6] *The Apostolic Digest* (Irving, TX: Sacred Heart Press, 1987): 242.

[7] Ibid, 249.

[8] Ibid, 157.

[9] Ibid, 59.

[10] ENI, (31 August 2001).

[11] The World Seen From Rome (27 November 2001), http://www.Zenit.org.

[12] *The Sword and Trowel*, 196.

[13] *Los Angeles Herald Examiner* (19 September 1987).

[14] Praise The Lord program on TBN (17 October 1989).

Chapter 14—The Kingdom of Antichrist

[1] Jeremy Rifkin, *Algeny* (New York: Viking Press, 1983), 112.

[2] Ibid., 244.

Chapter 15—Stories Given From the King

[1] This article gives a digest of two other articles: Mike Stallard, "Hermeneutics and Matthew 13—Part I," *The Conservative Theological Society Journal* 5 (August 2001): 131-54; "Hermeneutics and Matthew 13—Part II," *The Conservative Theological Society Journal* 5 (December 2001): 324-59. In those articles, the reader can study the arguments presented in this article in greater technical detail.

[2] The present writer is not succumbing to the temptation, just asserting its existence. The fact of the matter is that within the argument of the chapter, the genuine understanding of the disciples is set over against the lack of understanding of the Jewish leaders due to their unbelief.

[3] This article takes for granted that literal interpretation, understood as grammatical-historical interpretation, is the accepted approach in interpretation. An honest effort should be made not to read one's preconceived notions, including theology, into the text, but let the details of the text yield their own story.

[4] Mark Bailey, "Guidelines for Interpreting Jesus' Parables," *Bibliotheca Sacra* 155 (January-March 1998): 29-30. In general, this article by Bailey provides a brief, but excellent, survey of current studies of parables.

[5] Ada R. Habershon discusses the extravagances of the Church Fathers but argues for a realistic and complete use of the details. See Ada R. Habershon, *The Study of the Parables* (reprint, Grand Rapids: Kregel, 1975), 10-12.

[6] R. C. Trench reminds us that many of the Fathers such as Chrysostom, Theophylact, and Origen tried to maintain a balance between details and the big idea of a parable. Yet, Fathers like Augustine pressed the details. See R. C. Trench, *Notes on the Parables of Our Lord* (reprint, Grand Rapids: Baker, 1977), 15-16.

[7] There are many contextual factors that help the interpreter to maintain balanced focus in his interpretation of the parables.

Sometimes, Jesus gives the interpretation Himself. Other times the Evangelist gives additional comments about what is going on. Special clues can also be found in the prologue or epilogue to the parable (see Bailey's summary with scriptural examples, "Guidelines," 30-31). At times there is a combination of these factors, especially if there are several parables clustered together to convey truths linked to some common theme.

8 This approach to the structure of Matthew 13:3-52 recognizes some elements of chiasm. Several other scholars have argued for a form of chiastic structure. See David Wenham, "The Structure of Matthew XIII," *New Testament Studies* 25 (1979): 517-18. D. A. Carson, following Wenham, does so also ["Matthew" in *The Expositor's Bible Commentary*, Vol. 8, edited by Frank E. Gaebelein (Grand Rapids: Zondervan, 1984), 303-04]. In addition, Craig Blomberg admits to some inverted parallelism in the chapter while simultaneously recognizing that a chiastic presentation of the subdivisions throughout the chapter does not necessarily aid in understanding the content [*The New American Commentary Series: Matthew* (Nashville: Broadman Press, 1992), 22:225]. Similarly, this present writer does not see a clear and comprehensive chiastic structure for all of the details in the entire cluster of the eight parables in the chapter. However, there are enough elements to aid interpretation by highlighting certain connections and chief emphases. Specifically, since the interpretation of the parable of the tares is located structurally in the middle of the parable cluster, its centrality to the interpretation of the chapter should not be disputed.

9 A discussion of other elements of the parable of the tares will be given below including the identification of the "sons of the kingdom" in verse 38.

10 Carson, *Matthew*, 304. See Luke 5:36; 6:39.

11 John Walvoord, *Matthew: Thy Kingdom Come, A Commentary on the First Gospel* (Grand Rapids: Kregel, 1974), 97.

12 See Stallard, "Matthew 13, Part I," *Conservative Theological Journal*.

13 This approach which sees unity throughout Matthew in the way that the term **kingdom** is used is contrary to emphases that allow

for a shift within Matthew from one kind of kingdom to another [Mark Saucy, "The Kingdom-of-God Sayings in Matthew," *Bibliotheca Sacra* 151 (April-June 1994): 175-97.]

14 Dispensationalists have debated the identification of this "nation." One leading view is that the nation to whom the kingdom is given is the future Jewish remnant during the tribulation, which will be alive to see the start of the eschatological kingdom when Christ returns. Arno Gaebelein would be one representative of this view. He argues "They had refused not alone the kingdom but the King; the Son they would soon cast out and therefore the Kingdom was to be taken from them. These men who stood there, the generation which had share and part in the rejection of the Kingdom and the King, will *never* see the Kingdom. . . . The nation to whom the Lord promises the kingdom is not the Church. The Church is called the Body of Christ, the Bride of Christ, the Habitation of God by the Spirit, the Lamb's Wife, but never a nation. The nation is Israel still, but that believing remnant of the nation, living when the Lord comes" [Arno C. Gaebelein, *The Gospel of Matthew: An Exposition* (New York: Publication Office Our Hope, 1910; reprint, Neptune, NJ: Loizeaux Brothers, 1961), 437]. This approach has the advantage of meshing well with the Olivet Discourse (Mt. 24-25). It also could then tie in easily to the end-of-the-age scenario that is mentioned in the parable of the tares (13:40-41) as well as keep kingdom truth associated with Israel, the main focus of the Old Testament kingdom idea.

A second prominent view of "nation" in Matthew 21:43 is that it refers to the Church. Toussaint, representative of this view, responds to Gaebelein's argument in the following way: "But the difficulty with this [Gaebelein's] explanation is seen in that 'nation' (ἔθνος) is used and not 'generation' (γενεα`) or 'offspring' (γέννημα). Gaebelein also states, 'The Church is called the Body of Christ . . . but never a nation.' This statement can be very seriously disputed. 1 Peter 2:9 and Romans 10:19 definitely refer to the church as a nation" [Stanley Toussaint, *Behold the King: A Study of Matthew* (Portland, OR: Multnomah Press, 1980) 250-51]. Toussaint's positive reasons for his interpretation are mostly theological. What makes this view attractive, however, is that it also appears to fit the flow of Matthew's narrative with the transition from a focus on Israel to the Gentile mission.

15 Toussaint, *Behold the King*, 181.

16 Note that there is no differentiation within this age of a "church age" followed by a "tribulation." No doubt, postribulationalists are pleased with this, but pretribulationalists would simply point out that Matthew does not deal with such matters. What is in view is anyone who is following Christ and spreading His message versus those who are not. This, of course, comes to a head during the tribulation period immediately prior to Christ's Second Coming.

17 Blomberg, *Matthew*, 222.

18 It is beyond the scope of this article to evaluate the term *son* as it occurs in Matthew's entire Gospel, although such an analysis would inform to some degree the discussion about the sons of the kingdom.

19 Blomberg, *Matthew*, 222.

20 For example, see Lorraine Boettner, *The Millennium* (Presbyterian and Reformed, 1957), 131. This view depends upon the idea that the kingdom as presented in this passage is associated with all or part of the present age. However, as has been shown, it is not necessary to view the time of the events described in this chapter as the actual kingdom. Even if it were, as many non-postmillennial theologies hold (including dispensationalists), there are alternative explanations available. In fact, premillennialists do not reject the idea of great success in outreach although they usually reject the idea that society will be overwhelmed by Christianity – an idea that the tares in the previous parable bear out.

21 Blomberg, *Matthew*, 220.

22 Toussaint, *Behold the King*, 182.

23 Louis Barbieri, "Matthew" in *The Bible Knowledge Commentary: New Testament*, eds. John F. Walvoord and Roy B. Zuck (Wheaton: Victor Books, 1983), 51-52; Cp., Toussaint, *Behold the King*, 183-84. It must once again be pointed out that Matthew's understanding of the Church is sketchy and anticipatory. In general, Matthew's focus in chapter thirteen is on the new, unexpected work Christ is doing after the First Advent and before the Second

Advent in light of Israel's rejection of Him. Matthew does not formalize it as the Church although in later chapters he begins to move in that direction (Mt. 16:18; 18:17). The Church was not in all respects a new revelation given to Paul although it was entirely unknown in the Old Testament. Paul himself states that it had been revealed to the apostles and prophets (Eph. 3:5). The details of Jew and Gentile together in one body (the Church) are fleshed out most comprehensively, however, in Pauline theology.

24 In this light, the parable may be related in some way to Jesus' teaching in Matthew 21:43.

Chapter 16—Stage-Setting of the Last Days

1 John F. Walvoord, *Prophecy: 14 Essential Keys to Understanding the Final Drama* (Nashville: Thomas Nelson Publishers, 1993), 1.

2 Ibid.

3 John F. Walvoord, *Israel in Prophecy* (Grand Rapids: Zondervan, 1962), 129.

4 John F. Walvoord, *Armageddon, Oil and the Middle East Crisis*, rev. (Grand Rapids: Zondervan Publishing House, 1990), 217.

5 Ed Hindson, *Final Signs: Amazing Prophecies of the End Times* (Eugene, OR: Harvest House Publishers, 1996), 36-37.

6 Ibid., 36–37.

7 Walvoord, *Middle East Crisis*, 21-22.

8 Arnold Fruchtenbaum, *Footsteps of the Messiah: A Study of the Sequence of Prophetic Events* (Tustin, CA: Ariel Press, 1982), 65.

9 Cited in David A. Rausch, *Zionism within Early American Fundamentalism, 1878-1918: A Convergence of Two Traditions* (New York: The Edwin Mellen Press, 1979), 117.

10 Walvoord, *Israel in Prophecy*, 26.

11 J. Dwight Pentecost, *Prophecy For Today: The Middle East Crisis and the Future of the World* (Grand Rapids: Zondervan Publishing House, 1961), 226.

12 Hal Lindsey, *Planet Earth–2000 a.d. Will Mankind Survive?* (Palos Verdes, CA: Western Front, 1994), 221.

13 Chuck Missler, *The Magog Invasion* (Palos Verdes, CA: Western Front, 1995), 121.

[14] Mark Hitchcock, *After the Empire: Biblical Prophecy in Light of the Fall of the Soviet Union* (Wheaton, IL: Tyndale House Publishers, 1994), 156.

[15] Hindson, *Final Signs*, 151.

[16] Charles C. Ryrie, *The Best Is Yet to Come* (Chicago: Moody Press, 1981), 124-25.

[17] Thomas Ice and Timothy Demy, *The Coming Cashless Society* (Eugene, OR: Harvest House Publishers, 1996), 85-87.

[18] Charles H. Dyer, *The Rise of Babylon: Sign of the End Times* (Wheaton, IL: Tyndale House Publishers, 1991), 208-09.

[19] Joseph Chambers, *A Palace for the Antichrist: Saddam Hussein's Drive to Rebuild Babylon and Its Place in Bible Prophecy* (Green Forest, AR: New Leaf Press, 1996), 66.

[20] Ibid., 19.

Chapter 17—Sequence of End-Time Events

[1] *The Wall Chart of World History*, published by Banes and Noble, Inc., by arrangement with the Third Millennium Press Limited (Chippenham: England, 1997). *The Wall Chart of World History* can be purchased through Thy Kingdom Come, Inc., with an explanatory graph relating it to Bible prophecy, at www.thyking-domcometulsa.com.

[2] Some other examples of a clear time sequence in Bible prophecy include Luke 17:24-25; Acts 15:14-16; 1 Peter 1:11

[3] This passage found in Daniel 9:24-27 is called the 70 Weeks Prophecy. It states that 70 "sevens" (weeks) of years would elapse from day one until the establishment of the Kingdom of Jesus Christ. The prophecy says that 69 of these "sevens" would elapse from day one until Jesus' public ministry as the Messiah. After that, He would be crucified ("cut off"). History would continue, but the calendar would not resume its final "seven" (7 year period) until the end of this age. The 7 year period is the timeframe for what is called the Tribulation. Since all of the events of the 70 Weeks Prophecy have been fulfilled in terms of years, then the "weeks" or "sevens" are sevens of years meaning that the prophecy encompasses 490 years (70 x 7). Day one of the prophecy is 444 BC (exactly 69 sevens) or 483 years before Jesus

officially declared Himself to be the Messiah in fulfillment of the prophecyin Zechariah 9:9 (Lk. 19:35-44). There is a gap to incorporate the church age, which was a "mystery" (or unknown) when this prophecy was given. After the Rapture of the church to heaven, the final 7 year frame of prophetic time will commence as the Tribulation period.

4 The Abomination of Desolation is referred to in Daniel 9:27 where it is said to occur in "the middle of the week" (7 year period). Other references include Matthew 24:15 and 2 Thessalonians 2:3, 4.

5 The Abomination of Desolation occurs at the midpoint of the 7 year Tribulation. In Matthew 24:15-21, the abomination links the flight of the Jews with the start of the Great Tribulation. In Revelation 12, the flight of the Jews is said to last 1,260 days (Rev. 12:6), or "time, times and half a time" (Rev. 12:14). Thus, these two time terms are equal beginning with the Abomination of Desolation. The abomination is the key event which causes the Jewish Temple to be "tread under foot" by the Gentiles in Revelation 11:2. Since this "treading under foot" is said to last for 42 months, then this particular time term is connected to the other two time terms. Therefore, all three time terms are triggered by the Abomination of Desolation in the middle of the Tribulation; they span the final half of the 7 years. Two of these time terms are used of the length of the Antichrist's persecution of the saints (Dan. 7:25; Rev. 13:5-7), which we know to be the time of the last 3 1/2 year period called the Great Tribulation. Finally, in the context of Revelation 11, the two witnesses are seen lamenting (sackcloth) the abomination that desecration the Temple. Therefore, all three time terms ("time, times and half a time," "1260 days," and "42 months") in every occurrence refer to the same period of time, which is the last half of the 7 year Tribulation.

6 Jesus said in Matthew 24:15-21 that the start of the Great Tribulation would be signaled by the Abomination of Desolation.

7 Since there is a false peace covenant enforced for the first half of the 7 year Tribulation, then there will be relative "peace" in Israel. Therefore, the attempts to kill the two witnesses (Rev. 11:5) and

the Jewish remnant (12:13) must take place in the second half of the Tribulation.

8 The "sky sign" is mentioned in such passages as Isaiah 13:10; 34:4; Joel 2:31; Matthew 24:29; Mark 13:24, 25; Luke 21:25; and Revelation 6:12-14.

9 See my book *The Assyrian Connection* (Lafayette, LA: Prescott Press, 1993) for a detailed discussion of the sequence of end time events and the evidence to support the chronological placement.

10 See Revelation 7:1-8. Since these Jewish believers are said to have been "purchased from among men as first fruits to God" (Rev. 14:4), then they would have to precede the saved Jewish remnant during the second half of the Tribulation (if that term means the first of the Tribulation Jews to be saved); this would place the 144,000 witnesses in the first half of the Tribulation. If the term means the first to be martyred, then they would still have to arise during the first half of the Tribulation because the martyrdom of the Jews begins at the midpoint and continues during the second half of the Tribulation.

11 See Revelation 7:9-17. This scene of the Gentile believers takes place during the last 3 1/2 years because it is said of them, "These are the ones who come out of the great tribulation" (Rev. 7:14). According to Matthew 24:15-21, the Great Tribulation begins with the Abomination of Desolation.

12 As for the destiny of the Jews, someone has to fulfill the prophecy of Matthew 24:9 which says of Jewish believers during the Tribulation, "Then they will deliver you to tribulation, and will kill you." If this is not the 144,000 witnesses, then who is it?

13 These are the first four seal judgments of Revelation 6 that parallel Matthew 24:7, 8.

14 For the Antichrist to be in full power during the last 42 months, as described in Revelation 13:5, he will already have received the "gift of the kingdom" from the 10 kings of the Revived Roman Empire, as stated in Revelation 17:17.

15 Clearly, these two events occur in conjunction with the declaration by the Antichrist that he is "god on earth." This event immediately sets the one world religion in opposition with the one "who opposes and exalts himself above every so-called god or

object of worship" (2 Thess. 2:4); it is for this reason that the Antichrist destroys the religious system (Rev. 17:16). For the same reason, the mass defection of lip synching "believers," who are under pain of death, defect to the Antichrist in a worldwide "apostasy" (2 Thess. 2:3; Mt. 24:10).

[16] See *The Assyrian Connection*, 181, where I have a variety of reasons on the timing of the ministry of the two witnesses. I believe they are "harm-proof" until their divinely commissioned testimony is completed (Rev. 11:5-7). During the first half of the Tribulation there is no official persecution of Israel, or the saints (Dan. 7:25; Rev. 13:5-7). On the contrary, the Jews are under the protection of a covenant enforced by the Antichrist. There is no harm to require protection as far as "war against the saints" is concerned. Thus, the possibility of harm must commence with the time when Jesus warned the Jews to flee persecution, that is, the "Great Tribulation." This, of course, places the timing of the two witnesses during the Great Tribulation (the last 3 1/2 years) when they will require God's protection in order to survive.

[17] Lehman Strauss, *The Book of the Revelation* (Neptune, NJ: Loizeaux Brothers, 1969), 205.

[18] The bowl judgments represent the "last" of the wrath of God (Rev. 15:1). The scope and severity of the bowl judgment would not permit life on earth to extend beyond a few days. The entire vegetation and all water on the planet is dried up or poisoned (Rev. 16). Therefore, the bowl judgments must fit within the 75 days that surrounds the Second Coming of Christ.

[19] This period is known as the "Day of the Lord" in Scripture. It is timed precisely by the words, "immediately after the tribulation of those days the sun...moon...stars...they will see the Son of Man coming" (Mt. 24:29, 30) and then the words, "the sun...moon...before the great and awesome day of the Lord comes" (Joel 2:31).

[20] See the *Assyrian Connection* for a wider discussion on the timing of the sixth seal. Also see David Reagan, *Wrath And Glory* (Green Forest, AR: New Leaf Press, 2001), 68.

[21] It is impossible that the sixth seal could occur during the time of the Tribulation because the passage clearly shows that it is only

the Lord who will be exalted at that time. This is made explicitly clear by the panic driven cry of unbelievers ("...who is able to stand?"). The parallel passage to this scene in Isaiah 2:10-21 says, "the Lord alone will be exalted in that day" (2:11,17). Yet, the Lord is not exactly exalted by unbelievers until they are forced to do so at His return. It will be the Antichrist who will be exalted in that day, according to Revelation 13:4; it is there that the unbelievers exclaim, "Who is like the beast, and who is able to wage war with him?" How can these two statements come from the same mouths at the same time? They cannot and will not because the sixth seal does not happen during the Tribulation, but "immediately after" as recorded in its parallel passage in Matthew 24:29, 30.

22 The Millennial Kingdom is characterized as such, especially in many Old Testament passages such as Isaiah chapters 2, 9, 11, 25, 35, 65-66.

Chapter 18—Controversy Over Prophetic Fulfillment

1 R. C. Sproul, *The Last Days According to Jesus* (Grand Rapids: Baker, 1998).

2 Ibid., 203.

3 Ibid., 23.

4 Martin Lloyd-Jones, *The Church and the Last Things* (Wheaton: Crossway Books, 1998), 109.

5 Ibid.

6 Ibid.

7 Ibid., 110.

8 Ibid., 111.

9 Ibid., 112.

10 Ibid., 108.

11 Ibid., 109.

12 Louis A. DeCaro, *Israel Today: Fulfillment of Prophecy?* (Philadelphia, PA: Presbyterian and Reformed, 1974), xii.

13 Ibid., xiii.

14 Ibid., 218.

[15] Adapted in part from a privately published paper by Tom McCall entitled *Dallas Seminary Says: Don't Take A Stand For Israel* (Sherman, TX, September 2002).

[16] Charles Hodge, *Systematic Theology* (Grand Rapids: Eerdmans, 1977), 3:377.

[17] Ibid., 1:187 88.

[18] Louis Berkhof, *Systematic Theology* (Grand Rapids: Eerdmans, 1994), 714.

[19] Robert L. Reymond, *A New Systematic Theology of the Christian Faith* (Nashville, TN: Thomas Nelson, 1998), 2009.

Eternal Ministries is a discipleship and
evangelistic ministry dedicated to
teaching and proclaiming the Word of God.
For more information on the Christian life,
or to contact Ron Bigalke, Jr. please
do so through our website.

www.eternalministries.org

Printed in the United States
1292100005B/82-162